Althurian

Mystery of the Stones

by

Antony Barmew

Copyright © Antony Barmew 2023
<u>antonybarmew@gmail.com</u>

Cover art by Barty

Apart from references to actual historical events, this novel is a work of fiction. Names, characters and incidents have been created from the author's imagination and any similarity to actual persons, living or dead is entirely coincidental.

Other novels by Antony Barmew

Tumblewick

Love never dies

♦

Saving Innocence

♦

Eastaris

The journey begins

Antelogium

All I needed to do was to take just one more step and that would be the end of it; the end of pain, the torment, the need for explanation, the end of the struggle. I closed my eyes. I could hear the might of the sea below, feel its power thundering inside my chest, and taste its saltiness on my lips. Mariners knew it demanded respect and were right to be afraid. For me it was different; for this brief moment I had the courage to step towards the unknown, become one with the elemental forces all about me. What was there to fear anymore? I smiled inexplicably; my recent fatalistic view of life didn't help as I teetered on the edge of oblivion. I opened my eyes and leant forward, the sheer sides of the black Cambrian façade plunged deep into the white, frothing turmoil of the sea, churning menacingly below. I lifted my arm and squinted at my watch; its face was now covered with a fine mist; spray carried by the wind. I brushed a fingertip delicately across the glass, its vintage luminous dial still glowing eerily after all these years. It was 3am. I shivered. Several of my coat buttons had come unfastened and the chilly easterly breeze cut through the thin fabric of my exposed shirt; it occurred to me I should have put something warm underneath, like a jumper. I smiled again; a ridiculous thought considering my intention. What was I waiting for? Why did it matter? Alcohol does that, doesn't it? Confuses things, right? I took my last conscious breath, closed my eyes, and prepared to take the final step.

My life had been quite sweet until I arrived at Althurian; it should have been a life changing event for all the right reasons. Oh, yes, it was life changing all right.

Chapter 1
Inheritance

The man sitting before me had a gaunt, thin face, neatly trimmed hair; cut short, back and sides. I guessed he was no more than thirty, far too young looking to be a solicitor, and a little too audacious for my liking. 'You're now a very wealthy man, Mr Warrener,' he said, closing the file. 'Have you made any plans for the future?'

I could feel my eyes narrow as I looked at him. Fortunately, the words that came from my mouth were not the ones I was thinking. 'Did you know my cousin?' I asked.

James Parminter leaned back in his chair, interlacing his hands behind his head; he looked surprisingly relaxed for a man of law. He smiled. 'Not personally.' He paused. 'My father did, though. They were very good friends, apparently.'

I raised an eyebrow. 'Apparently?'

Parminter seemed not to notice my irritation. 'Well, according to Mr Simpson, my father's business partner, they were.' I got the feeling he wanted to roll his eyes, but sighed instead, nodding as if I understood his frustration. 'Mr Simpson still feels the need to come to the office twice a week.'

'And your father?' I asked, somewhat reluctantly.

'He passed away three months ago.'

As old as my face was, I could feel it blush. 'I'm sorry I...'

Parminter raised a hand and smiled. 'Thank you.' His face softened, then looked thoughtful. 'He'd been poorly for some time.' He paused again. 'It was still a shock, though.'

I nodded slowly. 'I can imagine.' I was now feeling awkward because I really wanted to know more about Sylvia but didn't want to appear rude or uncaring.

A grin developed across the solicitor's leonine face. In a way, I think he sensed my discomfort. 'Mr Simpson said my father and Ms Forsyth were great sparring partners. Politically, they were polar opposites, and he was surprised they ever managed to remain friends after the heated exchanges he observed.' Parminter unlinked his hands and leaned forward as if to share a secret. 'Of course, it may have had something to do with the volume of business Ms Forsyth brought to this firm.'

I felt myself frown. 'What sort of business?'

'Ms Forsyth became quite a canny investor after she inherited Althurian.' This time, it was Parminter's turn to frown. 'I'm sure all this must have come as a complete shock to you, Mr Warrener.'

I stared at him for a moment. It was more of a shock than he realised. I had no idea my great grandfather had a brother. I knew my great grandmother's name was Rosemary and had died from a rare form of polio well before I was born but that was about it. And to be honest, my interest and expertise in social history didn't extend to genealogy, as odd as that may seem.

I nodded, trying not to smirk. 'You could say that, Mr Parminter. Being the sole beneficiary to an estate once owned by a relative I didn't know existed, was…er…quite a surprise, I must say.' I thought that was a cool answer; I didn't want him to know I was absolutely floored by the huge sum Sylvia had left me. However, I was still intrigued how she had made so much. A "canny investor" was a stunning understatement.

Parminter looked at me, the way someone does when they don't completely believe you. 'Yes. Quite,' he mumbled, eyeing me a few seconds before gathering up a number of papers from his desk, neatly grouping them together. He glanced at a vintage clock hanging from an adjacent wall. 'Right, Mr Warrener, I'm afraid we'll have to leave it there for the time being, I have another client due in ten minutes.' He got to his feet in seconds, holding out his hand in a well-rehearsed, silky smooth action. 'It's been a pleasure to meet you at last. I hope you will consider using our services in the future. My door is always open, you know.'

I shook his hand. It was surprisingly firm and dry. Why I expected something different I'd rather not say. 'Thank you,' I said, 'I appreciate that.' And I meant it, even though I knew in my heart it was all about the fat fee he was hoping to receive.

Parminter led me from the office and ushered me through to the sharply furnished reception area. Skye's head was buried in a magazine. As I wandered in, she looked up, smiled and mouthed the words 'All right?' I nodded enthusiastically and glanced at my watch out of habit. She had been waiting for almost two hours and was not going to believe what I was about to tell her.

Almost as soon as the half-glazed door to Parminter and Simpson had squeaked shut, Skye was chomping at the bit, almost squealing the words, 'Well? What did he say?'

I looked at her; I knew I had a silly grin on my face, you know the sort: the ones that make your cheeks ache. I pointed to a coffee shop on the other side of the road. 'I think you'll need to sit down for this one, love.' I could feel my heart thumping in my chest as the words left my mouth. Strangely, my very next thought was: Please God, don't let me die of heart failure before I've seen my first bank statement. It's funny what money can do to the soul.

She looked at me with those, I can't wait that long, eyes. She knew I was rubbish at keeping secrets for longer than a nanosecond and was waving a sign the size of Europe saying so. Pouting playfully, she said, 'Spoilsport. It's your turn to buy then.'

Thankfully, Brannagans, a small family run café, was virtually empty apart from an elderly couple sitting by the window, each silently tucking into a sausage roll. The last thing I needed was someone listening, so we grabbed a table in one of the corners. Skye was now almost beside herself and was leaning across the table with her eyes popping out. 'Well?' she hissed.

Like some shady character from an old black and white movie, I glanced surreptitiously from side to side before answering. For someone who was trying not to draw attention, I was doing remarkably badly. I rummaged inside my jacket pocket for the envelope Parminter had given me earlier. Shakily, I handed it to her. 'Read this.'

'What is it?'

'Just read it.'

I watched as she fumbled in her excitement to open the heavy manilla envelope. After carefully unfolding the three sheets contained inside, she sat back, her eyes swivelling from side to side as if in some frenzied dance. She read no further than the first page before looking up. For the first time since I'd known her, she was stuck for words.

'So, what do you think?'

She glanced down again, massaging her forehead with her fingers. 'Is this for real, John?'

I knew how she felt. I still have difficulty believing it. I nodded. 'Yep, it sure is. I think even Parminter was surprised.'

She quickly flicked through the rest of the pages. 'But this lot must be worth a bloody fortune. This really wasn't what I expected.' She paused. 'If I was expecting anything.' She laid the papers on the table, shaking her head in disbelief.

'I know,' I said. 'Althurian is hardly a retirement bungalow in Eastbourne, is it?'

'Can I get you good people anything?'

I looked up with a jolt, as did Skye. For a split second I almost shouted at the source of the intrusion, completely forgetting where we were, and why it was perfectly natural for someone to ask such a reasonable question. It was a café. I noticed the man took a backward step as our eyes met. Instinctive self-preservation, I guess. I did my best to cover my initial reaction and smiled. 'Two Americanos, without milk, please.'

The waiter smiled back, albeit strained. 'Will you be wanting any food as the kitchen closes in half an hour and our Audrey has to get off early on Fridays.'

I thought it quite sweet the man needed to furnish me with more information than I really needed. I then felt guilty and wanted to apologise for putting the poor man on edge. 'No. Just the coffee, thank you,' was all I could manage; always the one to buckle to my ego.

The waiter, quite rightly, ignored my selfishness and turned to Skye. 'And the lady,' he asked, with more than just a raised eyebrow. He clearly had me weighed up correctly.

Skye had scooped up the papers and was protectively holding them close to her chest when our eyes met. She had spotted my embarrassment and, annoyingly, was grinning like a chimpanzee. She had developed a habit of doing this recently. 'The coffee will be more than enough,' she answered sweetly. 'But thank you for asking.'

The waiter too, looked pleased with himself as he scribbled the order in his notebook. I'm sure I caught sight of a self-satisfied grin on his face as he walked back to the service counter.

Skye quickly regained her composure, her expression changing back to one of shock. 'How much do you think the estate is worth? The house alone must be worth a million, maybe more.'

I jerked my shoulders. I really didn't know an exact figure, and nor did Parminter. Of course, he gave me a list of names to contact, investment managers, accountants, buddies lining up to make a quick buck. 'The total value of the estate hasn't been calculated yet. There'll be inheritance tax to pay, of course, so I'll have to find someone to look at the accounts sooner or later. Apparently, Sylvia had a share portfolio, a big one.' I dipped a hand into one of my side pockets and removed a business card. I flipped it over and tapped the fancy corporate logo with my finger. 'Parminter suggested I have a chat to this woman. She's some sort of stocks an' shares expert; works at the local Lloyds.' I nodded in the general direction. 'Just down the road here.'

'Wine bar pals?'

'Probably.' I smiled, raising an eyebrow. 'It's how it all works, isn't it?'

She nodded soberly. 'What are you going to do?'

I leaned back, folded my arms and slowly shook my head; the sort of thing you do when your sensibilities are caught between incredulity and disbelief. 'I have no idea. Parminter asked me the same question.'

'Early days yet, I suppose,' she said philosophically. 'Are you excited though? I know I am.'

I pulled a silly grin. 'When we get somewhere far from public view, and well out of earshot, I'm going to wail like a banshee and dance round like someone possessed.'

She chuckled. 'Now there's something I'd like to see.' She paused. 'You could sell the house and buy something smaller. You could easily retire on the equity. Like I said, it must be worth a fortune.'

'But I like teaching.'

'Really? So, your constant grumbling about funding cuts, student attention spans, and not being appreciated, is your idea of fun, then? You could always teach part time. Do it for nothing if it makes you feel any better.'

'Two Americanos,' announced the approaching waiter.

I had a feeling he was playing it safe and decided to warn us; not that I'm likely to kick off you understand, physical confrontation has never been my thing; I was preoccupied with the current situation and knew it was making me jumpy. The waiter carefully placed two large, white cups and saucers on the table, together with a receipt torn from his pad. Foolishly, I tried to make up for my earlier blunder. 'Thank you, they look great. By the way, I love the colour scheme you have here,' I blurted, just a little too quickly. I winced as the last word left my lips.

He looked at me with the kind of expression usually reserved for canvassing politicians; from the corner of my eye I noticed Skye had cupped a hand to her mouth. This didn't look good.

Almost indifferent to my lame attempt to redeem myself, he looked round the room before answering. 'It was the wife's choice, never liked it much me-self. Might give it the once over after she's been to pick up the rest of her stuff.'

I stared at him for a moment, struggling to find something, anything, that might sound remotely fit for purpose. I gave up easily. 'Oh…right,' I said. Although I didn't dare look at her, I knew Skye was enjoying every second. After a brief moment of immobility, the waiter shrugged indolently and, without uttering another word, marched off.

'Well done,' she said, doing that chimpanzee thing with her mouth again. 'That'll learn ya.'

Her grin was infectious, as was her wicked sense of humour. It's what I loved about her from the very beginning. 'You're enjoying this a bit too much, Tolhurst,' I said, trying extraordinarily hard to keep a straight face. I failed miserably as usual, and we both started to laugh like drains.

Life never seemed as serious when I was around her. Maybe it was her wandering spirit, her need to be free, unencumbered by convention and material possessions that released her from the anxieties of the modern world. She was one of a kind, and I was supremely grateful.

'Penny for them?' she asked, her pale blue eyes fixing mine; I think I may have been staring at her.

'Oh nothing,' I lied. 'Perhaps we should take a look at Althurian. It *is* ours now.'

She smiled. 'Yours,' she corrected.

'Oh, you know what I mean,' I snapped. 'You're as much a part of this as I am. Whatever decisions I make, affect you as well.'

'Soppy old fool.'

'Maybe I am. Well? What do you think?'

She took a delicate sip of coffee. 'I'd love to, but it depends where it is. Is it doable this afternoon, because I haven't brought anything with me if it means an overnight stay?' She gave me a serious look. 'You *do know* where it is, don't you?'

I chuckled. 'Of course, I do.' I hesitated, and the nerd in me took over. 'Well…sort of. Parminter said if we take the main road out of town and keep heading towards Otterburn, it's the third turning on the left after the second roundabout. About ten miles from here, he reckons. It's quite isolated, on the outskirts of a village called Feldingham.'

'You remembered directions, that makes a change,' she scoffed.

She was right of course; I'm usually rubbish at geography, as I am at taking criticism. 'This is different,' I grumbled. 'Well?'

14

She smirked. 'Then it would be rude not to, wouldn't it?'

The waiter, who earlier, I'd painfully established as the owner, was also licensee of the local social club. I discovered this to my cost because I had to stand behind the old couple as they took an interminable amount of time to pay for their two hot sausage rolls, a delicacy they gushed about for at least ten minutes before being equally complimentary about their tea. I also discovered to my cost, that bookings for the various functions held at the said social club were taken by Mr Brannagan at any time regardless of whom they held up. Skye had collected the car and was waiting for me outside. I climbed in the passenger seat and closed the door.

'Did you have a problem with your card again?' she asked.

'I paid cash.'

'Really?' She frowned. 'But you were ages. Did you go to the cashpoint?'

'No.'

Chapter 2
The Manor

The turning for Althurian was exactly where Parminter said it was and we found it easily; I'd even impressed myself for once. The gated entrance was marked by a large millstone standing to one side of it; the name boldly engraved and inset with bronze. Skye pulled off the main road and parked on the gravelled entrance so I could open the five-bar gate. I was astonished how beautifully maintained everything looked. For reasons unknown, I half expected it to be run down. The gate opened easily, and I took a moment to look up the driveway before returning to the car. The property was at least two hundred yards from the road.

Between us there was a silent but palpable excitement as we slowly approached this exquisitely beautiful manor house; all that could be heard was the crisp sound of gravel beneath moving rubber as the car crept along the hedge bordered drive. Neither of us uttered a word until we'd rolled to a stop. We sat with our mouths open for some time, just gawping.

Skye was first to speak. 'It's bloody enormous.'

'I know.'

'Are you sure Parminter,' she paused, 'has got the right person?'

'No.'

'He did know it was you, right?'

'I'm not so sure now.' I felt like a fraud, an imposter sitting outside a stranger's house after assuming their identity, and ready to take over everything that rightly belonged to them. Somehow it didn't seem right. I turned to look at her; she was wide eyed and staring out the window. 'Shall we go in?' I asked.

'Aren't you scared?'

I pulled on the car door handle, giving her a sidelong glance. 'Terrified!'

♦

I stood, paralysed, in awe of the double fronted, seventeenth century pile I'd just inherited, my eyes following the white Portland stone steps as they swept majestically up to the front door. I mindlessly checked my watch; I think I may have been procrastinating: It was almost two o'clock.

Skye locked the car and sidled up next to me. 'I know you can be an old romantic fool sometimes, but do you intend staying out here until we see the sun rise?'

I jolted slightly. 'Eh?'

'Have you got the keys, John?'

'Of course, I have.' I rummaged in my pocket. The single iron key of indeterminate age was tethered to a crisp white laundry tag with the word "Althurian" printed on it. I held it up, so it danced like a marionette. 'I hope it isn't fitted with a burglar alarm.'

'Well, it won't take us long to find out.'

It hadn't. The heavy wooden door opened easily; the lock as smooth as silk. I still expected it not to be like this. The hinges didn't creak, there wasn't a pile of unopened post, and everything wasn't covered in a thick layer of dust; in some respects, it was spookier because of this. We both stood in the hall trying to take it all in.

This grand entrance, easily the size of my flat, must have been at least as long as half the width of the house, the ceilings, I guess, twice as high as average. Enormous was an understatement. Sylvia must have rattled round like a pea in a wheelie bin.

'Wow!' gasped Skye. 'It's stunning. Look at all those paintings. I wonder if they're originals.'

I followed her gaze. 'I wouldn't be surprised.' To be honest I hadn't noticed the paintings until then; I was still overwhelmed by the spectacle of it all, as well as beginning to show the early signs of surprise fatigue; if there was such a malady.

A polished timber floor served five identical, six panel doors, two on either side of the adjacent walls, and one at the far end facing the front entrance. Each door had matching brass furniture and finger plates. The air was rich with the smell of scented bees wax, and just a hint of bleach.

Skye squealed, 'Where shall we go first?' Her excitement had gone up a notch and she was behaving like a hyperactive eight-year-old. 'Left, or right?' she asked breathlessly.

I can't honestly admit to being any different. 'You choose,' I said. We were like children on a wintery Christmas morning just as the presents were about to be handed out; it was as if a kind of nervous confusion had overtaken the rational centre of my brain. However, the love of my life didn't need to be asked twice and marched off; opening the first door she came to. Once inside, her reaction was somewhat predictable.

'Bloody hell! Wow! You gotta come and see this, John. Wow!'

As I entered, she was standing by an ornate and intricately carved fireplace, running her hand along the arm of a large fabric sofa; one of two facing each other at the centre of the room. 'These are exquisite, John. Your…er…auntie must have been quite a socialite; this was definitely furnished for entertaining.'

'She wasn't an auntie, Skye. She was a sort of a cousin, well…third cousin, actually.' I winced; the nerd in me was becoming vocal again. 'Maybe she just liked stretching out with her feet up.'

'Who told you that?'

'Just a guess, it's what I would do.'

'I meant the cousin thing, you Wally.'

I pulled a face. 'I kind of worked it out when I was talking to Parminter. I guessed she was a cousin, or at least something along those lines. A third cousin because she was, well, the third generation from my great granddad's…er…brother. I could be wrong.' I gave a crinkled smile. Yes, even I thought it sounded confusing.

'I'll Google it later,' she said. Kicking off her shoes, she did a neat pirouette and flopped onto the sofa. Drawing her knees to her chest, she hugged them like a small child. Inclining her head, her pale blue eyes fixed mine. 'I could get used to this, couldn't you?'

'You never say that when you're in the flat.'

She snorted. 'The ambulance has more room than your flat.'

I looked at the floor and shuffled my feet. If I'd been outside, I would have probably kicked a small pebble across the concrete or something. I knew she was right, even though it was an exaggeration. 'Academics need their books, you know.'

'Books, papers, carrier bags full of clothes, a decade of National Geographic magazines, and should I say, more furniture than you can shake a stick at.' She raised her eyebrows. 'Do I need to go on?'

I was outsmarted as usual, but wasn't going down without putting up some form of defence. 'You have to remember,' I said sombrely. 'I had a much larger property before I was divorced.'

She let out a hoot. 'But that was over ten years ago. Come on, admit it, you can't bring yourself to throw anything away. True?'

I silently wandered over to the other sofa, took a deep breath and sat down, clasping my hands together in my lap. 'I was saving it for when I got a bigger place.' I tried not to look smug. 'As you can see, it was only a matter of time.'

'Smart arse.'

'Ha. You're just a bad loser.'

She pointed towards the back wall. 'I wouldn't get too cocky; you'll have a problem squeezing those magazines between that lot.'

My eyes widened as they followed her well-manicured digit. I'm surprised I didn't spot them, being the bookish sort of bloke I am. Before me stood a bibliophile's wet dream; from floor to ceiling an entire wall of rare, and probably almost extinct, timber was rammed full of deliciously bound volumes of literary art, many rarer than the wood they were sitting on. I was staring open mouthed.

'Impressive, aren't they?'

I nodded. My eyes were still scanning from side to side like an organic form of Lidar. If I had a group of genes within my countless strands of DNA that could help me deal with this, they needed to start expressing themselves pretty soon.

'I've just noticed something weird,' she said.

'Eh?' My focus returned; she was staring towards the door. I automatically glanced over my shoulder. 'What sort of weird?' I could see nothing out of the ordinary.

'There are no stairs. I can't remember ever being in a house that didn't have stairs in the hall.'

This at first seemed improbable until I gave it some thought. 'You're right, neither have I, how odd.'

She slipped from the sofa, wriggling her feet into her shoes. 'Come on, let's explore. They have to be somewhere.'

Her impatient excitement could be infectious, and I did my best to smile. 'I'm sure the stairs can wait a few minutes, love. No one is standing over us with a stopwatch.'

Her shoulders sagged visibly. 'I'm getting over excited, aren't I?'

I pinched a finger and thumb together. 'Only just a weeny bit.'

She sighed. 'I feel that someone is going to walk in and tell us it's all been a mistake. I've always been the same, even when good things happen to me. When I got my first new bike, I thought Santa had delivered to the wrong house. It was more of a boy's bike, and I was convinced it should have been for the lad at the bottom of our street, not me. It's sad how these things stay with you.'

I could feel my face soften as I looked at her. Yep, I now felt a bit of a git. 'Come on, let's see if we can find those missing stairs.'

The door at the other end of the hall, although made in the same style, was appreciably larger than the others. It opened into a lobby, possibly a little smaller than the hall, it was difficult to tell. Another door immediately opposite looked older, as if it had been reclaimed from an earlier building, and clearly an entrance to the rear of the property judging by the intense shaft of sunlight coming through the fanlight above. A tiled floor replaced the timber and, although looking the same as the hall, had a slightly different layout, inasmuch, as there were two equally spaced doors to our left and one to our right. But, as our shoes clattered across the black and white slate floor, there was still no sign of the elusive stairs.

'I reckon your cousin must have had a cleaner, there's no way someone of her age could have managed a house of this size.'

I pulled a face. 'I couldn't do it now.'

'I wouldn't want to,' she said, with a chuckle. 'How old was she?'

'She would have been seventy-six on July 29th.'

'Shame. It's a pity you weren't invited to the funeral.'

I shrugged. 'They were probably trying to trace my whereabouts. It couldn't have been easy.'

'I'd like to know how she knew about you in the first place.'

'Yeah, me too.'

She gripped the brass handle to the first door and looked back at me. 'Shall we?'

The hollow rattle of empty space was unmistakable. The entire room was bathed in a warm, reddish glow; the double aspect windows devoid of curtains. A bare timber floor covered at one end by several large dust sheets spoke of work in progress. From the look of it, none had started in earnest; apart from two large drums of paint standing idle, waiting for a wall to inhabit, there were no other signs of any recent activity.

Skye stood inside the doorway with her hands on her hips. 'They must've been stood down when the old lady died.' She wandered over to the paint, inclining her head to read the label. 'French Lavender. Nice choice.' She paused. 'It's a really strange feeling when you experience a moment frozen in time. It's like…this place is waiting for it all to get back to normal.' Her face saddened visibly. 'You won't sell it, will you? Say you won't.'

This was another side of her I hadn't seen before. I was momentarily taken aback. 'I haven't really thought that far ahead.' I smiled. 'There goes my retirement fund.'

Her face remained stubbornly rigid, her eyes…different. 'I'm serious, John. You cannot, and must not, sell Althurian.'

I frowned. 'What's brought this on? Selling it was your idea, remember?'

She looked down at the floor like a scolded child. 'I…I know I…' She appeared to be struggling for an answer, nervously touching her forehead with her fingertips.

I took a step towards her. 'Are you all right?'

'I…I don't know. My head feels a bit woozy.' She was now beginning to rock unsteadily from foot to foot.

23

I took off towards her, and not a moment too soon. I caught her just as her knees were about to buckle. As slight as she was, her dead weight was quite a shock, and I almost toppled to the floor, taking her with me. I eased her into a sitting position with her back against the wall, trying my best not to panic; I've never have been very good at that sort of thing. Her breathing was deep and rasping as if she were fighting for breath, her eyes rolling round like they had a mind of their own; it was very, very scary. I patted the sides of my jacket and cursed when I realised my mobile phone was in the car. I was now caught between not wanting to leave her and the need to call for help.

'J-John,' she groaned. I jolted at the sound of her voice; it was unexpected but reassuring at the same time. She frowned, eyes narrowing like she was trying to identify who I was.

I stroked the side of her face. 'I'm here, lovey,' I soothed.

Turning her head slowly from side to side, she looked lost, bewildered. 'W-where am I?'

'Althurian. Don't you remember?'

The corners of her mouth quivered as if she were about to smile. 'Yes. Yes, I think so,' she mumbled softly. 'Yes. Althurian.'

'Will you be okay if I leave you for a moment?'

'Why? Where are you going?' she asked anxiously.

'Only to the car.'

Rocking her head from side to side, she mumbled, 'I...I don't understand.'

'I need to get my phone.'

She stared at me in a really odd way. 'John?'

'I'm here. Are you okay?'

'I...I think so.' She shifted her weight slightly.

'How do you feel now?'

She smiled at last. 'Better. Yes, definitely better.'

I slowly got to my feet so as not to distress her. I noticed some of the colour had returned to her cheeks. 'Right. I'm now going to get my phone. Okay? Stay there, do not move, I won't be long.' I winced inwardly: I was talking to her like she was a child.

'Okay.' She reached out to touch my hand. 'I won't move an inch, I promise. Thank you.'

I wanted to smile and frown at the same time. Smile because she appeared to be on the road to recovery, and frown, because there was something different about her, something I couldn't quite put my finger on. I hoped it wasn't serious.

When I returned, it was of no real surprise to see her standing by the window looking out. She had wrapped her arms round her chest, hugging herself; it appeared to be an action of pure joy judging by the expression on her face. She turned to look directly at me. 'The garden looks so beautiful at this time of the year, don't you think, John?'

'Er…yes…I suppose it does.' I inclined my head. 'Are you sure you're okay?'

'Of course, I am. I've never felt better.'

She sauntered past me and into the hall like nothing had happened. It was bizarre, then some.

'Come on, John,' she said, 'we have a house to explore.'

I looked at my phone as she disappeared from view. What was I to say if I were to call someone? "My girlfriend had a funny turn, but now she's all right, but I think there's something strange about her" Right. I know how that conversation would turn out.

Skye was exploring the room opposite when I caught up with her; it looked very much like a study. She was staring up at a heavy gilt framed painting above another fireplace. It was a portrait of a very noble looking fellow wearing a top hat, jacket and waistcoat, his proudly curled moustache, reminiscent of bygone Victorian extravagance. There was an assertive air about him, and I sensed a discernible melancholy in his eyes. 'I wonder if people's lives in his day were any different to ours,' she mused.

'It depends on their circumstances.'

She turned her head. 'In respect to what, John?'

'Health, wealth, social status, to name but a few; the world hasn't changed much since his day. Regardless of this wonderful technology we see all round us, an embarrassingly high number of people still live hand to mouth.' The gentleman's hands were clasping the top of a very fancy walking cane, and from the look of them, not to have endured much hard work. I felt slightly irritated by his pomposity. 'I doubt if he lacked many of the comforts the world had to offer.' My eyes started to wander round the rest of the room.

'He looks like a good man, I think,' she said.

'Really? What makes you think that?'

'He has kind eyes.'

I coughed a laugh. 'Trust you. I thought they looked a bit sad.' My heart skipped a beat. Skye, the one I knew best, had returned. I wanted to tell her what had just occurred but thought better to leave it.

I left her to ponder our Victorian friend's character and went off to explore the rest of the room. It was all very odd. If you can imagine visiting a National Trust property, or maybe a museum, and were allowed to pick up stuff, lounge about on the furniture, and generally treat it like home, well, that's what it was like. The thing was, it felt so wrong; we were intruders, illegal aliens, invading a world not belonging to us.

Opposite the fireplace, on the other side of the room, and centrally placed in front of the window, stood the grandest pedestal desk I'd ever seen. I'm no expert, but I believe it was constructed from walnut, the colour fabulous. The top was covered in unmarked green leather, framed by an intricately carved edge. Sylvia certainly had an eye for quality. The surface was surprisingly uncluttered apart from a worn leather blotter, a letter opener, and a modern Biro. A Mont Blanc certainly wouldn't have looked out of place.

Skye suddenly chimed, 'I'm surprised by the lack of photographs. I haven't seen any yet.'

I jumped slightly. I was lost in my own little world, as usual. 'Maybe she kept them in an album.'

'But you'd think there'd be at least one somewhere.' She frowned. 'People have photos, they put them out to show them off, it's what normal people do.'

I walked round the desk, the chair behind was in complete contrast, apart from the Biro, to it, and the rest of the room. Modern it was, inferior quality, it wasn't. It was also extremely comfortable, tilting and rotating in every possible way; this was a long-distance chair. I sat down, avoiding the temptation to hoist my size nines onto the desk.

'Well?' Her impatience had returned.

I shrugged. 'Perhaps she didn't like photographs. Perhaps she had an aversion to technology.' I knew I was clutching at straws.

She pulled a face. 'Photographs are hardly modern tech, John. Old ladies keep photographs, it goes with the territory. It's how it is. My grandma had loads of them. Every available horizontal surface was crammed with photo frames. It's just not normal.'

I absent-mindedly pulled out one of the drawers and was instantly jabbed by a sense of guilt; I was now entering someone's personal space. The guilt didn't last. I have a theory that you can tell a lot about a person from the state of their desk drawer. Okay, it's weird, I know that.

'It'll be a shame if we can't find a photo of her,' she said. 'Be nice to know what she looked like.'

'Eh?' I glanced up. 'What do you mean, what who looked like?'

She shook her head. 'You're hopeless. Sylvia, of course.'

'Yes…yes, it would be good to know,' I mumbled vacantly, pulling out the drawer a little more. It was a little disappointing. Writing pads, a stack of them, the sort my mum would have bought in Woolworth of all places. I was almost ready to move to another drawer when I spotted a sealed brown envelope. It had probably slipped to the back at some point and was too good to ignore. I turned it over and made an involuntary gasp. On the front, neatly written in ink, was a name. John. Nothing else, just the name.

Skye caught the look on my face. 'What's up now?'

I held it up for her to see. 'I think this was meant for me.'

We both stared at the elegant script, its blue ink, fresh as the day it was written. 'It could be for someone else, I suppose.' she said. 'A common name is John.'

I was transfixed. 'I know it is.'

'Are you going to open it?'

I could feel my pulse quicken. 'I don't know why, but I think I should.'

'Well, do it then. Don't just look at it.'

I didn't need to be told twice. I grabbed the letter opener, scything through the upper edge of the envelope in one smooth movement. I kind of felt rebellious. The faintest smell of lavender wafted out as I carefully separated the two cut edges. I was nervous, my palms moist. Inside, two sheets of rich, cream vellum were folded separately. I seemed to lose control of my hands at that moment; they started to shake as I fumbled to open the first of them. Skye was remarkably silent, never one to miss an opportunity to extract some comical relief at my expense. I must add a note here: If the time is right, I too am equally guilty of this childish crime. The content of the note was written in the same hand. I read it out loud.

Dear John

I have anticipated, indeed, dreamt of this moment many times over the years. My only regret is not to have met you in person, as I'm sure we would have much to talk about, you and I.

I would also like to apologise if this sudden knowledge of me has left you overwhelmed, and I hope you can find it in your heart to forgive me. Unfortunately, my circumstances left me no other choice.

You have already met young Mr Parminter. It's a shame Mr Parminter senior was unable to see you. His failing health and ability has been worrisome recently......

'This is so weird,' she said. 'It's like it was only written yesterday.'

'She was right about being overwhelmed.'

......You will at some point be required to return to the office, there are papers you will have to sign. This is normal so you're not to worry.

I have also arranged for you to be contacted by an old friend of mine. She will be a valuable resource over the next few weeks. She has my complete trust and you should feel free to ask her anything you are unsure about. She will make herself known to you in due course. I have left you a list of account numbers you may use until full financial authority has been granted. Access codes, passwords and PIN numbers for these accounts will be revealed to you very soon.

I wish you the very best life has to offer.

Kindest Regards

Sylvia

We both stared at the letter. I was the first to speak. 'No, this is stranger than weird, love.'

'So, she already knew of your existence; and for quite some time by the sound of it.'

'I know, and before Parminter senior died.'

'What do you mean?'

'The old man croaked it three months ago. Spooky stuff, eh?'

'Jesus.'

I nodded. 'Difficult to get your head around, that.'

Skye looked as perplexed as me. 'I'm not going to even try.' She paused. 'I wonder who this friend is? Handy if she'd left her name.'

'Odd this letter was tucked away in the drawer. How could she be sure I'd find it? Better to have left it with Parminter.'

'You did though. Maybe you just got lucky. Perhaps giving it to Parminter was the plan all along.'

I put my elbows on the desk and rubbed my face. Skye picked up the other sheet and whistled. 'One of these is a number for a Swiss bank account.'

'How do you know?'

'I recognise the prefix. My uncle Ted, dad's brother, was a banker. He used to work for Credit Suisse International. The silly old sod was always bragging about it, he must have shown me the same bank statement over a hundred times.'

I puffed out my cheeks. This was getting too much. I was beginning to feel as if I were living between the pages of a spy novel. 'Shall we see if we can find the kitchen? I could murder a cuppa.'

She hooted. 'Now that, my lover, is one of the best suggestions I've heard all week. I have a feeling it might be next door.'

I smiled. 'Female intuition?'

She jerked her head towards the opposite wall. 'Pipes! I reckon those are hot and cold supplies.' She paused, raising her eyebrows. 'Although it could be a bathroom, I suppose.'

I shook my head. 'Don't tell me, your other uncle was a plumber.'

'No, he was an electrician, my aunt was the plumber.'

I followed in silence as we filed from the room. The kitchen was indeed next door. It was an odd, narrow room, with a door at the far end. Don't get me wrong, when I say narrow, I mean it in the sense it was narrow compared to the rest of the house. This could hardly be called a galley kitchen. Anyway, best of all, it had a kettle. Skye soon found a couple of mugs and some teabags, and I managed to stumble across a few loose bourbons lurking in a sealed jar. There was even a fresh carton of milk in the fridge, and my world had just become a little happier. Soon, we were back in the drawing room slumped on one of the sofas.

'What time is it?' she asked.

I looked at my watch. 'Ten to six.'

'When shall we make a move?'

'I hadn't really thought about it.' And I hadn't. I was more than content where I was. 'Why? Are you in a hurry to get back?'

She wrinkled her nose. 'Not really. I'd like to see the rest of the house first. You?'

'The same.' Which was partially true. If I'd thought to bring a change of clothes, I would have been happy to stay the night. 'We do need to eat at some point.'

'We could nip to that pub we saw on the way in,' she said. 'It must do food; it had a menu board outside.' She chuckled. 'You could even chum up with the landlord now it's your local.'

I took a mouthful of tea; it was almost impossible to wipe the smile from my face. She seemed funnier, more animated than usual, and I had this warm, cocooned sensation washing over me. If I were listening to someone other than me saying this, I would suspect they may have consumed a little too much of that amber coloured highland water.

'What a great idea,' I said. 'We'll do that.'

She gave me one of those looks, the one I get when she thinks I'm not being entirely truthful. 'But you don't like pubs.'

'I know I don't, but I still think it's a great idea.'

'You're using reverse psychology, right?'

I laughed. 'How could you think such a thing?'

Chapter 3
The Jolly Archer

A little after seven, we pulled into the car park of The Jolly Archer. Our car was only one of three. The pub's sign, a Robin Hood looking character eyeing some unseen target, pulling the string of an equally unseen long bow, swung back and forth in the gentle south easterly. An eerie half-light made the fifteenth century coach house look even shabbier than it really was. The lack of any meaningful external lighting didn't help. Even the brass lamps illuminating either side of the sign needed a good polish.

'Looks a bit dingy, doesn't it,' said Skye.

'Sign of the times, I guess. These days, people prefer to sit in front of the telly with a six pack and a takeaway. It must be tough to get punters to drive out to these isolated pubs when they can slob out at home. If you don't fancy it, we could always drive into town, find something a little more appealing.'

'Seems a bit mean now we're here. Anyway, my stomach is anticipating sustenance.' She chuckled. 'And I'm not sure I can hold out for much longer, its insistence that I eat is overwhelming.'

I laughed. 'The Jolly Archer it is then.'

♦

It was chillier outside than first appeared; mercifully, the walk from the car short. I opened the solid, fairly modern, oak planked door and ushered Skye ahead of me. As she pulled back the inner door, my nostrils were assaulted by the delicious smell of fried food as it wafted past us in a bid to escape to the wider world. Now, I have this thing about fried food. I'm not actually a great fan of it, but when hungry, the smell can make me salivate like a Labrador waiting for a treat. I'm the same if I pass a hot-dog stall or burger van, and I don't even eat meat! Anyway, enough about me.

The interior was a different story, and a pity the outside didn't reflect that. The first thing we saw as we walked in was an inglenook with a grate full of blazing logs. I could feel the heat on my face as I closed the door, and the faint smell of wood smoke made the experience even more inviting. I was surprised to see what was basically a large room divided into about a dozen intimate units; each one comprising of four comfortable looking arm chairs enclosing a small round table. The bar ran from one side of the inglenook to halfway along an adjacent wall. It had neither staff behind, nor customers in front. However, there were more people seated than I expected to see, and most were couples. I could only guess some of them must have walked or hitched a lift. We found our own little space in a cosy alcove.

Skye took off her coat, hanging it over the chair opposite. She rubbed her hands gleefully and pulled one of her excited to be alive faces. 'This is so, so good, John,' she squealed. 'And to think we nearly went somewhere else.'

We picked up a menu each. 'They say you should never judge a book by its cover,' I said.

'I'd like to meet these individuals we call 'they'. How can such a unique group of people know so much?'

She snorted a laugh but didn't look up as her eyes continued to search for the perfect gastronomic delight. 'Mmmm,' she purred. 'Nut roast, fries, and a side salad. That'll do.'

'Nut roast and fries? Now there's a novel combination.'

'Don't knock it until you've tried it, I say.' She peered over the menu. 'What about you? Seen anything you fancy?'

'Baked potato with a mixed bean and lentil salad; I just hope there's plenty of it.'

'Good evening, people. Would you like to order now, or shall I leave you to ponder for a little longer?' I looked up. The gentleman standing before us seemed to have appeared from nowhere; difficult to believe considering the robustness of his size. His round face beamed happiness, the corners of his smile almost touching each ear. The term "people" seemed to be used a lot in this part of the world. Nice though it is, I still found it odd.

I held up the menu and tapped a finger on my meal of choice. 'Is that a sweet potato?' I asked innocently.

He looked at me seriously. For a minute I thought I'd crossed an invisible line. He nodded equally seriously. 'Our potatoes are some of the finest around,' he boomed. 'We only buy ones with the sweetest attitude possible.' He leaned forward as if to share a secret; I detected a quiver at the corners of his mouth. His eyes narrowed as he paused for the dramatic finish. 'You won't find an angry one amongst them.' This was followed by a bellow of laughter Friar Tuck would have been proud of. This attracted the attention of a number of other customers and a hushed murmur of polite tittering seemed to travel round the room. The man coughed. 'You'll have to excuse me, people, I can't help myself sometimes, drives the wife crazy, it does.' He frowned and ran a hand over his billiard ball smooth head. He then tutted. 'Now I've clean forgot what it was you wanted.'

I smiled. This sudden burst of unexpected humour had almost the same effect on me. 'It...er...' I stumbled. 'It was a baked sweet potato.'

The man rolled his eyes. 'Ah, that was it.' He began to scribble furiously in the small notepad he was holding. He looked up. 'Anything else?'

Luckily for us he refrained from any further demonstrations of amateur stand-up humour, took both our orders and scuttled through a doorway on the other side of the inglenook.

'Perhaps they have an open mic night at the weekends,' said Skye.

I pulled a face. 'Then I'm more than happy to only come here during the week.'

No sooner had the man disappeared, he was on his way back again, this time, carrying our drinks. I was having a soda and lime, and Skye, because I was on the tame stuff, and driving, had a large glass of Sauvignon Blanc. He set them down on the table, together with fresh mats and paper napkins. He stood up, eyeing us both for a second.

'Not from this neck of the woods, then?'

I glanced up. 'Eh?'

Skye answered. 'We're from Kent.'

'A long way from home then. Where are you staying?'

'At a guest house outside East Skelling.'

The man whistled. 'That's almost forty miles from here.' He checked his watch. 'You're leaving it a bit late to get back, aren't you?' He shook his head. 'I can't be driving at night these days. Every taillight looks like a triangle. Bloody awful, it is.'

'We'll probably leave once we've eaten,' I said.

'Must have been something special to have brought you this far,' he said.

I could feel his eyes boring into me, and I was trying not to look at him. I wanted to tell him to mind his own business but couldn't. He was such a happy man it would have been rude, even though he was being incredibly nosy. I gave in easily. 'We were visiting a place called Althurian.'

He inclined his head. 'Althurian, you say?'

I nodded. 'It's about five miles from here.'

He tutted. 'I knows where Althurian is. Are you thinking of buying it?'

I laughed nervously. 'Goodness me, no,' I answered a little too quickly, but it was the truth.

'Ah,' he said, holding his gaze. I could almost hear the wheels turning in his skull as he deliberated what to say next. 'Then you must be the fella who's related to Sylvia Forsyth.'

I raised an eyebrow. 'News travels fast in this neck of the woods.' I smiled at my weak sense of humour. 'I am indeed.'

The man held out his hand. 'Gerome Phillips, me friends call me Gerry.'

I took his hand. It was huge. Not the sort of man to have a disagreement with. 'John. John Warrener.' I gestured with a turn of my hand. 'This is my partner. Skye.'

'Pleased to meet you at last, John,' he said. He nodded at Skye but didn't shake her hand. 'And you, Miss.' His eyes shifted back to me. 'Will you be moving into the old manor, John?'

Suddenly, I felt important. I have no idea why. 'We haven't decided yet…er…Gerry. There's still a lot of paperwork to sign. You know how it is.'

He nodded sagely, pulled up one of the chairs and sat down. Gerry was in for the long haul. I just hoped he would move on to someone else before we got our meals, the last thing I wanted was to eat in front of a relative stranger. 'So, John,' he said, 'if the rumours are true an' you're planning to convert it to a guest house you'll have to be watching your back. There are dark forces at work in that place.'

I wanted to laugh but chose not to. For whatever reason Gerry thought it sensible to believe idle gossip and rumour was his problem. But making the claim that some supernatural energy was conspiring against me for an act I hadn't considered, was beyond the pale. I said the only thing I could say. 'I think you should be careful who you listen to, Gerry.'

'So, it's not true?'

'It's just a rumour, Gerry,' I snapped. 'Nothing more than that.'

I think Skye sensed I was becoming irritated by his questions, and asked, 'So, Gerry, how long have you been in the pub business?'

There were two possible reasons why he broke from the interrogation so quickly. One: he knew he'd possibly overstepped the mark and Skye had offered him a way out, or two: he preferred talking about himself. I had a feeling it was the latter. I did, however, have one plan I was prepared to execute almost immediately.

'Excuse me, Gerry, can you tell me where the toilets are?'

♦

The food was good. No. It was bloody delicious. If the jolly Gerry was the chef, then I take my hat off to him. Luckily, he chose not to bother us again; possibly because the pub started to fill up not long after a young woman, of very similar build and demeanour, came out with our meals. It was half past eight when we finally emerged. The breeze had died down to almost nothing, the sky was clear and the air freezing; our warm, sated breaths plumed like equine thoroughbreds. A frost was in the making, even an old townie like me could tell as much.

Skye hesitated before climbing in the passenger seat; she looked over the roof as I was removing my jacket. 'I know you think all this talk of the supernatural is mumbo jumbo, but what if there's something more to it?'

I casually threw my jacket onto the back seat. 'There isn't, trust me. It's just small-minded piffle.' Before she had time to answer, I continued. 'Someone, as usual, has started a rumour because they had nothing better to do. And rumours, no matter how ridiculous, soon become known as fact. This one has done just that, grown legs and started a journey of its own.'

'Okay, but why all the spooky stuff? That bit doesn't make sense, and it frightens me.'

I leaned my head back and sighed. Skye was always like this after a glass of wine; acute alcohol fuelled paranoia (also referred to as wineoria in the Warrener household) took over, and whatever I said was likely to be scrutinised to the nth degree. 'Look,' I said grumpily, 'a few people who have local guest houses have got wind of it and are now spreading a rumour about witches and warlocks just to put the willies up us, that's all.'

'You shouldn't joke about that stuff, John.'

Just as I was about to answer her, a grey shadow appeared across the windscreen, followed by two sharp raps on my driver's door glass. We both almost jumped out of our skins; I might even have shrieked. Well, twice actually. The car park spirit turned out to be none other than our grinning landlord; he was waving what looked like a newspaper and was looking slightly sheepish. I powered down the window.

'Can I help you, Gerry?' I asked calmly. It was a tame response, and not exactly the one I had in mind.

'I...er...sorted this out for you,' he said, holding up what was indeed a newspaper. 'It's our local rag from a few years back. You might find the article on page five...er...rather interesting.'

I reached out and took it. 'Thank you, Gerry,' I said, trying to nod enthusiastically. 'That was very sweet of you. You can't beat a local newspaper when you move to a new area.' I had no idea what I was talking about and was making it up as I went along. Anyway, Gerry seemed happy enough with the answer, even though at one point he did frown. I wound up the window, started the engine and lobbed the paper over my shoulder.

I could feel Skye staring at me. 'So, when did you decide to move in, then?'

I waved a dismissive hand. 'I just told him that. What else could I say?'

'Well, you told him earlier we hadn't made a decision yet.'

'Did I say that?'

'You did.'

'Oh.'

I took a left out of the car park. The moon was bright, and all about was cast a grey bluish hue; the roads just beginning to sparkle in the headlights.

'I thought we were going straight to the guest house.'

I shook my head, briefly closing my eyes, it had completely slipped my mind. 'Damn. I wasn't thinking.'

'We could stay the night.'

'But what about our stuff?'

'I'm sure we can rough it for one night.' She chuckled. 'It might be fun.' If it has been Sylvia's home for the last seventy-six years, then it's good enough for us.'

'What about the guest house?'

'Once we get sorted, I'll give them a call. Just as well we booked for three nights or we'd have to go back anyway.'

'Are you sure about this? I don't mind driving.'

'I know you don't, John, but why spend the next two hours cooped up in the car when we can choose not to. Anyway, I'd rather spend a bit more time exploring the house, wouldn't you?'

♦

She was right of course; it was madness driving all that way, especially when we were both tired. Like I mentioned earlier, I was more than happy to stay a little longer; there was something comforting about Althurian I found hard to define; in a funny sort of way I felt at home. As we turned from the main road, a series of lights along the entire length of the drive came on automatically. I pulled alongside the steps and turned off the engine. To me this was a real luxury as my flat in Whitstable had no dedicated parking, and some days I had to walk miles.

A waft of warm air came to greet us as I opened the door. I was surprised to see the hall light was on. At first, I was a little spooked by it until I discovered the switch had a programmable timer. Skye went through to the kitchen and put the kettle on while I set about finding somewhere to sleep. But first, I had to find the stairs.

Fortune smiled on me, twice in fact. A brief search of the hall revealed the most important discovery of the night: a downstairs bathroom. And after further sleuthing, I found the stairs lurking behind the door opposite. Skye came through with the tea just as I was about to pat myself on the back.

'I found the bathroom, and the stairs,' I declared triumphantly.

'You are a good boy,' she said, handing me my tea.

'And not a moment too soon,' I said, with a snort.

She chuckled. 'You should have gone before we left the pub. Just as well we didn't go back to the guest house, eh?'

'Yes, yes, I know that.' I think I may have scowled. I remember my mum using words arranged in a very similar order when I was about eight years old. Well, apart from the word pub, that is. I lifted the mug. 'Where shall we have this?'

'Drawing room?'

'Why not, we could do with a change.'

'Very funny. Did you bring the newspaper in with you?'

I rolled my eyes. 'Ah!'

'Shall I take your tea?'

She was waiting by the bookshelves when I returned. 'Found anything good?'

'If you like business and finance, you'd be in seventh heaven.'

'Really?' I wound my way to the nearest sofa and flopped onto its heavily upholstered interior.

She pulled out a book and opened the front cover. 'Some of these are decades old, John. On each of these shelves you could probably find an answer to every question about commerce there is.' She paused a moment. 'Beautiful, but hardly stimulating unless you're an accountant.'

I chuckled. 'I might just give them a miss then.' Unfolding the newspaper, I began to read out the headline.

"PRICELESS BRONZE AGE CHALICE STOLEN FROM LOCAL MUSEUM"

'I remember this story,' I said. 'I think it was part of a hoard found by a metal detectorist; turned out to be worth a fortune. They never did get it back.' I paused. 'This paper must be at least two years old.'

'Gerry did say it went back a bit. Some people have all the luck. I found a bag of pound coins on Skegness beach once.'

I looked up. 'Sorry?'

'It doesn't matter.' She tutted. 'You obviously weren't listening.' Slipping the book back on the shelf, she made her way to the sofa opposite. 'He said you should take a look at page five.'

I flipped over to the page in question. Nothing of consequence stood out until my eyes settled on a short article nestled near the bottom, and obviously an update to an earlier headline.

CRAVEN WOOD BODY IDENTIFIED

> *Police have revealed the identity of the person whose remains were discovered at Craven Wood. Detective Chief Inspector Russ Patrick said, "The discovery of James Dixon's body only deepens the sixty-two-year-old mystery surrounding Althurian Manor" Dixon, fifty-six, went missing in 1972; nineteen years after the previous occupant had also disappeared in suspicious circumstances. Chief Inspector Patrick added, "We are at present speaking to a number of retired officers, who were at the time, involved with the earlier investigation."*

'You're remarkably quiet, John.'

I leaned forward and handed her the paper. 'Maybe there is more to Althurian than we realise,' I said, as I watched her eyes zigzag across the lines of print.

She looked up. 'My God, do you think he was murdered?'

'Well, if the police were opening another investigation, it's more than possible.' I paused. 'I'm surprised his body wasn't found earlier; forty odd years is a long time to lay undisturbed.'

She shuddered visibly. 'What a horrible thought.'

'Shocking for whoever found him,' I said.

'Maybe the woods were being cleared for development.'

I nodded. 'It's not the first-time builders have stumbled across the grisly remains of some poor soul. More likely to have been a dog walker, though.'

'Your cousin must have known this Dixon guy if Althurian was her childhood home.'

'I don't really know if it was. Parminter said she inherited it in the late nineties. He didn't say from whom.'

She looked pensive for a moment. 'I think she lived here all her life. I can feel it.'

'If you're right, then she was certainly a witness to both disappearances. Be interesting to know how Dixon was related to the people here; if at all. Sylvia *was* a Forsyth, remember.'

'Perhaps he was the gardener.' She smirked. 'Lady Chatterley an' all that.'

I chuckled. 'I wish I had been a little more patient with Gerry when he gave me the paper.' I leaned back and briefly stared at the ceiling. 'He probably knows a lot more than what's written here.'

'We could always pop back tomorrow.'

'We could.' It wasn't what I had in mind, but it made sense. I really wanted to spend as much time at the house as possible. If there were any secrets to be found, Althurian was where we'd find them. She spotted my hesitancy.

'Not keen, then?'

I shook my head. 'Sorry, I was miles away.'

'I can see that.' She smiled. 'It has been a long day, sweetie. Perhaps we ought to sort out where we're going to sleep, or at least find some blankets so we can curl up down here. I know you think I'm a hardy girl, but even I need to cover myself up with something.'

I got to my feet, grinning feebly. 'I think I was supposed to have done that earlier.'

'Well, if you're going to explore upstairs then you're not going without me.'

She had already jumped from the sofa and bounded across to the door before I had time to move. I sometimes wondered where she found her energy; her parents seemed old before their time. I shrugged and followed her at my own speed; she was waiting for me in the stairwell, her arm draped round the newel post.

Once we'd reached the stair head the reasoning behind the orientation of the stairs became apparent. Well, sort of. The upstairs hall, landing, or whatever you wish to call it, ran from east to west. I kind of saw the logic in this. The house was wide, really wide, making the downstairs rooms disproportionately longer than their width. Upstairs, the rooms were still large but boxier, and there were more of them; eight, if you count the two en-suite bathrooms. Another landing ran from the front to the back of the house, or north to south. We turned south towards a window overlooking the back garden; halfway along there were two opposing doors.

Skye was still feverishly excited. 'Which one? You choose.'

I grabbed the handle and opened the one closest to me. It was pitch black inside and I had to blindly pat my hand round to find the light switch; two identical candlestick lamps with shades, lit up either side of a freshly made up bed. Two white towels, each with a small bar of soap and shower gel, were laid out just below the pillows. We both stood in silence. Skye was the first to break it.

'Do you get the feeling we were expected.'

I nodded slowly. 'I do now.'

'It doesn't make sense.'

'No.' I walked over and opened the door on the opposite side of the room; a light, and a hardly audible extraction fan, came on automatically. The en-suite shower room was immaculate, and if I were to make a guess, would say it had been installed fairly recently. 'Someone has been splashing out,' I said.

Skye squeezed past me. 'Oh, let me see,' she squealed, almost jumping up and down when she saw inside. 'This is so brilliant, John.' She turned to me. 'Why don't we stay for the rest of the week? You're not back at school until the twenty fifth.'

I smiled. It had crossed my mind, more than once. This latest discovery was the icing on the cake. 'Yeah, why not.'

'Yippee,' she cried, clapping her hands. 'I want the side closest to the shower room.'

I was unlikely to argue or win if I did. 'Someone definitely knew we were coming. Why would you bother preparing a room like this if you lived on your own?'

'Perhaps Sylvia *was* having Althurian converted to a bed and breakfast like Gerry said. Perhaps the cat was already out the bag before the old lady died.'

'But why would she,' I said. 'It's not like she was short of a bob or two.'

She giggled. 'You remind me of my dad when you use that old money speak.'

I snorted. 'But I like using old terms, leave me alone. What I said was true though, Sylvia didn't need to supplement her income by renting out rooms.'

'Perhaps the estate is worth less than we thought, John. Perhaps Sylvia was in hock to the bank?'

I shook my head. 'Parminter would have said so. Anyway, it costs a lot of money to convert a place like this, especially if it's a listed building. And at her age, why would she bother?'

She raised her eyebrows. 'She was obsessed with business? That room full of books should be a clue.'

'You have a point, but I can't really see it. With work still in progress, you'd hardly dress a room for guests before the rest of the house is finished.' I made my way to the door.

'Well, I suppose we'll find out soon enough.' She smirked. 'Do you fancy a little wager?'

'Ten bob says I'm right?'

'Oh, very funny.' She stepped to one side and ushered me through with a broad sweep of her hand. 'Age before beauty.'

♦

The door opposite opened to an empty room, newly decorated, but empty, nevertheless. We made our way to the other end of the landing; it was almost impossible to tell them apart. I suppose you could call this side, the north east wing. Skye tried the first door; it was another bedroom, and although it had a different colour scheme, was almost identical to the first had it not been prepared for guests. We wandered in anyway.

She opened one of the wardrobe doors. It was empty. 'Where is all Sylvia's stuff? She must have had personal belongings of some sort. I have loads, and I've been living in a converted ambulance for the best part of my adult life.'

She was right of course, so far, we had found nothing of any consequence. I sighed. 'Maybe you're right about the B & B and she had another house elsewhere.'

'I thought Parminter would have told you that.'

I gave a limp smile. 'It was just an idea.' I wandered out to the landing and tried the door opposite; I thought it had jammed until I realised it opened outwards. The room, if you can call it that, wasn't very deep, four to five feet at the most. Turning on the light revealed it to be a large broom cupboard, containing all the essentials: vacuum cleaner, mop and bucket, shelves with various products, dusters, that sort of thing. What I didn't immediately notice were the two Victorian travel chests tucked behind the shelving. Skye sidled up to me as I was working out what to do.

'Oh, great, a cupboard.'

'Not just a cupboard.' I stepped to one side, pointing to my find. 'What do you make of those?'

Her face had lit up like a beacon. 'Shall we take them back to the room and go through them in comfort.' She looked at me impishly. 'They could be full of dark, family secrets.'

'Or full of old clothes.' It wasn't high on my list of things to do. 'We need to move all this other stuff out of the way first,' I said grumpily. I know, it was stating the obvious, but clearing out a cupboard was something I really didn't want to do right at that moment. But before the last word had left my lips, she was already wheeling out the vacuum cleaner. As was usual, she had got her way.

It took less time than I thought. Fortunately, each brown and tan, tin plate chest had an iron loop handle at either end, and as they appeared to be locked or fastened in some way, we carried each one through to the bedroom anyway. I had visions of us sifting through musty old clothes and fox fur stoles until the sun came up.

I chuckled to myself as I made my way back to the cupboard. Skye had lost interest in anything else at this stage and was busy working out how to open the chests; unlike me, she was very adept at fixing anything mechanical. I returned the last of the cleaning materials, closed the door and brushed my hands together, feeling quite pleased with myself. Back at the room, I found her sitting cross-legged on the bed, head bowed and poring over a thick piece of card.

'Found something good, love?' I think I may have startled her.

She looked up suddenly. 'I think this is a photograph of Sylvia's father.' She held it up for me to see. The faded black and white image was of a man in his thirties, possible a little younger. He was dressed in a uniform, one of a pilot judging by the wings above his breast pocket; a handsome, proud looking man, with dark wavy hair and a strong jaw. I was strangely captivated by his dark, haunted eyes.

'How do you know?'

'Obviously I don't know for sure, but on the back, it says he's Pilot Officer Charles Forsyth, and it's dated the third of July 1940. He'd be the right age, I guess. Sylvia was born the same month, and if she was seventy-six when she died, born the same year.'

I sat next to her. 'I'll have to start calling you Sherlock. You're on a roll.'

She giggled and picked up another photograph. 'This was in the same envelope; it could be his wife.' The image was of a woman in her early twenties; it was difficult to tell because her hairstyle and clothes made her look a little older. I flipped it over. On the reverse was written the name Patricia. I stared at it for longer than I thought; this was a look Skye had seen before. 'She looks a bit like your mum, doesn't she?'

'Mum and dad's wedding photo, the one I keep on the fridge.' I shook my head. 'They could be twins. Creepy.'

She slid from the bed, took another handful of papers, and returned to resume her original cross-legged posture. 'You are so lucky to have the opportunity to do this, John. This is so much fun.'

I had to stop myself from laughing out loud; I was lucky to get a look in. But it was good to see her so animated, and so joyously excited. I looked skyward and thanked whoever made all this possible.

'Hang on, what have we got here?' She pulled out a limp piece of brown, parchment-like paper. To me it looked like a shred from the Dead Sea Scrolls. She slipped on her reading glasses and started to closely scrutinise the document; keeping it to herself a little too long for my patience to last.

'Am I in any danger of finding out,' I grumbled.

'You're going to love this.'

I sighed. 'This year?' Next year?'

'Sarcastic bugger. I'll let you have it in a sec.'

I was almost at my impatience fever pitch by the time she handed it over. This small leaf of paper was not as ancient as it first appeared and was in fact a newspaper cutting. There was no sub-heading like in the paper Gerry gave us.

> *After a country wide operation and several weeks of public appeals, police are now giving up the search for missing RAF war veteran, Flight Lieutenant Charles Forsyth, last seen after driving his car to the Seabrook filling station for petrol at around 8pm on Thursday 28th May this year. Mrs Patricia Forsyth, the missing man's wife, was not available for comment and is currently staying with friends. Detective Sergeant Arnold Berry, said yesterday, "We are treating the*

disappearance of Flight Lieutenant Forsyth as suspicious until we discover evidence to the contrary".

'It looks like he was the other missing person,' I said. 'Althurian seems to have a history of it. What's seventy-two take away nineteen?' Mental arithmetic has never been my thing.

She frowned. 'Fifty-three. Why?'

'Dixon went missing in 1972, nineteen years after Charles Forsyth. This article must have been written in 1953.' Then the gravity of the story hit me. 'Sylvia was only thirteen when he disappeared. 'Poor little cow,' I mumbled.

'If it was her dad.'

I rubbed my chin. 'I can't see who else it could be.'

'Then the lady in the photograph might be her mum.'

'Or just another relative.' I yawned noisily. 'I think we should call it a day.'

She cupped a hand over her mouth and yawned too. 'Ha! I didn't feel tired until you did that.' She smiled sweetly. 'I've had a really lovely day, John. Thank you.'

'Shall I see if I can rustle up a cup of cocoa?'

'Now you're spoiling me, Mr Warrener.'

♦

I was restless, very restless. New bed, unfamiliar surroundings, and a girlfriend who could do a realistic impression of a windmill, didn't help. I was envious too. Skye fell asleep as soon as her head hit the pillow, most annoying when you can't. When she finally stopped flailing her arms about, I was too awake to sleep. I lay on my back staring at the ceiling, my eyes now adjusted to the dim, curtain filtered moonlight. The house was deathly quiet, as was outside. Not a hoot, screech, or passing vehicle, broke the silence. I turned on my side for the fourth, or maybe the fifth, or even the sixth time; quite frankly I'd lost count.

I swung my legs from the bed, slowly, as not to wake the slumbering princess, although I sincerely believe the trumpets responsible for the fall of Jericho would have struggled. I sat up, getting to my feet without really knowing what I was going to do. I had thought about making some toast, perhaps a cup of tea; both standbys whenever I have trouble sleeping. I have often wondered, on those nightly occasions when I have too much time on my hands, if I need to eat to help me sleep, or wake up because I'm hungry. I padded across the carpet, opening the door as quietly as I could. I think screwing up my face must have helped because I didn't make a sound; this technique also worked on closing it again.

I tiptoed along the landing, aided only by the light coming from the two adjacent windows. I stopped at the top of the stairs and looked down into the dark well, it was like I was about to descend to the underworld. As a shiver unexpectedly shot up my spine, I got a whiff of lavender again, the same fragrance I noticed on opening Sylvia's letter. I know this sounds a little absurd, but I sensed it had drifted from somewhere behind me; I also had an overwhelming feeling I wasn't alone.

Without thinking, I turned to look towards the west wing of the house; I had an irresistible urge to explore a room at the end of the corridor. I took a step forward, and before I knew it was standing outside the door with absolutely no good reason to be there. The scent of lavender was stronger than ever, and I nervously wrung my hands together as I fought this seductive and weirdly familiar need to enter the room.

I looked back along the corridor towards the top of the stairs and the north south landing, and the room I had just left. A cascade of memories flooded my conscious thoughts as if I'd woken up and remembered every dream I'd ever had. I thought about Skye, our time together, the good, and the not so good. My hand reached out, then stopped, hovering just above the brass handle. I could feel my usually steady pulse quicken as my imagination began to anticipate what lay the other side. In some dark corner of my mind I believed I already knew. The wait was over, and my mind made up, I turned the handle and walked in.

The door closed behind me with a gentle click. From somewhere unknown, a thrilling sense of expectation seemed to saturate every cell of my body as I waited for whatever, or whomever, I had been sent to find.

'I know what you've been up to.' The voice was neither angry nor impatient. It was, however, the voice of a woman. My body stiffened. I tried to answer but could hardly breathe. I sensed she was behind me. She spoke again, her voice strangely familiar. 'You were a foolish man to believe your dirty little secret was safe.'

I attempted to move my feet, turn around and face my accuser, but it wasn't to be. I filled my lungs as best I could and, as every sinew in my chest strained to breaking point, fought to cast away whatever was holding me. I toppled forward into absolute darkness, an abyss without apparent end. The horror of falling into nothingness was terrifying, beyond anything I'd ever experienced. The last thing I remembered before blacking out completely was an intense searing pain behind my left ear.

Chapter 4
Secrets

My eyes snapped open. A shaft of dazzlingly intense sunlight had cleaved through a gap in the curtains and formed a bright vertical column on the wall next to the door. I groaned, lifted my wrist, squinting as I tried to focus on my watch. It was 10am. I groaned again, as I tend to in the morning, turning myself over so I could impart the drama of my terrifying ordeal to my mate. My heart skipped a beat when I found I was on my own; the other side of the bed was empty and surprisingly cold. I inclined my head, straining to hear any familiar sounds of movement. After a minute or so I concluded, and hoped, she had gone downstairs to make coffee.

Not that I was paying too much attention to my surroundings at that particular moment, but the room looked different somehow. A subtle difference, but different, nevertheless. I slid from the bed and stood up, rolling my shoulders, and my head, as I did so. This wasn't, as it turned out, a good idea. The pain that shot through the back of my skull was like I had been whacked by a hammer. My legs buckled under me and I collapsed onto the bed as consciousness slipped from me.

'John!'

At first, I couldn't make out what this sudden shock of sound was. I knew I should recognise its complex structure, but I couldn't, I just couldn't. I wanted to shake my head, the head I wasn't sure I had. My mind, the me, who occupied this strange moment in time and space, was happy in this woolly, black nothingness.

'John, please wake up!'

This time, the collection of sounds meant something to me, as did their creator. Whatever this mysterious energy holding mind and body together was, it had begun its journey back. 'Skye, is that you,' I mumbled.

'My God, are you all right?'

I wasn't sure how to answer. 'I...I think so,' I mumbled. My eyes flickered open. Skye was leaning over me; her expression was one of fear.' I lifted my hand, I wanted to touch her, show her I was okay.

'I'm going to call an ambulance.'

'No...Please don't.' I think I may have shouted the words. 'I...I just had a bad dream, that's all.' I pushed myself up on my elbows as she was about to get off the bed. I grabbed her arm. 'I really am okay.'

She gently pulled away from me, her bottom lip trembling slightly. 'This was more than a bad dream, John. I think you need to see a doctor.'

Whatever it was had scared her enough to want to call for help. An unexpected memory of her in an empty downstairs room flashed into my head. I made a mild attempt at humour. 'I didn't call an ambulance when you had a funny turn.'

She looked at me as if I was talking gibberish. 'And what funny turn was that, John?' she asked calmly. Now she was beginning to sound like a psychiatrist.

I was on the road to nowhere and knew it. I took a deep breath. 'Look, once I've had a shower and livened up a bit, I'll tell you all about this weird dream I had.'

She looked unconvinced but nodded reluctantly. 'Okay.' She gave me one of her piercing looks 'Only if you promise to book an appointment with the doctor the moment you get home.'

'I will, I promise.' Not that I had any idea what I was to consult the doctor about. Maybe she was right; maybe it was more than just the stuff of nightmares.

She did her best to smile as she got up to leave 'And don't lock the door.' She knew me well; I have always locked the door, a habit I just can't break. I feel a kind of naked vulnerability if I don't. Perhaps I do need to see a shrink! As she turned to leave, she said those words a man like me always wants to hear. 'I'll see if I can find some coffee.' Her face brightened a little. 'An' boy, do I need one.'

Personally, I could have done with something far stronger, but hey ho. The door clicked shut and I was suddenly on my own again, the bedroom was back to how it was the night before, and I was beginning to think clearly again. Yes, my world had returned to relative normality. I was apprehensive about getting to my feet again, avoiding any movement of my head just in case; when I did finally stand up, I was surprised not to feel at least a little wobbly.

My shower experience was delicious. No expense had been spared on the fittings; I spent the first few minutes trying to work out how to turn off the three pairs of body jets, nice as they were, and get the satellite dish sized shower head to work. When I finally did have it, all figured out and stood motionless under the deluge for probably longer than I should have, I realised I'd left the shower gel and towel in the bedroom. If my head could have endured such things, I had the perfect excuse, and opportunity, to have a good rant; I was clearly feeling better than I had earlier. Luckily, Skye returned to get her reading glasses as I started to emerge from the shower, saving me from the inevitable funny walk and subsequent wet footprints across the bedroom carpet.

I find the smell of coffee intoxicating, as it always is when one is addicted to the stuff like me; especially when the aroma saturating every molecule of air has the flavour of freshly roasted beans. Not true in this case, of course. Anyway, the smell was delicious, and I was unnecessarily torturing myself before going downstairs. I closed the bedroom door and wandered to the centre of the landing. I gave more than a cursory glance along the corridor towards the room that had appeared so real in my dream. I felt a sudden, cold whisper of uneasiness as I stood there. A dream it might have been, the fear, well, that was something completely different.

Skye had only just removed the percolator from the hob when I came into the kitchen. She gave me a look of concern. 'How you feeling?'

'I'm okay. You really shouldn't worry.'

'Easy for you to say.

'At least I didn't drown in the shower.'

She scowled. 'It isn't funny.'

'Sorry.'

'So, you should be.'

Thankfully I detected a ghost of a smile. 'Are you taking that through to the drawing room?'

'No,' she said, her smile turning to a smirk. 'As the sun has blessed us with its presence today, I thought we might have our refreshments in the garden room.' She knew something I didn't. I could tell.

'Althurian has a garden room?' I asked.

'Oh yes. And you won't believe how wonderful it is. I've already laid everything out for breakfast.' I could see she had already settled to the ways of country life. 'It has those really expensive wicker chairs and a lovely bleached wood table. You'll love it.'

And she was right, I did. It was beautiful. I expected it to be a recent addition to the property, but it wasn't. Looking extensively refurbished throughout its history, the structure appeared to be late Victorian; accessed from the kitchen through a solid, split stable door, and attached to the east side of the main building. I stood by the twin, half glazed doors looking out; the view to the south was stunning, although a little hidden by a line of mature elder trees running from the east to west towards the lower end of the visible garden; it was difficult to tell how far the estate boundary extended and where the rolling hills began. I had that feeling of being overwhelmed again.

'Don't let your coffee get cold, John,' she said, clutching a pillow to her chest, and for a brief moment, looking sublimely content. Her earlier fear for my health appeared to have evaporated, or so I thought. She took a sip of coffee and returned the cup to its saucer. 'I was really worried about you this morning.'

I smiled. 'Like I said, it was only a dream.'

Her face hardened. 'It wasn't like that, John. You were unconscious. I couldn't wake you up.'

I wandered over to the chair opposite and sat down. Picking up my coffee, I shrugged. 'I must have been in a really deep sleep, that's all.'

'Not with your eyes open, you weren't. When I woke up, I thought you were dead.' She wiped the corner of her eye with the back of her hand. 'It was horrible, you have no idea.'

It took a moment to sink in. 'What did you say?'

'It was horrible?'

'No,' I huffed impatiently. 'Before that?'

'I'm not sure what you mean.'

I rolled my eyes. 'You were in bed when this happened? Yes?'

'Of course, I was. Where else would I be?'

My head swooned a little. 'B...but when I woke up earlier, you weren't there.'

'Don't be silly. I slept like a log; I hadn't moved.'

I stared at her. None of this made sense. I couldn't have made it up, or could I? I began to doubt my sanity. 'Was I under the duvet?'

Her eyes levelled with mine. 'Under the duvet with your head on the pillow, normal, the way you always sleep.' I caught an undertone of irritation in her voice. I realised my version of events didn't quite fit hers. 'It could have been sleep paralysis; I suppose. A friend of mine used to suffer from it quite frequently. It used to scare her to death.' She laughed nervously. 'Scares me to death just thinking about it.'

'If it was that, I would have known about it,' I snapped unnecessarily. We were going around in circles, and I was about to suggest we drop the subject when there was a loud clack, clack, clack, at the front door. Both of us jumped. 'I'll go,' I said, glad of the interruption.

The short, smartly dressed man holding a brown paper parcel was a courier and staring at his phone when I opened the door. He looked up and gave me the most cheerful of smiles. 'Mr John Warrener?' he asked politely.

'Yes, that's me.'

He handed me the parcel. 'Sign here please.'

This may be a mark of advancing years but I'm beginning to find signing a screen with my fingernail irritating. I scribbled what looked like a Picasso snail and handed the device back to him. He seemed pleased, but indifferent to my writing style, turning to leave with a wave of his hand.

'Thank you, Mr Warrener,' he said. 'Have a nice day.'

I closed the door and looked at the address; it had been handwritten. According to the printed label attached by the courier, it had been accepted for delivery two days ago. I wandered back to the garden room; Skye was reading a copy of Horse and Hounds. She leant forward as I placed the shoebox sized parcel on the table. I sat down, picked up my coffee and took a sip. It was cold and I pulled a face. 'Yuk!'

'I told you it would get cold.'

'I know you did.'

'Is it for you?' she asked, nodding at the parcel.

'It appears so.' I stared at it for a second. 'I wonder what it is.'

She laughed. 'You'd know if you opened it.'

I've never been one to open anything in a rush, cherishing the moment of anticipation for as long as possible. When I was a kid my mum and dad had very little money, so Christmas time was always a bleakly austere event. Making the most of the few presents I received was part of the excitement; patience really was a virtue. I think this strange habit started then. I tore a strip of wrapping from the parcel and tried again to guess what was inside.

Skye sighed, picked up the percolator and got to her feet; I knew this frequent ritual drove her crazy. 'I'll make another coffee. Probably grow some beans while I'm at it.'

I completely missed the humour. 'Yeah, okay. Thanks, love.' Finally, the need to know got the better of me. After removing the rest of the wrapping, the plain cardboard box told me little. Even now I hesitate before removing any lid or covering flap. Perhaps I really do need to see someone! I rubbed my fingers and thumbs together in a kind of nervous excitement.

Inside, there were three bundles of papers, each neatly tied with ribbon, two thick brown envelopes, and a small square box; the sort you might put trinkets in. I took out the first bundle, and the one looking the most recent; the others had a yellow tinge to them. Underneath the bow there was another envelope. I could feel my pulse quicken as I began to untie the ribbon. Skye came in with the coffee, looking over my shoulder as she put down the percolator.

'Now, they look interesting,' she said.

I took out the unsealed envelope and removed the single velum sheet inside. The paper was identical to the one left in the desk drawer and written in the same hand.

'It's another letter from Sylvia.' I sat back and began to read.

Dear John

This box contains the Land Registry papers and deeds to every property you now own. This, I know, will come as a surprise to you as I instructed Mr Parminter (Junior) to withhold certain details of my estate at the time of reading. This was my wish. Also contained in the box are a number of share stock certificates that have already been transferred and are now in your name. If you decide to cash them in or keep them, the choice is now entirely up to you. Mr Parminter would have already given you the names of brokers who are trusted enough to do this for you......

I let the letter fall limply in my hand. Looking up at Skye, I said, 'I don't get it. It chills me to think Sylvia must have organised this in the knowledge she was about to die. It's so controlled and well thought out, it borders on spooky.'

'This whole business is spooky if you ask me' she said. 'What does it say?'

I raised an eyebrow. 'Althurian is one of several properties Sylvia left to me, and somewhere in this lot, a wad of share certificates.'

'So, she did have somewhere else to live.' 'My God, the estate must be worth a small fortune.'

'Not so small by the look of it.'

She pointed to the small trinket box. 'What's in there?'

'Let me finish this and we'll have a look.'

……Some of them may be worth keeping, at least until their value increases. I have listed those I believe may have some life left in them. The small box contains a key. Keep it safe, you will be told its significance in due course. Just a small note regarding the vehicles you may have already discovered in the garage. If not, you'll find the keys to the Aston and the garage doors hanging underneath the cupboard to the left of the kitchen sink. I have arranged for the Silver Wraith to

be refurbished by a local company and have agreed for it to be picked up at your convenience......

I looked at Skye, my excitement obvious. 'You'll never guess what's in the garage?'

Her eyes widened. 'A Rolls Royce?'

'Well yes, there is one of those,' I said flippantly. 'Only an old one though. But listen to this.' I now looked smug at this point. 'There's only a bloody Aston Martin parked in there.'

'Really?' Now I had her attention. 'Which model?'

Only someone who has spent a considerable amount of time travelling the length and breadth of Britain and Europe would ask such a question. To be honest, I know I like the look of them, but could I tell one model from another? No. 'It doesn't say,' I said, grinning. 'We could go and take a look.'

Her face lit up. 'Even better, we could take it out for a spin.'

'I'm not insured to drive a car like that.'

'Of course you are. You're covered third party if you have the owner's permission to drive it. Now, you might not be the keeper yet, but you're certainly the owner. Just be careful not to break it. You could always give your insurance company a call and extend your cover just to be on the safe side.'

I sometimes envied her grip on the world; she either knew the answer or had a way of breaking down the toughest of problems into manageable pieces, making the whole process look easy. Very rarely have I seen her stumped for an answer. 'I might just do that,' I said.

'Well if you're not game, I know someone who is.'

♦

The share certificates would have to wait. I found the keys and had a very peculiar sense of déjà vu as I unhooked the fob bearing the Aston Martin marque. I smoothed the soft brown leather between my thumb and forefinger. This vehicle, if the fob and key were anything to go by, had seen some life. I smiled to myself; I was beginning to realise this distant cousin of mine was not a victim of a fad society. She calculated everything, right down to the smallest detail, looked for quality not quantity, and sought out the best money could buy, not only because it was well made or fit for purpose, but because it would stand the test of time. The line in her letter about the shares was an example of a shrewd investor, and not someone out to make a quick buck. I stuffed the keys into my pocket and went to catch up with Skye, who no doubt was already waiting by the garage, hands on hips. And I was right.

'What took you so long?'

I laughed. 'Impatient people always seem to have a different perception of time to everyone else.'

She poked out her tongue. 'You're just slow, Warrener.'

I gave a derisory snort as I removed the heavy padlock. The double width garage door consisted of five individual sliding sections that moved effortlessly across the opening with the lightest of touch. I found it impossible to lose the feeling I was a visitor to a world I didn't belong. We stood gawping at the spectacle before us.

One of the vehicles was completely covered with a remarkably white cover sheet. The other was not. A metallic blue Aston Martin was parked front end in, its sleek, rakish lines unmistakable.

I thought her eyes were about to pop out. 'You lucky sod,' she said. She bounded over to it and immediately began to run her hand over the paintwork even before the thought of moving had entered my head. Personally, I've never understood the need to know a car so intimately. I think it must be a petrol head thing. 'You know this must be worth close to half a million, don't you?'

I wasn't quite sure I'd heard right. 'Sorry? What did you say?'

'A DB6 sold at auction for just under half a million pounds.'

'You...are...kidding.'

'I'm not, as it happens.'

'Bloody hell,' was all I could say. Three weeks ago, I was trying to work out how I could afford the repayments on a second-hand replacement for my twelve-year-old Toyota Yaris. I wiped the bead of sweat from my top lip.

'Well, are you going to open it or stand there like a lemon?' It was more of a demand than a question.

'I think you'll need the key, love.'

Too late, she was already waiting by the driver's door. 'Just DO IT from where you are. Come on, hurry up.'

I sighed, wandered to where she was standing and held out the key. 'There's no remote central locking on this baby. You have to do it the old-fashioned way.'

She took the key, grinning sheepishly. 'I knew that.'

For one brief and terrifying moment, I thought the huge door was about to hit the garage wall as she swung herself into the driver's seat. I should have known better. I can't imagine Sylvia overlooking the possibility of such an obvious calamity. I watched as she performed almost the same ritual inside the car as she did outside. First, she ran her hand across the wooden dashboard, then in one non-stop, flowing action, applied the same treatment to the light tan, leather passenger seat; every action seamlessly executed while her face appeared to be in a state of meditative bliss. It was uncanny to watch.

She looked up at me, her face as serious as I had yet seen. 'We have got to take this out, we really have.' She returned her gaze to the brass riveted wooden steering wheel, delicately massaging it with both hands. 'My dad said that if he ever won the lottery, he'd buy one of these.'

'You could always take him out in it,' I said. 'Let him have a drive. He'd love it.'

She turned her head suddenly, her eyes meeting mine. I thought she was about to cry. 'Y…you'd let me do that?'

'I can't see why not. Be a shame not to get the most out of it.'

Her eyes filled. 'I…I…don't know what to…' she stammered.

I laid a hand on her shoulder. 'Start her up, let's go for a blast.'

She sniggered between tears. 'You are so old fashioned sometimes.'

♦

The Aston grumbled to life as only a car of its pedigree could. She carefully reversed it from the garage, turning so it faced up the drive; it looked smaller than I thought. She powered down the window, her grin almost as wide as the front grill. 'You can drive her first, if you like.'

I chuckled. 'It's a she, is it?'

Her brow furrowed. 'Of course, it is,' she said indignantly. 'It's far too beautiful to be a man.'

I closed the garage doors, wandered over to the car, and opened the passenger door. 'I just need to lock up the house. I'll meet you by the front steps.'

'You are driving, right?'

I shook my head. 'I'd like to check out the insurance first, if you don't mind.'

She grinned again. 'Disbeliever.'

I think she was secretly pleased; in fact, I know so. I'm a complete wimp when it comes to such things, I need to see things in black and white, or get someone in authority to give me the nod. My father was the same. Inherited genes, I guess.

I checked the doors to the garden room, and I picked up the box from the table; it wasn't something I was happy to leave lying round. I did, however, remove the key from the trinket box and slip it into my pocket. I could be wrong, but it looked very much like it was meant for a safe.

The Aston was parked just ahead of our car. Now, in comparison to the Toyota, it looked huge. As I walked towards it, I could see Skye's head bobbing up and down, no doubt exploring every nook and cranny. I think I startled her when I opened the door. 'Having fun?' I asked.

'Well, your cousin didn't smoke; the ashtray is as clean as the day it was made.'

'Perhaps she used to have a crafty fag outside.'

She glared at me. 'I don't think she was that sort of woman. If she was a smoker, she'd do it anywhere she damn well wanted. She was her own woman, make no mistake.'

Her sudden, defensive response surprised me; Sylvia had already made quite an impression on her. I climbed in and closed the door. 'Where shall we go, then?'

She tapped the fuel gauge glass with a fingernail. 'We need to get some gas before we go too far. I wonder if the petrol station Sylvia's father used is still around.'

I thought for a moment. 'Seabrook's?'

'That's the one.'

'Be great if we knew where it was.'

'It can't be far.' She adjusted the rear-view mirror. 'We can always ask someone.' She slipped the Aston into drive and eased on the accelerator. The deep, but gentle burble coming from the engine seemed to vibrate the inside of my chest as the car began to creep slowly along the drive. 'I can't believe I'm driving this…this beautiful machine,' she oozed. 'Even though I reckon this car must be at least forty years old, it feels like brand new.'

'How many miles has it done?'

She leant towards the speedometer, narrowing her eyes. 'Forty-five thousand four hundred and fifty-two.'

I whistled. 'It's done less than mine.' I paused. 'I suppose it could've been round the clock a couple of times.'

She shook her head. 'Too clean, too tight, I'm surprised it's done that much.'

We were less than halfway along the drive and I was beginning to feel a tiny bit envious, this was indeed, a beautiful machine. She pulled up before the gate. 'We should go right,' I said. 'I can't remember seeing a garage on our way in.'

'Me neither. Right it is.'

To say the Aston took off and flew like a low flying jet aircraft would probably understate the experience. Skye regaled me with various facts and figures about Aston Martin's long automotive history as the miles dissolved beneath us. She even knew that only eighteen hundred were ever made. It was…I suppose…interesting to a point. Don't get me wrong, I was thrilled to be the new owner of this wonderful beast, but not quite as thrilled as she was to drive it. It was, however, my over enthusiastic chauffeur who first spotted the petrol station.

'There it is,' she cried. 'I knew it wouldn't be far.'

Apart from the two modern looking pumps, the forecourt, and the three buildings behind it, appeared to have changed little in decades. Their shabby, olive green painted corrugated iron walls, and roofs of faded burgundy, did nothing to suggest this isolated plot had seen much investment since the fifties. Even the door leading to the office had a large hand painted sign next to it declaring, "This site is not self-service" and to "Wait in your vehicle to be served". Charles Forsyth would certainly have recognised it.

She pulled up, hesitating a moment before turning off the engine. 'It's weird having the handbrake next to the door.' She chuckled almost mischievously. 'This is so cool.'

'I can't remember the last time I had to wait next to a petrol pump for someone to serve me,' I said.

She moved the mirror, inclined her head, and wiped a minute smear of lipstick from the corner of her mouth. 'I never have. It's quite nice in a way.'

'Nice if someone bothers to come out,' I said grumpily. 'Sound your horn. They may be out the back or something.'

'I'm not doing that,' she hissed. 'They might tell me off.'

I reached for the chrome door handle. 'I'll see if I can find an attendant.'

She grabbed my arm. 'No, wait, John, I can see movement.'

Sure enough, within the shadow of the open doorway I could see the outline of someone lurking inside. Unfortunately, it didn't appear as if they were making an effort to reveal themselves. 'What are they doing?' I grumbled. 'We'll be here all bloody day at this rate. Just drive off, we'll find somewhere else.'

'We can't.'

'Why?'

'Because the fuel gauge shows the tank is empty and unless there's a really long hill before the next one, I'd rather wait here.'

'Okay.' Although I wanted to, it was pointless trying to dispute the sound logic of her argument. Instead, I started to mindlessly drum my fingers on the seat squab; an annoying habit at the best of times.

With our eyes fixed on the shadowy figure, the unexpected, and loud, rat-tat-tat on the rear quarter light took us completely by surprise. In the second or so it took to recover, the source of the intrusion had sidled up to the driver's door. A thin, mousy looking man, with hawkish eyes, thin face, and grinning yellow teeth, peered almost salaciously through the glass. Skye gave me a sideways glance before powering down the window.

'Afternoon,' he said, his eyes continuously jerking from Skye to me. 'Want me ta fill her up for ye, duck?'

'Yes, if you could, please.' He loitered for longer than was comfortable. Skye shifted awkwardly in her seat. 'Do I need to do anything?' she asked innocently.

'No, no. I was just wonderin' how ye came by this fine vehicle, that's all.'

'Why do you want to know?' I snapped.

The man stepped back, raising his hands defensively. 'I didn't mean nothin' by it,' he said apologetically. 'It's just that I'm used to seein' someone else behind the wheel.' The earlier leering gaze returned as his eyes settled back to Skye. 'An' someone quite a lot older than you, Missy.'

'Just fill up the car, will you,' I barked. By now you have guessed I have a problem with busybodies. Unfortunately, this town, village, or whatever it likes to call itself, appeared to be full of them. Okay, so I exaggerated a bit, but you know what I mean.

The man touched the side of his temple with a finger and dodged from view. We silently listened to the sound of a rattling petrol cap and scraping nozzle; the man was at least familiar with the car and knew where everything was. The whine from the pump and the gushing of fuel seemed to go on forever, and I was soon to discover why.

'Ninety-seven pounds,' I shrieked. So as not embarrass myself further I adjusted my voice down an octave. 'How can it be that much?'

I detected a ghost of a smirk before the man spoke. 'Sixty-nine litres, sir. You can go an' check thee pump if ye like.'

'My God, how much is it a litre?'

'A pound an' forty pence, sir.'

I wanted to blurt out phrases like, "Daylight robbery" and "You've got to be having a laugh" but thought better of it. 'Do you take credit cards?'

The man frowned. 'Yes, of course we do, lad.'

Now it was my turn. I think I droned on about the evils of capitalism for at least four miles, a somewhat longer distance than it took for me to learn about the motoring excellence of a British automotive legend. Skye said very little in response to my rant, possibly because she wasn't really listening. I consoled myself with the misguided belief that George Clooney was unlikely to have done any better. I sat quietly and watched the world go by until a series of carefully arranged words immediately drew my attention from the blur of passing hedgerow.

'What say you we find a pub, John? I could murder a baked potato and half a Guinness.'

'Good idea. I could murder both of those, twice.'

♦

After we passed a promising, gold lettered sign pointing to a hostelry called The Royal Oak, we left the main road, turning right onto a lane no wider than the Aston, praying not to meet anything coming from the opposite direction. We must have broken the world record for two people holding their breath simultaneously for the mile and a half it took to get there. Set on the edge of woodland, the nineteenth century inn was as charming as any pub could be. Unlike our visit to The Jolly Archer, parking spaces were at a premium, and narrower than expected. Several aborted attempts later, Skye thought it safer to park on the road; and after grinding away most of my tooth enamel I was inclined to agree with her.

The sound of muted exchanges, the odd burst of laughter, and musical hits from the eighties, drifted invitingly in our direction as we approached the freshly painted, solid wood entrance door. We stopped to check an adjacent menu board before going in.

'I fancy pasta,' she said.

'I thought you said you could murder a spud.'

'I know I did. I've changed my mind.'

I chuckled. 'Potatoes too common for you now, are they?'

As she brushed past me to open the door, I think she may have deliberately jabbed me in the ribs with her elbow. I yelped appropriately and followed her inside. It was noisier than expected, although I noticed a slight drop in volume as a few people decided we were briefly more interesting than the current topic of conversation. We chose to sit in one of only two vacant snugs.

Skye slipped off her jacket, tucking it neatly at one end of the settle. 'I like this place more than the other one.' She wrinkled her nose and snuggled down 'This is far cosier.'

'I'm sorry to disturb you, but do you mind if I ask you a question?'

Here we go again, I thought. We've only just sat down. I looked up and smiled as sweetly as I could. The bespectacled man staring down at me smiled back. I guess he was roughly my age, maybe a little older, had grey flecked, collar length hair and a neatly trimmed beard. He stooped slightly and peered over his spectacles as he spoke. I guessed he was a geography teacher. 'Be my guest,' I said.

'It's to settle a small wager I have with my friend.' He paused and raised his eyebrows as if he needed my permission to continue.'

I nodded. 'Right…Okay.'

'Well,' he said, pointing towards the window next to us. 'My friend says your DB6 is one of the later models, and I'm pretty sure it's an earlier one.'

Oh Lord, I thought, why oh why didn't we bring the Toyota? I had the urge to palm my face.

'I'm afraid you've lost your bet, my friend,' chimed Skye. 'It was one of the last six's to be built.'

I looked across at her. How did she know this stuff? I turned back and eyed our guest. Even though Skye had just delivered news he probably didn't want to hear, he was still smiling. I had the feeling this wasn't his only question. And I was right.

'Is it fitted with the ZF five speed manual gearbox or the Borg Warner three speed auto?'

I stared at him. I could see the words silently drifting across my field of vision. I'M NEVER TAKING THIS BLOODY CAR OUT AGAIN. Oddly enough, his question was, in fact, one I could answer. 'It's an auto,' I said, perhaps a little too sharply.

He stroked his chin thoughtfully. 'Right,' he said. 'How interesting…um…I wonder if…'

I raised my hand. 'I'd love to continue our little chat, but if you don't mind, we're rather hungry, and we haven't ordered yet. Do you mind?'

The man gasped, clutching a hand to his mouth. 'I'm dreadfully sorry, how rude of me. What must you think?'

'Please, at any other time it wouldn't be a problem,' I lied.

'Of course, of course,' he mumbled. 'Yes, another time.' With the last word trailing behind him, he turned on a heel and made off.

My eyes followed him until he was out of sight. I turned to look at Skye. She was smiling. 'What?' I snapped.

'I was impressed how restrained you were. You're not usually so polite with uninvited guests.'

I sighed. 'I'm trying my best to get used to it. I have a feeling this may happen quite a lot here.'

'Thinking of staying, then?'

I pursed my lips. She was very perceptive, but I honestly didn't know. There was something about Althurian I couldn't quite pin down, and it wasn't just curiosity. 'Ask me the same question in a few weeks. What about you, sweetie? Could you give up your life on the road and settle down?'

She coughed a laugh. 'Is that a proposal, Mr Warrener?'

'You know what I mean. Well?'

She slowly rocked her head. I could see from her expression she'd given it some thought. 'I must admit the

81

travelling life is beginning to lose its appeal, more so since we've been together. I suppose if you'd had the same wandering bug as me, and we were doing it together, I may feel differently.' She raised her hands. 'And I know you'd never stop me from doing what I want, but...' She paused. 'It's just that...I've been travelling on and off for the best part of fifteen years and it may be time to do something different.'

'At least you'd have a base to work from if you ever got the wanderlust again. You could even trade that old ambulance for something a little more...er...comfortable.'

She looked horrified. 'No way. Daisy has shared too much of my life to end up rotting in a scrap yard, cannibalised for spares.' She paused thoughtfully. 'I might take some time out to do her up, though.'

I wanted to shake my head. 'Ah, yes, Daisy. Well, there's plenty of room for her at Althurian.' I turned and scanned the room. 'I'm surprised someone hasn't come to take our order.'

Skye tapped the vase standing in the centre of the table; it contained a wooden spoon with a green number seven painted in its bowl. 'I think you have to take this to the bar to place your order, John.'

I got to my feet, probably shaking my head again. 'I'll get a bloody menu then.'

♦

'My God that was good.' I wiped the corners of my mouth with a napkin. 'How was the lasagne?'

She leant forward. 'Better if they'd put a little more salad with it. Pubs always seem to go overboard with the chips, as nice as they were, and skimp on the healthy stuff.' She patted her stomach. 'Not that I'm complaining, mind.'

It was quieter now. The Royal Oak was clearly a lunchtime destination for many. I carefully looked round to see if I could spot the geography teacher. Now we'd finished our food we could be a target for another salvo of questions I was ill prepared for. In fact, it appeared, as far as I could tell, we were one of only three couples left. From the corner of my eye I spotted a smartly dressed woman making her way towards us; I hoped she was a member of staff coming to collect our plates.

The tension in my shoulders evaporated when she asked, 'Did you enjoy your meals?'

We both nodded in unison. Skye spoke first. 'It was brilliant, thank you.'

I followed her praise almost instantly. 'Yes, very tasty, just what we needed, thank you.'

'That's good. I shall pass your compliments to our chef.' The woman quickly scooped nearly everything from the table, deftly supporting each item in a carefully coordinated balancing act. She stood back and seemed to dither slightly. I thought she was about to ask if we wanted something else. Her question caught me by complete surprise.

'You're Ms Forsyth's cousin, aren't you?'

Suddenly, I became aware of this person standing before me. I have a habit of not fully engaging with people of a transient nature. I'd be hopeless as a witness if I had to give evidence concerning the identity of a person I'd only met briefly. This woman could have looked like Quasimodo and I wouldn't have remembered. As it turned out, she didn't. Her name badge said she was known as

Rachael. A slim, sporty looking woman, with short hair and a round face. She may have been a little younger than Skye, but not by much. The corners of her mouth quivered as if she was struggling to smile. I frowned. 'Why do you ask?'

'You're driving her car,' she said. 'An' she told me you'd be coming to Althurian.'

I felt my eyes widen. 'She told you? When was this?'

'After she got sick. Said you'd take over the running of the place an' you'd look after those who worked there.'

I puffed out my cheeks; this was an unforeseen turn of events. I wasn't sure what this woman was expecting from me, if anything. Her manner suggested she was waiting for an answer, and I was struggling to respond. 'How did you know Ms Forsyth?'

'I clean for her,' she said, matter-of-fact. 'I do Mondays, Thursdays, and Fridays, eight 'til four thirty. Ms Forsyth said I should make myself known to you.'

'Right,' I said. 'And…em…do you live locally?' Yes, it was a ridiculous thing to ask, but it was all I could think of. Luckily Skye began to see the panic in my eyes.

'May I ask you a question, Rachael?'

'Sure.'

'When was the last time you were at Althurian?'

'Thursday, Miss.'

'This week?'

'Yes, Miss.'

'And you've been working there every week since Ms Forsyth passed away?'

'Yes, Miss. Apart from the Monday before last when I had to go to the dentist.'

'Rachael! The call was loud as it was clear. It came from the bar area, delivered by a man wearing a white chef's jacket and black skull cap.

The woman's head spun round. 'Yes, Mr Coleman.'

'Tables twelve and nine need to be cleared. Chop, chop.'

'Yes, Mr Coleman, right away, Mr Coleman.' She gave us a brief, nervous smile, curtsied awkwardly, and left.

I waited until she was out of earshot. 'Well, what do you make of that?'

Skye looked as dumbfounded as I was. 'It explains why the house is so tidy. I feel like Sylvia was trying to manage everything beyond the grave. If you know what I mean.'

I nodded. It was exactly how I felt. 'The odd thing is, for someone so organised, it's a shame she didn't think to keep me in the loop.'

I paid the bill and we wandered back to the car in silence. I think we were both weighed down with the one hundred and one questions flying about inside our heads. The Buddhists speak of the monkey mind; well, my head must have had an entire jungle of them. I automatically went to the driver's door, fumbling inside my trouser pocket as I did so.

'I'm driving, remember, John,' Skye said, holding up the key.

'Mr Forsyth. Mr Forsyth, sir.' The voice sounded urgent.

We turned to see Rachael jogging across the car park in her working clothes. She was quite out of breath when she got to us. 'H…have, have you…got a minute, Mr Forsyth?' she panted.

'Yes, of course I have, Rachael. And please, call me John.' I wanted to correct her assumption as to my surname but thought better of it; it was likely to confuse matters more than they already were. 'What can I do for you?'

Rachael glanced over her shoulder before speaking. 'You do still want me to work at the house, don't you?' She glanced back at the pub again.

What could I say? I was now well and truly on the spot. Her eyes were boring into mine, pleading almost. 'Don't worry, your jobs safe for the time being,' I said.

Her face instantly brightened. 'Oh, thank you, sir.'

Skye asked, 'Does the boss know you're out here, Rachael?'

She shook her head. 'He's on the phone to his brother, he'll be ages yet.'

'Well, don't get yourself in any bother, you can always talk to us another time.'

'I'll be okay, Miss, Mr Coleman's bark is worse than his bite.'

'If you don't mind me asking,' I said. 'How have you been paid for the work you've done so far?'

'Ms Forsyth see me all right before she left us, paid me cash, she did. Said you'd do the same.'

Skye asked, 'How many of you work at Althurian?'

'Five, Miss. Thomas Coley and Ted Ferris do the gardens, Stevie Watkins is the handyman, although he's hardly ever there because he's usually doing things at the other houses, and Mrs Redland is the housekeeper, although she's off with her hip at the moment.' She chuckled. 'And there's me.'

I realised I had committed myself to keeping all five of these people on the books; I could hardly promise work for one and not for all. I just hoped I could afford it. 'Have any of you been laid off?'

'No, Sir John, Ms Forsyth did the same for all of us.'

I smiled at my elevated status, choosing not to look in Skye's direction. 'And where and when can I meet these colleagues of yours?'

'Rachael! Rachael! Where the bloody hell are ye?'

I could just see Mr Coleman's skull cap bobbing along the roofline of a Range Rover. It was unlikely he'd spotted his errant waitress yet.

'I'd better go,' she whispered. 'Thank you again, Sir John.' With that, she turned and scampered off.

I glanced at Skye. I knew I had to at some stage; I also knew she'd be grinning impishly. 'Okay, get it over with if you have to.'

'Would Sir John like me to drive him back to the manor, or has Sir John got another engagement he wishes me to fulfil?'

It was difficult not to laugh, impossible in fact, and that's precisely what we did, all the way back to Althurian.

Chapter 5
The Althurian Circle

We turned onto the drive a little after three thirty. The afternoon had warmed considerably, the sun dazzlingly bright against a canvas of cobalt blue. Now on its westerly descent, its warming glow was just beginning to climb the spires of the majestically tall conifers lining the estate's eastern boundary. I had a kaleidoscope of butterflies flapping around inside my chest as the house came in view. It really did feel like I was coming home.

As we passed the Toyota, I noticed an old wooden wheelbarrow standing at the end of one of the gravel tracks that led away from the garage block; it had certainly seen better days. I couldn't remember seeing it when I opened the garage, not that I was looking; four wheels trumping the one easily. 'It must be the gardeners' turn today,' I observed.

Skye brought the Aston to a stop and craned her neck. 'It looks like you might need to open your wallet judging by the state of that wheelbarrow. Are you going to make yourself known to them?'

'Be rude not to. Can you remember their names?'

'One of them was Ted, I think.'

I tugged the chrome lever to unlatch the door. 'I'll do it now; they might be on their way home soon.' I grinned. 'And while I'm at it, you can do that thing you do so well with the percolator.'

'Oh, I can, can I? Would Sir like me to run his bath while I'm at it?'

I gave her a sidelong look. 'You can if you like. Make sure it's not too hot, you know I have delicate skin.'

She laughed. 'Be off with you, Warrener, before I pull that crown around your ears.'

I made my way along the track towards the wheelbarrow; it seemed to me a good place to start. I shivered involuntarily, I had that eerie sense of déjà vu again, and a prickling sensation that made the hairs on the back of neck stand on end. Ignoring it, I carried on. At first glance, I thought the wheelbarrow might have been abandoned until I spotted several gardening tools laid neatly on a pile of bramble cuttings. I straightened up and surveyed the area. There was not a soul about, nor could I hear anything. No idle chatter, the sound of metal upon stone, the grunts of effort. Nothing. It didn't help the fact that I had no idea how large the estate actually was; these men of the soil could have been anywhere. I was considering the possibility they may have gone home and forgot to put the tools away, when my eyes settled on something looking very much like the roof of a shed; it was peeping over an adjacent hedge line, south of where I was standing. This looked promising; sheds and gardeners always go together. Another gravelled path led the way.

It was farther than it looked, and getting chillier by the minute, even the sky had darkened appreciably, the air strangely oppressive. I shivered inwardly, chastising myself for leaving my jacket in the car. When I got to the hedge, an arch made from finely woven willow twigs was the only visible way through. Once on the other side the grounds opened out to the largest vegetable plot I had ever seen. It was huge. Sylvia either owned a greengrocery store or had a voracious appetite for plants. As I stood, taking it in, I caught the musty aroma of burning pipe tobacco; a distinct, earthy smell, unlike cigarette smoke.

'Can I 'elp ye, laddie?'

Jumping out of my skin was becoming a habit. I swung round. Standing between the open double doors of the shed, was a man, looking as it he had been plucked from the pages of an Edwardian novel. A short, sprightly character, possibly in his mid-sixties, dressed in brown baggy trousers and matching waistcoat, white linen shirt, and flat cap; he watched me intently as I recovered from the shock. 'Hello,' I said. 'You must be Ted.'

He frowned, eyeing me suspiciously. 'Who do ye say, lad?'

I winced. 'Ted?'

'Na, lad. There's nowt 'ere with a name as such.'

'Okay.' It was likely Skye must have misheard. I tried a different tack. 'Who else works on the estate with you?'

'Ye mean auld Tom.'

That name chimed a little bell in my head. 'Yes, that's him. Is he about today?'

'Na, lad. E's down at yard.'

'Right. Well then, I'd better introduce myself.' I stepped forward and held out my hand. 'I'm John Warrener.' The man met me halfway, his grip was iron like, and I did my best not to whimper as his huge calloused fingers pressed into mine.

'Albert Ferris. Pleased ta make ye acquaintance.'

Yes. I was sure Ferris was one of the names Rachael mentioned. Progress at last, I thought.

Unfortunately, Mr Ferris still had a look of suspicion about him, and so far, I had done nothing to help allay that. 'Do you work here every day, Albert?'

'Aye.'

I waited, expecting more. Sadly, it was not to be. I nodded morosely. 'Well, that's good.' I paused, feeling awkward. 'So, I suppose you'll be knocking off soon, won't you?'

Ferris' eyes narrowed. 'Does thee mind tellin' me what business ye 'ave 'ere, lad?'

I almost kicked myself. The old man was right to be suspicious; I'd completely forgotten to tell him why I was there. 'Sorry Albert, I should have said earlier.' I took a breath and smiled. 'I'm the new owner of Althurian.'

His tanned, lined face crinkled round his brown, kindly eyes as he lifted his cap to scratch his head. 'New owner, ye say?'

'Yes. I arrived today. I spoke to Rachael earlier; she said you'd be here.' I watched for a sign of recognition. 'And when I saw the wheelbarrow, I thought I'd come down and make myself known to you.' I knew I was beginning to ramble. I do that when a conversation becomes one sided. I was hoping the "new owner" bit might have swung it.

Ferris gave me a sidelong look. 'But I only see's Mr Bradford this mornin' an' e' said nothin' about a new owner. Who did ye says ye were?'

I tried not to roll my eyes. 'My name is John Warrener and I am Ms Forsyth's third cousin. I inherited the estate after she passed away last month.' I frowned. 'Has no one told you yet?'

91

The man waved his hand, I thought dismissively. 'What's this nonsense ye speakin' of, laddie. Lady Forsyth was only 'ere a few hours back, spoke to her me-self, I did.'

I stared at Ferris. My first thought was to run back to the house and scream rather loudly. Yep, that would do it. Now, there were two possibilities to this mystery. I had either fallen asleep on the way back from the pub and was dreaming, or, I had someone in my employ who was suffering from severe delusional psychosis. I pinched myself on the arm. Thought so. 'Right then, Albert,' I said. 'I'd better make a move and let you get on.' It wasn't the most creative of excuses, but it was all I had. I gave him a limp wave and left before he had time to speak. As I passed through the arch, I suddenly felt nauseous, slightly giddy, and a bit fluffy headed. I hadn't had any alcohol, so it wasn't that. I wobbled slightly and grabbed one of the arch supports to steady myself. After a few deep breaths the fog began to clear. I gave it a few more seconds before I was confident enough to let go and make my way back to the house.

I could see Skye standing outside the garage as I turned onto the track by the wheelbarrow. She had her arms folded and looked cross. I tried to look as jolly as I could, it sometimes worked when I was in trouble. 'Are you okay?' I asked.

'No.'

'Why, what's up?'

'You, John. I couldn't find you anywhere.'

I pulled a face. 'I was only up by the shed. I found the gardener.'

'What shed?'

I thumbed over my shoulder. 'The one behind the hedge.'

She looked confused, narrowing her eyes. 'I didn't see a shed...or a hedge. Are you sure?'

I scoffed. 'The guy was inside it when I spoke to him. It was a shed all right.'

'Show me.'

'Really?'

'Yes, really.'

'Okay,' I huffed. 'Come with me. But I'm not going back there, the bloke is as mad as a hatter.' As we passed a row of head height conifers lining the track, I turned and pointed to where I had met Ferris. I gasped. All I could see was a beautifully smooth lawn, flanked either side by beds of carefully tended shrubs and small trees. I took a step backwards, holding the top of my head with both hands; the nausea had returned. 'This can't be right,' I mumbled. I think she realised there was more to this than a silly prank. Her earlier anger evaporated, and she wrapped an arm round my waist, I think more for support than comfort.

'I need to get you indoors, John.'

I could feel my body go limp as she held me. In a few minutes I felt like I had aged thirty years. I wanted to speak, say something glib, but had lost the power to do so. She walked me back to the front steps, stopping before them. 'I need the key, John. You took it with you.'

I fumbled in my trouser pocket, pulling out the still labelled iron key by its string. I gave a limp smile. 'I'm really sorry about this.'

♦

I sat mindlessly staring at the portrait above the fireplace. I'm not sure if I was thinking anything in particular. The whole episode in the garden was like a dream. No. This was worse than a dream. I've woken up from dreams before and, for a few seconds, believed they were real; I think we all have at some point. But this was real, I know it was, and now my head had cleared, I wanted to go back outside and check one last time; to regain my sanity somehow. The clatter of Skye opening and closing the interconnecting door shook me from my solicitude. She came in carrying a tray.

'I've made us some hot chocolate.' She closed the door with her heel. 'And I found an unopened packet of chocolate biscuits in the cupboard. They're still well in date, can't have been there long.' She laid the tray on the cushion and handed me a mug. 'How are you feeling now?' Her face was one of concern; I really had scared her.

I picked up a biscuit, then smiled. 'Better now I've got one of these. Thank you.'

I could see from her expression as she sat down, she had a million and one questions and didn't know where to start. 'Has anything like this happened to you before, John?'

I took a sip of chocolate, it was hot. I shook my head. 'Never.'

'This had something to do with that funny turn you had this morning. I should have called someone. You might have had a stroke.'

'I haven't had a stroke,' I snapped. 'I don't know what happened this morning,' I jabbed a finger in the general direction of the garden 'I know what I saw, Skye.'

'But there was nothing there, John.'

'You saw the wheelbarrow.'

'That doesn't prove anything.'

'It had tools in it,' I huffed impatiently. 'You would have seen them if you'd bothered to check.' I was becoming defensive and knew it. 'Sorry.'

'Did you feel dizzy or have a headache when you got out of the car?'

'No. I felt fine earlier.'

'Perhaps you went to a different part of the garden, a part I haven't seen yet.'

I guessed she was now grasping at straws. I wanted to nod my head, agree, and forget all about it. But I couldn't. 'I didn't stumble on some secret garden, if that's what you mean. The shed was behind a hedge, and behind that was a huge vegetable plot. I can't explain how it turned into something different, I really can't.'

'How do you know this person was the gardener?'

'He told me his name was Albert Ferris. The name Rachael gave us.'

'I think she said his name was Ted.'

'She could have got it wrong.'

'I somehow doubt that. What did you say to him?'

'I told him I was Sylvia's cousin and had inherited Althurian.'

'What did he say?'

'He said I was talking nonsense because he'd only spoken to her this morning.'

Her eyes widened. 'He actually said that?'

'Well, not exactly, he referred to her as Lady Forsyth.'

'Didn't you think that was strange?'

'Of course, I did.' I scoffed. 'Probably came as a shock to someone deluded enough to believe they spoke to a dead person.'

'That is bizarre. Did you see anyone else?'

'No, but Ferris said he worked with someone called old Tom.'

'How did you leave it?'

I inclined my head. 'Rather quickly. I saw no merit in continuing a conversation with someone who was away with the fairies.' I drained my mug and placed it back on the tray. 'So, what do you think, Doc, has the Lord of the Manor finally lost his marbles?'

'It could be stress. Makes the brain think and do all sorts of funny things.'

'I've never known stress to cause hallucinations.'

Two very loud raps on the front door turned both our heads. Neither of us jumped this time, we were obviously getting used to noisy surprises. I got up and peeked round the edge of the curtain.

'Who is it?' she hissed.

'I can't see.' I sighed. I'd had enough of people for one day. Our visitor announced their impatience by hammering on the door again. I screwed up my face as the clash of iron on iron seemed to rattle every cell of my brain. 'All right, all right, I'm coming,' I grumbled.

I concluded the person standing before me was incapable of such loud door bashing and glanced from side to side, expecting to spot someone else lurking in the shadows; possibly a much larger, barrel chested individual, with arms like tree trunks, and hands the size of spades. It was not to be. The man was very much alone, and barely an inch over five feet; a wiry, intense looking character of about forty, his round, jowly face somewhat out of proportion to the rest of him. The smile I met as I opened the door appeared a little false.

'Good evening,' he said. 'I'm sorry to call unannounced, but I didn't know how else to contact you.'

I stared at him. 'Do you know me, then?'

'Well, no.'

'So how did you know it was me you wanted to contact?'

He stared back. 'Well, I didn't, I suppose. Look,' he said impatiently. 'I heard that Althurian had changed hands and I was hoping to ask a favour of the new owners.' He gave an awkward smile. 'I assumed...er...you...were the new owner?'

I thought I'd have a bit of fun. 'It depends what the favour is.'

'Ah, yes, I can see why that would help.' He scratched behind his ear. 'Well, I'm a bit of a history buff, you see, and I wondered if it was possible if I could pop round one day and have a look at your stones.'

I inclined my head. 'My stones?'

The man nodded enthusiastically. 'Yes.'

'And these stones are where exactly?'

He looked puzzled. 'Why, here, of course.'

I had that queer, detached from reality feeling again. I leant against the door frame and folded my arms. This could be a while. 'I'm not entirely sure what these stones you speak of are. Are they in the soil, can I see them lying around, are they big, are they small? Can I tell fortunes with them?'

His puzzlement turned to incredulity. 'But...but, you must have seen them. They're not the easiest things to miss.'

'Sorry, Mr...er...?' I raised my eyebrows.

'Ah.' He stared at me. 'Apologies. Larry. Larry Talbot.'

'Larry,' I sighed, 'I have absolutely no idea what you're talking about. We only arrived yesterday. We haven't even managed to look at all the rooms yet.'

'Oh.' He looked genuinely surprised. 'I didn't know that.' I noticed his face had coloured a little. 'I'll call back another time. I'm really sorry.' He turned to leave.

'Wait, Larry,' I said, feeling a little guilty. 'I'm more than happy for you to take a look at these stones. Just tell me what and where they are.'

Larry looked pleased to have been asked; his answer seemed a little rehearsed. 'Some believe the site is Neolithic, whereas I tend to think it was built a lot later, possibly as late as the fifth century AD. It's been hotly debated at the local archaeological society for years.'

'Right.' I couldn't believe my ears. 'Are you telling me we have a Stonehenge somewhere on the estate?'

'Not Stonehenge exactly, but impressive, nonetheless. The circle isn't huge or the diameter wide, but what is interesting, is how the stones have been shaped and laid out. I have to be honest I...' He stopped mid-sentence. 'I don't know your name.'

'My fault, Larry,' I said, holding out my hand. 'I was distracted by the talk of stone circles. I'm John.' Luckily, his grip was nowhere near as fierce as the mysterious gardener. 'Are you an Archaeologist, Larry?'

'Not by profession, more of a hobbyist. I've been interested in the ancient past for as long as I can remember. I'm even a member of the CBA.'

I frowned; to my rather childish mentality, this acronym had a completely different meaning to me than it did Larry. 'What's that, then?'

He smiled proudly. 'The Council for British Archaeology; it's a charity. I joined them about ten years ago.' He pulled a face. 'Now I've forgotten where I was.'

'The stone circle?'

'Ah, yes. Well, it's not entirely accurate to call it a circle, more of an ellipse really. Although its existence has been known about for years, very few people have seen it up close. The Forsyth family guarded it for generations without anyone knowing why. I've only ever seen a few grainy photographs of it, and only just recently, several minutes of drone footage.'

'Why the interest, surely there must be easier sites you could explore?'

His expression darkened 'In my view, none even come close to The Althurian Circle. Legend has it the stones were once used by the Druids. Sorcery and magic were practised here, they say.'

I raised an eyebrow. 'And you believe in all this stuff, do you?'

Larry smiled sheepishly. 'I must admit, some of the stories I've heard take a bit of believing.' He inclined his head. 'Others, however, are in need of serious investigation before ruling them out as old wives' tales.' He held my gaze. 'Were you serious about me taking a look round?'

'Of course I was. I was going to stumble across them sooner or later and having someone around with a bit of knowledge can only be a bonus. When were you thinking of coming?'

'Would tomorrow be okay, say about ten?'

'I don't see why not.' I smiled. 'Ten it is.'

♦

I watched Larry amble along the drive until he disappeared from sight, I was surprised he didn't bring his car up to the house; assuming he had one and hadn't come entirely on foot. I closed the door and wandered back to the drawing room, taking up my position on the sofa. Skye was poring over an old book. She looked up. 'That was interesting.'

'You were listening?'

She grinned. 'You bet I was. Where do you think this stone circle is?'

I shrugged. 'Could be anywhere. If it wasn't so dark, I'd be outside trying to find it.'

'You wouldn't be on your own. I can't believe we have a genuine archaeological site on the estate. It's so cool. You do realise we'll have to buy ourselves a couple of long white robes and learn to whittle a flute from a piece of willow that once touched a virgin's thigh.' She paused. 'Okay, so I made up the last bit.'

I snorted. 'I don't think he fully understood why generations of Forsyth's wanted to keep it secret. Can you imagine how many wannabe Druids you'd have wearing a path across the lawn during the winter and summer solstice.'

'I have a feeling he's already on the phone bragging to his mates. And once the word gets out, it won't be long before we have a queue forming outside our front door. We'll have to start charging admission.'

I grinned. 'I've noticed you've started saying we instead of you.'

'Have I?'

'Yes, more than once. I have a feeling you can see yourself in this house.'

She looked thoughtful for a moment. 'Yes, I can. It's funny, I didn't to start with. When we first arrived all I could see was this huge pile of masonry that belonged to someone else. To me, it seemed too big to be a home. I couldn't believe Sylvia used to rattle round inside these walls all by herself.' She sighed. 'I can now, though.'

I could feel the warm glow of a smile cross my lips. 'I know, it kind of wraps itself round you when you're not looking.' I nodded towards the book.' Any good, is it?'

'No idea. I was too busy earwigging. Weirdly prophetic, considering it charts the rural history of Feldingham.'

'Where did you find it?'

She frowned. 'It was on the sofa where you left it.'

I stared at the book. 'Not guilty. It wasn't me.'

'You must have done. It was here when I came in with the cocoa.'

I really couldn't remember seeing it. One of us was losing their mind and it appeared as if she was beginning to suspect it was me. I couldn't blame her either. I raised my hands submissively. 'Okay, maybe you're right. I probably wasn't thinking straight.'

'You worry me, John.'

I smiled limply. 'I worry myself.'

'It's not funny, I mean it.'

'I know you do.' This was getting out of hand; I changed the subject. 'See if you can find anything about Althurian.'

'You won't get away with it so easily next time.' She gave me one of her looks and started to thumb through the book.

I stretched out and closed my eyes. But not for long.

'This has to be some kind of joke,' she cried.

'W-what?'

She was shaking her head. 'Unbelievable.'

'Are you going to keep this to yourself or has my current fragile mental state made it unsuitable for me to hear?'

'Not hear, John, see.' She held it up.

I couldn't quite make out the grainy black and white image. I took the book from her. The photograph showed a small group of people gathered in front of a hedge. The man in the centre looked very familiar; to either side, and surprisingly taller, if he was without his top hat, were three men dressed in the working clothes of the time. I scrutinised their faces carefully. 'It's definitely our man over the fireplace. Well spotted, love.'

'I know that,' she huffed. 'Look what's behind the hedge.'

A sudden intake of breath caught the back of my throat; how could I have missed it? Outlined against the sky, and just above the hedge line, was the unmistakable shape of a shed roof. The short descriptive at the foot of the page confirmed it.

Sir Edmund Forsyth in the grounds of Althurian Manor with three of his workers
c1934

I tapped the photograph with my finger. 'This is exactly what I saw.'

'Is there any way you could have seen the photo before we went out today?'

'I didn't imagine it,' I snapped.

'I agree, you must have seen something. Do any of the men look familiar?'

'No.' I shook my head. 'Only the clothes they're wearing. So you believe me now?'

'I didn't say I disbelieved you, John. Just because you've had an experience I can't explain, doesn't make it a lie. I'd like to get to the bottom of it though.' She paused thoughtfully. 'I wonder if you're somehow related to Edmund Forsyth.'

'Why?'

'Just a guess.'

I stared at the man in the photograph. He looked nothing like anyone from my side of the family. 'I doubt it.' I grinned. 'He's not good looking enough.'

'On that note.' She stood up, stretching luxuriantly. 'I'm going to grab a shower before I get too tired to bother.'

'Good idea.'

'Perhaps we ought to get something to eat when I come down? I'm not sure my stomach can hold out until breakfast.'

I smiled. 'I'll see what I can rustle up.'

'I was hoping you'd say that.'

♦

In the silence, I could just make out the gentle creak of stair treads as she made her way up to the bedroom. Although I was still a little ruffled by the day's events, I was beginning to feel a certain inner calm. I opened the book, turning once again to the photograph. The narrative associated with it was on the facing page.

> ***Althurian Manor is believed to have been built on a far older site. Local historians have suggested it could have been the original location of the Monastery of the Forgotten Saints. A deed of works kindly shown to the author by Sir Edmund Forsyth indicates that some of the stonework used in the construction of the seventeenth century manor was known to have been found at the site when it was first cleared. Of course, this cannot be taken as proof, as no specialist investigations have been made to ascertain provenance of such material.***

'Monastery of the Forgotten Saints, eh,' I mumbled. Now there was a brotherhood I'd never heard of. I flipped to the cover sheet. The book was printed in 1938 so it was entirely possible further research now existed. I was quite excited by it all. A circle of standing stones, and a monastery; I couldn't wait to tell Skye. She'd be out there with her metal detector every day if she had brought it with her. I closed the book, yawned and checked my watch. I was surprised to see it was after 9pm. Time had an uncanny ability to disappear at Althurian. I clapped my hands on my knees and got to my feet. I was hoping someone had left a couple of microwave dinners in the freezer, the thought of cooking at this late hour, or eating, had lost its appeal. Not that I could say anything to Skye.

I wandered through to what I thought was the kitchen and opened the door to the study. I cursed silently to myself, but as I turned to leave, I noticed a faint glow coming from outside the window. I thought it was the moon until I closed the door. It appeared to be emanating from an area lower than the horizon, but still some way from the house. It was difficult to tell exactly. The colour was strange too, a kind of iridescent green and not particularly bright; if the moon had been out, I doubt I would have spotted it. Suddenly, as if someone had thrown a switch, it vanished. I cupped a hand round my face, pressing my nose against the glass to block out any light leaking from the door frame. I thought I'd missed something. I hadn't, the light had disappeared completely. There had also been a perceptible change in the feel of the house. If asked, I'd struggle to explain it easily. The atmosphere had become unexpectedly vibrant. This will probably sound "out there", but it was like Althurian had gained energy.

I jerked with a start as the sound of running footsteps careered across the ceiling above me. Naturally my first thought was of concern for Skye; for whatever reason she found to be in such a hurry, it sounded urgent. I reacted immediately, bolting through the interconnecting door, and turning from the front hall straight into the stairwell. I thought I was almost keeping up with her as I neared the foot of the stairs. The speed at which she was coming down them was frightening. My heart thumped wildly as I swung round the newel post, stumbling on the first tread as I looked up expectedly. What I saw made no sense. I blinked, then blinked again. I sprinted up the stairs and met her coming out from the bedroom. Her expression was one of wide-eyed puzzlement. We both tried to speak at the same time. I raised my hand. 'You first.'

She gulped twice before she uttered a word. 'Did you hear them?' she hissed.

'Them? I thought it was you running across the landing.'

'It wasn't me, John. I'm talking about the children.'

I stared at her. 'I didn't hear any children.'

'They were right outside the door.'

'Where did they go, then?'

'I don't know. It suddenly went quiet. It's why I came out to check.'

'Did they say anything?'

'They weren't talking; they were shouting and laughing their heads off. I think they were trying to hide from someone,' she said breathlessly. 'They were scared in an excited way. But one of them did shout the name Jemma.'

I puffed out my cheeks. 'Bloody hell.'

'Do you think Althurian is haunted?' She looked a little pale, and I didn't have an answer for her.

'Christ, I wish I knew.' I palmed my jaw. 'How do you feel?'

'Spooked if I'm honest,' she said, her voice quavering slightly. 'It was terrifying.'

I laid a hand on her shoulder. 'We can go back to the digs tonight if you want.'

'No chance. It'll take more than a couple of kids running about to scare me off. Anyway, we'd never make it in time, and I'm tired and need something to eat.' She pulled a face. 'I wouldn't make the sweetest of travelling companions, I'm afraid.'

'Okay, as long as you're sure.'

'Perhaps sure isn't the right word, John.'

♦

Our unease lifted temporarily after we discovered a pack of tortellini and a bag of microwave veggies in the freezer. Not a banquet by any stretch, but it did the job, and we gobbled it down far too quickly. After a quick clear up, Skye made another cup of cocoa and we went back to the drawing room. Although both tired, we were still buzzing from the day's events. I was pleased I wasn't the only one to experience something strange; if I was losing my mind it was a relief to know I was in good company. We both avoided talking about anything supernatural; it was a subject that could easily spiral out of control without specialist knowledge, or experience.

Skye picked up the book we were reading earlier, and I started to sift through the box of papers Sylvia had sent me. Most of it I didn't understand, and clearly needed advice from someone who did. To be honest, my thoughts kept drifting back to my encounter with the gardener.

'Do you know what I think is weird?'

I looked up. 'What's that, sweetie?'

'If Edmund Forsyth owned this house back in 1934, how did you end up inheriting it from someone I assume was his granddaughter?'

'The family connection must be from Sylvia's maternal side.'

'Yes, her mother could have been a Warrener?' She looked thoughtful for a moment. 'Do you feel strange being the last one left, the last of the family blood line?

I sat back. 'I do a bit.' I hadn't actually thought about it that much and I suddenly felt sad. There was little chance of me passing on my genes. It would end with me.

'Are you okay, John?'

'Yes. Why?'

'You were staring.'

'I was thinking about Sylvia's mother,' I lied.

She chuckled. 'I think there's a song about her.'

I rolled my eyes. 'Perhaps it's time we went to bed.'

Chapter 6
The Last Guardian

I was wide awake the moment she slapped me in the face. I knew the time must have been between half past six and seven. You see, Skye is like an alarm clock. At about this time, she starts flailing her arms round again. Yes, I know what you're thinking. I quietly slipped from the bed so as not to wake her; she was good for at least another hour, and enough time for me to make a cup of coffee and take a stroll outside. I had this compelling desire to find this stone circle for myself.

Considering the day we'd had, I slept remarkable well and felt quite refreshed. I grabbed my clothes and silently made my way from the bedroom, padding down the stairs in my socks; apart from the obvious, I never take them off, my feet having been perpetually cold since I was a child. I dressed quickly in the hall before going to the garden room to check the weather. My luck was in; blue skies, little cloud, and a large planet warming sun. Perfect. I found some instant coffee in one of the cupboards, which was lucky, because I was in too much of a hurry to wait for the percolator. It wasn't the worst I'd tasted, but it was close. I scribbled a note for Skye, put on my shoes and checked my watch. It was 7:05am.

I walked south across the lawn in shadows cast by the row of tall conifers. The air was crisp and fresh, every lungful a breath of joy. As I had not the foggiest idea where this so-called circle was supposed to be, I thought

I'd start where I'd spotted the light; at least I had a back-up plan in the guise of Larry Talbot. After about a hundred and fifty yards the lawn came to an end and where a rough, grassed area of common land began. As this border was not fenced, I assumed this was still part of the Althurian estate. I stepped from the neatly manicured sward and glanced back towards the house; I could just make out the top sash of each of the ground floor windows. I hadn't noticed the path I had taken was on a gentle downward slope and explains why, from the garden room window, I was only able to see the crown of the trees standing ahead of me. It was also likely that the source of the light was hidden behind them.

As I drew closer, the line of leafy elders turned out to be more like a wood; the density far greater than it looked from a distance. I stood for a moment, working out if it was easier to find a path through them or make one of my own. I didn't want to be out for too long or Skye would begin to worry. I decided that if there was nothing immediately beyond the woods I'd turn back. I checked my watch again and frowned. It was still 7.05am. I tapped the small screen, then shook my wrist; my go to solution for watches regardless of technology. Although the sun had barely moved, I guessed I must have been outside for no more than fifteen minutes. I chose what I thought was the quickest route: a straight line.

The ground under foot was a soft, springy bed of fallen leaves and woodland foliage; small gatherings of rare blue campion were clustered haphazardly as if sown by a carefree hand. Rooks cawed loudly, sounding their displeasure at this sudden human intrusion. Red and grey squirrels scurried up trunks and skipped along fallen boughs, one stopping in the cleft of a branch to eye me suspiciously as I picked my way in the gloom. Fortunately, my decision to go through the wood rather than round it was the right one, and soon a clearing appeared a little way ahead. With only a few yards to go I saw something that made me stop in my tracks. I could clearly see the outline of what I can only describe as a tall, upright rock. My heart quickened; was this one of the ancient stones our local archaeologist was so desperate to see? I had to shield my eyes as I stepped from the wood, and as they adjusted to the glare, was blown away by the sheer magnificence of what I saw before me; and covered an area much larger than I expected. Larry was right when he said the stones were interesting; although in my view, this was a gross understatement.

Having been carefully hewn from a dark, grey rock of unknown identity, the shape of each individual piece, and its precise positioning, was unlike anything I'd seen before. Not only were all nine of these ancient artefacts sculpted in a way that suggested a high level of technical know-how, they were arranged in a pattern that indicated the builders had some sort of alignment in mind. Several were well over six feet tall, and as broad as three people huddled together. The larger stones were arranged in an ellipse, some thirty feet in diameter; the smaller ones appeared to be strategically placed in and around this rather elongated circle. I shuddered. I had that peculiar "been here before" feeling.

I must have stood with my mouth open for some time. So absorbed in the spectacle of it all I completely missed an unexpected detail in the landscape; unexpected, because I believed I was alone. At first, I thought I was seeing things. The man was wearing a grey two-piece tunic and trouser combination, the colour blending remarkably well with that of the obelisk he was facing; this, and the distance from me, was possibly why I hadn't spotted him immediately. His head was tilted back, displaying a shock of white, silky hair that cascaded over his shoulders, and appeared to be looking at something higher than the stone he was in front of. I was unsure if he knew of my presence. My first impulse was to quietly slink away, in my head I was the trespasser.

Dogged curiosity got the better of me; I was fascinated why someone would spend so much time staring into nowhere. I stepped from the partial cover afforded by one of the smaller upright stones and began to walk toward him. It soon became evident the man had closed his eyes and was completely unaware of me. Or so I thought. I slowed my pace as not to scare him and stopped a safe distance to wait. He was not a large man. His fine boned, unlined face looked remarkably calm, a faint smile forming at the corners of his mouth as he continued with what I assumed was a form of quiet meditation; his hands pressed together in Anjali mudra. I noticed he wore a wide gold band on his right ring finger; possibly engraved with some form of text. In an odd way I was strangely captivated by this enigmatic man's tangible serenity.

'I'm glad you could join us, John.'

I stepped back. 'What?'

He turned and opened his eyes; they were a striking iridescent blue, so blue and clear I felt as though they were looking into my soul; know everything there was about me. He smiled gently, sweeping his hand in a slow, wide arc. 'These artefacts have silently watched over this holy place for over twenty-seven centuries. A more than fitting testament to those who built them, wouldn't you say?'

'How do you know my name?' I barked.

He chuckled softly to himself. 'A question for a question, John?'

'Yes,' I said. 'And one you need to answer.'

He sighed. 'Your presence here is part of the natural law of things. You function in a process as old and predictable as the ebb and flow of the tides. It was only a matter of time.'

This man was beginning to unnerve me. 'Just who are you?'

'I am the last Guardian.'

'Right. So, do you have a name?'

'Julius Becket, if it is of any consequence.'

'So why are you here?'

Becket turned and summoned me to follow. 'Come, let us sit a while. I've been standing for far too long.'

The man walked with an unhurried, graceful ease, reminding me of the monks I saw in a rare visit to a Tibetan Buddhist monastery. I followed, still keeping a safe distance from him. He wandered out of the circle and headed towards a large recumbent stone I had not yet seen. It was flat topped, about two feet high, and the length of the double sofa; an equally large vertical stone leaned against the back, making the whole edifice look like an oversized chair. I was surprised when he eased himself into a normal sitting position, I kind of expected him to assume a full lotus. I continued to stand; arms folded. I suspected he might be a friend of Larry Talbot and sought to pip him to the post and would explain how he knew my name. Even though she hadn't met Larry in person, Skye usually had people weighed up within minutes. Her guess about him bragging to his mates was probably accurate. More than once I regretted not listening to her advice about someone.

'Do you live locally?' I asked.

He made a quiet chuckling sound again; a frequent reaction to my questions I was to find irritating. 'You could say that I do.'

I was getting nowhere. He gave me the impression he wanted to sit and chat, and then did the opposite. This wasn't a conversation; this was a wind up. I decided to use a touch of psychology and turned to walk away. 'Sorry, pal,' I snapped, 'if you're not prepared to answer any of my questions, then I'm not prepared to hang around in the vain hope you might.' Feeling very pleased with my cleverness, and probably sporting one of those smug expressions reserved for special occasions, I walked back towards the wood. I had travelled no more than a few steps.

I heard him sigh. 'You need to be patient if you are to fulfil your destiny.' This time, I detected a little urgency in his voice. My tactic appeared to be working.

I waved my hand dismissively as I continued to tramp a path between the stones. 'Whatever,' I answered indolently.

'Would you like to know why you can see and feel the past, John?' His voice sounded closer than expected.

I stopped dead. This moved his knowledge of me to another level. I was never in control, and he knew it. I swung round and was caught totally off guard. Becket was standing with folded arms, leaning against a stone no more than a few yards from me. It seemed impossible for him to have moved so fast. I felt slightly disorientated. 'How did you...' Suddenly my ability to assemble an intelligible collection of words had simply vanished. I was immobile, and all I could do was watch as he unfolded his arms and slowly moved towards me. He stopped directly in front of me, so close I could have reached out and touched him. 'You inherited far more than a house. The site on which it stands has been a place of pilgrimage for millennia, and for good reason. Those of us who have the ability to see the rhythm of life, he traced the air with an outstretched hand, 'its past, present, and future, have the rarest of gifts, John.' He stepped to one side. 'This gift, as you can imagine, is one to be protected. In the wrong hands the consequences of an action at the wrong time, or place, could have disastrous consequences.

I found it hard to look into his eyes, staring at a space just above his temple. My voice croaked. 'S-sorry, you've lost me.' I tried to shake my head but couldn't. I managed to frown. 'W-what has this got to do with me?' I asked, for the second time.

He lifted his right hand and the ring he was wearing touched the centre of my forehead. 'You will see it with your own eyes, John.' The instant this last word left his lips the world round me blinked out. I was still fully awake and conscious, yet in every direction, all I could see was empty blackness. Suddenly, I toppled like a stone, falling towards some unseen pit, far, far below me.

A sudden current of cool air lightly brushed my cheek. I groaned. I just wanted to turn over and go back to sleep, but wherever I was lying was unforgivingly hard. An earthy, damp smell tickled my nostrils as the memory of my existence started to return. I took a sudden deep breath and coughed violently; this caused my eyelids to flicker uncontrollably for a second or two before they opened fully. The brightness of everything around me seemed to burn the back of my eyes as I tried to focus on anything familiar. My ability to move, or at least the sense I could, began to seep into my muscles and joints. It was only when my fingers began to massage the ground, I realised I was still outside, and the material pressing into the side of my face was a patch of damp, rough grass. I hoisted myself up on my elbows and looked round. I was about halfway between the wood and the circle. Getting to my feet was a bit of an effort, feeling wobbly when I finally stood upright. Although I was in no condition to make my way back to the house, I knew by now Skye would be up and beginning to worry. I decided it best to take my time, recover fully, and leave my little adventure between me and the stones; I was doubtful she'd believe me anyway. I squinted at my watch; the screen was blank.

♦

The incline I had hardly noticed on the way down was not so easy to ignore on the way back, and I arrived at the garden room exhausted, and not a little out of breath. The house was quiet. I was expecting, and hoped, to be greeted by the smell of freshly brewed coffee. But it was not to be; the percolator was stone cold and my note still where I had left it. Now it was my turn to feel anxious. I looked at my watch again, silently cursing under my breath. I had no way of knowing what time it was, as if it really mattered. Not that I'd been particularly looking for one, but I'd not seen a clock, or any other timepiece, in the house so far. I made my way up the stairs, carefully cracked open the door to the bedroom and peeked in. I could swear she hadn't moved an inch, an unusual turn of events, if not a miracle. I quietly made my way to the other side of the bed, trying my best not to make any noise; it was very unusual for her to stay asleep for so long. I leant close to her face, just to check if she was still breathing. It was at this point her eyes snapped open.

'Jesus Christ,' she screamed, contorting her body into a defensive knot 'You scared the living crap out of me!'

I leapt back; arms extended protectively. 'S-sorry, sweetie, I just wanted to know if you were okay.'

'Well now you know,' she barked. 'You could have tried something less bloody creepy.'

'I thought you were asleep.'

'I was until you got out of bed.'

'Eh?'

'You could at least have brought a coffee with you.' She paused. 'And you can stop looking at me like that.'

'I left you a note.'

Her brow furrowed. 'Why?'

'In case you wondered where I'd gone. I didn't want you to worry.'

Pulling back her chin, she said, 'What *are* you talking about, John?'

'I went for a walk.' I gave a limp smile. 'I was longer than I thought.'

She looked at me askance. 'You can't have done. I've only been awake for a few minutes.'

I laughed. 'You must have fallen back to sleep. I was out for ages.'

She picked up her phone from the bedside table. Touching the screen, she held it up for me to see. 'I last checked this ten minutes ago.' She took a breath. 'Come on, smarty pants, tell me what it says?'

My mouth dried as I stared at the phone's luminous white digits, seconds scrolling like the beat of its electronic heart. I swallowed nervously. 'I-I don't know what to say.'

'Say nothing and make the coffee.'

Again, I had nowhere to go, and no way could I argue with the evidence; I had left the bedroom for no more than ten minutes. I lifted my wrist, tutted, and tapped the blank face of my watch. 'You know, I thought the battery was on its way out,' I blathered. 'I should have changed it.'

'More like you were dreaming.'

My face coloured up. 'Do you want your coffee up here?'

She stretched luxuriantly 'Tempting, but no. I'll come down for it. We have that guy turning up at ten, and I'd like a little time to chill before he arrives. Will he be on his own?'

My mind darted back to the stones and wondered how much, if anything, Larry knew of the enigmatic Julius Becket. 'I don't know. He might like to keep the first visit to himself. Steal the glory.'

'I thought we might take a look for ourselves.'

I bit my tongue. 'I doubt we have enough time.'

'You're probably right.' She paused. 'And we need to pick up our stuff from the guest house.'

I nodded. 'We can leave as soon as he's gone.'

'Do you mind if I keep out the way?'

'Are you sure?'
'Oh yes.'

♦

Larry turned up on the dot of ten o'clock. Dressed in tan baggy trousers, safari jacket, and a wide brimmed, leather hat, he looked as if he were auditioning for *Raiders of the Lost Ark*. He had brought with him a large canvas holdall which, by the way he staggered over the threshold, was rather heavy. I tried my best not to smirk as I closed the door. 'Would you like something to drink before we start, Larry?' I asked.

'I need to get on with it if you don't mind, but thanks anyway.' He lifted the camera hanging from his neck. 'I brought this with me, I hoped you wouldn't mind if I took some photographs.'

'Not at all, Larry, I'd be surprised if you didn't.' I opened the interconnecting door and ushered him through. Larry huffed and puffed his way past me, quickly dumping the holdall on the lobby floor. I was intrigued to know what he had in there, and how he expected to hump it all the way down to the circle, not to mention the long haul back; a journey, I doubt he was up to.

Larry swivelled his head round, taking a brief, but interested note of each of the paintings. 'What a lovely place you have. Do you intend to make it your home…er…, John?'

I could feel my eyes narrow. I tried to work out if this was a reasonable question or not. I shrugged mentally. 'Yes. Yes, we do.' Curiosity, again, got the better of me. I looked down and nodded at the holdall. 'The bag looks heavy, Larry.'

He gave me a shifty glance. 'Ah, yes. I have another little favour to ask. I've brought some test equipment that I'd like to leave here overnight. It's to monitor the magnetic resonance radiated by iron like materials embedded in the stones.'

'Right,' I said. 'And this will tell you what exactly?'

'If they were deliberately cut and placed in their positions to create some form of energy field.'

I stared at him and started to feel a tension creeping from my neck to the back of my head. I had a brief but vivid image of Larry wearing a tin foil hat. I shook the thought from my head. 'This…er…equipment, is it waterproof?'

Larry's expression became intense; I was obviously asking the right questions. 'Absolutely yes,' he enthused. 'I've used it to monitor a number of sites now. I left it overnight at the Callanish Stones when a rainstorm blew up from nowhere. It worked perfectly.'

'Well, I think you might need a hand with it.'

He gave me a confused frown and shook his head. 'Thanks for the offer, but I've set this equipment up so many times I could do it with my eyes closed.' He looked down at his feet. 'You'd probably get in the way.'

'I meant to carry the bag, Larry.'

'Ah, yes,' he said, smiling sheepishly. 'That would help.'

♦

I left him in the garden room, happily tinkering with some sort of electronic gadget, while I nipped upstairs to see if Skye was okay. I caught her standing in front of the mirror admiring a pair of light blue, denim dungarees she was wearing. She turned and beamed. 'What do you think?'

'You look great,' I hesitated. 'I thought you didn't bring anything with you.'

'I didn't. I found these rolled up in the wardrobe with three tee shirts, and a pair of white trainers. And they're all my size. Cool, eh?'

'Well yes, but not the sort of things I would associate with Sylvia.'

'Me neither. Not that I'm complaining, there are only so many days a girl can be seen in the same clothes.'

'Yeah, don't I know it,' I said, with a snort. 'We'll go as soon as I get Larry on his merry way. Will you be okay for a while?'

'If I find any more stuff like this, I will.'

♦

My archaeological companion was waiting for me outside the garden room doors, idly drawing patterns in the gravel with the toe of his shoe. His sullen, bored expression lit up when he spotted me emerging from the kitchen. As we met, I wrung my hands vigorously and looked up at the clear, blue canopy above. Yes, I did feel guilty I'd kept him waiting. 'Looks like we've got a good day for it,' I enthused. I thought it best to play dumb. 'Have you any idea where these stones are?'

Larry pointed south. 'According to the drone sequence, they should be somewhere in that direction.' He smiled limply. 'I'm not entirely sure how far though.'

Grabbing a strap each, we headed off, carrying the holdall between us. We were silent for a while, and it was Larry who spoke first. 'Do you know much about stone circles, John?'

'Not a lot,' I said. 'I know they're old.'

'Most are very old, and most are Neolithic, and why it's generally believed the one at Althurian could be at least four thousand years old.'

'But you believe it's later than that.'

'I think it's entirely possible. Early written historical records seem to suggest the stones were erected by the Druids. If this is so, they can't predate the people who conceived them, and why I believe they date between three hundred and five hundred AD.'

'Could they be older than that?'

Larry nodded. 'Equally possible, a lot of history is speculative. Just because someone wrote it down years ago, doesn't mean it's true. Most of what we know about the ancient past is based on a knowledgeable best guess. Archaeology is no different.'

'What about two thousand seven hundred years?'

Larry glanced at me; his brow furrowed. 'Late Bronze age, what makes you think that?'

I smiled. 'Just a guess.'

'I doubt it. Heaving massive stones around went out of fashion after the late Stone Age. If they are older than the Druids, you're looking a lot earlier if anything.' Larry turned his head. 'Ah, the trees.'

I was mildly shocked how quickly we'd got there, and slightly guilty for not sharing my earlier experience with him. I almost made the mistake of pointing the way.

He turned, checking our route from the house, possibly to align ourselves with the circle. 'Well, we're in the right place, John. They should be on the other side of these trees.'

I nodded. I knew he was right, of course. 'We could go through that way,' I suggested helpfully.

♦

I was more than happy to see the holdall find a place on the grass; I swear my shoulder was about to part-company with my arm. Larry looked like a child who had been given the keys to a toy shop and told to help himself. It was quite sweet in a way.

'Wow!' he exclaimed. 'They're more beautiful than I imagined.' He lifted his camera and started to snap away, taking several different shots before he'd even moved very far, and nothing dramatically artistic, I thought. Then I watched as he slowly strolled round the outside, running his hand lovingly over each stone as he passed them. He looked almost bewitched.

I kind of expected the white-haired guy to turn up, and it was strange to be back so soon. The whole experience had stuck in that woolly part of my brain, the place where dreams usually sit for less time than it takes to draw breath. Remnants of them remain but are soon to vanish completely.

'Nine is an interesting number, John.' Although he was on the other side of the circle, his voice carried remarkably well.

'Is it?'

He came out from behind the stone opposite. 'Yes, it's a number that seems to pop up everywhere. Like the number of segments in an orange, that sort of thing.'

I smiled. I love oranges, but never had the slightest inclination to count how many segments there were. 'Is that right? Well I never. Do all stone circles have nine...er...stones, then?'

'A few do, not all of them, though. Did you know, if you multiply any number by nine, the digits in the answer always add up to nine, or the sum of them is divisible by nine?' He raised his eyebrows. 'Fascinating stuff, eh?'

'Yes, very intriguing,' I said. For some really irritating reason, I actually started to do the arithmetic in my head while he continued to regale me with even more bizarre encyclopaedic facts.

'Nikola Tesla once said, *"If you only knew the magnificence of three, six and nine, then you would have the key to the universe"*. It's quite an amazing number, yes?'

I pulled an impressed face and did my best not to yawn. I wanted to look at my watch, but knew it was a waste of time, and probably rude. 'So, this equipment of yours, how does it work, and what do you actually do with it?'

I caught a look in his eye as he made his way back to me, a worryingly, gleeful look. I knew I'd made a mistake. He put his hands on his hips. 'Basically, it's a device that records data from a number of carefully selected inputs depending on the site; magnetic variation sensors in this case. These small, encapsulated coils of wire pick up changes in magnetic flux which is then recorded by the logging unit in real time. I can even download an hours-worth of data to my smart phone just to see if everything is working okay.'

'Clever stuff,' I said. He'd lost me after he used the word flux.

'I've also included a sound and vibration sensor for good measure. You never know what you might pick up.'

'Yes, you never know, Larry.'

He squatted and unzipped the holdall. I was impressed how neatly everything was packed; each piece wrapped in a soft, cloth like material. I watched with interest as he skilfully fitted the various parts together, unrolled cables, and placed each of the sensors in positions he had unquestionably calculated beforehand. When finished, he stood back, brushed his hands together, looking very pleased with himself.

'I can see why the bag was so heavy,' I said.

Larry wiped his mouth with the back of his hand. 'It's those magnetic sensors; they have a great lump of iron in them.'

'Right,' I said. 'So, what happens now?'

Larry checked his watch. 'It's set to start recording in an hours-time. We don't want to be detecting our own presence before we've left the site, do we?'

'Heaven forbid.' I was pleased not to be lugging the equipment back up the hill for at least another twenty-four hours. 'Is that it, then?'

'Not quite,' he said, rummaging in the holdall again. He removed a large surveyor's tape measure, and a hammer like tool with a point at either end of the head. 'I need to take a few measurements.' I could see another hand-wringing request in his eyes. 'Only if it's okay with you, John, I'd like to take a tiny sample of rock so I can analyse its crystalline structure and magnetic properties. It's a material I'm not familiar with.'

I shrugged. 'Sure you can, Larry. I doubt if one small chip will make any difference to its historical value.' I now concluded the man was obsessed. He sauntered off towards the closest stone, unwinding the tape as he went. I watched as he carefully sized up each piece, jotting down its measurements in a small notebook he balanced on his knee. I decided to ask him about my mysterious visitor. 'Do you know a chap called Julius Becket?' I watched his face carefully for any tell-tale signs of recognition.

'Hang on a sec, John,' he said. 'I'll just get this last one down before I forget.' He scribbled a couple of notes, looked up and smiled. 'Right, I'm all ears.'

'Julius Becket?'

Larry pulled a genuine puzzled expression, slowly shaking his head. 'The name sounds familiar. Is he a local man?'

'I think so.'

Larry gazed skyward as if in thought, then shook his head again. 'Perhaps he's new to the neighbourhood. Why do you ask?'

'A guy at the pub told me about him,' I lied. 'He said that Becket was known as the Guardian. I wondered if you knew what that was.'

Larry snorted. 'In my experience, and depending on who you talk to, pubs tend to be a breeding ground for misinformation, rumour, and half-truths. Was this The Jolly Archer by any chance?'

'Yes,' I lied, again. This was becoming a habit I wasn't comfortable with.

He chuckled. 'I thought it might. Was it the landlord?'

I was now firmly on the back foot. Lies do that. 'I don't know who he was.'

Larry gave a knowing nod. 'I bet it was him. Gerome comes out with all sorts of tall stories to keep the punters entertained. A few years back he was telling people he was related to Robin Hood.' He held up the pointed hammer. 'I'll just get that sample, and I'm done.'

Fortunately, Larry was in a hurry to get away once he'd bagged his sample. To be honest, for a while there I thought he was one of those types who could talk for England and likely to keep me there all day. So I was pleasantly surprised when he stuffed what was left into the holdall and moved it to the edge of the wood.

'What time are you back tomorrow?'

'Ah, yes, tomorrow.' Larry fumbled in his jacket pocket. 'Probably about the same time,' he said, handing me a slip of paper. 'Here's my mobile number.'

♦

I waited by the front steps, watching Larry until he disappeared behind the tall trees at the end of the drive. I decided my conscience would not allow me to do the same tomorrow; I would give him a lift, and I might even use the Aston.

Skye sidled up to me, encircling my waist with her arm. 'You weren't very long.'

'The stones were closer than I thought,' I lied; a half-truth, but a lie, nevertheless.

Her eyes widened. 'Really?'

'Only a short walk from here. Larry knew exactly where they were.'

'How exciting. What did he say about them?'

'They're old, made from stuff he couldn't identify.' I hesitated. 'And he had a thing about the number nine.'

She pulled a face. 'Nine?'

'It's a long story.' I rolled my eyes. 'We'll know more tomorrow.'

'Why tomorrow?'

'He's coming back to pick up a device he left to monitor magnetic activity in them.' I shrugged. 'It was a bit too technical for my ears.'

'What are they like?'

I made a shape with my hands. 'About this big and had a wire coming out at either end.'

'Not them, you Wally, the stones?'

'Sorry.' I laughed and may have blushed a little. 'They're quite something.' I paused. 'We could take a look if you like?'

'I'd love to, but I think we need to stick to our plan before it gets too late.'

Chapter 7
Past Lives

It was twilight when we pulled onto the drive; thin, grey cloud with smudges of deep red hung quietly above the trees as the Aston grumbled its way towards the house. The light above the front door flickered and came on. I turned off the engine, arched my spine, rubbing the back of my neck. I looked across at Skye; she had fallen asleep about an hour ago. I was glad to be back, and not just because the eighty-mile round trip was a congested hell on earth.

Perhaps it's an age thing, but I was expecting a little more from the owner of the guest house. We paid almost four hundred pounds for a three-day break and stayed for one. Now, in my eyes, he was quids in. He, on the other hand, thought differently and actually implied we had somehow taken advantage of his hospitality. Yes. It was good to be home.

I gently stroked her cheek. 'We're back, sweetie,' I whispered.

She smiled without opening her eyes, snuggling into the cardigan she had rolled up as a cushion. 'I'll be down in five minutes,' she mumbled. 'Put the coffee on an' I'll…'

'Skye,' I said, 'you're not in bed, my lovely, you're in the car.'

Her eye's blinked open. 'W-we're home?' She sat up, rubbing her face. 'What time is it?'

I looked at the luminous hands of the analogue clock. 'Half past eight. You've been asleep for over an hour.'

'Have I? Oh, dear,' she said, with a chuckle. Suddenly, her eyes looked past me as if distracted. Her expression darkened and she grabbed my arm. 'There's someone lying on the steps, John.'

I swung round. The grey, slumped outline of a body covered the upper three steps, and halfway across the top slab. It was immobile and face down. I almost fell out the car, skidding on the gravel as I scrambled to get a grip. My heart was almost in my mouth. I heard the passenger door slam as I arrived at the bottom step. I was now in shadow and laid my hand on what I assumed was the lower leg of whoever it was. 'Are you all right?' was all I could think of to say. Skye was right behind me by then.

'They're not…dead, are they?' she said, cupping a hand to her mouth. I could hear the panic rising in her voice.

I climbed up a couple of steps and knelt down. 'I don't know.' The head was covered by some form of hood which fell to one side as I attempted to turn the body over; revealed was the face of a young woman. I tried to calm my breath as I pressed my fingers to the side of her neck, feeling for the carotid artery. She was still warm, but not that warm. Seconds passed. A bead of perspiration formed on my top lip as I tried to determine if the pulse in my fingers was mine, or that of the woman. I cursed as my own heart pounded in my ears. Then I heard it: A weak, gurgled sigh. I held my breath. Another followed, longer this time. I fumbled for my front door key and handed it to Skye. 'Get the door open and call an ambulance.'

'Is she breathing?'

I nodded. 'Yes, thank God.'

Skye was already tapping the screen of her phone as she stepped over me. I'd never seen her face so grim. She rattled the key into the lock, opened the door and switched on the hall light. 'There's no bloody signal.'

'Jesus,' I hissed. 'Try mine, it's in the car.' The woman unexpectedly opened her eyes, turning her head so she was staring directly at me. I found her sudden look of terror intensely unnerving, and for a brief moment I thought she was about to scream. Her hand reached up and grabbed my wrist; I'd forgotten to remove my fingers from her neck, and she must have wondered what I trying to do. 'It's okay, love, you're amongst friends,' I soothed. Again, under the circumstances, it was the best I could come up with. She continued to hold my wrist, her wide, accusing eyes, fixed. I heard the car door close behind me.

'It's the bloody same,' cried Skye. 'What are we going to do?'

'Well, she can't stay out here. We need to get her inside somehow. If you hook your arm under hers, we'll get her to her feet and see if she can walk.'

After a bit of manoeuvring, we got the woman to her feet. Although she seemed out of it, her legs didn't buckle beneath her, and she still had the wherewithal to walk, albeit, hesitantly. We took her to the drawing room and carefully laid her on one of the sofas; in a rushed an improvised recovery position. Her eyes were now closed, but she looked comfortable. It might have been my imagination, but sure I caught a whiff of lavender again; a fresher, sharper fragrance, but lavender, nevertheless.

'Do you think she'll be okay, John?'

I shrugged. 'I don't know. I can't believe we can't get a signal. I thought you could call 999 from anywhere.'

Skye touched the woman's cheek with the back of her hand. 'She feels cold. I'll get her a blanket.'

I leant down and brushed a few loose strands of hair from her face. She looked to be in her early thirties, and not a large woman, fortunately for us. I was at a loss of what to do. It did occur to me that one of us could drive to the pub, our nearest neighbour, and use their landline. But for some obscure reason I felt this was not what the woman would have wanted.

Skye returned and covered her with a heavy tartan blanket. 'I wonder who she is.'

I pulled a face. 'Should we…er…try and find out?'

'Search her pockets, you mean?'

'What else can we do?'

'It doesn't seem right.'

'I know.'

'She looks well to do, although her clothes look a bit out of date.' She paused. 'Well, a lot, actually. I'm surprised she's not carrying a handbag, it kind of goes with the style.' Skye gasped, cupping a hand to her mouth. 'You don't think she's been mugged, do you?'

I rocked my head from side to side. 'I can't see any injuries, not that that means anything.'

The woman opened her eyes again, groaned and started to move her arms about, she was trying to pull off the blanket. Skye immediately laid a comforting hand on her shoulder. 'You're safe, darling,' she soothed. 'Try to rest.'

'W-who are y-you?' she stumbled. 'W-where's Pattie?'

'There's no one here by that name, darling,' replied Skye. 'You must have come to the wrong house.'

The woman anxiously glanced at me, then back to Skye. 'W-what do you mean?' She propped herself up on her elbows. 'I-I can't have.'

I asked, 'Do you remember what happened to you?'

'Happened to me?' The woman shook her head, looking confused. 'No. I-I don't know.' Frowning, she continued to stare at Skye. 'Who-are-you?' she repeated.

'My name is Skye,' she made an open-handed gesture towards me, 'and this is John. We're new here. Would you like to tell us your name?'

'The woman touched her lips and frowned. 'Skye?'

'Yes. And this is John.'

'Where am I?'

Skye glanced at me, then back to the woman. 'Althurian. You're at Althurian.'

The woman was beginning to show signs of trauma, shaking her head vigorously. 'B-but I can't be. Y-you're, you're, lying to me.'

'Please calm down. I'm not lying to you.' Skye tried a different approach. 'Where have you just come from? Where do you live?'

The woman's bottom lip trembled, then she opened and closed her mouth as if she were struggling to speak. Her taut, wide eyed expression could only be described as one of terror. She gulped for air. 'Alth…urian?'

Skye threw me a sharp, puzzled look. 'Yes. Althurian.'

The woman closed her eyes, slowly rocking her head. 'No. You don't understand. I'm from Althurian, from here. Don't you see? You can't be here. This...is my home.'

I touched Skye's shoulder. 'Can I have a word, love,' I said, jerking my head towards the door. This was getting out of hand. I had a distinct feeling we had a complete fruitcake in our midst, and there was nothing we could do about it. We were, as the Cherokee Indians may have said on numerous occasions, up the creek without a paddle. The lack of a phone signal didn't help, and it was beginning to look as if my plan for a trip to the pub was the only sensible course of action.

We left our "guest" and scurried to the hall. I closed the door behind me and pulled a face, just as Skye did the same; we looked as if we were competing in the world gurning championships. Skye spoke first. 'What are we going to do?'

'We need help with this one, and I think the police might be the favourite. It wouldn't surprise me if she's escaped from a secure unit. It might account for the strange choice of clothes. We could always go to the pub.'

'Great. Now you want to go to the pub.'

I rolled my eyes. 'To use their phone,' I snapped.

She shook her head. 'Sorry.'

The door clicked open. We both turned. The woman was standing, slumped against the door frame, her face, pale and drawn. 'I need to use the bathroom,' she said.

Skye straightened. 'Yes, of course you can, darling. I'll show you where it is.'

The woman rounded on her. 'I do know where my own bathroom is, thank you.' She took a step forward, wobbled slightly, grabbing the top of the cast iron radiator. Instinctively, Skye went to help her. The woman raised her free hand defensively. 'Don't you touch me,' she barked. 'I don't need your help, and I'm not your darling.' She began to slowly inch along the wall holding on to anything for stability. We watched, as without any hesitation, she went straight to it, opened the door and stepped inside. I can't really say who was the more shocked, and it was a while before either of us said anything.

Skye gripped my arm. 'How did she know where to go?'

I blew out my cheeks. 'I've no idea, but there has to be a plausible explanation for it.' This was becoming an overused anaphoric. 'Perhaps she used to work here and now has delusions it was once her home.'

'I think she meant it in the present tense.'

I shrugged. 'But it isn't, is it?' I huffed. 'Look, the woman is probably barking mad and that's all there is to it. What's taking her so long?' I grumbled.

'John!' she exclaimed. 'Don't be so impatient. I hope you don't time me when I'm...in the bathroom.'

I grinned. 'Only if you're longer than five minutes.' My misplaced humour fell short and was subsequently ignored.

'Actually, she's been in there quite a while. Shall I give her a knock?'

'You could, but when you do, I wouldn't hang around for too long.'

'Great. You do it then.'

'Okay. Give her another couple of minutes.'

'Chicken.'

'Yep.'

'This is ridiculous; she could have passed out and banged her head or something.' She marched over and lightly tapped on the door. 'Are you okay in there?' She inclined her head to listen. After a moment or two she looked at me and shrugged. 'I can't hear a thing.'

'So much for a quiet night in,' I muttered. 'You'd better try the door.'

Skye gingerly turned the handle, cracked it open and peeped through the gap. She lingered for less than a second before walking straight in without saying a word. I expected the worst and waited for the inevitable scream.

Skye stepped out and stared at me. 'She's gone.'

'What do you mean? Gone?'

'The room's empty.'

'It can't be.'

'See for yourself.'

The bathroom was hardly a place large enough to lose yourself. I sat on the edge of the bath and stared at the wall. 'This is bonkers.'

'Could she have climbed out the window?'

'Not unless she was able to lock the sash from outside.' I paused. 'I think there's stuff going on here we're doing our best to ignore.'

'I know there is,' she said, edginess to her voice I'd not heard before. 'If I hadn't seen it with my own eyes, I wouldn't have believed it. I know she came in here, and I know she didn't leave. Well, not by the door.' She combed her fingers through her hair. 'I-I can't get my head around what has just happened. I really can't.'

I saw a tortured look in her eyes. She was struggling to explain the same incongruous reality as I was. 'Are you okay?'

'I'm not sure to be honest. I feel like my understanding of how the universe works has just taken a huge knock. Do you mind if I sit down? I feel weird.'

The drawing room had become our room of choice. Our unexpected visitor had discarded the blanket, leaving it in a heap between the two sofas. As Skye bent down to scoop it up from the floor, a small, light blue leather purse flipped from one of the folds and dropped on the rug. She picked it up.

'Is there anything in it?' I asked.

'It's got some weight to it' she said, holding it up for me to see, the soft leather moulding into her cupped palm. 'It's certainly not mine.'

'Aren't you going to open it?'

'Do you think we should?'

'Well, I doubt if the purse police will mind too much.'

'You know what I mean,' she snapped. 'What if it's…hers?'

'It's hardly likely to belong to anyone else, and I stopped using one after the age of five.'

She gingerly opened the brass coloured zip and emptied the contents onto the seat cushion. There was a collection of silver and bronze coins, including two, shiny half penny pieces, some folded paper currency, and a dog-eared piece of card. 'My dad keeps some of these in a jar,' she said, holding up three, fairly fresh-looking pound notes, and a rather battered ten shilling one. 'These went out of circulation ages ago.'

I took one from her; it was in remarkably good condition considering it was around fifty years old. 'And before either of us were born. What about the card?'

'It's an address and telephone number for a Janice Bergan.'

'Cool. So, we have name for her. Is she local?'

'Cramerly. I'm sure I saw that on the way here.'

I nodded. 'Yes, just as we came off the motorway.'

'We could drive there tomorrow?'

'We should try to call her first.'

She waved her hand dismissively. 'Ring her when we get there. If she doesn't answer we can knock on the door.'

'But we don't know for sure it's her, do we?'

She shrugged indolently. 'Maybe not, but she might know who she is if we give her a description.'

'And say what exactly? We found this unconscious woman who woke up and vanished after going to the bathroom. Oh, and we found your address and telephone number in her purse. She'd probably call the police like we should do.'

'You're making this more complicated than it needs to be.'

'I'm not sure that's possible.'

'And what would you tell the police, something different?'

I looked down at my feet. 'We should have called them when we found her.'

'We tried, remember?'

I could feel we were entering one of those cycles of no return, an endless ping pong of argument and counter argument. And I was losing. I sighed. 'What do you suggest?'

'We call Janice Bergan and say we found the purse and wish to return it.'

'Okay, have it your own way.'

'You know it makes sense.' She gave a smug grin of triumph, and picked up the purse, squeezing it between her fingers; I saw a brief change in her expression. 'I think there's something else in here, I can feel it. It's in the lining.' She started to manipulate the fabric inside. 'Got it.' She held up a narrow, rose gold wedding ring. 'Well, I never.'

'Perhaps she was married once,' I said, 'kept it as a reminder not to make the same mistake again.'

She chuckled. 'Spoken like a true cynic.'

'You wouldn't have me any other way.' I folded my arms. 'Do you think this woman has anything to do with the old guy I saw in the garden?'

She lifted her hands in the air. 'I don't know what to think. I can't explain any of it.'

'I saw someone else this morning.'

Her eyes narrowed. 'What do you mean?'

'I wasn't going to tell you, but whatever is happening here involves the both of us now. When I told you, I'd been out for a walk this morning, I didn't tell you everything. I found the stone circle.'

'But you were only gone for a few minutes.'

'It was longer than that, maybe an hour.' Suddenly, my skin started to prickle, like an electric current had shot from my fingers, up through my arms, and into the very core of my body. It was like I'd grabbed hold of a cattle prod. Seconds later every one of my five senses closed down completely.

♦

'For goodness sake, wake up, you lazy good for nothing.' The woman's voice was strong, assertive, and not in the least bit feminine. It was the sort of demand you'd want directed at someone else. I thought if I kept my eyes closed, she would go away. A physical aspect to this intrusive salvo of invective soon developed and I was about to feel my whole body being shaken violently.

'What is it? I grumbled. I wanted to gasp, the words, and my voice, seemed that of a different man; sounding shriller, and at a pitch my ears were not accustomed.

'Get up,' she growled. 'I'm not making excuses for you this week.'

My eyes snapped open. I was suddenly, and rudely, very awake. The snarling face before me, and clearly the source of my discomfort, was taking no prisoners. I stared at her. Part of me was trying to remember a life that was not this, an anomaly, not quite hidden. I spoke in a strange tongue again. 'Who the devil are you?' I cried.

'Don't start all that nonsense, you're not a child. I warn you now, any more of it an' the master will hear of it, mark my words.'

'What are you talking about, woman?' I barked.

She took a step back, her expression now one of horror; I'd obviously said something she was not used to hearing. 'I will not allow you to address me in such a manner.' She made off towards the door, glaring at me with the haughtiest of expressions. It was not until the door slammed behind her I began to realise the seriousness of this sudden, and life changing, development.

I was in bed, the room was somewhat familiar, and I felt lighter, less rigid physically. Although it was the oddest of feelings, it kind of felt normal. I went to pull the covers from me and caught sight of my fingers, not appendages I usually take a lot of notice of unless I've had an unfortunate mishap with a hammer or super glue. They were smoother, neater, less wrinkled, and remarkably free of the liver spots I seem to be collecting lately. The big surprise, however, came when I swung my legs from the bed and got to my feet. Not only was the action astonishingly easy, but I noticed a large proportion of me had simply vanished, allowing me to see my feet from a new, vertical perspective. There was something else worth mentioning. I was wearing a pair of blue, candy striped pyjamas, an item I'd not worn since the age of twelve.

A voice inside of me was telling, or possibly shouting, that I had slipped out of my time, landing in a world I didn't really belong. I padded to the window in my bare feet and looked out; the curtains already pulled by, I suspect, my earlier, not so happy intruder. Weirdly, I was not surprised to see the grounds had changed little from when I viewed them last, albeit from a different window. Several people were milling around, one was pushing a wheelbarrow of the type I'd seen before my encounter with Albert Ferris. The line of trees extending south along the eastern boundary, were thick and lush as I remembered them. It was still not possible to see the stones, or interestingly, the trees before them.

My thoughts were interrupted by a light knock at the door, and my immediate response surprised me.

Possibly because I was fairly confident it was not the woman from earlier. 'Yes, what is it?'

The door cracked open a little. I could just make out the shadow of a face hovering on the other side. 'Is it all right if I come in, Wills?' It was the voice of a woman; a soft, somewhat strained, but refined voice.

Strangely unfazed by the unfamiliar name, but taken by a brief moment of shyness, I called out, 'Er...Yes. Yes, please do come in.' It was an unusually polite response.

She hesitantly opened the door. Framed by the darkness of the landing, the woman looked to be in her early twenties or late teens. Her chestnut, bobbed hair, dark brown corduroys and sleeveless, green jumper reminded me of grainy monochrome photographs I'd seen of wartime Britain. I also thought I recognised her from somewhere. She cupped a hand over her mouth and gasped. 'No wonder Mrs Hughes was in a two an' eight, you're not even dressed yet. You know she takes her housekeeping duties very seriously.'

I stared at her, unsure how to answer. I had no idea what time it was, or why it was such a big deal. Uncharacteristically, I did, however, decide not to say anything clever and make myself look an arse. 'Is it late, then?' I asked innocently.

'Almost eight o'clock,' she hissed. 'Charles will go mad if Mrs Hughes goes blabbing off to him. You know what he's been like lately.'

I looked at her blankly. My brain tried to assimilate the information I had gathered so far. Mrs Hughes must have been the odious crone who threatened to report me to the master, who I now suspected to be a man called Charles, a person recently stricken by anger issues it seemed. The only character I'd yet to identify was the one in front of me. 'What do you suggest I do?' I asked, a little too blandly under the circumstances.

'Getting dressed might be a good start, Wills. And I suggest the quicker you're out of this room the better.' The young woman rolled her eyes. 'Charles will be on his way back from Crownhurst shortly, so you need to make yourself scarce for a while.'

'It's that serious, eh?' I answered glibly.

She gulped nervously. 'Please, Wills, do it for me.'

'How could I refuse?' I smiled. 'Leave it to me,' I said confidently.

'Just make sure you do,' she said, backing from the room. The door closed with a gentle click.

'Oh, lord,' I mumbled, my eyes settling on an ornately decorated wardrobe in the corner of the room, opposite the window; my immediate problem had shifted from who I had now become, to finding some clothes to wear. When I look back at this sudden and bizarre physical transition, I sometimes question why I accommodated it so easily and not lost the plot completely. It was certainly a lot to take in, as you can imagine. Some of it was due to feeling weirdly at home in what can only be described as an alter ego, an avatar not of my choosing. At least I was still at Althurian. I opened the wardrobe door.

The grey baggy trousers with turn ups looked too small but fitted perfectly. It was the same with the white linen shirt and sleeveless burgundy jumper. But the tan brogue shoes did it though. I probably looked like a *Great Gatsby* wannabe. All I needed was a mirror. My heart stepped up a pace as I reached for the door handle; I was now about to travel even farther into the unknown.

The landing had changed a little; it looked shabbier than when I saw it last, and the polished wooden floorboards were definitely in need of some restorative work. But in the main, the general layout, paintwork and decoration appeared to have remained the same, familiar in some respects. One addition I had not seen before, was a full length, gilt framed mirror fitted to the wall just before the stair head. I hesitated, taking a deep breath before stepping in front of it; my relationship with mirrors began to wane after the size of my waistline began to closely follow my age. If the experience of waking up this morning was strange, looking at my reflection had got to be one of the weirdest. Not only did I look half the man I used to be, I looked a third of my age. The most shocking aspect though, was the face staring back at me; it was mine, but wasn't at the same time, and my ability to find a plausible explanation for the change took a dive at this stage, and all I could do was walk away and hope there was a reason for it all.

I detected the sweet, but earthy scent of coal smoke as I turned to go downstairs; I kind of expected Skye to meet me halfway with a steaming mug of coffee. I silently chuckled at my absurd attempt at wishful thinking. Sounds of occupation coming from below stopped me in my tracks. I waited, my foot lightly touching the top step, my fingers tapping out an unfamiliar beat on the newel post; scary implications about the formidable Charles had made their mark.

'Master William?'

I turned on a heel. A smartly suited man in his late forties, stood halfway along the east to west corridor. His clothes and formal air suggested he was a servant of some kind. 'Yes,' I said. 'Can I help you?'

He smiled benignly. 'Is everything all right, sir?'

'Yes, it is. Why?' I bluffed.

He took a few paces forward, cupping a hand in front of his mouth as if to share a secret. With his voice scarcely above a whisper, he said, 'I took the liberty of saving you some breakfast, sir. You'll find it in the pantry wrapped in a linen cloth.'

'Why…thank you...I…' It was agony not to address someone by name, especially when they appeared to be operating outside their remit. 'I can't wait,' I mumbled, briefly catching sight of the man's bemused expression as I quickly hurried off down the stairs.

I wandered into the hall; the sounds I'd heard from upstairs were coming from the direction of the kitchen. As I stood facing the front door, deciding if it was wise to quietly slip away unnoticed, a voice from behind called out. I froze. Its tonal quality and power was scarily similar to the formidable Mrs Hughes. Not that I'm a coward you understand.

'Master William, sir.'

Preparing to bolt at the first sign of danger, and not wishing to fully turn around, I took a deep breath and glanced over my shoulder. 'That's me,' I said. My defences relaxed a little when I saw the source of my anxiety. A short woman of around fifty, and carrying considerably less bulk than my earlier adversary, was holding open the interconnecting door. Her kindly eyes and broad smile was a reassuring relief. It felt safe enough to completely turn around.

'I was wondering if you an' Mistress Forsyth will be coming home for lunch.'

'Ah,' I said, my brain scrabbling round for an answer. Although I had no idea who she was referring to, I had the vague impression it may have been the young woman who had given me the warning. 'I think you ought to ask her, she may have arranged something different today,' I added quickly.

The woman frowned. 'But Mr Jameson told me you were both going to the meeting at the town 'all after your stint at Boxford.'

I slapped my temple. 'Oh Lord, I'd forgotten all about that,' I lied. 'I'll try to catch up with her and find out what we're doing.'

The woman shook her head. 'You'll forget your own name one of these days, Master William. By the way, Mr Jameson left something for you in the pantry.' She grinned mischievously. 'Just so you don't forget.'

'Yes, he told me.' I gave a limp smile. 'I guess I'd better take it with me then.'

'Well, that was the idea, Master William.'

I followed the woman through to the kitchen, a room twice the size as the one I remembered, and now with a spectacular view of the back garden; I feel slightly awkward referring to the experience as a memory, because I'm not entirely sure where I was in relation to the time I used to know, if that makes sense. Luckily, the woman, whom I assumed was a cook, went straight to a tall, solid looking cupboard attached to the wall next to the window, and retrieved a neatly bound cloth package. She turned, smiled, and handed it to me. I tucked it under my arm. 'Thank you.' I hesitated. If this young woman was the one from earlier, and I was supposed to be going to a meeting with her, I ought to at least get to know my travelling companion a little better.

'Would you know where I'm likely to find Mistress Forsyth?' I had suddenly become strangely eloquent. And the really crazy part of all this was: I was getting used to it.

'I think she's in the library, Master William.'

I tried to nod convincingly. 'Ah, yes, the library,' I said. Shit! I had no idea where the library was, and in danger of looking like a complete idiot if I went about trying each door to find it. I was back to the, not so reliable technique: the best guess. I wandered back to the hall for a think. Noting the study had vanished and morphed into becoming part of the kitchen, made it a little easier; at least one room was eliminated from my search. I stood stroking my chin, pondering. There were some bookshelves in the drawing room, quite a few if I remembered correctly. Then it dawned on me, as long as the cook didn't see me, I could try as many doors as I liked. With my strategy set, I boldly made my way to the drawing room and went straight in. It was odd to see how much the room had changed in such a short space of time, relatively speaking. With shelves bending under the weight of hundreds of books, and fitted against nearly every wall, it did indeed look like a library. At a table at the far end, by the window, sat the young woman I'd met earlier.

She looked up. 'Shouldn't you be at Boxford?'

I lifted up the package. 'I had to get my breakfast from the kitchen.'

'Jameson spoils you.'

I nodded. 'I know.' I decided to take a gamble. 'The cook wants to know if we're coming home for lunch.'

She frowned. 'You mean Mrs Campbell?'

I could feel myself wince. 'Sorry. Yes, I meant Mrs Campbell'

'We could have done if you'd got yourself out of bed earlier. As it is, I doubt we'll have time.'

'Right.' I smiled limply. 'Mea culpa.'

'As usual.' She rolled her eyes. 'You'd better get going; you're already an hour late. Have you enough money for petrol?'

'Petrol?'

'You said you had an empty tank, remember?'

This time I knew I was running out of bluff. 'I…um…I.'

She tutted, leant to one side and picked up her handbag. 'You should have asked me earlier,' she said, opening her purse. 'It's your own fault for staying out late with this Lipton girl you've been courting.' She shook her head. 'Mother was right, God bless her, when she said you have your head in the clouds most of the time.' She held out her hand. 'Here's a pound. Try to make it last the week, will you? Charles is already asking me where all my money is going.'

I ambled over to her, placing my cloth covered breakfast on the table; I felt like a scolded child as I reached out my hand. For a brief, fleeting moment I remembered the woman on the steps and the money in her purse. With a part of me believing I should know the answer, I so wanted to ask her who Charles was. 'Thank you,' I said. I stood there, feeling a bit of a lemon and not knowing what to do next, when a solution came from an unexpected quarter. The door burst open, and a man, who looked too young to be wearing green plus fours and tweed shooting jacket, walked in with a bullying swagger. I now had my answer.

He eyed me suspiciously. 'What are you still doing here, boy?' he snapped.

From the corner of my eye I saw the woman duck her head down, surreptitiously dropping her handbag from sight. 'I came to say goodbye,' I said.

'That's not what I asked,' he snarled.

'I'm to blame for that, Charles,' the woman confessed meekly. 'I asked William to do some errands for me. I didn't realise it was so late.'

He glared at her. 'Don't lie to cover for your brother's laziness. You know very well Mrs Hughes had to get him out of bed this morning.'

I had a hard time listening to this upstart in man's clothing, ripping into a woman I now understood to be my sister. 'Your right, Charles, the buck should stop with me,' I said.

He turned; his face now contorted in rancour. 'It's about time you admitted your indolent ways, boy. Your father may have put up with it, but I damn well won't.' He then cackled derisively. 'You'll be lucky if the Royal Air Force allow you to even look at a Spitfire.'

I looked at Charles through narrow eyes. Vaguely familiar, and looking no more than twenty-five, he had an arrogance that beggared belief and a face you could easily slap, and trust me, I was tempted. I had no idea what he was talking about, and probably just as well I didn't. I shrugged as if I cared less. 'I'd better go.'

He cackled again. 'Lost your nerve for combat, have you?'

I was in no mood to argue with a bully. Balling my hands into fists, I left the room in silence and leant my back against the closed door. I hung my head down, with eyes screwed shut as I listened to the continued sound of conflict; Charles had turned his attention to another victim. I could feel my temperature, as well as anger, rising as his language became cruder and more threatening. I took a deep breath and was about to go back when a hand lightly touched my shoulder.

♦

'Where have you been, I've been worried sick.'

For a second, I didn't quite recognise the voice. It had also gone deathly quiet. I took another deep breath and opened my eyes. I knew the face, the shoulder length brown hair, the slightly upturned nose.

'John?'

'Y-yes.'

'Are you all right?'

I could feel myself frown. 'Skye?'

She smiled. 'You know how to worry a girl, don't you?'

I wiped a hand across my mouth and looked into her eyes. 'What happened?'

'You disappeared, John. I couldn't find you anywhere.' She laughed nervously. 'I thought for a minute you'd taken the same route to the bathroom as our mystery woman.'

'I-I'm not sure if I…' I stammered.

'You don't remember, do you?'

'I remember sitting on the sofa, then it went a bit crazy.'

'We were talking, and you got up without saying a word and walked out the room. It was the oddest thing. I couldn't have been more than a second behind you, but when I got to the hall, you'd gone. I didn't know what to think.'

'How long?'

'Over two hours.'

I stared at her. I needed to think; difficult, as my brain was surrounded by a blanket of fog. I turned to open the door. 'I need to sit down.' The sofa, the blanket, everything was how it was. I sat down, feeling numb. She sat opposite.

'Where did you go?'

'I'm not sure I went anywhere, at least in the physical sense. If I tell you what I believe happened, I know you're going to think I've lost my mind. It really is crazy, trust me.'

'As crazy as our vanishing woman? Tell me first, then let me be the judge.'

'Okay.' I took a deep breath. 'I think I might have slipped back in time, but not in a way I can explain easily.' I waited for the anticipated reaction. I was surprised when it didn't come. She just watched me intensely.

'Go on,' she said.

I told her everything I could remember, although the memory of it, once spoken, seemed to evaporate into nothingness, like the hazy recollection of a dream after waking.

She was silent for a moment. 'What year do you think it was?'

Suddenly, my head started to clear; the world I thought I'd left behind came flooding back. 'Those photographs, the ones you were looking at the other night, the ones you found in the chest. Where are they?'

'I put them on the bedside table. Why?'

'I want to see them again. I need to know who the woman was.'

'I thought you said the staff referred to her as Mistress Forsyth.'

'Not to her face.'

♦

Skye came to the room carrying a small bundle of envelopes. 'I think they were in this lot,' she said, retaking her place on the sofa. It was unsettling to think that for a brief moment of time I, or whoever I'd become, had just walked from a completely different room, occupied by people whom I knew nothing about. She opened the ends of each envelope until she found the one containing the photographs and handed it to me.

As I slipped the first one out, the face looking up at me was unmistakable. The young woman in the photograph, the one we had decided was Charles Forsyth's wife, was the woman I had met, the woman who had defended me in the very room we were now sitting. I smiled. And now I had a name for her. I removed the second photograph, with it came the newspaper cutting. I held them side by side. Those sharp, dark eyes, bony cheeks and tight-lipped smile meant something to me now. I re-read the story. Something inside me wondered if Charles had pushed his bullying ways a little too far. I handed Skye the photograph of Patricia. 'It must have been before Sylvia was born. She only looked a kid herself.'

'Did she look pregnant?'

'Not that I noticed, and I'm sure I would have.'

'How old did she look?'

'No more than about twenty, I guess.' I was humbled by Skye's ability to accept such an unbelievable turn of events. Her focus and enthusiasm was palpable. It was uncanny.

'We could really do with some dates. At least we know it was before the war.'

'I have a feeling war wasn't far off. Charles mentioned something about Spitfires.'

'Late thirties, then?'

'Possibly.' I leaned back, looked up at the ceiling and sighed. 'I wonder what this is all about. There has to be a reason for it.'

'But don't you find it exciting, John? We may have stumbled across something extraordinary here.'

I puffed out my cheeks. 'Personally, I was hoping for a quiet life.'

She laughed. 'That's age talking. This house might be a gateway of some kind. Think of all the possibilities if you could travel through time at will.'

'I don't know if it works like that.'

'But what if it does?'

'Then,' I shrugged, 'we'll cross that bridge when we come to it. What time is it?'

She checked her watch. 'Nearly midnight. Where did the day go?'

'It's all right for you, I feel like I've just got up!'

Chapter 8
Old Times

I listened to the birds outside the window singing their hearts out. Life sounded so normal, predictable, although my short time at Althurian had taught me differently. I sighed. I knew Skye had embraced this contradiction of reality more than I had. She was excited; I, on the other hand, was frightened by it. I opened my eyes and turned over; part of me expected her not to be there. As I have already pointed out, the love of my life is also my alarm clock, so it was an unexpected sight to see her so quiet and so still. Today was a special day, she was on a mission to discover the identity of our mysterious vanishing lady and had insisted we drive to Cramerly and attempt a meeting with Ms Bergan.

I slipped from the bed and padded across to the chair on which I'd dumped my travel bag; the prospect of a hot shower and fresh, clean clothes was an exciting one. I flinched as the zip made a noise akin to an ice sheet breaking up. I glanced across to my slumbering mate and breathed a small sigh of relief; as I have mentioned before, it was unusual for her not to stir a little, she was the lightest of sleepers. I checked my phone and frowned. It was 07:05. I felt a shiver run down my spine as the events from yesterday flooded back to the present. I wondered how long I could cope with life at Althurian if it was always going to be like this.

She was still asleep when I eventually emerged from the en-suite; I had taken longer than usual. I decided not to wake her and snuck off as quietly as I could. I was more than happy just to sit on my own in the garden room with a cup of coffee, watching the shadows shorten across the lawn. It was about two hours before Larry was due to pick up his equipment and I felt like I had all the time in the world; I had decided against going anywhere near the stones beforehand.

I placed the percolator on a tiled mat in the centre of the table next to my mug, turned the chair so I could get a good view of the garden, and fluffed up the cushion. I shivered suddenly, it was still a little chilly, although the gentle and reassuring, tick, tick, tick of the radiator as its metal jacket expanded with heat, cheered me greatly; the boiler must have started its early morning cycle. I poured myself a generous mug of coffee and put my feet up. I closed my eyes and took a sip, careful not to burn my lips.

'I thought I'd find you out here.'

It was quite a shock; I didn't even hear the kitchen door open. I jumped with a start, spilling some of my coffee onto the red, quarry tiled floor. I looked down and cursed under my breath. It was only at this point I realised all was not as it seemed; on every other visit to the garden room the floor had been covered in rush matting. I slowly raised my head. 'You?' I whispered.

Patricia was standing with her hands on her hips. 'Who else did you think it was?' she replied acidly.

I nervously scratched a place behind my ear. 'I-I don't really know,' I blathered.

'Head in the clouds again?'

I think I may have blushed. 'It's not a bad place to be,' I said glibly.

'You don't want Charles to hear you say that.' She paused. 'Mr Jameson is looking for you.'

'Oh, right.' I was still a little shocked to be back so soon. 'Do you know what he wants?'

'He didn't say.' She looked at me inquisitively. 'How did you get on at Boxford?'

I sighed. 'Great.'

'Really?'

When she looked as shocked as I felt, I knew my answer was probably suspect. 'No. I was being facetious. How is Charles?'

She pursed her lips, looked away, then back again. 'He's a little better this morning.'

'What does that mean?' I could feel the bile rising in my throat. 'Is he still asleep?'

Patricia cupped a hand over her mouth and sniggered. 'Wills, you are a fool.'

'Well?' I had become unexpectedly protective.

She nervously massaged the back of her neck. 'He had to catch an early train to London.' She smiled limply. 'It's not his fault. He has a lot on his mind lately. We all have.'

'So, that gives him the right to bully you, does it?'

She brushed an eye with the back of her hand. 'Please, Wills, don't do this.'

'Sorry.' I took a breath. 'Look, I know it's none of my business.' I'm not sure why I said that. It was my business in a way, but not in another. Crossed paths, I guess. 'But I wouldn't be much of a brother if I didn't care about how he treats you.'

'I know that.' She folded her arms, wandered over to the door and looked out, her face drawn. 'Charles believes Chamberlain will soon appoint Churchill to First Lord of the Admiralty. He says it won't be long before Hitler marches into Poland.' She did nothing to disguise the fear in her voice. She turned to look at me directly. 'All this talk of war frightens me, Wills.' Her brow creased. 'Is it really possible we could go to war with Germany?'

I wanted to reassure her, say everything would be all right, but if the world, at this juncture, was as close to war as I thought, then comforting words from me were likely to be short lived. 'I think we need to prepare for the worst, Patricia.'

Her lips trembled, but I noticed a ghost of a smile. 'You only call me Patricia when you're angry.'

'No. Not angry,' I said. 'I'm just resigned to the inevitable.' I guessed a change of subject was needed. 'What have you planned to do today?'

Her face softened. 'Well, as Mrs Campbell is taking her usual jaunt into town today, I suggested we go together. I fancy a change of scenery, and it'll save her waiting for a bus. Anyway, the Alvis could do with a run.'

'Sounds like fun.' At least I now knew who Mrs Campbell was. 'Could you get me a newspaper while you're out?'

Patricia snorted. 'Since when did you start reading newspapers?'

I raised my eyebrows. 'This morning.'

'Things are looking up. Well, if you're that keen, yesterday's Telegraph is in the library.'

'Thank you. What time are you leaving?'

'About ten, I should think.' She grinned. 'I have to wait for Mrs Campbell to put on her best frock. I think she has one especially reserved for going out in the car. Still no news from Doncaster yet?'

Here we go again, I thought. 'Doncaster?' I asked, trying my best not to look puzzled.

Patricia rolled her eyes; I noticed she was good at that. 'Aircrew Selection Board?'

I guessed this had something to do with Charles' remark concerning Spitfires. I assumed William must have applied to join up in some capacity. 'No. Not yet,' I said, hoping this would satisfy her curiosity.

'But it must be almost a month now. Charles was only waiting two weeks.'

'Perhaps more people are applying.' I smiled. 'These things can take time.'

'You've changed your tune. Yesterday, you were pacing up and down the floor about it.'

I shrugged. 'They'll call me when their ready.'

Patricia howled. 'Don't be daft, Wills, you'll get a letter like everyone else.'

My face reddened. 'That's what I meant.'

Patricia glanced at her watch. 'I'd better get myself ready and move the car to the gate. Mrs Campbell will be here way before she needs to be.'

'You could just go and pick her up.'

Patricia shook her head. 'I think she's embarrassed about where she lives.' She paused. 'You could come with us if you like. We might go to the Plaza; they're showing the Wizard of Oz every day this week.'

I tried not to pull a face. 'Thanks for the offer, but as it's such a nice morning, I thought I'd go for a walk round the garden.'

'Reading newspapers and walks in the garden,' she scoffed. 'You'll be playing bowls next. You're getting old before your time, my lad.' She looked at me with her large, intensely blue eyes. 'Are you sneaking off to see that Lipton girl?'

'Perish the thought.' I chuckled guiltily for absolutely no reason I could think of. Clearly, whoever this Lipton girl was, she meant something to William's latent memory. 'I do have to rest at some point, you know.'

Patricia inclined her head. 'In that case, perhaps you can give Albert a hand sawing up that fallen horse chestnut.'

'Albert? Is he...er...working today?'

'Albert works every day. You are a funny boy sometimes.' She walked over to me and held out a hand; in her palm was a small, gold amulet and chain.' I'd like you to have this. Sorry it's not in a box.' She swallowed noisily. I thought it might keep you safe. You know,' she glanced towards the ceiling, 'while you're up there.'

I carefully took it from her. 'I don't know what to say.'

'Well, don't say anything then,' she said softly. 'I'd better make a move.' She winked. 'Don't forget to say hello to Daphne for me.'

'Ah, Daphne...er...yes...her.'

I watched as she left the room, taking a long sighing breath, the effort of maintaining this pretence was draining. I stood up, went to the door and looked out. I wondered if the "Albert" Patricia was referring to was the same gentleman I'd met the other day. I closed my eyes. The sun was just peeping over the treetops, its rich golden light beginning to flood the garden room; I could feel its warm rays on my face. A prickling sensation made the hairs on my forearms stand on end.

♦

'I hoped you were making one of those for me.'

I spun round, my breath catching in my throat. 'S-Skye,' I gasped. 'You scared the life out of me.'

'Makes a change.' She was standing by the chair, wearing a white, towelling robe and slippers. 'Well? Where is it?'

'I was just about to make a fresh one,' I lied. 'Have you been up long?'

'Long enough to have a shower,' she said. 'I thought for a minute you'd gone for another one of your long walks.'

'Not this time.' I didn't feel up to explaining myself just yet. 'Sleep well?'

'Better.' She picked up the percolator, carefully touching the side. 'Is this your second one?'

I shook my head. 'I've only just made it.'

'I'll get a mug.' She hesitated. 'Are you okay? You seem a little distant.'

'It's nothing, sweetie, I'm still a little worn out from yesterday.'

'I'm not surprised. You do feel okay though?'

'Would I lie?'

'Yes, that's why I asked. 'We've got a busy day ahead of us.' She grinned. 'Can't be having you throw a sickie.'

'Very funny. I thought you were taking Mrs…' I stopped myself. 'It doesn't matter…I was thinking of something else,' I lied.

She looked mildly puzzled but didn't pursue it. 'Don't forget Larry will be here at ten.'

I looked down. Weirdly, I could still feel the impression of the amulet in my palm. 'No. I hadn't forgotten.'

♦

Larry was rubbing his hands and stamping his feet noisily as I opened the door. I didn't realise how cold it was until I was nipped by the frigid air wafting in from outside. He stepped into the hall, still wearing the same outfit as yesterday. 'You could have brought better weather with you,' I said.

He chuckled politely. 'I can't believe how bloody parky it is out there.'

'It won't have damaged the equipment, will it?'

'Some of the plugs might have frozen in their sockets but it won't have affected the readings. I can't wait to upload the data to my tablet, there was certainly something going on last night.'

'Really? How do you know?'

He held up his phone, tapping the side. 'I pulled off a random sample last night. It showed a massive spike in the electromagnetic footprint, way above ambient. There was quite a lot of noise in the signal, but that could have been interference.' He nodded sagely. 'Definitely something going on,' he mumbled.

'What time was this?'

'Between eight an' nine, peaked about eight thirty, dropped off slightly, then levelled out. Won't know how long it continued until I upload the rest of the data.'

I shivered as my flesh turned icy cold, I could feel the hairs on the back of my neck begin to prickle. When is this likely to happen?'

'I only need to unplug the logging unit and bring it inside to do it. I brought my tablet and a fresh set of batteries, just in case.' He nodded towards the back door, there was an aura of childish excitement about him. 'So, John, shall we see what we've got?'

♦

We spoke little as we walked towards the tree line. I was intrigued with the sudden activity recorded by Larry's instruments; my usually sceptical stance on such things had taken a massive knock in the last few days, although in my head I could still find one hundred and one reasons to explain the coincidence. Larry glanced over his shoulder as we started through the wood. 'I was talking to a pal of mine last night; I mentioned the name of that chap you told me about.'

'Julius Becket?'

'That's the one. 'What were you told about him?'

'Not a lot. Just that he was known as the Guardian, whatever that is.' We scrambled through the last of the leafless shrubbery to the clearing, and the stones; everything was as we left it.

Larry put down the holdall and straightened up. 'It was just as well I'd jotted down the name.' He tapped a finger on his temple. 'The old memory's not as good these days. Anyways, this Becket fella has some history at Althurian.' He paused. 'No. Not Althurian exactly. This was way before Althurian was even conceived. Did you know there used to be a monastery here?'

'So I believe.'

'Well, Julius Becket used to make frequent trips to meet the brotherhood, a really obscure group known as the Forgotten Saints. He wasn't on his own either; it was a journey many from all over Britain frequently took, some even making their way from the continent.'

Although I found this information interesting, the man Larry was talking about was clearly not the man I had in mind, or met; a spooky coincidence, nonetheless. 'Becket was a pilgrim, then?'

Larry nodded. 'Apparently so, he was a religious eccentric, and a brother of Thomas, no less.'

'Thomas Becket, the saint?'

'The very same; Julius was eight years younger and, some say, influenced Thomas' decision to oppose Henry's attempt to regulate relations between state and church.'

A little far-fetched I thought; my knowledge of the period was thin to say the least, but I was sure Thomas Becket was an only child. 'That's some story, Larry. So, what happened to him?'

'No one knows. He made his last trip to the monastery in 1171 and simply disappeared. A document discovered a little while ago, and written by a political scribe of the time, seems to suggest he was pursued by the same knights that murdered his brother.' Larry scribed an arc with his hand. 'There's a good chance his bones lay somewhere under all this earth.'

'Nice. And the monastery?' I asked.

'Looted and torn down during the reformation; allegedly one of the first.'

I puffed out my cheeks. If true, it was hard to believe so much had happened in one place. 'Any idea why they were called the Forgotten Saints?'

'Ah, now I know this one. Although the evidence is a bit sketchy, the twelfth century monastery was built over another religious site, one believed to have been occupied by a Druid hierarchy. Scholars wrote at the time that during preparatory excavations a number of unmarked graves were discovered, each one filled with objects they attributed to that of the saintly. Hence, the Forgotten Saints.'

I was tempted to ask more questions; Larry was obviously a mine of information. I was, however, aware of the time. I nodded at the data logging unit. 'It's a pity your machine can't read what this lot have seen.'

Larry inclined his head. 'The stone tape hypothesis. Many have tried.' He grinned. 'Including me.' He raised his eyebrows. 'And many, like me, have failed. Perhaps we'd better get this data logger indoors.'

♦

I watched, fascinated, as Larry plugged a device similar to a memory stick into a small aperture on the side of the unit; a small, green indicator flashed twice. 'Good, that seems to be working okay,' he mumbled.

With his wayward, windswept hair, and glasses perched at the end of his nose, he looked every bit the mad professor; tutting and shaking his head worryingly as he tapped the screen of his tablet. 'Something wrong?' I asked.

'I'm not sure.' He turned the tablet for me to see; the screen displayed a graphic waveform, showing a series of spikes, each one falling to a real time base line, then up to a peak again; there were several of these overlapping each other. 'What I'm seeing here is extraordinary.' He paused. 'So much so, I'm wondering if it could have been caused by something man-made.'

'Like what?'

He shrugged. 'Could be anything electrical, even a poorly shielded domestic appliance can affect sensitive measuring equipment.'

I continued to stare at the screen. Everything I'd experienced in the last twenty-four hours seemed to coincide perfectly with the timing of each spike. 'But what if it isn't?'

Larry stroked his chin. 'Then it's probably the most active site I've ever measured.'

'And that means what exactly?'

He sighed. 'I was asked by a friend of mine to monitor a house he'd recently bought. He was convinced the place was haunted. All sorts of strange things were happening to him, it got so bad he had to move out and rent somewhere. I have to be honest; I've never been so freaked out as I was there.' He looked at me steadily. 'The electrical and magnetic activity I recorded then was nowhere near what you have here. I've never seen anything like it.'

I shuddered. Skye's words from the other night came back to me. 'Are you saying the stones are haunted?'

'Quite frankly, John, I don't know. Parapsychology is not a field I'm entirely comfortable with. Not that I doubt its existence, you understand. I'm very aware strange events occur that are beyond rational explanation. It's just...' He was thoughtfully silent for a moment. 'It's just that I need to find evidence based on science. A few grainy photographs of a shadow someone purports to look like a recently departed uncle, or a case file full of ghostly anecdotes, are not convincing evidence in my book.'

I was feeling a little frustrated. Larry seemed to contradict himself. To me the evidence was staring him in the face, possibly interpretation was the problem. 'So, what would be your best guess?'

I saw the corners of his mouth twitch; a memory of our earlier conversation perhaps? 'Apart from being places where people worshipped everything from trees to planets, most ancient stone circles are thought to have been used to predict various astronomical events. Now, what is interesting is how their geographical location, and alignment with other significant objects, was chosen to begin with. Many, including me, believe these ancient sites are accurately positioned within a web of criss-crossing lines of energy, using techniques that are now lost to us. What I do with my equipment is to try and discover what that energy is.' He went across to the window and looked out. 'The energy I picked up around those stones was more than just a line of force. It was more like a modulated signal.'

'You've lost me, Larry.'

He turned, pressing his hands deep into his pockets. 'The signal was carrying intelligent information, John. Like a radio or television broadcast, or the internet through our phone cables.'

He'd now got my attention. 'You mean we can decode them?'

'It's not quite as straightforward as that. Without knowing the language or the key to deciphering the language, it's like trying to understand an Egyptian hieroglyph without a Rosetta stone.'

Frustrated, and now a little deflated, I was beginning to think Larry's faith in his technology may be misplaced. 'So it was a waste of time, then?' I snapped, probably a little rudely.

He sighed 'No. Not a waste of time,' he answered emphatically. 'These data need careful analysis and comparison. There are a countless number of variables that could explain the anomalous nature of those signals.' He smiled wearily. 'You did ask for my best guess.'

'Yes, I know I did. Sorry.' I felt bad; Larry was such an unassuming man, eager to help in many ways.

'I can let you know my conclusions in the next few days, if you're interested.'

'Oh, I'm interested all right.'

♦

Larry accepted the offer of a lift, but insisted I drop him off at a junction with an un-adopted road, about two miles from Althurian; he said he was worried that the unmade cinder track may damage the underside of the Aston. I struggled to believe he had manhandled that heavy holdall so far. I returned just after 11.30am.

I found Skye in the drawing room; she had brought down one of the travel chests and was in the middle of arranging several neat piles of envelopes and various papers either side of where she was sitting. She looked up and smiled. 'I hope you don't mind, John, but I thought I'd make a start on this lot.

'Of course I don't mind, it has to be done at some point. Anything good so far?'

She shook her head. 'Nothing of any consequence. You were quick, I didn't expect you home so soon.'

'It wasn't far.' I smiled; she had referred to Althurian as home.

'So, what's Larry's verdict on our stone circle?'

'I think the word is inconclusive. He reckons something is going on but has no idea what's causing it.' I flopped on the sofa opposite. 'He'll let us know for sure in a few days. When do you want to leave for Cramerly?'

'I'm ready when you are.'

♦

I turned into Shaftesbury Road, pulling up a safe distance from the junction. I leant forward and tapped the glass of the fuel gauge; the needle had fallen dangerously below the quarter tank mark. I remembered the ninety-seven pounds of petrol we had poured into its voluminous tank only a day ago and shuddered; this was no Toyota Yaris. 'We'll need to find a petrol station before we make our way back,' I said.

Skye was otherwise occupied; she had already entered Janice Bergan's number into her phone and was waiting for it to connect. It bleeped twice. 'It says the number isn't recognised.'

I looked at the card we'd found in the purse. 'I think there might be a "one" missing from this number, love. Maybe it's zero one six, it could've been written down wrong.'

'It's worth a try.' She squinted at her phone and redialled. It was switched to speakerphone.

'Hel...lo.' The voice was hesitant, a little shaky, and sounded somewhat older than we expected.

'Is that,' Skye glanced at me, 'Ms Bergan?'

'Who...is...this?'

'My name is Skye, I live at Althurian Manor, I found something that may belong to you.'

'Althurian?' repeated the woman.

'Yes. This *is*, Janice Bergan I'm speaking to?'

After a moment of silence, the woman answered, 'I used to be, dear. What is it you've found?'

'A purse.'

Really?' She paused. 'But I haven't lost my purse. Are you sure it's mine?'

'We found a card inside with your address and telephone number.'

'Well, I don't know how it could be, dear. I suppose it might belong to one of my friends. What does it look like?'

Skye covered the phone's microphone and whispered, 'Should I really be describing it to her?'

I chuckled. 'It was us who rang her, remember. It would be different if it was full of payment cards instead of a few pre-decimal coins.'

'And a ring.'

'Just tell her.'

'It's made from light blue leather and has a brass zip.'

'Did you find this purse at Althurian, dear?'

Skye glanced at me again. 'Yes.'

Her voice dropped. 'Is there...a...ring inside?'

'Yes, Janice. Yes, there is.'

We both heard a sudden intake of breath. 'Oh Lord,' she said. 'I-I don't know what to say.' There was a long pause. 'If I pay for the postage, is it possible you could send it to me?'

'I assume you still live in Shaftesbury Road?'

'Yes, dear.'

'Then we can do better than that, Janice. We can drop it off to you, we're only around the corner.'

'Are you sure? That's very kind of you.'

'Honestly, it isn't a problem.'

'Well, in that case…I'd better put the kettle on. See you shortly. Bye, bye.'

Skye cradled the phone in her lap. 'It looks as if we've found her, John.'

'She sounds a lot older to me.'

'Some people do over the phone.' She raised her eyebrows. 'She knew about the ring.'

I started the Aston, put it in drive and released the handbrake. 'True,' I said.

♦

Shaftesbury Road was longer than expected and finding a property without a house number was to try my patience, especially when I had one eye glued to the fuel gauge. After turning around for the second time, tolerance was becoming scarce. 'What the hell is a Badgers Rake, anyway,' I grouched. Skye came to my rescue, and hers!

'I'll ring her again,' she said.

♦

The sign outside the property was big enough to see from space, how on earth we both missed it (Okay, it was me), was a mystery. The fine, mid twentieth century property, set back some way from the road, was in need of a little tender loving care. We turned onto the drive and pulled up behind a car suffering from the same level of neglect as the house; it's once white paintwork, a grimy, watermarked green, each tyre flat and down to their rims. It is a sad reflection of life to see the accumulation of dreams, and hard work, reduced to a state of slow decay. I shrugged and climbed from the driver's seat.

A minute or two after Skye had rung the bell, we heard shuffling footsteps coming from within; it took a further minute of rattling bolts and scraping locks before the door finally swung open. The woman was short and slight of frame, with a small, plate round face, and a neatly tied bun of pure white hair; her dark hazel eyes missed nothing. I glanced at Skye; we were both thinking the same thing: Janice Bergan was not our woman.

'You found us, then?' she said, with a cackle. Janice left the door open and walked back along the hall. 'You'd better come in or the neighbours will talk. And close the door behind you, if you will.' The interior was a dull mixture of faded, embossed wallpaper of various colours, and cream painted woodwork. As we followed her through to a back room, I detected the faint aroma of stale tobacco smoke. She stood by the open door and gestured towards a pair of matching winged armchairs. 'Sit yourselves down, and I'll get the tea.'

Skye asked, 'Would you like some help, Janice.'

Turning awkwardly until she faced us, Janice said, 'Lord no, dear. I've been doing for myself for almost twenty years now.' She cackled again. 'Not that Bert, bless him, was much of a help when he was at home.' She hesitated. 'I'd better get that tea.'

Janice emerged from the kitchen carrying a tray which tilted alarmingly as she hobbled towards us. I could see from the corner of my eye, Skye preparing to leap from the chair at the first sign of impending disaster. Luckily, the tray, three china cups and saucers, and a plate containing three chocolate biscuits, arrived at the coffee table without incident. Janice flopped heavily onto the chair opposite, clasping her hands neatly on her lap. 'So, where did you say you found the purse?'

Unfortunately, the one thing we forgot to do was rehearse a story that made sense, and not sound as if it had been plucked from an episode of the *Twilight Zone.* 'It was jammed down the side of one of our sofas,' I said.

Janice's eyes widened. 'They must have been quite old, these sofas.'

Skye said, 'They were in the house when we moved in.' She glanced at me and started to fumble inside her bag. 'You're right, they're hardly new.'

'How do you know Althurian?' I asked.

'My father was head gardener for over thirty years. I used to spend most of my summer holidays there as a youngster.'

Skye asked, 'You must have known Sylvia Forsyth.'

'Oh yes. We were inseparable once.' Janice sighed. 'But that was a long time ago.'

'You didn't stay in touch?' I asked.

Her hazel eyes fixed mine. 'Some friendships last, others are not meant to,' she said glibly. We both outgrew each other, I suppose. Sylvia found other friends, and so did I. We still saw each other from time to time, but that too fizzled out.'

Skye got to her feet and handed Janice the purse. 'I've left the note with your name and address inside.'

Janice examined the purse carefully, a slight smile appearing on her face as she massaged the soft leather between her fingers; I could see from her expression she recognised it. I watched as she carefully unfastened the zip and peeked inside.

'So, Janice…is it your purse?' I asked.

She laid it on her lap and took a moment to consider her answer. 'It was once. I gave it to Sylvia as a gift. We didn't have much money, you see, and it was her birthday, and I knew she liked it.'

'And the ring?' I asked.

'Ah, now there's a story.' Her expression suddenly darkened. 'May I ask you a question first?'

'Yes, sure you can.' I said.

'I assume something must have happened to Sylvia or you wouldn't be here.'

'She passed away a little over three months ago.' I felt my heart sink. 'I'm sorry to be the bearer of such bad news.'

She sighed. 'Just lately, bad news has become an all too common bedfellow. Tell me, how did you know Sylvia?'

'I didn't actually know her. I inherited her estate.'

She frowned. 'You're a Forsyth?'

I shook my head, smiling limply. 'No. I'm a Warrener. Sylvia was a cousin.'

'Ah, from Pattie's side of the family,' she said solemnly.

'I glanced at Skye, then back to Janice. 'Pattie?' I repeated.

'Sylvia's mother was a Warrener.'

'I see.' I paused. 'But you called her Pattie.'

Janice shrugged as if it were obvious. 'Everyone did, including Sylvia. I thought it was odd hearing her call her mother by her Christian name. My father would have boxed my ears if I'd done the same.'

'Do you remember what happened to her brother? William?'

Her expression changed again; I could see sadness this time. 'I do indeed. William was a lovely boy, a local hero.' She momentarily appeared distracted. 'Unfortunately, his bravery got him killed.'

My heart seemed to somersault in my chest, suddenly this became incredibly personal. 'My God, what happened to him?' I barked, unable to hide my shock.

'His plane was shot down over the North Sea. He was only nineteen. I don't think Pattie ever got over it, they were very close. Not that I was around at the time.'

'When was this?'

'During the war.'

'Sorry,' I said, 'I meant, when during the war?'

Janice stroked her lips, her eyes distant for a moment. 'June 1940, I think.'

I stared at her. I couldn't come to terms with what I'd just heard. It was as if I had been given a death sentence with no chance of appeal. I may have had my mouth open. 'Do you remember the date?'

Janice inclined her head. 'No. Sorry, dear, you have to remember I was barely a year old at the time. Everything I know about William came from Sylvia.'

'You were about to tell us about the ring, Janice,' said Skye.

'Ah, yes,' she said, 'the ring. I don't know the full story because, quite frankly, it's all a bit of a mystery and anything I do know has come from several different people.' She paused. 'It belonged to her grandmother. It was her wedding ring, Sylvia told me that much. How she came by it was a story told to me by others, though.'

'Why was that?' I asked.

'Sylvia was cagey about her past, and with good reason. Rumour had it her grandparents got into financial difficulties during the great depression, made some unwise investments in the stock market and borrowed a significant sum of money from Edmund Forsyth, Sylvia's paternal grandfather. When Edmund died in thirty-four, his son took over the family business and began to call in the debt.'

Skye interrupted. 'But he was their son in law, for Christ sake. What a bastard.' She immediately cupped a hand over her mouth. 'I'm so sorry, Janice, it just slipped out.'

Janice chuckled. 'I couldn't have put it better myself, dear.' She sighed. 'You have to remember, this is second-hand information, and you know what that can be like.'

'But I thought Edmund already owned Althurian,' I said.

'As far as I know, he did. I think her grandparents were tenants for a while.'

'So, how did they pay the money back?'

'They couldn't. Pattie returned to the house one afternoon and found a note on the kitchen table, and they were never seen again.'

'What do you mean?' I frowned. 'They just ran off and left the children to fend for themselves?'

Janice shrugged. 'Yes, I suppose so.'

'And the ring?'

'Left on the edge of a washbasin.'

Skye exclaimed, 'My God, those poor children!'

'So that was why William was at Althurian,' I mumbled.

Janice frowned. 'I'm sorry, what did you say, dear?'

I bluffed. 'I'm guessing William and Patricia stayed together.'

'Yes, I believe so.'

Skye asked, 'And these people were never found?'

Janice shook her head. 'Never.'

I waited for the old woman to look away before giving Skye a vague nod towards the door. Luckily, she understood my surreptitious gesture. I made a show of looking at my watch. 'Oh, dear,' I said. 'I'm afraid we need to be making a move.' I began to get to my feet. 'It's been lovely talking to you, Janice.'

'Me too, I've enjoyed the walk down memory lane.' She rocked a few times and gingerly rose from her chair. 'There's still a few around who remember Althurian, you know.'

'Is that right,' I said. 'Locals, are they?'

'Some are. I can get them to give you a call if you're interested.'

'Yes, I'd be happy to talk to them,' I said, fumbling for my wallet. 'I'll give you my number.'

'No need, dear. Unless it's different than the one you used to phone me.'

Skye glanced at me. 'That one's fine, Janice.'

'Good.' Janice held out the purse. 'I think you'll find this belongs to Althurian, dear.'

Chapter 9
A Gathering Storm

After reversing the Aston from the drive, we were several car lengths along Shaftesbury Road before either of us uttered a word. Janice had looked genuinely sad to see us leave, and we promised to go back at some point to "have a natter" about old times. I had a feeling there was a lot more to the Althurian story than we realised or feared.

Skye chuckled. 'She's all there, isn't she? Funny how we can get a completely different impression of someone by the way they sound on the phone. I thought it was going to be hard work.'

'We may not be quite so lucky with some of her friends,' I said.

'It's worth it, though, the more I find out about Althurian, the more intrigued I become.'

'I feel the same. It's like trying to find the missing pieces to a giant jigsaw puzzle.'

'So, our mystery woman knew Patricia Forsyth?'

'It looks like it.'

'But why would she ask for someone who must have died years ago?'

I pulled up at the junction, resting my hands on the steering wheel. 'Perhaps she didn't know Patricia was already dead.'

'Do you believe that?'

I took a deep sighing breath. 'Not really. Janice said everyone called her Pattie, including Sylvia.' I looked at her briefly. 'Are we both thinking the same thing but too frightened to say?'

Skye nodded slowly. 'The woman we saw last night was Sylvia?'

'It's too bizarre for words. If it wasn't Sylvia, then why did she have her purse?' A driver in the car behind us impatiently sounded her horn several times. I checked the rear-view mirror, raised my hand apologetically, and mouthed the word, 'Sorry.' I turned the Aston and accelerated along the main road, leaving only the foolhardy to keep up.

'And as bizarre as it sounds, John, it happened to you as well.'

'Yes, but I ended up in the body of William.'

'True.' She paused. 'It might work in different ways depending on where you are.'

'How do you mean?'

'Well, you disappeared from the hall and woke up in an upstairs bedroom. Perhaps you have to be in a certain place at a certain time for it to work.'

'It doesn't explain where my body went, or why it hasn't happened to you yet.'

'I can't explain the vanishing trick, but it might have something to do with genetics. You're related to Sylvia, I'm not.'

I raised an eyebrow. 'It's possible, I guess.' As I was pondering the imponderable, I looked down at the fuel gauge; the needle was barely above empty. 'Shit,' I cursed. 'We're almost out of gas.'

Skye thumbed over her shoulder. 'Then it's lucky we've just passed a petrol station.'

♦

I dropped her at the steps before parking in front of the garage. I locked the door and looked across at the Toyota; part of me felt guilty, and a little unfaithful. I'd spent almost two hundred quid in just two days filling the Aston with petrol, more than I usually spend in three months. It was becoming a mistress.

Taking the gravel path running along the back of the garage, I crossed to the front of the garden room, stopping outside the twin, half-glazed doors. I turned towards the garden to take in the view; the sun had dropped below the tree line marking the estate's western boundary, casting long shadows across the lawn. It had been warm during the day, but as evening drew near there was a marked chill in the air; I pulled up my jacket collar and took a deep lungful. Somewhere unseen, a blackbird serenaded a song of exquisite beauty, for those who had the time to stop and listen; this was soon interrupted by a quarrel of noisy sparrows that appeared from nowhere, dropped onto a patch of grass almost at my feet, and did as their collective name suggested, completely unaware of my presence.

Although we had chattered non-stop about Janice and our experiences at Althurian, we had not spoken of the emotional toll it was having on us. The horrifying news of William's death troubled me deeply; more than I would care to admit, even to Skye. To me, William was still alive, and to think otherwise, was mentally shocking.

The door cracked open behind me. 'A penny for them?' she asked. I recognised the voice, thankfully familiar; a whisper of a kiss brushing my cheek. Resting her head on my shoulder, she slipped an arm gently round my waist. 'Maybe we should get married.'

I coughed a laugh. 'What?' These five words were in an order I would have laid good money not to hear from her. In fact, in the eight years we had known each other, not one of us had mentioned the possibility at all. It's funny when I come to think of it; both of us had spoken at length about the importance of freedom and personal choice: Skye, with her need to travel alone and see the world, and me, well, to have an untidy flat and eat pizza on more days than was good for me. I suppose in the circumstances we had both found ourselves, it was easy to see marriage as a threat to the status quo.

'Oh, come on, it's not such a strange idea.' She raised one of her neatly trimmed eyebrows. 'Is it?'

'Did I say it was strange?'

'No, but I can tell from your eyes, you think it is.'

I laughed again, and probably not a good idea as her expression had an accusing edge to it. 'I'd like to know what brought it on.'

'Eight years is a long time for a thirty-seven-year-old to call her man a boyfriend.' She grinned. 'It must be worse for you, you're almost forty-five.'

'Not really, I don't have to call you my boyfriend.'

'Very funny,' she said, playfully pinching my midriff. 'So, it's a no, then?'

'There you go again, putting words in my mouth.'

'You still didn't answer the question.'

'Won't you miss taking off for days on end when the mood takes you.'

She pulled a face. 'Damn, I forgot about the kitchen sink. And there was me thinking nothing would change.'

I winced inwardly. 'I just thought…'

She interrupted. 'I'd take up knitting and flower arranging?'

There was no escape; I'd backed myself down a blind alley. I raised my hands in a gesture of surrender 'Okay, I admit it was a thoughtless reaction.'

'Well?'

'Well what?'

'Yes or no?'

'I'll have to think about it. Ouch, that hurt!' I'm such a wimp when it comes to pain. 'Okay, okay. Yes.'

♦

She sat on the sofa opposite, embracing her knees with her arms; resting her head upon them, she wore a smile as wide as her face. She watched me for a few seconds before speaking. 'I feel different now. You know, like I belong. Weird when you consider all that's been going on.'

'Whose fault is that? You should have asked me to marry you years ago.'

She giggled. 'You didn't have money then.'

'Very funny.'

'You know what I mean, though.'

I did. Althurian seemed to have acquired this ability to make you want to stay, regardless of its chequered and murky past. I smiled. 'What's it like to see yourself becoming Lady of the Manor.'

'Pretty cool,' she said. 'I might start wearing a tiara.' She eyed the travel chest; it was still open, the envelopes and other papers in neat piles at the other end of the sofa. 'I was going to carry on sorting through that lot.' She sighed. 'But I can't be arsed.'

'There's always tomorrow.'

She tutted. Unfolding her legs, she reached over to pick up a few sheets from a wad of papers. 'Bad language and laziness are hardly qualities worthy of a lady.' She settled back to read them.

'What are they?'

'Seventy-five-year-old shopping receipts, would you believe. Who keeps receipts for that long?'

'My dad would. He kept a ticket from Woolworth for a watch he bought with his first wage packet.'

'That's different, and quite sweet in a way.' She waved one in the air. 'But a receipt for a bunch of chemicals with names I can't pronounce is just weird.'

I chuckled. 'Perhaps they were a present for someone. Are they all the same?'

She looked down. 'These ones are.'

'Let me see one.' I held out my hand. I felt a weird familiarity with the limp, yellowing paper, and in remarkable condition for its age; the dark blue ink of the handwritten receipt looked as fresh as the day the scribe first held the pen. Just two items were jotted down, to which the princely sum of four pounds was paid, and a lot of money in those days. 'Blackouts and air raids didn't do Blandford Apothecary much harm,' I said, handing them back to her.

'I'm not surprised at those prices. Let's hope it wasn't the going rate for cough mixture.'

I chuckled politely, put my feet up and turned onto my side, resting my head on the low arm. 'What else have you got?' I said, watching her through half-closed eyes. It had been a very long day.

♦

'William, William, wake up.' I knew it was my name, and not my name; if that makes any sense at all? The demand was not particularly urgent; no one was shaking me this time, and the voice, thank God, was not that of Mrs Hughes. If anything, the source of this demand appeared muffled, and may even have been coming from another room. I opened my eyes. Patricia was leaning over me, and she was smiling. 'Hello,' I answered feebly. 'Is everything all right?'

'Yes, yes.' She was beaming. 'Listen, Wills, I thought you'd like to be the first to know.'

I sat up and rubbed my face. I was surprised to find myself on the sofa; it was like I hadn't moved. I made a cursory glance opposite; I'm not entirely sure what, or who I expected to see, the room was different in a number of fundamental ways and was a library when I last encountered Patricia. 'First to know what...er, Pattie?'

She took a deep breath. 'I'm expecting a baby, Wills,' she panted excitedly. 'Isn't it wonderful? Doctor Roberts said I should be due about the second week of July.'

'That's fantastic news.' I tried to smile; be happy for her. 'Does Charles know yet?'

She shook her head. 'No. I was going to ring the station, but I thought it might not be such a good idea if he's busy. I'll wait until he gets home.'

I noticed two small marks on the upper part of her left arm, both a vague, greenish blue, tinged with yellow. I pointed to them. 'How did you get those?'

She became flustered suddenly, pulling down the sleeve of her blouse. 'Oh, they're nothing. H-have you read the paper this morning?'

I could feel my eyes narrow as I looked at her; she was hiding something, and I didn't need to be a detective to guess what it was. 'No,' I said curtly, unable to disguise the rising anger. 'Did he do that?'

She turned the arm away from me, covering it with her hand. 'I-I w-walked into the kitchen door,' she answered defensively. 'Please, William, don't cause another scene with Charles. I can't bear it.'

I took a deep breath, several in fact. I needed to calm down; I was in danger of directing my ire in the wrong direction. She was now pregnant, and in her eyes, this changed everything; and it did, in many ways. I raised my hands placatingly. 'Okay.' I was biting hard on my bottom lip, the last thing I wanted was to cause her anxiety; she had enough of that already. 'I won't say anything this time.'

'Thank you, Wills. I'm sorry it has to be like this, I really am.'

'Yeah, me too,' I replied sharply. 'You can't keep taking it from him, Pattie. He'll make your life unbearable.'

'Please, William.'

'Okay. Sorry.' I struggled to change the subject. 'So, what's in the newspaper, then?' Although the question was a little abrupt, she looked relieved.

'The Admiral Graf Spee has been told to leave Monte Video.'

'Is that right,' I said, my interest piqued.

'It was even on the wireless.' She eyed me seriously. 'Jameson said Langsdorff will probably try to cross the estuary to Buenos Aires.'

This headline news, and a part of world history, was not lost on me. As a child I knew of this particular event; a chance encounter with a book from the school library describing a battle that took place on the River Plate, had fired my interest in history. This news also indicated World War Two must now be underway, although I was not entirely sure how far. 'I wouldn't be surprised if Langsdorff scuttles her and takes his own life,' I said. Yes, I know, it was childish.

She pulled in her chin, 'Well, Jameson believes he'll fight to the bitter end. People are flooding to the waterfront to watch. I read that some boat owners are making small fortunes taking sightseers out to get a closer look.'

'Really?' I chuckled, glancing round the room. 'Is this…newspaper anywhere handy?'

'In the back room,' she said. 'Wait there and I'll get it for you.'

'As I got to my feet to stretch my legs, I noticed they were feeling unexpectedly heavy and achy; I caught sight of the neatly pressed, blue grey, worsted trousers enclosing them, and felt a shiver run down spine. My fears were now confirmed: William had been accepted into the Royal Air Force. I stood motionless for some time trying to get my head round the gravity of the situation I now found myself; I was even struggling to adequately describe who I actually was. Was I John Warrener, or William Forsyth, or a composite of both? Patricia broke the spell I'd cast myself when she returned with a copy of the *Daily*

Telegraph. She was wearing a stylish, turquoise and navy, camel coat.

'There you go,' she said, balancing the paper on the arm of the sofa. 'There's a pencil inside if you fancy doing the crossword. I'm nipping out for a couple of hours. Mrs Campbell has left some of that chocolate cake you like in the pantry.' She grinned. 'Mrs C says it'll help with all that square bashing you're doing lately.'

'Ah, right. Thanks. So, where are you heading off to?'

'To see Emma Bergan's new puppy, it's only eight weeks old, and ever so cute.'

My ears pricked up. 'Emma Bergan you say?'

Patricia pulled a face. 'You know, Fred the gardener's wife.'

'Ah, yes. Fred. Of course,' I mumbled. A puppy to train, and baby Janice on the way, I wonder if she knows yet, I thought.

'When is your appointment for the dentist? I'm sure it's this week some time.'

'Eh?' I must have looked confused. I had no idea what she was talking about.

Patricia rolled her eyes. 'You know, to have those fillings changed, the ones they said were unsuitable for high flying.'

'I can't remember right off hand. I'll have to check my diary.'

'Make sure you do; we can't be having you in pain while you're up there.' She came over and kissed me lightly on the cheek. 'Leave some of that cake for me, won't you.'

After she left, I went to the window, just out of her line of sight, watching as she made her way down the steps, along the drive until she disappeared from view. As I walked back to the sofa, I started to clench my teeth as I imagined what it was like to experience mid-twentieth century dental technology.

I picked up the paper and sat down. I smiled as the pencil slipped to the floor; it was such a sweet thought, not that I had any great love of word games. It was odd how few pages there were, and astonished to see the cover price was only a penny, and an old one at that. As Patricia had alluded, the front-page headline was all about the German pocket battleship. I found the experience unsettling. Not one inch of column space contained anything but stories and news of the war; even a surprising number of advertisements mentioned it in one way or another. What did come as a bit of a shock was the date: Monday, December 18, 1939. It was seven days before Christmas, yet no signs of this festive time were evident in the Forsyth household. However, it was good to see the crosswords on the back page, although a glance at the clues suggested the answers, unsurprisingly, were of a military nature. I chose the quick crossword; I've never understood anything cryptic. I folded the paper to a manageable size and nibbled the end of the pencil as I deliberated over the answer to one across, and possibly the only one I was likely to get right. I held the nib over the small square for a second or two before committing myself. Yes. It looked right. Suddenly, the absurdity hit me. I put down the paper, took a deep breath and closed my eyes; I think I was willing myself to return to normality, whatever that was.

'What are you still doing here?'

My hackles raised immediately; his voice unmistakable; I may have delayed opening my eyes deliberately. The sight of his face was beginning to sicken me. 'Morning, Charles,' I said.

'It's afternoon,' he said bluntly. 'Where's Patricia?'

'Gone to see a friend, I think.'

He gave me a morose, almost malignant, scowl. 'Which friend?' he growled.

I jerked my shoulders; the rudeness of the man was beyond belief. 'No idea,' I lied.

Charles' jaw clenched visibly, his lips tightly pursed, resentment oozing from every pore. 'Are you going to sit around here all day?'

I looked at him coldly. 'And what if I do?'

'Don't get lippy with me, boy,' he barked. 'Remember who keeps this roof over your head.'

I'm not a violent man, but I was seconds away from thumping the arrogant bastard. Unfortunately, he had me at a disadvantage, and knew it. I had no knowledge of William, or his circumstances, to build a defensive argument. My alter ego, for that was what William had become, was an innocent victim of a cruel turn of fate, and one I was helpless to do anything about. Charles, however, had the upper hand, and, I either had to kowtow to his narcissistic driven superiority, and walk away, or try to find a weakness in this apparently impenetrable wall he had created round himself.'

'Cat got your tongue, boy?'

I looked into his cold, grey eyes, and continued to do so as I swung my legs from the sofa and got to my feet. Carefully, and wordlessly, I folded the newspaper, placing it on the arm where I had found it. Tapping the paper with my forefinger, I said, 'There's an interesting article about boat trips, Charles, you should book one before it gets too late.'

'What are you talking about?' he said, almost spitting out the words.

I kept a steady eye on him as I picked my way round the sofa and headed towards the door. The man looked totally baffled by the remark and surprised me when he stepped to one side to let me pass; I found it almost impossible to keep a straight face even though I'd won nothing. I walked into the hall feeling quite pleased with myself. I decided as a reward, a piece of Mrs Campbell's chocolate cake was the order of the day.

♦

Before I got to the kitchen, I could already smell the enticing aroma of a freshly baked loaf; the choice between chocolate cake and warm, buttered bread with strawberry jam was likely to be a difficult one. I loved both, as did William, it seemed.

Mrs Campbell was a neat, trim woman, and dressed in a white, full length, wrap round apron and matching mop cap. She was just removing a loaf tin from the oven as I walked in. She laughed heartily when she saw me. 'I knew it wouldn't be long before you followed your nose, Master William,' she said, placing the tin on a wooden block next to the range. 'I've already got the butter an' jam out of the pantry for you.'

'You spoil me, Mrs Campbell,' I said, beginning to salivate at the thought.

Her smile withered slightly, and for a minute I thought I'd said something to upset her. 'Did I hear Mr Forsyth earlier?'

I nodded; I think I may have inadvertently pulled a less than complimentary face at the mention of his name. 'He was in the...' I stumbled; I was beginning to forget which room was which.

Mrs Campbell raised her eyebrows. 'The library?'

I smiled impishly. 'That's the one.'

She nervously glanced at the door 'May I speak in confidence, Master William?'

'Yes of course, Mrs Campbell. What's on your mind?'

'Is Miss Pattie.' She closed her eyes, quietly cursing under her breath. 'Sorry, Master William, I forget where I am at times.' She paused. 'Is Mrs Forsyth all right? I mean, is she well? She's been looking rather pale lately.'

'I think so.' I was guessing there may be more to her concern than she was letting on. 'Is there something bothering you, Mrs Campbell?'

She nodded and took a deep breath; whatever was troubling her was weighing heavily on her mind. She sidled up to me, and lowering her voice to hardly a whisper, she said, 'I think Mr Forsyth isn't being very nice to her, Master William.'

I sighed. 'In what way do you mean, Mrs Campbell?'

'He's been pushing an' shovin' her around, he has. Does it when you're not here.'

I wiped a hand across my mouth; my fears were confirmed. 'Have you seen him do it?'

'No, but Mr Jameson has. Walked in on them when he heard her screamin' an' hollerin' one afternoon. Thought she was being murdered, he did.'

'When was this?'

'A little over a week ago,' she said, shaking her head angrily. 'He's always shouting at the poor sweet thing.' Her eyes began to fill. 'I wished he'd never set foot here; we were like one big happy family before she got tangled up with that monster. The man is evil.' She cupped a hand over her mouth. 'I'm so sorry, Master William. I didn't mean to…'

I gently laid my hand on her shoulder. 'Don't apologise for recognising him for what he is, Mrs Campbell.' I paused. 'From now on, and when we're on our own, you may call me William, and I, shall call you by your first name. Is it a deal?'

'Oh, I don't know if I can, Master William. It's not my place to be addressing you in such a fashion. What would people say?'

'No one needs to know; it'll be our little secret. Now, you know my name, are you going to tell me yours.'

She frowned, drawing in her chin. 'Are you playing one of your little jokes on me, Master William?'

'Why would I do that?'

'But you know my name's Elizabeth; you've known it since you were a wee nipper.'

I was confused; if this was a Forsyth family home, how could she have known William as a child? I could only conclude Patricia must have brought her to Althurian. 'Yes. Elizabeth. Of course, it is. It must be all these people I've had to meet recently,' I blathered. 'Just put it down to my age.' I knew at this stage I was only digging a deeper hole for myself. I smiled lamely. 'It must have slipped my mind. Sorry.'

'Yes, it must.' She inclined her head. 'What are we going to do about Miss Pattie?'

'I don't know yet, Elizabeth, things became a little more complicated this morning.'

'She's in the family way, isn't she?'

'How did you know?'

'It's not difficult to read the signs when you're a woman, Master William. I knew for sure when she made an appointment to see Doctor Roberts this morning. She hardly ever goes to the doctors, even when she's really poorly.'

I nodded solemnly. 'The baby's due in July,' I said, pleased to have an ally at last.

'I thought as much.' She slowly shook her head and sighed. 'Not the best of times to have children, I would have thought.'

'Maybe she didn't have a choice. I think we all need to keep an eye on her. Is Mr Jameson likely to help us?'

'Oh yes, Master William. He said he'd rather swing at the end of a rope than see anything untoward happen to Miss Pattie.'

'Good, we may need him if this all turns nasty.' I wondered if Jameson had moved to Althurian under the same circumstances, although it was hard to believe Charles would have allowed it. I wanted to ask her but would have only made myself look a bigger fool than I had already. I suddenly became aware of a sound from behind me, followed by a peculiar, prickly sensation that made the hairs on the back of my neck stand on end; the kind of feeling you sometimes get when walking alone at night. I noticed Mrs Campbell was staring over my shoulder towards the door; I saw a dreadful fear in those eyes. I turned to see Charles leaning against the frame.

'Wasting another's time with your mindless banter, Warrener? Have you nothing better to do?'

'I was just making Master William a sandwich, Mr Forsyth,' said Mrs Campbell.

Charles rounded on her. 'Did I ask you to speak, woman?' he snarled.

Mrs Campbell didn't answer him, but I heard her take a sharp gasp of breath; nervously wringing the towel she used to remove the baking tin. I had the feeling he may have been listening to our conversation, and I suspected Mrs Campbell may have thought the same. Again, I tried to remain calm. 'Steady on, Charles,' I said. 'Mrs Campbell was only carrying out my instructions.'

'The woman is an employee, my employee, and I will say and do what I want. No one tells me what to do in my own house, do you understand?' he screamed. 'Now, get out of my sight, the pair of you.'

I stared at him. Two thoughts occurred to me: was he completely insane, or was it me? I found it difficult to believe a man with such a volatile nature had managed to fool the Royal Air Force into giving him a commission, or any job for that matter. Again, I backed down; I saw no merit in standing up to him. I held out my hand. 'Come, Mrs Campbell, we'll take a walk in the garden.'

Charles stood triumphantly erect, his arms tightly folded to his chest; he watched us leave via the garden room, with a smug, acid like smile across his lips. It was a look of victory.

We walked for a while in silence, just listening to the chatter of a skylark somewhere high above us. Mrs Campbell was the first to speak. 'I'm ever so sorry I got you into trouble, Master William. I didn't know what to say to him.'

'You have nothing to apologise for, Elizabeth. I think the man's deranged.'

'Please call me, Lizzy, Master William; it reminds me of happier times.'

'Lizzy, it is then.' As I looked at her, I had an idea, a hunch. 'In that case I think we shall talk about those happier times, Lizzy, and forget all about Mr Forsyth.'

Mrs Campbell clapped her hands together, as would a child. 'Oh, please do, I'd like that, William.' She covered her mouth and giggled. 'Hark at me calling you William.'

I laughed with her. 'Now, I'm sure you've told me this before.' I sighed. 'How did you end up working in domestic service?'

She smiled. 'Of all the questions you've asked me, young William, and there have been many, you've never asked me that one.' She took a few steps in thoughtful silence. 'I was an orphan as well. My mother and father both died of the influenza when I was fifteen. I was a little too old to be placed in an orphanage but ended up in one anyway. I stayed there until one of the benefactors spotted me and found me a position in his household as assistant to the cook. I worked there for about two years, not a particularly joyful time, I must add, when a friend told me there was a vacancy for a cook at Althurian.'

I interrupted. 'What year was this?'

Mrs Campbell touched her cheek. 'This would have been 1912.'

'And you've worked here since then?' I have to be honest here: I thought she looked a lot older than her forty-four years; the slightly greying hair, tied into a neat bun, didn't help (She removed the mop cap when we left the house).

'Twenty-seven years this August just gone.'

I almost missed the relevance of this; I had been looking at her face wondering what on earth had caused her to age so quickly. Something about her story didn't add up. 'So, who did you work for when you first came to Althurian?'

'Why, your father and mother, of course! Didn't you know that?'

The plot just thickened. 'No. No, I didn't.' I stroked my chin. The two questions I most wanted to ask, were the ones I should already know the answers to, unless I had total amnesia: How Charles got his greedy little hands on the family estate, and what had happened to William and Patricia's parents; their sudden disappearance was deeply suspicious. 'How long have you suspected Charles was violent?'

I could see she was uncomfortable with the question, and I couldn't blame her; it was me who suggested we talk about happier things. A small muscle in her cheek flexed visibly 'The first week he was here. He's got worse since he's been in uniform.' She turned to look at me. 'You must have seen that for yourself.'

We came to the line of elders shielding the stone circle; a path had been cut through them, and two of the upright monoliths were clearly visible. 'Why didn't you say anything, tell someone?' I winced inwardly; I was vocalising twenty first century thinking, a time when domestic abuse was to become a serious crime. It was too late to take it back, and the pain was already showing in her eyes.

'There was no one to tell, William.' She wiped a tear away with the back of her hand. 'You were barely sixteen, and the only two people who could, and would have done something were not with us anymore, were they?'

Sadly, it appeared one of my questions had now been answered. I looked up at the sky; thick, nomadic quilts of cumuli were drifting aimlessly across a canvas of deep cobalt. I suddenly felt very tired, and the need to close my eyes overwhelmed me.

Chapter 10
The Celopea

There was a strange tension growing in my neck, it started just below my left shoulder blade. I felt strangely calm though. 'I'm really sorry, Lizzy; I had no right to lay that one on you.'

'Sorry, what did you say?'

The tension was turning to pain, and it was getting worse by the second; my thinking had become muddled, Mrs Campbell's voice sounded different, softer, younger, more refined. My whole body jerked as if I'd stepped from an invisible kerb. A hand lightly touched my shoulder. 'Are you all right, John?'

'Eh?' I opened my eyes but couldn't move. Skye was standing over me. I didn't expect to see her grinning; the circumstances didn't seem right somehow.

'Were you having a little dream,' she cooed in a child-like way.

Feeling started to flood back into my hands and arms; evidently, I had tucked them under me. I flexed my fingers and tried to sit up. My back was stiff. 'How long have I been asleep?' I asked, groaning wearily, trying not to yawn.

'About ten minutes, fifteen at most.'

'Are you sure?' I asked, somewhat incredulously.

She raised her eyebrows. 'I was being generous.'

'It feels like hours. Did anything happen while I was asleep?'

'Apart from you mumbling to yourself. No.'

'Ah.' I found the lack of drama strangely disappointing; my exploits to the past had been accompanied by the unfathomable. I felt cheated, possibly because I didn't want it to be just another dream.

She frowned. 'Are you sure you are all right? You look a bit weird.'

I sat up and rubbed my eyes. 'I thought you were my friend.'

She chuckled. 'Your face is telling me you could do with a coffee.'

'I could do with something stronger.' I paused. 'Is it too late to give Janice Bergan a call?'

She checked her watch. 'Ten past seven. She might be watching a soap. Can it wait 'till the morning?'

I sighed. It could, but after speaking to Mrs Campbell I was impatient for an answer; the content of our conversation had a significant bearing on the past. I must have looked a little vacant, for a little too long.

'Well?'

'It might take a while to explain.'

She sat down and listened without interruption; I was aware in the telling, this particular excursion to the past could have a plausible explanation. 'I'm not saying this didn't happen, John, but are you sure this wasn't just a dream?'

I shrugged. 'It seemed real enough, as real as you are to me now. It's why I need to speak to Janice. So far, she's the only one who can confirm some of the things Mrs Campbell told me.'

She slipped her phone from a back pocket. 'Then ring her if you must.' She got to her feet. 'I'll make the coffee.'

I tapped in Janice's number, and she answered quickly. I smiled. I could hear the television blaring away in the background. 'Hello, Janice. John Warrener. You know, from earlier.'

'Yes, dear,' she said. 'I know who you are. I've got your wife's number on my phone.'

'Ah, right,' I answered sheepishly. 'Look, I won't keep you long. I just wanted to ask a couple of questions. Is that okay?'

'Hang on, I'll turn down me telly.' I imagined the remote control, phone, and ash tray, perhaps even a copy of the *Radio Times*, were all in easy reach. 'Okay, John, I'm all ears.'

Skye came in, handed me a mug of coffee and sat down; I nodded and mouthed the words, "thank you". She smiled, leant forward, cupping her hands under her chin.

'Do you remember when Pattie's parents went missing?' I asked.

I heard her take a breath. 'Now let me see.' There was quite a long pause, and I thought I heard the click, click sound of a lighter. She took a breath. 'That's an easy one to answer. It was the year Roosevelt became president. 1933.'

'A year before Edmund Forsyth shuffled off,' I mumbled.

'Sorry, dear.'

'Nothing, Janice. Do you remember Elizabeth Campbell?'

'Lizzy Campbell, the cook?'

'Yes. How well did you know her?'

'Very well.' She chuckled. 'Lizzy was a wonderful woman. Whenever the two of us went for a ramble, she would make us the most wonderful packed lunches. Her chocolate cake was my favourite.' I smiled. Suddenly, I had my proof. I was also touched by the way Janice recalled the fond memory of her. 'How did you know about Lizzy?' she asked.

'We came across her name in an old diary,' I lied. 'How long was she at Althurian?'

'She was there until she died in sixty-two.' She paused. 'I know that because it was exactly ten years before my dad retired.'

'Right,' I said. 'Just one more question. How was Sylvia after her father disappeared?'

There was another long pause. 'When we heard he had gone missing, mum and dad thought he'd gone on another bender. It wasn't unusual, you see. Sylvia didn't seem bothered, if anything she seemed happier.' She snorted. 'Patricia was much the same. I think they preferred him not being around if the truth be known.'

'What about later on?'

'I didn't notice much of a difference in her really.' She paused again. 'I remember there was some sort of argy-bargy with the finances. Everything was in Charles' name, and it was all a bit grim for a while. I think Pattie had to wait until he was presumed dead before she got any money. They never did find him, you know.

'So I believe.' I suddenly remembered the missing person story in the newspaper, the individual Skye thought was the gardener. 'Who was James Dixon?'

'Husband number two.'

'She married again,' I exclaimed. This news caught me by surprise, and for reasons I can't explain, really shocked me.

'Not long after she got the nod from the judge.' She wheezed, coughing a chuckle. 'He disappeared as well; it's why some folks reckon Althurian has a curse.'

'Is that so,' I said. 'And what do you think?'

She chuckled again. 'Well, it's not the place you want to be if you're a man. You know they found his bones in Craven Woods.'

'Yes, I was aware of that.' Janice clearly relished the more macabre aspect of the story. 'What was Dixon like?'

'I think he may have been little better than the first one. But there again, I didn't see much of him, he was always away on business; quite rich by all accounts. My dad liked him though.'

'And Sylvia?'

'Although she never said, I had a feeling she was wary of him. She was definitely happier when he wasn't there, and a little disrespectful to him when he was. I think she saw him as a threat. I put it down to her relationship with Pattie, they were very close.'

'Did Pattie ever marry again?'

'Not that I know of, you see, most of the news came from my dad until he retired. I'd met Bert, got married, and moved away by then.'

Skye spoke for the first time. Janice was remarkably unflustered by her unannounced interruption (I'm quite envious of people who can calmly deal with the sudden vicissitudes of life; I'd like to use the excuse of age, but Janice was considerably older than me). 'Hello, Janice. Was there anyone special in Sylvia's life?'

'Oh, hello, dear. There was someone she used to talk about. Quite taken with him, she was, can't remember his name though.'

'How old was she at the time?' I asked.

'About twenty-four, twenty-five. Something like that.'

'Was it a proper relationship?' asked Skye.

'Lord no, dear. I think it was more of an infatuation. I had a feeling he may have been married, or a lot older. She kept him to herself, I know that much.'

'You didn't get to meet him, then?'

'No, dear, I wish I had.'

I glanced at Skye and nodded. 'Okay, Janice,' I said. 'I hope you didn't mind me ringing tonight. You've been so patient with me.'

'Not at all, John, it's been rather fun. Call me any time you like. Goodbye, dear.' She ended the call almost immediately.

Skye was staring at me. 'What does this all mean, John? I've always been open minded about many things, but this is just plain spooky, and worrying at the same time. I've never been superstitious, or spiritual to any great extent.' She pursed her lips. 'But what if she's right and there is a curse?'

'Religious mumbo jumbo if you ask me. People will always find an excuse for stuff they don't understand.' Even though I can hardly call myself spiritual, I always have this feeling I'm about to be struck down for saying such godless things; I often wonder if I'm alone in thinking this, or if others feel the same. 'There's a rational explanation for everything,' I said confidently. 'We just have to look for it.'

'I very much doubt we'll find a scientific explanation for this one, John. This is beyond science.' She suddenly yawned, covering her mouth. 'Oh dear.' She giggled. 'I think it's all finally caught up with me. Perhaps we ought to call it a night.'

♦

I lay awake for some time; I really wasn't that tired. Skye, on the other hand, was almost comatose before her head touched the pillow. It was a damp, blustery night; sash windows clanked in their frames, roof tiles rattled, and timbers creaked. If I were writing a ghost story, Althurian was the perfect backdrop. Interlacing my hands behind my head, I stared at the ceiling; the room glowed with an eerie bluish hue, as slivers of moonlight squeezed through the finely woven curtain fabric. It had indeed, been a long day; longer for me in many respects. Fortunately, sleep came when I least expected it, and I slept undisturbed by dreams, real or otherwise. Skye also reported nothing unusual and agreed that we were both remarkably well rested.

We were out of bed and showered before nine. I left Skye in the bedroom sorting out some clothes, while I made my way to the kitchen to carry out that all important function: making the coffee. The winds had dropped to almost nothing, and a clear cloudless sky promised a warm garden room, once the sun had dared show itself.

Skye, whose timing was rarely imperfect, appeared just as I was carrying the percolator to the garden room. Wearing a pair of faded blue jeans, white tee shirt, and the white trainers she had found in the wardrobe, it was a uniform, apart from the shoes, she was hardly ever out of. As I was pouring our first cup of the day, she wandered to the door, looked out. 'Do you know what, John; I think I'd like to explore the rest of the estate today.'

'Really? What's brought this on?'

'It just feels right.'

'When?'

'Soon.'

'After breakfast?'

'Yes, I'd like that,' she purred.

'I can show you the stones. You'll love them.'

'It would be rude not to go, then.' She glanced back at me. 'I know you said they were close, but how close?'

I chuckled. 'Just a stone's throw from here.'

♦

It was warm and still when we set off, even the birds were quiet, eerily so. The sun was peeping over the trees, although we walked in their shadow for most of the way. I caught the aroma of freshly cut grass just before we got to the treeline; I strained my ears to listen for the sound of a distant mowing machine.

Skye took a deep lungful, and said, 'I love that smell, it so reminds me of summer.'

'Yeah, me too, it's a pity it's nearly over.' I pulled a face and looked round. 'I'll soon need to start cutting some of this back before it gets much longer.'

'Looking at the rest of the garden,' she said. 'I think you already employ someone who does that, John.'

'Ah, yes,' I said. 'Ted Ferris.' I pointed out the route through the wood. 'It's that way. And mind the brambles.'

The stones were more impressive than I remembered; they were smoother, darker, more refined, and seemed to be emitting, or so I sensed, a form of benevolent energy. I say benevolent, because I can think of no better word to describe it: a kind of comforting presence beyond inanimate. I stood motionless, staring, oblivious to the rest of the world, until Skye broke my revere.

'These are magnificent.' Her eyes wide with surprise, her voice scarcely above a whisper. She looked totally spellbound for several minutes. 'It's even quieter here. I can't hear a thing, can you?'

I took a breath and held it; we both did, waiting for as long as one breath can last; and still we heard nothing. So profound was the silence I could feel the gentle throb of my heart behind my ribs. After all I said about my beliefs, or lack of them, I had an overwhelming need to treat this place, this sacred site, with reverence. I quietened my voice. 'So, what do you think?'

'I love it. It's quite, quite beautiful. I would have come here every day if I'd known. How long have these stones been here, do you know?'

'According to Larry: anywhere between two and five thousand years.'

She whistled. 'I can't even comprehend that amount of time. It's amazing to think people from long ago once stood where I am now.'

'Many thousands of them, I guess.' I remembered Julius Becket. 'Perhaps we should bring a picnic next time.' I turned to look at her. 'Maybe even bring some chocolate cake.' Her expression remained fixed and she appeared not to have heard me. 'Skye,' I said, 'did you hear me, love?' She continued to stare ahead as if frozen in a moment of time, like a rigid, three-dimensional snapshot. I grabbed her forearm and recoiled; her flesh was as cold and hard as marble. I can find no words to adequately describe the horror I experienced in that instant; she had turned into a lifeless mannequin, a soulless statue, another upright stone, and I had not the faintest idea what to do next.

'Hello, John.' The voice was soft, measured, and familiar.

I twisted round. 'What are you doing here?'

'Waiting for you,' he said. 'It was only a matter of time until we met again.'

I pointed at Skye. 'What have you done to her?'

'I have done nothing.' He smiled. 'You are a man of many questions. I will endeavour…'

I interrupted him. 'Look,' I snapped, 'I've had enough of this inscrutable sage shit, just tell me what you want.'

He either ignored my outburst or was immune to it. 'We need to talk, John, and we need to talk soon.'

'Okay.' I pointed to Skye again. 'Let her go, then we'll talk.'

Becket smiled. 'Unfortunately, what you request is impossible, or I would gladly do as you ask.' He sighed. 'You and I at this moment exist in a space inside time itself.' He swept his hand in an arc. 'We are now outside this world you call reality.'

'Great. So, I'm trapped here,'

'No. Not trapped, John. We are both bound by the same rules, rules set by the nature of time itself. You are as tied to the place you occupy as I am to mine. We only get to meet like this because there are windows of opportunity where our paths cross.' His expression hardened. 'These can be rare, and not always stable, or continuous, so it is critical we use this time effectively.' He smiled. 'It's a case of carpe diem, my friend.'

I looked at him. Nothing had changed, my first encounter with Becket confused me, and now the same had happened again. 'So, we only meet by accident, then?'

'To begin with, yes. But this time, although you may not have been aware of it, you sensed an opening in the continuum and made your way here. This gift of recognition, and one of many, is known as the Celopea. At present your sensory awareness is weak and will only gain strength from use; as would a young child when it first learns to walk.'

It was a lot to take in, and Becket was right, I was a man with many questions. I glanced at Skye; her eyes appeared to have closed slightly; clearly, for her, time had not completely stopped. As I stood looking at this man, I seemed to be developing an unexpectedly warm, inner calmness; this was not something I was used to, trust me! Becket was smiling like he knew. 'What is it I have to do, Julius?' This was the first time I had addressed him by name; it was as if somewhere deep within me came a need to show respect.

'In this century you were not the only one to inherit the Celopea, John. There were two others. One is believed to have attempted to use its power for good, the other,' he raised his eyebrows, 'not so. The consequences of this misuse have been far reaching and history needs to be realigned because of it.'

I was now confused more than ever. 'How can history change?' I asked. 'Surely, once an event has occurred, that's it, isn't it?'

'History is a process of continual change, recorded by those who live through it, and participant in those changes. The Celopea allows a certain amount of movement within this process.' He nodded sagely. 'Without this gift, without the ability to see the outcome of an action, or non-action, how would you know history had been altered?'

I shook my head. 'I find that almost too incredible to believable.'

'It is the truth, whatever you choose to believe.'

'Who are these others you speak of?'

Becket shrugged. 'I do not know.'

He didn't elaborate, and I didn't question it. 'Let me get this straight,' I said, taking a breath. 'Are you suggesting I can somehow undo a misdeed perpetrated by a long-lost ancestor?'

Becket shook his head. 'The Celopea is inherited from continuum; it has nothing to do with family. Somewhere buried in Althurian's past, an unidentified individual has changed the course of history, and you need to find out who they are and what they did.'

I could feel the calmness beginning to ebb away. 'But how will I know?' Thinking I should have studied theoretical physics. 'And what do I do if I find out?'

Becket raised a hand and looked away as if he had been called. 'Our time is short, John.' He returned his gaze. 'You will know all these things when the time comes.

Allow the Celopea to guide you. It is not fully revealed yet, so you must tread carefully. You must also be on your guard for those who bear false witness. They come in many guises, so be warned.'

It had to be seen to be believed. I watched as his image dissolved right in front of me; it was the eeriest thing I'd ever experienced with my own eyes. Within seconds I noticed the renewed chatter of birdsong, the evocative smell of freshly cut grass, and the brush of warm, clean air against my face. I knew I was back.

'I'm up for it.' Skye hooted. 'But I'll only allow you to buy chocolate cake if I can have a bottle of Australian Shiraz.' She clapped her hands together. 'We'll nip out later and get some supplies, we could even buy one of those throw away barbecues.'

This sudden leap in time was extraordinary and left me reeling. All I could do was watch and listen as she continued to describe the delicacies we should consider for our picnic. It was uncanny how she was totally unaware of what had just occurred. I smiled. 'I can't wait,' I said.

She hurriedly made two complete circuits of the stones before suggesting we went back to the house; she was eager to get to the shops, and on the long haul up the slope, spent most of the time regaling me with horrendous stories of various barbecue disasters she had while on the road. To be honest, it hardly filled me with confidence; I was more than happy to share a sandwich if it came with a hefty lump of chocolate cake. Putting her predisposition to burn food to one side for a moment, I really did have every intention of telling her about Becket; it was the right and proper thing to do.

I was surprised how quickly we arrived at the garden room, and how out of breath I was. Skye is shorter, weighs less, and, annoyingly, so much fitter than me; my preference for takeaway pizza may account for some of it! I had a few minutes to myself while she went upstairs to get a jacket. My earlier state of calm was beginning to dissipate; I was hoping it would last a little longer. I slumped onto one of the wicker chairs, put my feet up, and started to fiddle with an errant loose thread on one of the cushions. Becket had said something interesting: two individuals, apart from me, had inherited the Celopea. I needed to think. Leaning back, I stared up at the white, timber framed glass roof, and into the blue, cloudless canvas beyond. I had a list of people in my head, and all of them were possible suspects in a crime not yet obvious; perhaps I needed a degree in criminology as well as one in theoretical physics.

Skye wandered in from the kitchen carrying my phone. 'You've had a missed call.'

'Who from?'

She handed it to me. 'No idea.'

I chuckled. 'You just don't like my phone,' I squinted at its screen.

'Let's face it, John; they went out of fashion before Noah built the Arc.'

'You like the Aston.'

'That's different. Well, who was it?'

I may have scowled; I rather liked my phone. 'Larry Talbot. He must have finished his analysis.'

'Are you going to call him back?'

'I don't know,' I said, tapping the phone against my lips. I wanted to, but not looking forward to the long-winded conversation beforehand. Yes, he had found some interesting information about Becket, if I was to believe the guy was almost eight hundred and fifty years old! I also remembered his enthusiasm for the number nine; and yes, I do admit to using the calculator on Skye's phone to test all those divisions and multiplications Tesla found so intriguing; and yes, I did find it bloody baffling. Yet, after all that, I still couldn't find it in me to ring him.

'But it might be important,' she said.

'I'll do it later. I'm sure it can wait.' I frowned. 'Have we had this conversation before?'

'About a call from Larry?'

'I think so.' I blinked, then blinked again; her image was fading, and I started to feel unimaginably nauseous. 'I'm…'

♦

'So, Alexander, when exactly is this deal of yours likely to come off?'

'Next week, maybe the one after, I can't be sure.'

I could hear what was being said, but not who, or where they were. My head swam with thoughts, idle, dream like thoughts, about everything and nothing at the same time. Suddenly, as if a light had turned on, all about me came in to view. I was sitting in, and almost engulfed by, a huge, winged armchair; it was facing a vaguely familiar open fireplace where a few smouldering embers still glowed in the grate. Opposite me, two men stood facing each other. One was tall and stout, the other, shorter, thin and wiry; both wore smartly tailored suits of a style I was not familiar with. The taller man had a smug air of arrogance and authority about him. With one hand propped against the white stone mantel, and the other casually tucked into a waistcoat pocket, he appeared to be the one in control, and was the next to speak.

'You told me the same story last week, and the week before that.'

I watched as the other man looked down at his feet, rocking his head from side to side, the way someone might if they were about to tell an untruth. 'This one is different, Edmund, I've put everything I have left into it. It's a sure thing, mark my words.'

The mention of his name (I thought he looked nothing like the photograph) brought everything into perspective; up until then I hadn't been aware of where I was, or who I was. I kind of knew I was at Althurian, although the room was not one I had visited often, if at all (This, as it turned out, was the large back room that was in the process of being decorated). It occurred to me this event must have been way before 1939, and possibly, if Janice Bergan was correct about Edmund, before 1934. I also started to realise something else: I was much smaller than I remembered. My skinny white legs hung off the cushion like those of a child, my feet barely touching the floor. As before, this unreal circumstance bothered me little, although knowing how old I was would have been useful. Anyway, it was what it was, and all I could do was sit in mild amusement at my predicament.

Edmund threw his head back and gave a derisory cackle. 'Your overconfidence in your ability to spot a sound investment got you into this mess in the first place, Alexander.' His face darkened, as did his manner. 'Remember, my friend, you are living on borrowed time. I will require payment of what you owe by the first week of

October, or I will double the interest. Do I make myself clear?'

Alexander started to wring his hands in a way that looked quite pitiful. 'It will be here, Edmund, you have my word on it,' he said, dipping his head obsequiously.

Edmund smirked. 'For your sake I hope you're right, Alexander.'

'Of course,' I cried, jabbing a finger in Alexander's direction. 'You're Patricia's father.' I froze instantly. Both men turned and stared at me, each wore an expression of complete shock; I had a feeling this was a decade when children were to be seen and not heard.

Alexander's response was immediate. 'What on earth are you babbling about, boy?' he shouted.

I pulled a face. 'I-I'm sorry.' I said, the words gagging the back of my throat.

'Address me properly, boy, or not at all.'

My mind whirled and I started to feel hot, I had no idea what he wanted from me. I took another best guess; it had worked before. 'Sorry...Father?' Even I wasn't convinced.

'Go to your room. I'll speak to you later.'

I slipped from the chair, an interesting experience when my legs were less than half the length they used to be, and padded across the room in short, springy steps. I did my best to look the sorriest I'd ever looked, as I slunk from the room; William was now in trouble and it was all down to me.

'Hello, young Master William, what have you been up to?'

I smiled. It was the delightful, and somewhat younger, Mrs Campbell. I grimaced. 'I think I may have upset someone, Lizzy.'

She lowered her voice. 'Have you been rude to Mr Forsyth again?'

I shook my head. 'I spoke out of turn. It was...er...Father who took it badly.' I puffed out my cheeks. 'I should have been more careful.'

She inclined her head. 'Have you been hanging around with those children from the camp again, Master William?'

'Er...I don't understand what you mean, Lizzy.'

She pulled back her chin and frowned. 'You have a strange tongue about you.'

'Ah.' I hesitated. 'I've been reading the newspaper a lot just recently. It does that I believe.' It was time to use a distraction tactic. 'Have you baked some of that lovely chocolate cake recently?'

She gasped, looking shocked. 'How on earth did you know I was about to make a chocolate cake, Master William,' she whispered hoarsely. 'It was supposed to be a secret, so don't you dare say a word to Miss Pattie.'

I decided against asking the obvious and jerked my shoulders instead; If I was going to be treated like a child I may as well act like one. I raised my eyebrows. 'Bread and strawberry jam?'

A voice called out from behind. 'Don't give him any, Lizzy; he had two helpings of porridge this morning.'

I spun round. Patricia was standing by the back door with her hands on her hips; apart from the pretty floral dress she was wearing, and a slightly plumper face, she had changed little. I thought she looked about fifteen. I can't tell you how odd it is to see people change in a kind of reversed chronological order, especially when we're programmed to accept that time, and ageing, only move in one direction. 'Hello, Pattie,' I said cheerfully. 'You look well.'

'I think you must have worms,' she scoffed. 'You're always hungry.'

'Aye, he's a growing lad, Miss Pattie.' She glanced at me. 'I'll leave out some bread an' dripping for you, Master William.'

'Er…lovely,' I said, inwardly heaving at the thought. 'Thank you, Lizzy.'

Patricia asked, 'Is Father in the drawing room?'

I sighed; at least this was a question I could answer fully. 'Yes, he's with Edmund Forsyth.'

'You are funny.' She pulled a face. 'Are they shouting at each other yet?'

I shook my head. 'No. Should they be?'

'You know they do,' she snorted. 'I wanted to speak to Father but I'll wait until Mr Forsyth leaves.' She glanced past me as if she were looking for someone. 'Is Charles with them?'

'No.' My heart sank. 'Are you looking for him?' I asked, knowing she probably was. Apart from my suspicion Charles was the rotten apple in the bag; I had a somewhat morbid fascination with how they ever got together in the first place. Her answer surprised me.

She protectively wrapped her arms round her chest and shuddered visibly. 'No, I'm not, and if you see him, and he wants to know where I am, don't tell him.' This was a good sign, I thought.

'Are you hiding from him, then?'

She sighed and nodded. 'He's becoming a pest.'

'Why don't you tell…Father?'

'I have.'

'What did he say?'

'He told me not to say or do anything to upset him.'

'He actually said that?' I gasped. 'Why?'

'You wouldn't understand, Wills.'

If I were to choose four words and arrange them in an order, I found intensely irritating, it would be those. 'How do you know that?' I snapped. 'You could at least try.'

She sighed audibly. 'Father has come to some sort of arrangement with Mr Forsyth and said I could ruin it for him if I caused any ill feelings.' She jerked her shoulders. 'I guess it's easier to keep out of his way.'

This went some way to confirm my suspicions: Charles was predatory, and Alexander was prepared to do nothing to protect his daughter from him; it was a disaster in the making. It saddened me, but I could find no words to comfort her; I knew what was in store. 'What are you going to do?'

She leant forward, lowering her voice. 'I'm going to the linen room; he won't find me up there.' She touched a finger to her lips. 'Remember what I said.'

'We have a linen room?' I asked.

Patricia tutted and walked past me shaking her head. 'I'm surprised you ever find your way to school, Wills.' She opened the door to the stairs, looked back, and gave me a little wave before she disappeared.

I stared into empty space, feeling helpless. I couldn't understand why she would at some stage in the future, change her mind about him. I had to somehow warn her, make her realise what a mistake it would be. I sighed. I was in the wrong place, at the wrong time, and in the wrong body; Becket had failed to mention I could one day find myself wearing a pair of badly fitting shorts, over tight braces, and a white frilly shirt, and look as if I was about to attend a wedding dressed as a page boy. It was doubtful she'd listen to a younger brother, whose age had only just entered double digits, even if he did have a convincing argument; an argument unlikely to make any sense considering her present attitude towards Charles. I knew there must be another way; I just had to find it. I glanced at the back door; I needed air, and somewhere to think.

Chapter 11
Forsyth House

The cold, damp cloak of autumn seemed to wrap itself around me from the moment I closed the door; dark, forbidding clouds threatened an imminent downpour. Luckily, I had found a coat of suitable size hanging from a stand in the hall; I had to remove another, much larger coat to get to the one I was about to wear, my newly acquired little legs almost buckling under the weight of it. I realised there was a lesson to be learned here: my forty-four-year-old mind was now occupying the body of a child; this was quite a turnaround, as my ex-wife used to frequently assert the complete opposite.

I pulled up my collar, skipped down each of the stone steps to the gravel path, and made my way round to the garden room. As all small boys are prone to do, I pressed my nose against the glass and shielded the light from behind me with cupped hands. The room was furnished in a much grander style; huge winged armchairs in bright, floral fabrics, dressed with vivid cushions, stood elegantly round a beautifully carved occasional table; even the rear wall had been covered with richly woven tapestries. I whistled at the sheer opulence.

'What are you doing, boy?'

I closed my eyes and sighed; how could I be this unlucky? I slowly turned; I was in no hurry to see this sorry excuse for a man so soon. I looked at him curiously; although he must have been about twenty, he only looked a child himself. For one thing I was certain, it was evident he had been honing his malevolent nature for some time. As young as I was, I could feel the bile rising in my throat. I took a deep breath. 'Hello, Charles,' I answered politely.

'Mr Forsyth to you, boy,' he growled.

'Okay, Charles, Mr Forsyth, it is.' This was probably ill-advised. Charles' face looked fit to explode, and I had nowhere to run. I turned; my back was now against the glass and timber wall, the only escape route blocked.

He took a step towards me, thrusting a finger so close to my nose my eyes crossed; I caught the foul stench of spent alcohol on his breath, as he rasped, 'You show me some damn respect, churl.'

I gulped. I was tiny compared to him, and my choices few. 'Sorry, Mr Forsyth,' I whined. 'It won't happen again, I promise.' I wished I could say I was trying not to laugh, but I wasn't. Charles unexpectedly took a step back. 'That's more like it, boy.' He thrust out his chin, and pulling a sort of a grimace, he ran a finger round the inside of his collar as if it were irritating his neck. 'Where's your sister?'

I jerked my shoulders indolently. 'I haven't seen her since breakfast.'

His eyes darkened, narrowing in a way that suggested he was about to kick off. His teeth bared between tight drawn lips. 'You'd better be telling me the truth, boy,' he snarled.

'Why would I lie to you…?'

He scowled, ground his teeth, and was silent for a moment; I had a feeling he wasn't quite finished with me yet. 'When my father takes what's rightfully his, you will find out what it's like to live on the streets.' He laughed. 'You may even end up in the workhouse.'

I was wrong about Charles. He wasn't any old narcissist; he was a very cruel one; a malignant personality of the highest order. I can't imagine the damage that could be done to a mind of someone as young as William if they had to endure bullying like this.

'Ah, there you are, Wills. Hello, Charles. How are you?'

The transformation of Charles' expression was magical; it changed as soon as he recognised the lilt of Patricia's voice. I was astonished how quickly the face of this monster appeared almost virtuous by the time it took to turn his head. 'I'm very well, Patricia,' he answered politely. 'It's so lovely to see you at last. I looked everywhere for you.' He gave me a sneering glance. 'Even your brother was unsure of your whereabouts.'

'I was in the garden, you must have missed me,' she said. 'Maybe another time, yes?'

The corner of Charles' mouth twitched. 'Another time?' he growled. I could see the mask beginning to slip.

Patricia smiled convincingly. 'Yes, your father is leaving soon and asked me to come and find you.' She made a sweep of her hand and grinned. 'And here you are.'

Charles grunted contemptibly. 'Very well,' he said, turning to leave. 'You won't get away from me so easily next time, my dear.' Those words, although tempered by Charles' standards, concealed hidden menace.

We both watched as he marched off with sharp, rapid steps. Patricia was first to speak. 'I hope Father changes his mind.' She slowly began to rock her head from side to side. 'Why does it always come down to money,' she mumbled softly.

I looked at her. 'I don't understand, Pattie. What do you mean?'

She rolled her eyes. 'Oh, don't take any notice of me, Wills, I'm thinking with my mouth again.'

'No, don't do this, Pattie,' I pleaded. 'You're being used as some kind of bargaining chip.' I took a short, sharp breath. 'And that bastard,' I jabbed my finger to where Charles had been standing, 'is just biding his time until he collects the grand prize.'

Patricia covered her mouth. 'William!' she gasped. 'You mustn't use language like that, someone might hear you.'

I knew I'd gone too far but waved a dismissive hand anyway. 'Bah! You know very well I'm right, don't you?' I snapped.

She nervously massaged her temple. 'B-but, how do you know this?' Her expression was one of shock, as well as surprise; an understandable reaction considering where this sudden, and possibly unusual, outburst had originated. Her eyes widened. 'Have you heard something?'

'I didn't need to,' I rasped. 'It's bloody obvious. Look, you can't let this happen, Pattie. Alex…' I took a deep breath; I was allowing emotion to overtake rational thought. 'Father has used Althurian as security for a loan and is trying to buy himself time because he can't pay it back.' I calmed my voice. 'He's using you, Pattie.'

Patricia looked drained; her voice barely audible. 'Is this really true, Wills?'

'As true as me standing here, I heard Father pleading with that snake Edmund this morning.'

Her brow furrowed. 'But was my name mentioned?'

'Well no. No, it wasn't,' I said, wondering if she had secretly guessed as much. 'But I think there's a very good chance he could lose this house. Lose Althurian.'

She slumped against the door, covering her face with her hands. 'If only I could speak to Mother,' she mumbled. 'She'd know what to do.'

'What's stopping you?'

She removed her hands and stared at me, her eyes were red and puffy. 'You know very well that's impossible.'

I was tempted to ask why but chose not to; I was aware my credibility was already close to the edge. For whatever reason Patricia was unable to speak to her mother meant she was virtually defenceless. I pondered the problem for a moment. 'What about Uncle Stanley and Aunt Rosemary, could you not speak to them?'

Patricia stared at me. 'What are you talking about?' she cried.

I briefly closed my eyes; this wasn't going well. 'Father's brother?' I raised an eyebrow. 'You know, Stanley Warrener?'

'I don't know who you mean, Wills, Father hasn't got a brother.'

I puffed out my cheeks, this was becoming complicated. I could hardly argue with her and say I knew it for a fact. I decided to lie instead. 'I heard Father talking about them once, I thought you already knew.'

Patricia shook her head. 'Something has happened to you, Wills. You're different.'

'Ah, there you are.' The voice was harsh, uncaring, and familiar. 'Come inside, the pair of you.' Alexander was outside, standing at the corner of the main building. 'And hurry yourselves,' he said coldly. 'I haven't got all day.'

We followed him to the drawing room; a strong smell of coal smoke hung in the air; the fire had been made up and slivers of orange flame were just beginning to lick and dance against the blackened fire brick. Alexander checked his pocket watch before tucking it back into his waistcoat. 'Sit down, this won't take long,' he said, his manner remarkably indifferent; he could have been talking to anyone. We both silently complied; I sat in the same chair as I had before, Patricia in the one next to me. Alexander picked up a cut glass tumbler from the mantelpiece and took a small sip of the amber liquid it contained. He returned the tumbler and stood with his back to the fire; not once did he look at us directly. 'I have to go away on business for a while, and as it's impossible for you to be left here on your own, I have asked Charles Forsyth if he'd be kind enough to look after you until I return.'

Patricia groaned, and not quietly either. 'But, Father, we don't need anyone to look after us,' she pleaded. 'We have Mrs Campbell in the kitchen, Mr Jameson looking after the house, and Ted Bergan and old Albert in the garden. I think you forget, Father, I am almost sixteen.'

Alexander brushed her protest aside with a sweep of his hand. 'This is not a debate, Patricia, my mind is made up. Charles will be here the week after next. He will use mother's old room for the time being.'

'B-but, you can't, Father. You said we'd keep her room as it was.'

'Be quiet, child,' he rebuked. 'I will not tell you again.'

'Will you be leaving Althurian soon, Father, sooner than the arrival of Mr Forsyth?' I asked politely.

The question appeared to surprise him (As it did me!). 'Yes, William. Charles and I are following slightly different agendas that week. I will leave early Monday morning and he will arrive late on Tuesday.'

Deliberate or not, the way he used the word "agenda" made my stomach churn. I glanced at Patricia; her face had turned deathly pale, her bottom lip trembling uncontrollably. I knew what she was thinking, and I knew this was more than just a premeditated relationship that would eventually turn bad. Perhaps it was time I pushed my luck again. 'We could go and stay with Uncle Stanley, Father?'

He rounded on me. 'What did you say?' he roared. His shock was palpable.

Oddly, I felt no fear, as I had with Charles. I continued. 'You remember, Father, your brother Stanley,' I said calmly. 'I'm sure he'd be more than happy to look after us.'

'Did your mother put you up to this, boy,' he snarled menacingly.

Patricia looked at Alexander, then to me, then back to Alexander. 'Is this true, Father, do we have an uncle?'

Alexander's face had turned crimson. I turned and looked at Patricia. 'And an aunt. Her name is Rosemary, isn't it, Father?' I knew all this was unlikely to change his mind, or his temperament. What I did hope, however, was its effect on Patricia; and a tiny seed of doubt was all it might take. I blinked, then blinked again; a tingling sensation that started behind my left ear began to travel down my neck. I suddenly became incredibly tired and could hardly keep my eyes open. In a way I can't explain, I kind of knew what was happening; I just hoped the William I was leaving behind could cope with the fallout.

♦

Rocking forward unsteadily, I took a couple of faltering steps to right myself, my head felt heavy, muzzy, not fully conscious of what was around me. I inhaled deeply and bent down, grabbing my knees for support. I allowed myself a moment or two before straightening up; the lower part of my back and right hip, seemed a little stiff and pained me. I had a vague memory of a conversation I was having with Skye before being whisked away again. I rubbed my eyes and looked round. The garden room was empty, and looked different somehow; grey, melancholy, lacking in its previous lustre. The weather didn't help; it looked dull and dismal outside, rain a distinct possibility. I guessed from this sudden change, it was later in the year than when I left.

I wandered through to the kitchen, through the lobby, then to the hall; Skye was probably upstairs sorting out even more clothes. I smiled. I was looking forward to seeing her; this time I was going to tell her everything. I blindly took the same route towards the stairs, on autopilot, my head somewhere in the past; the door was already open, held back by the weight of an old smoothing iron. It was only after arriving at the foot of the stairs, did I begin to suspect things were not entirely the same as when I left. I'd just come from the kitchen, a journey usually accompanied by the clatter of leather on tile or timber. I looked down. The floor was covered wall to wall with a rich, deep red carpet; the hall was the same. It didn't make sense, because I was sure I had returned to my own time. I padded up the stairs.

'John, is that you?' I stopped halfway; the voice echoing from somewhere below was older, deeper and more melodic, and one I recognised instantly. I hesitated before I turned. The woman looking up at me smiled. 'Have you been in long?' she asked.

At first, I found it almost impossible to speak; the slight figure with the pale gentle face, and brown, slightly greying hair, was equally unmistakable. 'About five minutes,' I said. It was hard not to stare at her.

'I was about to make lunch,' she said. 'Is a cheese salad okay?'

'Er…' I pursed my lips. 'Cheese salad would be good. Thank you.'

She frowned. 'Are you all right, John? You look a little spaced out.'

'Do I?' I forced a chuckle and patted my stomach. 'It's probably the thought of food.'

'It'll be ready in ten minutes. I know the weather is a bit rubbish, but thought we'd take it in the garden room. I've turned up the heating.' As she went to leave, she looked up again. 'Make sure you don't forget, John.'

An odd thing to say, I thought, but she left before I had time to reply. I had just enough time to check the mirror on the landing. It was evident I had moved forward to an unknown future; how far, it was difficult to tell. I was pleased to be in my own body again, even if it was older; and intrigued to see how it had fared over the years. Strange beast, the ego. I should have known better, the mirror had gone, or maybe never there in the first place. I smiled. Strange thing, time. There was, however, one in the bedroom, and where I remembered it. As before, I hesitated before stepping in front of it. I closed both my eyes, then squinted at my reflection through one of them; as if it was likely to make a difference.

The image before me wasn't quite as horrific as I'd expected. My streaked, grey hair looked surprisingly distinguished, even for me, and I had clearly lost a considerable amount of weight at some stage; I was thinner than I can ever remember, and hardly recognisable from almost any angle. Overall, although I wasn't too keen on the flappy loose bits below my chin, I didn't look too bad for a man of advancing years; not that I had any idea how advanced those years were.

I strolled into the garden room. Skye must have heard my approach and was about to pour the coffee; it was good to see some things hadn't changed. I watched as she carefully, and gracefully, filled each cup. There was something very elegant in the way she moved, the years had not only been kind to her, they had actually improved the perfection that was already hers. I sat back, feeling very pleased with myself. Skye was first to speak.

'So, how did you get on today?'

The "I was feeling very pleased with myself" quickly faded. I winced. 'Not too bad, I suppose.' It was a lame answer, I know. I picked up my cup and took a sip.

Inclining her head, her eyes seemed to be evaluating my every move. 'Have you travelled again, John?'

I puffed out my cheeks. I had been rumbled; my experiences appeared to be unexceptional. 'In a way.' I sighed. 'What year is it?'

She answered as if the question was perfectly normal. 'It's August 21, 2037.'

I whistled. 'Twenty years,' I mumbled.

'What year have you just left?'

'I don't know.' This conversation had started to become more than surreal. 'Patricia was almost sixteen and William was just a kid.'

She slowly nodded. 'This was around 1933. How do you feel?'

'Fine, I think.' Her confidence of the year surprised me.

'No injuries?'

I frowned. 'Should I have?'

She looked away, then back again. 'You must have changed something, interfered with the past somehow. What did you do?'

'Nothing remarkable. I spoke to Patricia, pissed off Edmund, and had an argument with Charles.' I gave a tight smile. 'And generally tried to fit in the best I could.'

'Nothing physical?'

It was a strange question. 'I didn't pick a fight with anyone, if that's what you mean.' She didn't answer and stared at me blankly, as if preoccupied with some unfathomable puzzle. I had a feeling she knew more than she was letting on. Something else was troubling me, as it had before: If I had travelled almost twenty years into the future, where in time was the "Me" from this decade, the one I had replaced? I looked her in the eye. 'How long has this been happening to me?'

'Since we moved here,' she answered softly.

I raised an eyebrow. 'How much?'

She sighed 'Too much.'

'Right.' Her reluctance to fully engage with me was worrying. Apart from obvious physical characteristics, I hardly recognised the woman sat before me. Much had changed; even the light that once burned behind those pale blue eyes had dimmed considerably. 'Do you know what happened to Patricia?'

Hunching forward, she spread her hands on the table, but didn't look up. 'There are some questions I'm not prepared to answer, John. I'm sorry.'

'Why?'

'Because,' she said, slowly rocking her head from side to side. 'You have no idea what you're about to get involved in.' She looked up. 'There are things in the universe you shouldn't meddle with, and the past is one of them.'

'Telling me what happened to someone is hardly messing with the past, is it?'

She looked up. 'No, you're right, John, on its own, it isn't. But what if you try to change that particular outcome because of something you've heard? Then what? And what if that goes wrong? Do you go back and try again?' There was a grave, dark look about her eyes. 'Errors are cumulative, make just one small mistake and it will spread through time like a ripple on a pond. The consequences are too terrifying to even contemplate.'

'H-how do you know so much?'

'It's been almost twenty years, John. For twenty years I've watched you try to rewrite history. In the beginning I believed it to be a just cause until it all started to go wrong, and now those ripples, those errors in time, have started to catch up with us. If you really want to make a change, look in the mirror and start there.'

Something wasn't right. 'I'd agree with you if I had a choice. I don't choose to go back in time; something makes that choice for me. I have no control over it.' I frowned. 'But you know this.'

'That may be true, John, but you have the freedom to choose what you do once you're there.'

This was so unfair. I was dumbfounded. 'What happened to you, Skye?'

Her eyes stayed fixed to mine. 'The past happened to me, John, and one man's obsession to change it.'

Those words hit home. She believed that I, and I alone, had done this to her. She was a bitter woman but hid it well. I had arrived at a crossroads where every route took me to the same place. If I were to return to my own time and leave Althurian, then I would change the very course of history she was part of, and her past, the one she had now, would simply vanish. I had broken her heart, perhaps even her soul. Could I carry on knowing that? She was right of course; the present situation proved I had not been a careful observer, the opposite in fact. On reflection, I would have done anything to have my life back to how it was before Althurian. It was at times like this I really needed to talk to the one person who would understand, and it wasn't the woman sitting before me.

We finished our lunch in relative silence, an odd event in itself. After we cleared away the plates, she left me on my own; she said she had to run some errands for a person with a name I didn't recognise. If I'm honest, I was quite hurt by the way she treated my presence with indifference; it was like we were an old married couple whose once solid relationship had drifted so far apart there was nothing left to keep it together. Maybe she knew everything there was to know about me and had become jaded with it all. She left the house by the front door without saying a word.

I returned to the garden room and stood by the door looking out. One thing was certain; I was not where I was supposed to be. My unsolicited trips to the past (And now the future) were becoming more frequent, but still lacking in purpose; if there was one, its meaning was unknown to me. What made no sense at all was the situation I presently found myself. What was there to learn from it? Was it a warning? Was my sudden appearance in a yet to be written future, a plot by some unseen agent provocateur, a threat to throw me into confusion, put me in fear of myself. If it was, it had successfully produced the desired effect; part of me wanted to walk away and forget the whole business; the other part, the stubborn, pig headed, not to be messed with part, said no.

For some bizarre reason, I really liked Althurian, loved it even, and the new life it promised. I loved its antiquity, its retirement, the early sunrise over the trees, its stillness; most of all, I wanted to call it home, and if that meant becoming embroiled in a fight for a cause lost in the shifting sands of time, then so be it. I sighed deeply, if only I had the power to choose where the battlefront was to be.

I left the garden room and took a gentle, aimless stroll alongside the exquisitely beautiful beds of carefully managed flowering plants and shrubs. Someone had spent a lot of time, or money, or both, cultivating rich palettes of colour, variety, and depth. From what I had seen so far, Althurian had changed little in two decades; it was a pity the same could not be said for its denizens.

The sun frequently dipped behind hurrying, smoke grey clouds; weather wise, it wasn't the best August day I'd known. I continued my absent-minded wanderings until I came upon the line of elder trees, their earlier blooms replaced with ripening berries. Separating the cultivated splendour from the land of ancient stones and uncut meadow, it looked as if this area of woodland had been neglected for some time; fallen, rotting boughs lay haphazardly amongst the tangled masses of bramble and briar; access through this jungle of growth and decay was virtually impossible, and maybe that was the point.

I started to make my way back, taking a more direct route; extensive excavation works had levelled out the sharp rise in the terrain leading up to the house. I could now almost see the entire ground floor from the tree line, its mottled, orange brick façade, and lines of dark windows reflecting that broken, metal grey sky. Whoever the architect was, I was eternally grateful; the gentle gradient made the hike back to the garden room far less of an effort.

As I opened the door and entered, I heard a muffled conversation coming from somewhere deep within the building; my first thought was Skye had returned with a friend. I removed my jacket, hanging it over the back of a chair, before making my way to find them. I pulled up sharply; an acute feeling of danger overwhelmed my senses, every cell in my body warning me of some, as yet, unseen threat. I scurried back to the kitchen and stood just inside, near the door. I could feel my heart thumping wildly in my chest as I tried to calm my breath. Althurian had changed, and not just physically, it had become hostile, and I had no idea why, or what the threat actually was; even the loose, congenial chatter had stopped, replaced by the most intense, empty silence. I was rigid, hardly daring to move, hardly daring to breathe; it was as if I were the quarry of a stalking predator. As the minutes passed, the need to escape became desperate. Holding my breath, I silently inched my way along the side of the worktop towards the door to the garden room.

'Tut, tut, we can't have you leaving just yet, can we?'

I froze instantly. The voice from behind was barely recognisable, and my assailant swift and sure footed; the blow to the back of my head was vicious, calculated, and accurate, and the world around me vanishing instantly as I fell into a black abyss.

♦

A penetrating, almost deafening whistle assaulted the inside of my skull as the initial trauma began to wear off. I attempted to lift my head from the floor, but the effort, and the pain it induced, was greater than I could bear. As my senses stabilised – the blurry beginnings of sight, the tincture of smell, taste, and touch – I realised I may not be where I fell. This place, wherever, and whatever it was, was grim, damp, earthy and cold. I was lying on my side, my head hurt like it was being squeezed in a vice, and my mouth was full of the most foul-tasting grit. I could not move one of my arms; trapped beneath my prostrate body, it had become numb and virtually lifeless, and I had to prop myself up using my one good arm. After a minute or two my vision began to clear, and although far from perfect, it was good enough to look round and take stock of my situation.

The room, if you could call it that, was a dim rectangle of white painted brickwork, the floor, earthen and hard. There was no door, and a small square window just below the ceiling was the only source of light. Once the feeling had returned to my other arm, I dragged myself to the closest wall and slumped in a hunched, curled up sort of way. I had lost all sense of time and dozed on and off several times until the fog inside my head cleared enough to reason my predicament; even so, I found it almost impossible to understand, or come to terms with what had happened.

As old as I was, I had never experienced a physical assault of any kind; as a child I can only remember being pushed and shoved round by the bigger boys at school. This may sound dramatic, but I felt as though I'd been defiled by it, never to be the same again. I moved my head forward and gingerly touched the back of it. What I found didn't make sense: there was no bloodied, matted hair, no lump, and no sharp, nerve searing pain as my fingers probed what I thought to be the impact point. I took a deep breath and carefully got to my feet. I stood with my legs bent and stooped over for several minutes, leaning heavily against the wall for support; I found my present circumstance, and the lack of any physical, or visible injury, baffling. Just to add to the puzzle, I was wearing a completely different suit of clothes.

Several minutes later, and somewhat revived, I straightened up, rolled my shoulders and tried to shake off the feeling of futility that had begun to seep into my thoughts. As I stood, muzzy headed, and struggling to think of a way out of this mess, I heard a pair of heavy footsteps walk across the floor above. I held my breath as they slowed to a stop not far from me; this was followed by the sound of furniture being moved, the odd grunt, more scraping, and the clatter of something heavy falling to the floor. I was about to cry out when a sudden dazzle of light appeared from above. My whole body stiffened as the memory of the assault came flooding back.

'Keep back if you know what's good for you.' The shouted order came from a man whose voice I didn't recognise. He then added, 'I have a gun and will use it if you try anything stupid.' Instinctively, I stepped back against the wall, my eyes riveted to the opening above. More scraping and banging followed as a thick wooden ladder was lowered to the floor. 'Right,' he cried. 'Up you come.' For a naturally stubborn man, I complied remarkably quickly. On closer inspection, the ladder was old, rickety and full of woodworm, and I was more than a little uneasy as I gingerly climbed each of the wear worn treads. However, unease was nothing compared to the terror I felt as I emerged from the opening; the man had taken up a position behind me, and no doubt had the gun pointed at my head. The top of the ladder barely cleared the floor and I had to make a rather inelegant scramble to get to my feet. As yet, I still had not seen my captor, and was unlikely to. 'Keep your eyes to the floor, do not look back, and do exactly as I say. Do you understand?'

I nodded uneasily. I had this dark, dreamlike image of being taken outside and executed.

'Did you hear what I just said?' he barked.

I straightened suddenly. I was expecting another blow to the back of my head. 'Yes. S-Sorry.'

He jabbed the muzzle between my shoulder blades. I gasped as it pressed into the fleshy area to the side of my spine. 'Now move,' he growled.

'Where are you taking me?'

'You'll find out soon enough.'

The opening was in the close boarded floor of a workshop. The first thing I noticed, probably because I'd been starved of light, was a line of metal framed windows down one side of the room; all were glazed with yellowing, wire reinforced glass panels. Under these, and along the entire length, a timber bench had been built; it had shelves below and above, three individual carpenter's vices, several racks holding chisels, set squares, auger bits, and other woodworking paraphernalia. Although the tools were from another era, they looked remarkably new and well maintained.

I had obviously slowed my pace and had a short, sharp reminder of this: a jab in the back. 'Move it, Sunshine, we ain't got time for no sightseeing.'

I found the man's ability to steer me in whatever direction he wanted me to go, terrifying; I was unconsciously grinding my teeth as we wended our way round each of the various timber projects under construction. We came to a halt by a pair of freshly painted double doors; behind these, a rectangular concrete hard standing had been set into the floor. I could hear very little noise coming from outside.

'Wait here,' he said. I heard him take a few steps to my left; there was a window to one side of the door, and I could only guess he was checking outside for some reason. I was in no hurry to turn my head and find out.

Two loud raps were followed by a cry of, 'Okay, unlock 'em, Harry.'

My faceless man now had a name. Harry prodded me in the back again. 'Slowly turn and face the bench. Do not move again until I say so. Got it?'

I nodded, but this time answered, 'Yes.'

The doors scraped and clattered noisily across the concrete floor as they opened. Seconds later I heard the unmistakable rattle of a diesel engine and the whine of a vehicle being reversed; it backed into the workshop belching out a thick cloud of choking fumes. Fortunately, the driver killed the engine before I suffered any permanent lung damage.

'Right, you, keep your head down, do not look up, and get in the back of the van.'

The rear doors to the black Morris Commercial were already open; I climbed in and sat down on the ribbed metal floor. A section of thin steel plate had been fitted as a bulkhead between the driver, passenger, and load space, and apart from a little extraneous light seeping round various panel joints; it was as black as pitch once the doors were closed, an unnerving experience at the best of times. As I sat hugging my knees, I noticed a luminescent glow coming from my wrist; at first, I was a little unnerved by it until I gingerly lifted my arm and realised it was coming from a watch I had not seen before, or aware of until then. I had a feeling it may have stopped working; the face was heavily scuffed, and I could feel a large dent on its rotating bezel.

Chapter 12
The Diary

Rolling round in the back of a vintage delivery truck was not my idea of fun, and not a journey, or a mode of transport, I'd choose if it were not for the Remington semi-automatic (Yes, I actually caught a glimpse of it) rammed into the small of my back. Now, as I bounced about, I had several important thoughts: My life was unlikely to be in any immediate danger (This was probably wishful thinking), and reasonably sure I had returned to somewhere in the past. What wasn't immediately clear, was who I'd become.

After slowly decelerating, the van turned sharply to the right and proceeded at a crawling pace for about a minute before coming to a dead stop. All was quiet outside; I didn't even hear the driver get out or move around, and wondered if he, or she, was on their own, as the usual chatter heard when people are cooped up together was non-existent. I didn't have to wait long.

The doors clanked open and the bright light of day flooded in, making me squint and shield my eyes. A dark silhouette of an unbelievably large man holding the door was all I could see. I had a feeling he wasn't the one from the workshop. I was right.

'Get out, and be quick about it,' he barked.

I complied immediately even though I didn't see, or feel, a gun this time (He was of a size few would argue with). The man grabbed my arm and frog marched me across a paved yard towards a large, box like concrete building; it looked more like an Art Deco inspired family home than anything commercial. Before being hustled through a pair of double doors, I noticed this was not a building in isolation and there were three others, identical in every way. After a short walk along a dark corridor I was left in a starkly decorated room, containing a cream enamelled table and two steel framed chairs; I'd seen this set up before, and it didn't look good. I tried the door, and it was no real surprise to find it locked. I wasn't going anywhere, anytime soon. I perched myself on the edge of the table and stared at the floor; the single incandescent light bulb suspended above me cast a forlorn shadow as I deliberated my fate. Reading this, you have already realised the gravity of my situation. Whatever the reason for my captivity, I was at a loss to explain it, and all I could do was wait until someone, somewhere could tell me. I was not to wait long.

I heard the distant creak of a dry hinge and the thump of a door left to close on its own. Soon, hushed, tinny voices and footsteps echoed along the corridor outside; my pulse quickened as the instinctive urge to hide or run overwhelmed me. I guessed there were two of them, and from the timbre of their voices, both male. They quietened just before unlocking the door.

'You,' I growled.

'Good to see you too, William,' said Charles. He nodded to an unseen companion before closing the door; the key turning in the lock almost immediately. Charles had a calm, confident air about him, he clearly didn't consider me a threat of any consequence. He folded his arms, leant back against the wall and scrutinised me for several seconds before he spoke again. 'Just a word of warning, old boy, if you try anything stupid you will be shot. Do I make myself clear?'

I didn't acknowledge the warning; I didn't need to. 'Why have you brought me here?'

'Why do you think?'

I stared at him. 'Oh, it's a guessing game, is it?'

His expression hardened. 'Where is it, William?'

'Is asking a stupid question the same as trying anything stupid?'

'What the devil are you talking about, man?' he said, curling his lip.

'Funny that, Charles,' I said dryly. 'You took the words right out of my mouth. If you'd like to tell me what it is you want, I might be able to help you?'

'You know very well what I'm talking about.'

I jerked my shoulders defiantly. 'We could be here a while then.'

'The bloody diary, you cretin,' he barked. 'Where have you hidden it?'

'Let me get this straight,' I said. 'You had me locked up in a cruddy cellar for God knows how long, then brought here in the back of a delivery van just to ask me if I know the whereabouts of a sodding diary. Tell me if I've missed anything?' I could see the anger rising in his eyes, and there was nothing I could do about it. 'You can't keep me here forever, Charles, people will start asking awkward questions.'

He sneered. 'Trust me, William; no one is out looking for you.'

I saw something in his eyes that unsettled me. 'They will at some point.'

'Not since you and your plane went down in the North Sea,' he said, laughing menacingly. 'Officially, you're now a casualty of war, William.'

My eyes hardened. 'What do you mean? How can that be?'

'It was easy to change the flight log when we have so many of these Czech pilots flying with us.' He grinned malevolently. 'You're already dead, my friend.'

A cold realisation swept over me; Charles had no intention of keeping me alive even if I was able to tell him what he wanted to know. As Janice Bergan had told me, history had already recorded William's demise. I was surprised he was so candid with me. 'Why are you doing this?'

His face contorted. 'I've already told you once. Give me the damn diary and I'll let you go.'

'I destroyed it.'

'Don't lie to me,' he barked. 'Destroy the only evidence you have? Bullshit!'

'Okay, you win, Charles.' I did my best to smile confidently, tightly crossing my fingers behind my back. 'I sent it to Parminter and Simpson for safe keeping; I thought something like this might happen.'

For a brief moment I saw a mark of fear in those dark eyes; they narrowed, and a small muscle twitched in his cheek as if he was trying to gauge his next move. I could see this unexpected twist had caught him off guard. 'You're lying again,' he said. I now detected a definite uncertainty in his voice.

I shrugged. 'My instructions, if anything happened to me, regardless of cause, were quite specific, Charles. They were to turn the package over to the police at their earliest convenience. I think you may have boxed yourself into a corner, old boy.'

He angrily jabbed his finger at me. 'You had better be telling the truth, churl.'

It was a strange accusation. I looked him directly in the eye. 'You'll find out soon enough, won't you?'

Charles anxiously wiped a hand across his jaw. 'You will write them a post-dated letter of instruction giving me authority to take possession of it.' He raised a finger to me again. 'And if you refuse, I shall personally guarantee your sister will suffer severely for it. Is that clear?'

My blood ran cold. 'You bastard,' I snapped.

'Precisely. I'm glad you understand what's at stake here.' He grinned arrogantly. 'Shall I get you a pen and some paper,' he raised an eyebrow, 'maybe an envelope or two?' Charles was a man who thrived on winning, defeat for him wasn't an option. I could only hope this distraction might buy me enough time to give me the break I needed. He rapped a knuckle on the door and smiled sardonically. 'I'll let you have a few minutes to think about what you're going to write.'

My heart sank on hearing the turn of the key. As the reader has probably gathered, I am a relatively peaceful man, and not one to cause a scene, even if provoked beyond reason. But it was becoming evident over the last few days that this had to change, and unless I got lucky, fighting my way out looked the only option. I glanced round at what had become my cell; escape was unlikely, unless it was through the door, solid walls and no windows saw to that. I really had run out of choices and would have to get away by fair means or foul. Charles had proved himself to be a ruthless psychopath, willing to do anything to get his way; the threat to harm Patricia was mind boggling as well as sickening.

It was surprisingly hot and took off my jacket, hanging it over one of the chairs. I tried to think why Charles was so interested in a diary, and desperate enough to use extreme measures to get it back. It occurred to me that William may have stolen it because it contained incriminating evidence of some hideous wrongdoing. It would come as no surprise if a narcissist like Charles bragged about his dubious triumphs between the pages of his own diary; if only this ephemeral residence in William's head allowed me access to his memories as well. My heart skipped a beat at the sound of footsteps. I was surprised when the door was opened by a short, broad shouldered man with black, close cropped hair, and spade like hands; his thick, muscular arms were slightly bent at the elbows as if he was preparing to execute a rugby tackle. His shifty, stone grey eyes watched me like a hawk. Another of Charles' flunkies you'd be insane to argue with. 'You're to come with me, fella,' he said, with a jerk of his head.

'Where are you taking me?' I asked. It was becoming a regular question.

'You'll find out soon enough.' He jerked his head again. 'Now move.'

I sighed and got to my feet, even hearing the same answer was becoming tedious. 'Just a second,' I said, turning to get my jacket. I'm not entirely sure what gripped me at that particular moment; maybe the unfairness of it, or maybe I had simply lost my mind. I curled my fingers round the top tube of the chair, and with every ounce of my strength, swung it in the direction of my jailer. It really was a lucky shot. One of the legs on its upswing caught him squarely under the chin with a sickening thud, his feet literally lifting from the floor as he flew headlong into the corridor.

I froze for several seconds. If I'm honest, this sudden burst of violence made me feel quite sick; I'd actually shocked myself. When the reality finally sunk in, and I had quickly gathered my thoughts, I realised it wasn't a good idea to leave the guard where he could be seen (I did check if he was still breathing). As I dragged his lifeless body through the doorway by his feet – he was a lot heavier than he looked – it did occur to me how thoroughly pissed-off this gorilla of a man would be when he woke up, and tried not to dwell too much on this inescapable fact as I locked the door.

I was tempted to see how far the corridor went in the opposite direction; the lack of lighting suggested the building may have been deserted. Potentially, it was a risk whichever way I chose, and could have easily been taken on the toss of a coin. I decided to go with the route I was already familiar with; the entrance doors were half glazed so I could check if the coast was clear before venturing out. I tiptoed towards them, wincing at the slightest noise, and staying within the shadows as best I could. As far as I could see, the yard was empty. I cracked open the unlatched door and listened; as was usual, all I could hear was my heart thumping in my ears. Everything seemed quiet. I pushed it open a little more and surreptitiously checked in either direction. I couldn't afford to hang round for too long, sooner or later the man I'd unceremoniously dispatched to the Land of Nod would wake up, and I guessed with some confidence, he was unlikely to stay quiet for too long. I checked one last time, crouched as low as I could, and scampered along the side of the building until I was able to duck behind what looked like an old rusty oil tank. 'So far, so good,' I mumbled.

'You all right, mate?'

I spun round; my heart was in my mouth. I had been concentrating so much on the yard I had missed a partially hidden entrance next to the tank. The man stood with one hand stuffed into a pocket, while the other held a thin, hand rolled cigarette. He looked about twenty-five, lean and wiry, with a flat cap, baggy woollen trousers, and a white shirt with braces. Scratching behind his ear, he said, 'You one of the blokes from next door?'

I nodded solemnly. 'Yeah, what's up?'

He jerked his head towards the door. 'We've fixed the electrics on your motor. You can take it away if you want.'

I stared at him. 'You've fixed it, then?' I winced.

He stared back at me. 'Yeah, that's what I've just said.'

My eyes widened. 'You mean I can just drive it away?'

He frowned but nodded anyway. 'That's the idea, mate. It's all paid for. We were expectin' one of your lot to come around for it about twenty minutes ago.'

I smiled, glanced over my shoulder, and brushed my hands together nonchalantly 'Yeah, we were a bit busy,' I said. 'You know how it is.'

♦

I put the Morris Eight in first gear, gave my newfound friend a wave, and pulled out of the garage as soon as the roller shutter door was clear of the roof. I looked in the mirror and watched the buildings as they diminished from view. I had just added another to the list of people I hoped I would never bump into again. Stealing a car, or driving one without permission, was not something I have done or ever contemplated doing, but here I was, happily driving along a narrow, hedge lined country road without any sense of guilt; although I can't begin to describe my fear of capture at this point, and I almost got a crick in my neck checking the rear view mirror every few seconds.

I was at a loss of what to do, not a clue where I was, and had no idea who was involved in this conspiracy with Charles. I had considered driving directly to a police station until I realised that turning up in a stolen car, possibly belonging to a potential war hero, may not go down too well; I had a suspicion that law enforcement in mid-twentieth century Britain was a remarkably different animal to what we have today. I pulled up at a junction and stared at the blank signpost boards opposite; I seem to remember reading these were defaced, or removed, to foil enemy invaders. I cupped a hand over my mouth as I glanced, first in one direction, then the other; it was down to a toss of a coin again. I took a chance and turned right.

If it wasn't for potholes, and the Morris' horrendously hard suspension, and notchy gearbox, I would have found it curiously pleasurable driving on roads as empty as these. After a few miles, I spotted the tip of a church spire poking through a dense tree canopy; and where there was a church; there were people, people I could ask for directions. This was to prove more problematic than it first appeared.

I pulled up outside a small, detached building, its white, stucco walls and blue painted timber framing were showing signs of neglect. I looked round before getting out, and apart from a slightly overweight ginger cat ambling lazily across the road, the place was deserted. The door was open, and I could hear the sound of big band music coming from somewhere inside. Stepping over the threshold and into a world I was completely unfamiliar with was a mixture of inquisitive interest and more than a little fear; this was like no shop I had ever visited before. It was tiny. A short countertop packed with jars, packets, and bowls of all shapes and sizes; most were empty. Several open wooden boxes, containing a grubby assortment of various root vegetables, took up what little space was left on the bare boarded floor. I had to almost shuffle in sideways to get to the counter.

'Hello,' I called. No answer, not even a peep. 'Hello,' I called again.

'Hang on, I'm busy at moment,' replied a distant male voice. 'Can ye call back?'

I think I may have tutted; twenty first century impatience clearly had no place here. 'I just wanted to ask for directions if that's okay,' I asked politely.

'What ye say?' he shouted.

I sighed. 'I want to know how I get to Feldingham.'

A man suddenly appeared behind the counter. (To this day I'm not sure how he got there) He looked like an older version of the man from the garage, and by the look of his hands, doing the same job; he was cleaning them with an old, and equally greasy, vest. 'Directions ye say?'

This looked hopeful. I nodded. 'Yes, please.'

He scowled. 'If I'd known I would have run all tha way here,' he said sarcastically. 'Are ye going to buy anything?'

'I patted my pockets (I had already checked them for anything useful). 'I'm sorry, I'm completely out of cash,' I lied guiltily.

The old man craned his neck; he first looked at the car, then eyed me suspiciously. 'So, ye drives a motor, but has no money on ye, eh?'

I shrugged. 'I left my wallet at home.'

'Is that right,' he said, narrowing his eyes. 'Where did ye say ye were from?'

I could feel myself backing into a corner. My voice went up an octave. 'Er...Boxford?'

'And ye want ta get ta Feldingham?'

Hallelujah. 'Yes.'

'So ye come from Boxford and ye need directions ta Feldingham?'

Oh Lord, give me strength. 'That's what I said.'

He scrutinised my face for a few seconds. 'But they're next ta each other.'

I nervously scratched behind my ear. 'Ah. I can explain that.'

The man folded his arms. 'Can ye now?'

'Yes...um...you see.' I puffed out my cheeks. In for penny, in for a pound, I thought. I leant towards him, surreptitiously glancing from side to side. 'I probably shouldn't tell you this.' I took a deep breath and beckoned him closer. 'I'm stationed at Boxford. I was only confirmed fit to fly and passed my night vision assessment test two days ago,' I said proudly, using my best, lying through my teeth voice. 'You see, my old friend, the boys took me out to celebrate, got me drunk, and left me the car so I could get home.' I shook my head. 'The bounders, eh?' I had suddenly adopted a "steady on chaps" accent. 'You see, I've got to get myself back to Feldingham pretty sharpish, so I can pick up the rest of my kit.'

At last, the man's face creased into a broad smile. He chuckled and rolled his eyes. 'Why on earth did ye not say so, lad,' he said, lifting a hinged flap in the counter. 'If ye move along, I'll take ye outside an' point ye in tha right direction.'

'I can't thank you enough, old man. Wouldn't want to end up on jankers before I get a chance to have a stab at Jerry, eh?'

The man laughed heartily. 'Lawd no, lad, 'eaven forbid.'

'Just one more thing,' I said. 'What date is it?'

♦

As luck would have it, I was already on the right road, and only three miles from the main highway leading to Feldingham; and one, although decades later, I had travelled before. I pulled up a few hundred yards from Althurian; there was a very good chance Charles could be inside. It was time to choose again, not that I had an abundance of options. It was obvious a confrontation with him was inevitable at some stage, whether this was now, or at some time in the future, was a matter for fate to decide.

I slipped the Morris in gear and was turning onto the driveway in less than two minutes. It was a strange feeling to be crawling towards the house almost eighty years before I'd be doing the same thing with Skye. I was relieved to see no other cars parked outside. I had to perform an eight-point turn, the heavy, unpowered steering being almost as bad as the gearbox, to get the Morris facing the road in the event I had to make a quick getaway.

Climbing the steps, I loitered by the door a few moments before knocking; it was unfortunate that, not only was I penniless, I was keyless. I rapped the cast iron ring twice and waited; I was fairly sure Charles was unlikely to answer even if he was standing in the hall. My pulse quickened when I heard the sound of scuffling footsteps coming from inside. A bolt rattled as it was pulled from its keep, and the door swung open.

A startled, and clearly shocked, Mrs Campbell raised a hand to her mouth as if she was in pain, she stared at me, her dark blue eyes frozen, caught in a trance. 'Good Lord,' she gasped. 'M-Master William.'

An odd reaction I thought. 'Is Charles here, Lizzy?' Still with her hand cupped to her mouth, she slowly rocked her head from side to side without speaking. I stepped into the hall and closed the door. 'Okay...well...er...any idea when he's due back?'

It took a moment for her to answer. 'About...an hour,' she mumbled.

I laid a hand on her shoulder. 'Are you feeling okay, Lizzy?'

'W-we were...told you...you had been killed, Master William.'

I closed my eyes, quietly cursing under my breath; it had completely slipped my mind. 'Yes. Sorry,' I said, fumbling for words. 'Look, Lizzy, I can't explain anything just yet. Is Pattie here?'

A tear rolled down her cheek as she looked at me, the corners of her mouth trembling as she attempted a smile. 'Miss Pattie is in her room.' She sighed. 'She hasn't come out since we heard. Oh, Master William, it's so good to see you.'

'You too, Lizzy,' I said softly. 'I could do with a brew and something to eat if it's not too much trouble.'

Mrs Campbell pulled a small lace handkerchief from her apron pocket and dried her eyes. She laughed nasally 'I think we could all do with something a little stronger than tea, Master William. I'll see what I can do.'

I slowly climbed the stairs, my heart beating faster than when I was standing by the front door. I got to the stair head, closed my eyes, and took a deep, calming breath; I wondered if my escape could be the act that broke the spell. History had changed to be sure. I could feel my face soften, maybe the beginnings of a smile as I opened my eyes; this was to be a happy, but tearful reunion, and one that was likely to change the world in a way hard to imagine. I straightened my back and took my first step.

♦

I had no prickly feeling on the back of my neck, no sudden nausea, giddiness, or warning; the room, the world about me, the smell of wood polish, the sound of Mrs Campbell fussing about downstairs, the feel of the floor beneath my feet, all disappeared like it never existed. I can't even say I fell anywhere, because for one brief moment, I was nowhere.

I first became aware of my gradual return to the real world when I sensed a mild feeling of pressure on one side of my face; it was also warm, cosy, and safe. I may have fallen asleep, because I suddenly woke up with a start and sat bolt upright. I was in bed, the duvet was in a heap on the floor, and daylight was filtering round the edge of the curtains; all very familiar except for one thing: this was no Althurian. I was back at my flat in Whitstable. I rubbed my face, got to my feet, and padded over to the mirror (this had now become an annoying, but necessary, routine). I was pleased to see the reflection looked equally familiar, and I was back to my old self. Although it was curious to find myself in the flat, I strangely gave little thought to it. I picked up my phone from the bedside cabinet and checked the screen. It was 9:30am, Saturday 26th May 2016. I had lost a few months and had two missed calls: one from my ex-wife, and one from a person called Zoe. The oddity of this didn't occur to me immediately, as I would only endure the pain of speaking to Clare (my ex), and the mysterious Zoe, after I'd had my fix of caffeine (or possibly two!).

Although the layout of the flat was identical to how it had always been, it was not so with the furniture, carpets, and almost everything else; luckily I found the coffee where I usually keep it (and an expensive brand I would never think of buying), and looked at my phone while performing the all-important duty. The call to Clare would follow a predictable pattern: she would talk endlessly about herself until my bladder ran out of spare capacity; after all these years I was amazed she still kept in touch. Zoe seemed a far better bet. I tapped in her number and waited.

'Hiya,' she said. 'Late night, or did you leave your phone in the car again?'

This was no stranger it seemed. 'No. Sorry, I didn't hear it,' I lied defensively.

She sighed. 'You don't change, do you?'

I was irritated by her familiarity. 'What did you call me about?'

'Wow! That was abrupt.' She paused. 'If you're not up to this viewing I can easily change it to another day.'

I stopped myself from asking the obvious. 'Yes, that might be a good idea.' I took a deep breath. 'Look, Zoe, I'm sorry if I sound a bit off today, but I have one monster of a headache. Can we talk about this tomorrow?'

'Sure, John,' she said. 'It can wait. Do you need me to drop round anything? I'm popping into town later.'

I think I may have gasped. 'No. No, that's okay…er…Zoe. I might just go back to bed for an hour or so.'

'Okay. Well, don't say I didn't offer,' she said. There was certainly a light-hearted nature to her answer. 'I'll give you a call in the morning. Take care.'

I puffed out my cheeks, wandered to the kitchen and eyed the full bottle of Sauvignon standing next to the radio. I shook my head; I needed my wits about me. I decided to give Skye a call; she was bound to know who this Zoe was. I flopped on the sofa and started to scroll through my recent call list. 'That's weird,' I mumbled. Her number was missing; unusual, because it's almost the only one I call. I checked my contacts; this was the same. I scratched my head, none of this made sense, and I could think of nothing remotely rational to explain it (Again!).

I got up, paced round and kept checking my phone in the vain hope that her number might suddenly appear. It was during one of these anxious, hand ringing moments I spotted a waste bin lurking next to the front door; it had been partially hidden by a curtain, and was full of unopened mail, and as unusual as Skye's number missing from my contacts. I have an obsession with opening mail almost before it hits the door mat, so to have a bin full of it was highly improbable, and extremely worrying (especially for someone with a hang-up like mine).

There were twenty-two envelopes in total, only five of these were junk; the others were plain, officious looking, and post marked with dates going back to the beginning of March. I wiped a hand across my mouth; I was almost too frightened to open them. I took this bundle of mail back to the sofa and laid them out in neat rows. I stared at each one in nervous anticipation before picking up the scariest one and tearing off the end.

Re: Flat 2. The Oysters, Harbour Way, Whitstable, Kent

Dear Mr J Warrener

It is with regret that I must inform you that it is the banks intention to seek a lawful repossession order through the court unless the charges and loans outstanding on the above property are settled on receipt of this letter, and in accordance with the terms and conditions stated in your original loan agreement. Please do not ignore this request.

Yours Sincerely

Charles Fordham

It was as if the letter was meant for someone else. My hand started to shake as I massaged my forehead, this was the sort of letter I always dreaded, but never thought I would receive. I felt sick. I stared at the signatory and couldn't even laugh at the irony. I balled the letter into my fist and threw it across the room; this had to be some kind of joke. I opened another, and another, then another; they were basically all the same: demands for money, a lot of it. I'd never let myself get in such a mess. I have always been a bit of a miser when it came to my finances. Skye would rib me mercilessly about my inability to spend money. Now, the complete opposite appeared to be the case, almost everything I owned was bought with debt. Not only did I feel sick, I now felt terribly alone.

I stood up, took a deep breath and paced round the room again, not knowing quite what to do with myself. I tried to think calmly, get things in perspective, but failed miserably, and the fact I couldn't speak to anyone made it worse somehow. I went to the bathroom, splashed my face with cold water and stared at the man looking back at me; whatever this other entity had done, I was the one who was stuck with the consequences, and sitting round doing nothing was likely to drive me insane. I marched back to the kitchen, grabbed what looked like a bunch of car keys from a hook below one of the wall units, and went off to find a jacket, a bag, and enough clothes to last me a few days.

Chapter 13
Reunion

Fortunately, my taste in cars had not changed, even though my sense of fashion had; the last thing I needed was to search the streets of Whitstable for a car I didn't recognise, wearing a pair of grey Farrah flares. The Toyota was not far from where it was usually parked; even the number plate was the same. It was certainly no Aston Martin but would get me there; which was probably just as well considering the present state of my finances. I also planned to drive through Faversham and swing by Skye's parents before joining the motorway; there was always a possibility she might be at home and not travelling.

The roads in and out of town were horrendously busy, the oyster festival didn't help; even taking the coastal route through Seasalter, it still took me a good forty minutes before I pulled up outside the Tolhurst residence. I stared at the empty hard standing James (Skye's father) had laid so she could park the converted ambulance in their front garden; I guessed she was out on one of her many road trips. I considered driving off, but I was curious to why her contact details were missing from my phone. I did wonder if this latest manifestation of me had two phones and picked up the wrong one (wishful thinking I hear you say).

I climbed from the car and slowly wandered up the garden path, as I had done many times over the last eight years. I was surprised to see the front door painted a rather bright red; a colour James swore was the sign of the Devil. I chuckled to myself and pressed the bell.

I heard a male voice shout, "I'll get it". It was an odd timbre, sounding nothing like the voice I knew so well. I was used to waiting, and surprised when the door suddenly swung open.

The man looked at me as if I had disturbed the most important moment in his entire life. 'Yeah, what do you want?' he growled. He was in his mid-twenties, wearing a white tee shirt, blue jeans, and scruffy, unkempt hair; he had a really pissed off, why are you here, expression.

I shrank back. 'Er…is…Skye here by any chance?' I asked feebly.

He eyed me suspiciously, twisting his mouth to one side. 'The geezer wants to talk to you, Skiz.'

A voice, one I would recognise anywhere, called out, 'What does he want?'

The man inclined his head and sneered. 'Well, you heard her.'

'I…just wanted to have a word, if that's okay?' I asked apologetically.

'What about, pal?' I sensed a threatening element to the question.

Just then, Skye's face appeared over his shoulder. She stared at me for a second and frowned; I thought she had recognised me. 'Can I help you?' she asked politely. Her manner was in complete contrast to the man who answered the door, and it seemed inconceivable they were a couple. I could feel my heart sink at the thought.

As our eyes met, I struggled to find an answer that made sense; it was obvious she didn't know me from a bar of soap. 'M-maybe I was mistaken...er...Sorry to have disturbed you.' I turned to walk away.

'No wait,' she said. I stopped and looked back, my heart skipping a beat. 'Why do I know you from somewhere? Were you at the Rumford rally this year?'

Watching the face of someone I loved struggle to recognise me was the saddest, most heart wrenching experience I'd ever had. I sighed. 'No, Skye, not at a rally.' It was impossible to hide how I felt.

The man glared at me, then back at Skye. 'I'm going back to the football,' he said grumpily. 'Remember it's your turn to pick up the Chinese.' He pushed his way past her, quite roughly I thought, leaving her to hold the door.

She pulled a face. 'Sorry about that. Can't choose your family, can you?'

I raised my eyebrows. 'Family?' I repeated, somewhat incredulously.

She gave a crumpled grin. 'My brother. He was only supposed to be staying a couple of weeks. That was three months ago, an' now thinks he owns the place.'

I hesitated. 'Oh, I thought...'

'Oh, Jesus, no.' She gave out a hoot of laughter. 'I would have murdered him by now if he was.' Her eyes levelled with mine. 'So where was it, then?'

'Sorry?'

She rolled her eyes. 'Where I know you from?'

My mind travelled back eight years, to that exceptionally windy day in August. I took a chance. 'We bumped into each other on Skegness sea front. You were trying to convince the guy running the donkey rides that you really were as light as a child.'

Her eyes widened, as big as I had ever seen them; she cupped a hand to her mouth. 'Oh my God,' she gasped. 'I remember that.' She examined my face a moment. 'That was such a long time ago.' She laughed again. 'What took you so long?'

I sighed. 'Time got in the way, I'm afraid.'

She looked at me curiously. 'How did you know where to find me?'

'You wrote your address on a chip wrapper.' (That was true). 'Last week I found it sandwiched between the covers of a book (That was a lie), and thought I'd drop by to see how you were. Are you still travelling?'

She shook her head. 'Gave up after my parents were killed,' she said solemnly. 'It never felt quite the same after that.'

'No!' I gasped. 'How did that happen?' I was shocked, but it was a question maybe I shouldn't have asked.

'Hit an' run.'

'I'm sorry. I had no idea.'

She frowned. 'Why would you have?'

I suddenly felt awkward; I knew more about her than she did of me. I ignored the question. 'Did they find who was responsible?'

Her face darkened. 'Yes, for all the good it did. It was never going to bring them back, was it?'

'No, of course not,' I blathered clumsily. I thought this might be a good time to leave; it was becoming far too painful. 'Well, it was great seeing you again.' I paused. 'Maybe we should go for that drink we talked about.'

'Did we?' She smiled impishly. 'Yeah, maybe we should.'

'I could give you a call sometime.'

'Be nice to know your name.'

I closed my eyes and winced. 'Yes. Sorry. It's John.'

She held out her hand. 'Pleased to meet you, John; I'll see if I can find something better than a chip paper to write my number on.'

♦

The last few seconds of our conversation changed everything, and I drove away feeling quite pleased with myself. That rare something, the spark that ignited our passion all those years ago was still there; it was inescapable, and I could feel it as if it were only yesterday. I turned onto the slip road, joining the motorway at junction seven. It was to take over seven hours before I pulled up at exactly the same spot I had parked the Morris all those years ago.

I picked up my phone, scrolled through my contacts, and sighed with relief when I saw Skye's number was still there; reality was becoming less dependable, and it was making me paranoid. I stared along the main road. Although I'd just driven over three hundred miles, I was still hesitant to what I should do next, these sudden transitions between the past and present were playing havoc with my head, and I had to keep reminding myself where in time I actually was. It didn't help that everything I identified as me seemed inextricably attached to the past as the duration of each visit increased. It also didn't help that my presence caused such a dramatic change in the future without any real conscious effort on my part. I had an uneasy feeling I was involved in something far beyond what I was capable of dealing with or understanding.

Possibly Skye's warning may have come a little too late. I put the Toyota in gear and pulled away.

Althurian hadn't changed, nor should it have done, I suppose I just expected it to have. I parked, made my way up the steps and rang the bell. The door was quickly opened by a slim, athletic looking man in his early twenties, his neatly trimmed hair with a bold parting, dating him a little. He smiled. 'Yes. Can I help you?'

'Yes…um…I think we may be cousins.' Not the best introduction I could have made; Ill-prepared as usual.

His eyes narrowed. 'Who are you?'

'My name is John Warrener.' I watched for a sign of recognition.

'And that's supposed to mean something to me, does it?' he asked sharply.

I was about to answer him when a hand appeared on his shoulder. 'Who is it, Richard dear?'

He turned, continuing to keep a steady eye on me; behind him stood a woman of about eighty. She was carefully examining my face; I suspected her sight was maybe troubling her. 'Don't worry, Grandma, it's just another time waster. And he's just about to leave.' He started to close the door.

'No wait,' I said. 'My great grandfather was Stanley Warrener.'

I saw the old woman frown. 'What did you say, young man?'

'My great grandfather was Alexander Warrener's brother.' I took a gamble 'We're cousins.'

The woman touched the man's arm. 'You'd better let him in, Richard.' He grunted and stepped to one side; I was surprised he capitulated so easily, although he watched with an expression that oozed suspicion as I walked in. 'Do you have a name?' she asked bluntly.

'John,' I said.

She turned to the man. 'Be a dear, Richard, make a pot of tea and bring it through to the library for me.'

'Are you sure, Grand...'

The old lady raised her hand. 'Please, Richard, just do it, will you. Come through, John.'

Childish, I know, but I really wanted to smirk at Richard as I followed her to the library; a room that had changed in name only. The old woman gestured towards the sofas. 'Take a seat, John,' she said, closing the door. 'Have you come far?'

'Whitstable. In Kent.'

She sat down. 'I know it well.' She paused. 'So, was this a passing visit or have you made a special trip?'

Now we were sitting opposite each other, I began to see a distinct family resemblance, and I was fairly sure I knew who she was. 'I drove straight here, Sylvia.' I raised my eyebrows. 'It is Sylvia, isn't it?'

The old woman seemed unfazed. 'Knowing my name proves very little.' She smiled. 'If you could tell me something you couldn't possibly know. Now, that would be interesting.'

'Your mother's name was Patricia, but you called her Pattie.'

She waved her hand again. 'Good research could have found that out. Tell me something else.'

You own an early Aston Martin DB6 in blue, that has forty-five thousand miles on the clock, and you were born July 29th, 1940, and had an uncle who was supposedly killed over the North Sea the same month. Shall I go on?'

Her eyes narrowed. 'How did you know about my uncle?'

'I know that William was abducted by your father.'

She slowly rocked her head. 'Who told you this?'

I'd shot my mouth off again, and was back in the corner I usually found myself. 'May I ask you a couple of questions first?'

She eyed me cautiously. 'If you must,' she said, a little tight lipped.

'Did William survive the war?'

Sylvia appeared agitated. 'Yes.'

'Did he stay in the RAF?'

'No. After the war he moved somewhere north of here and became a teacher, I believe.'

'A teacher?' I nodded slowly. 'Interesting. Did he have any children?' I'm not sure why I asked this; my kinship with William, I suppose.

'That's more than a couple, John.'

'Please, Sylvia.'

'Two. A boy and a girl.'

'Are they…still around?'

'One of them is, not that I see very much of Cousin Lilly now she lives with her daughter.' She tapped the side of her head and pulled a face. 'I'm afraid she's not entirely with us anymore.' Her eyes seemed focused somewhere distant. 'The other one,' she said, curling her lip, 'disappeared two years ago after being released from prison.'

I felt myself grimace. 'In prison?'

She sighed. 'Cousin Alistair was not a very nice man.'

'In what way?' I was now pushing my luck but couldn't help myself.

'He was an abusive drunk and womaniser for most of his life. Well, that was before he was sent to prison for murder.'

'Good grief,' I said. It took a moment to sink in before recoiling at the cruel irony; William's life had been saved, but his son was destined to take the life of another. 'And no one knows of his whereabouts?'

'No. Lilley received a letter from him three days after he left prison, saying he was going to punish those responsible for ruining his life. To this day he hasn't been seen since. Good riddance, I say.

I decided to change the subject. 'What about your father?'

She turned her eyes towards the window, her manner abrupt 'What about him?'

'What was he like?' I was clearly probing an area she was not comfortable with, and it showed. I'm still surprised she didn't ask me to leave. Curiosity, I guess.

'I never really knew my father, or what happened to him.'

I knew this to be a lie, and clearly an attempt to brush the question aside. I continued to dig. 'I'm surprised Pattie didn't tell you.'

'She would rarely talk about him. He was hardly ever around, and as far as she was concerned it was good enough for me to know he existed. What little I do know came from our housekeeper.'

I nodded. 'Mrs Hughes.'

She raised her hands. 'I don't know how you know all this, John. You speak with uncanny familiarity.'

I sighed; the truth was far weirder than the lie I was about to tell. 'Okay. Like you, most of what I know came from someone else.' I paused. 'My grandfather.'

'Your grandfather?' She frowned. 'It's strange Mother never spoke of him.'

'Perhaps they fell out,' I bluffed, then shrugged. 'It happens.'

'Possibly. Mother could be rather headstrong. Sylvia looked towards the door and chuckled. 'I think Richard must have either lost his way, or he's playing with that new phone of his.'

'Does he live with you?'

'Only when his mother has had enough of him.'

'You have a daughter?'

'Skye's not really my daughter.' She smiled. 'You could say we kind of adopted each other after her mother died. She was a friend of mine, you see.'

My stomach somersaulted. 'Skye?'

'Yes. Pretty name, isn't it? It was my idea, actually. Julie was going to call her Daphne, but I changed her mind, I thought it was so old fashioned.'

'What gave you the idea?'

She chuckled. 'You'll laugh when I tell you.'

I smiled. 'Try me.'

'A woman with the same name came to me in a dream.' She snorted. 'And I have to say, it was one of the strangest dreams I've ever had.'

I inclined my head. 'Sounds like a good dream to me.' This pretty much confirmed Sylvia was the woman we found on the steps. But, if this was so, it didn't explain how Skye was no longer in this new future of mine, when she'd have to be for Sylvia to hear her name in the first place. Confused? I know I was. 'I believe you have a stone circle at Althurian?'

Her face hardened. 'We have, but I won't go near the place. Never have.'

'Why is that?'

'I don't really know; probably because Mother used to tell me scary stories about the stones. She even hated the mention of them.'

'Really?'

'Well.' She paused. 'Mother blamed them for everything that went wrong in her life. She wanted to have the whole lot bulldozed but couldn't because they were listed as some sort of monument. She was very upset.'

'Superstitious, was she?'

'Not particularly. She had some crazy idea they had a malignant influence over what went on at Althurian.'

'Did she ever say what that was?'

'I remember her telling me the circle was where the past, present, and future crossed. I never did ask her what she meant by it.' She chuckled softly. 'It was after a couple of glasses of wine, and you know what that can do to your head.

I smiled politely. 'And what do you think?'

'Mother was a troubled woman for most of her life, and if I'm honest, I think she needed to hold something accountable for it. I'm surprised she managed as well as she did.'

'But you still won't go near them?'

She visibly stiffened. 'Some nights I can see them glowing from my bedroom window. That's enough for me.'

I had to stop myself from blurting out, that I too had seen the same thing. I felt an odd shiver of anticipation, a sudden and compelling need to be there. 'Would you mind if I take a look?'

'Of course not, be my guest, John,' she said, rising to her feet. 'I'll get Ferris the gardener to show you.'

'There's no need, Sylvia, I know where they are,' I said, maybe a little too quickly. 'I can make my own way.'

She raised an eyebrow. 'Your grandfather must have known an awful lot about Althurian.'

'Ah. I saw a map once,' I lied, chuckling nervously. 'And some drone footage.'

'I see. Well, make sure you don't get lost.

♦

The flower beds were full, almost overflowing; a heaving palette of riotous colour. Rows of tall, bright yellow sunflowers stood guard over blue hydrangea, purple and yellow lupin, and red fuchsia, while Brompton stocks and lavender aubrietia tumbled carelessly over the rocky boundaries. The air was fresh and slightly chilled, and I caught the thin, damp smell of a spent bonfire as I neared the tree line. I'm not sure why I felt so calm, my situation was far from rosy, this really wasn't the future I had planned for myself; maybe it was the small, and possibly overconfident, voice inside my head telling me that this alternate reality wasn't…actually…real, and change was just round the corner. I was hoping this visit to the stones may somehow expedite matters. It was all I had left.

A tall, panelled fence had been erected, separating the garden from the wood; the gate to the path I'd used before had been left open and was swinging to and fro in the gentle breeze. I wondered if Sylvia had ever ventured this far, or if anything beyond this point was only for those who worked the soil and cut the grass. The path (which had now been gravelled and edged) looked as though it had been used recently, as there were several deep tracks in the earth, like those made by a heavily laden wheelbarrow. I closed the gate behind me and wandered through to the stones. I wasn't sure what I was expecting to see, if anything. What I did see shook me rigid.

Sitting in the middle of the circle, legs crossed and folded arms, was Patricia (I thought she had aged somewhat, although it was obvious who she was). She half smiled as if she knew me (it didn't immediately occur to me that our previous encounter was through William). I stared at her, unable to speak.

She slowly shook her head. 'Your presence here is now beginning to worry me.'

'I don't know what you mean.'

Patricia got to her feet, unfolded her arms, and pushed her hands deep into the pockets of her brown corduroy trousers. She inclined her head. 'This must be early days for you, cousin.'

I suddenly felt irritated. 'You're talking in riddles.' I glared at her. 'I have no idea what you're talking about.'

Keeping her eyes on me, she slowly wandered over to one of the larger monoliths and casually leant against it. 'I suspect you were hoping to see Becket. Correct?'

I felt a shiver run down my spine. Was Patricia the one he had warned me about? If she was, maybe I should be careful with my answer. I shrugged. 'I was visiting Sylvia and thought I'd come for a walk. Personally, I didn't expect to see anyone. Is Becket the gardener?' I enquired innocently.

Her expression hardened. 'This is not a game you can win, John Warrener. The tide is already turning, and your fate is in the balance.'

Those words, especially coming from someone I thought I knew, made my blood run cold. It didn't seem possible the Patricia I knew could change so radically; if I had money to burn, I would have bet on her being one of the good guys. I needed to ask questions; she hadn't appeared within the circle for nothing. 'Why are you here, Patricia?'

'Ah,' she said, raising her eyebrows in surprise. 'So, you do know who I am.'

'Well?' I asked.

'I came with a warning: Do not meddle in things you do not understand. Past, present, and future are now in equilibrium, and any unnatural disturbance within time could affect this fine balance and will not be tolerated.'

'If it's in equilibrium, then why has my life changed so dramatically from the one I once knew?'

Patricia shrugged. 'Your life was not congruent with the past and had to be corrected. It is you who is out of step.'

'But how can that be?' There was something odd about her demeanour, it smacked of control, conceit, and a strange, dark superiority. She was acting more like Charles.

'It is what it is and cannot be changed,' she answered curtly.

I suspected she was now stretching the truth a little; if change is impossible, why the warning? I remembered what Becket had told me, and it was time to test her resolve. 'I have no control over my actions, Patricia, so what do you suggest I do?'

She bristled. 'Then you will suffer the grave consequence of your actions.'

Almost the instant the last word left her mouth she vanished in a blink. I stared at the vacant space for several seconds; I may not have even drawn breath. A moment later the sound of nature, in all its richness, erupted around me as if awoken from some deep slumber. Perhaps I've overused the word "uncanny" a little too much, but that was exactly what it was. One thing that did stand out was how Patricia, unlike Becket, appeared to have chosen when it was her time to leave. Possibly the Guardian was not as potent as I first thought, and why he needed a third party (Me) to act on his behalf.

I walked round the circle several times, loitered inside for more than an hour, and sat on the recumbent until my legs went numb, all in the vain hope that Becket would reappear. The unchanging chorus of nature suggested this was unlikely to happen any time soon. I reluctantly gave up the vigil. Slipping from the stone, I shook the circulation back into my aching limbs, and prepared for the walk back to the house. I know this isn't always the case, but waiting in solitude gives you time to think, ask questions, create wild hypotheses, and maybe solve some of life's more taxing problems. I concluded fairly quickly that Patricia was probably correct: I was meddling in things I had no chance of understanding. Basically, I knew I was winging it.

Like I said earlier, I thought Patricia was one of the good guys. Maybe this new incarnation was an example of a time travelling Jekyll and Hyde character; a dual personality, each fighting for control. I needed help, someone to ask, someone to bounce ideas off. Not easy when the only people in this recently acquired existence, were an ex-wife, a stranger called Zoe, and a number of faceless individuals doing their best to make me homeless. I wandered towards the tree line, taking one last glance at the circle before leaving. I needed answers, and maybe Sylvia was all I had.

Chapter 14
The Search

Wary to avoid another encounter with happy boy Richard, I kept close to the eastern edge of the garden until I hit the rear wall of the garage, then took the narrow gravel path to the garden room; for reasons I cannot begin to fathom, I took a chance, a correct one as it happened, believing I would find Sylvia inside. I peered through the window before gently tapping on the glass. Sylvia, who was reading a magazine, looked up, appearing unfazed by my sudden appearance. She got to her feet with remarkable ease, pulled a chair from under the table, and beckoned me to join her. She seemed pleased, her face brightening a little as I opened the door.

'Sit yourself down,' she said, then chuckled, 'and I'll make sure we get our tea this time.'

I did as ordered, watching Sylvia scuttle off to the kitchen. I began to look round; it was becoming a regular practice. I was searching for changes, additions, that sort of thing. Surprisingly, the furniture, decoration, and colour scheme, were unchanged from when I first arrived at Althurian. I found this weirdly reassuring. Sylvia padded in carrying a tray; she was light on her feet, nimble considering her age. And as you have probably realised, still in the land of the living; at the time, an astonishing twist to the tale even I had missed.

She sat down. Leaning back in the chair, she tucked her hands beneath the pretty floral tabard she was wearing. 'Well, are you any the wiser after your visit?'

I ignored the question. 'What happened to you, Sylvia, the night you lost your purse?'

She took a sharp intake of breath. 'How do you know about the purse?' she hissed.

'Because I found it, Sylvia, and inside, there was a name and address. It was given to you by your friend,' I raised my eyebrows, 'Janice Bergan?'

Her bottom lip began to quiver, a small tick just below her eye twitching uncontrollably. 'J-Janice?' she rasped.

I continued to stare at her.

'Is she still alive?' she asked shakily. Sylvia looked genuinely shocked at the prospect, and difficult to speculate in what way.

'She was when I last spoke to her.' This could have been a cruel play on words, although for my sake I hoped she was; Janice was a source of information I couldn't afford to lose. I was beginning to feel like a detective. 'She told me it was a birthday present.'

'What do you really want from me, John?'

I paused to think, even if she wanted nothing to do with the stones, or anything associated with them, or the many strange occurrences visited upon Althurian and its occupants, she must have been well aware of their potential. 'I want to know.' I hesitated. 'I want to know what happened here, Sylvia. I want to know what really happened to your grandparents, your father, and your mother's second husband, James Dixon.'

Sylvia looked away, a fixed, empty gaze to somewhere beyond mortal vision. There followed an uncomfortable silence, lasting several minutes, before she turned and looked at me. I thought she was going to tell me to mind my own business and show me the door. 'Where did you find my purse?'

The "it was down the side of the sofa" explanation was not going to wash, it had to be the truth this time, as implausible as it was about to sound. I took a deep breath; it was becoming a habit. 'After we found you unconscious on the front steps of this house, we took you into the drawing room and put you on the sofa. You must have dropped it then.'

She gasped, lightly touching her lips. 'How can that be?'

I nodded. 'I'm afraid it's true, Sylvia. After you came round, you went to the bathroom and disappeared.'

'We?'

'My partner and I.'

A flush of realisation crossed her face. She cupped a hand to her mouth. 'Skye?'

I gave a limp smile. 'Yes.'

'I thought it was you who had disappeared,' she whispered hoarsely. 'I-I thought it was a dream.'

Her somewhat moderated reaction surprised me, and I expected to be questioned. Instead she just stared at me. 'Do you remember when this was?' I asked. 'A date perhaps?'

Her expression hardened; she looked tense, uncomfortable. 'It was August third, nineteen seventy-two. Five days after my birthday. A day in my life I'll never forget.'

'What happened to you that night, Sylvia?'

'I was a victim at the hands of another of my mother's bad choices.'

'I'm not sure I understand you.'

'Mother managed to marry two complete bastards. On more than one occasion, I became the focus of their attentions.' She drew a bitter breath. 'Husband number two was the worst.' She looked at me carefully. 'It was a Thursday, the day we decided it had to end. Enough was enough.'

'They found Dixon's remains several years ago, didn't they?' The fact she used the word "we" was not lost on me. I decided not to press her on it though.

'It was 2013.' Her shoulders jerked indolently. 'I'm surprised it took them so long.'

I should have been shocked, but I wasn't; I kind of felt her pain and understood in a way. I wanted to know more but couldn't bring myself to ask, and perhaps it was best not to know. 'And your father?'

Her eyes darkened as if she had stepped on the shadow of the Devil. Her lips tightened across bared teeth as she began to speak, her pale green eyes empty of emotion. 'He was a violent thug. Nothing more, nothing less.'

There was hatred in her voice, the anger truly palpable. I shifted in my seat; Charles was a thug all right, I knew that from experience. He had also disappeared in suspicious circumstances. I could feel my eyes narrow, as I considered the possibility Sylvia was more than just a casual bystander in both cases. I had to ask the question. 'Do you know what happened to him?' I detected a ghost of a smile just before she answered.

Her eyes stayed fixed on mine. 'He went missing and was never found.'

She neatly avoided the question; I knew it, she knew it. 'Nor were your grandparents,' I said, watching for a reaction. 'I know about the ring, Sylvia.' The words caught in my throat, so I tried again. 'I know about the ring, Sylvia.' I blinked; my vision beginning to tunnel.

♦

'William, wake up, will you.'

I groaned, rubbed my face, and tried to open my sleep hungry eyes. My head told me I was pulling out of a dream. 'What time is it? I mumbled innocently. In an instant, after the words had left my mouth, the covers, the ones I had obviously cocooned myself at some stage, were savagely torn from me. I was rudely assaulted by a gust of chilled air round my feet.

'Charles is on the warpath, and the one place you really shouldn't be when he gets home is in bed. It's almost ten o'clock. He'll go mad if he finds you in here.'

I managed to open one eye. Patricia was flapping round the room, picking up things from the floor, opening drawers and cupboards, and generally making an unholy din while she was at it. I squinted at her; the sunlight streaming through the now curtain-less window bored into my retinas. Suddenly, I realised the woman before me, Patricia, looked completely different to when I saw her last. She was now heavily with child as folk of that era would say, and a lot rounder than I remembered. It was quite a shock.

'Should you be doing all that...,' I said.
'Doing all what?' she snapped.
'All that...er...tidying up.'

'I'm not an invalid.'

'Yes. Yes, I know that,' I blathered. 'But...but you're...er...you know.'

'It's known as pregnant, Wills, and yes, I am perfectly capable, unlike you it seems.' She waved a pair of socks at me. 'It only takes a minute to put things in their rightful place.'

I winced; it hadn't occurred to me that Patricia was tidying up *my* room. I didn't know what to say, I had no idea William was such a sloth. 'I'm sorry, Pattie, you're right, it shouldn't be down to you to tidy up after me, especially in your condition. From now on I'll be a changed man. You wait an' see.'

Patricia inclined her head, glanced at some imaginary place near the ceiling, and touched a finger to her lips. 'Now, where have I heard all that before?'

'Ah.'

She smiled triumphantly. 'Anyway, I have some errands to run so you'll have to deal with Charles on your own.'

'Why, what day is it?'

'What day is it!' she exclaimed. 'If you stopped coming home completely sozzled most nights, you'd know what day it was.'

'Please, Pattie, just humour me, will you.'

She glared at me; hands firmly planted on her hips. 'It's Monday, the day that follows Sunday, or had you forgotten that too.'

I smiled sheepishly. I really needed to know the date, but that would be pushing it, and a question likely to suggest my brain was even more fuddled by alcohol than she already suspected. Patricia's only concern was for my welfare, I knew that, and asking something she considered daft was only going to worry her (Okay, it was William, but you know what I mean). Anyway, judging by Patricia's advanced state of pregnancy, I suspected I had returned somewhere between June and July. I swung my legs from the bed, sat up, and frowned. 'What time is the idiot due back?'

Patricia stifled a smile. 'Within the hour, so you'd better get a wriggle on.' With that, she left the room, quietly closing the door behind her.

'Oh Lord,' I mumbled. Charles was becoming a pest, a bad penny who seemed to turn up at exactly the same time as I did. I sat there a moment, trying to think, I really needed to know if this was before, or after my abduction, or if I was following a completely different time trajectory altogether. I concluded, that whatever my current situation was, I needed to find the diary, and find it fast; although what to do with the secrets it contained, was a whole new ball game, and sitting around waiting for something to happen was not helping. William clearly had "things to do", a structure to his day, and one I could not possibly know. I had a sincere hope that this was one of his quieter days.

On a chair by the window lay a neat pile of carefully folded clothes; over the back hung a white cotton shirt, and recently ironed by the look of it. I was relieved it wasn't a uniform. Nevertheless, as with my earlier experience, it was really odd picking up and putting on garments which, in normal circumstances, would be far too small for me. I must be honest though, once I'd got them on, the collarless shirt, blue Fair-isle tank top, and grey Oxford bags, made me look quite dapper; I could get used to the Forties look. The next task of the day was to find a newspaper.

As I emerged from the bedroom, I could hear the tinny music of broadcast radio coming from downstairs, and a voice, unmistakably that of Mrs Campbell, singing along with it. I followed her not so mellifluous tones to what I assumed was the dining room. She was busy polishing the top of a large gate leg table as I pushed open the door.

'Morning, Lizzy,' I trilled, maybe a little too enthusiastically, and without thinking.

Mrs Campbell stood up suddenly, clutching her chest. 'Good lord, Master William, you scared me half to death, you did.'

'Sorry.'

'Never the mind, Master William. Late night again?'

'It appears so, Lizzy.' I did my best to look suitably guilty.

'I suppose you'll be wanting something to eat before you go?'

I frowned. 'Go where, Lizzy?'

Mrs Campbell rolled her eyes and started shaking her head. 'To the tailors.'

Now, as an astute observer of this story, you can see where I was about to make an erroneous assumption; Mrs Campbell, however, could not, and clearly thought I was losing the plot, or possibly still hungover, or worse. For a second, I thought I was being clever; what I should've done was to keep my mouth shut.

'Ah, the Taylor's,' I said. 'Yes, I promised to pop over for afternoon tea. Lovely couple, I'm quite looking forward to it.' It was after this last word left my lips; I saw the look of baffled confusion materialize on Mrs Campbell's kindly face. It took her a moment to gather her thoughts.

'Are ye havin' me on again, Master William? I thought it was Mr Duggan measuring you up for your number ones, an' I never heard anyone goin' there for tea before.'

The penny dropped, and I smiled sheepishly. 'Just one of my little jokes, Lizzy. Have you seen today's paper?' I asked, quickly changing the subject.

She neatly folded the polishing cloth she was using, slipping it into the pocket of her apron. 'I'll get it for you, it's in the library.'

I raised my hand. 'Please, Lizzy, you really don't need to. You shouldn't be so quick to wait on me like that.' I chuckled. 'Anyway, you'll make me lazier than Charles already says I am.'

Mrs Campbell cupped a hand to her mouth, her cheeks blushing slightly. 'Master William, you are naughty,' she whispered hoarsely.

'I try my best, Lizzy.' I paused; a thought had suddenly occurred to me. 'Do you know if Patricia has left yet?'

'I don't think so, Master William, she was off to the garden room the last time I spoke to her, an' I haven't heard the front door go yet.'

♦

Patricia was indeed still in the garden room and reading the paper. She had shifted one of the chairs away from the table and positioned it by the window, possibly to make the most of the early morning sunlight. She looked up as I entered the room, her expression was somewhat strained. 'I thought you had some errands to run,' I said.

She nodded, glumly I thought. 'I did until Ted Bergan brought me a note from Emma asking if we could go tomorrow instead.' Patricia pulled a face. 'She's feeling a bit icky this morning.'

I sat down. 'Nothing bad I hope.'

She shook her head. 'The joys of pregnancy, I'm afraid.'

I nodded. 'Yes. Yes, of course...Emma Bergan.'

Patricia frowned. 'I thought you had a fitting to go to.'

'Later. I'm not feeling too good myself' I smirked. 'Couvade syndrome, I guess.'

'What are you talking about, Wills?' It was obvious my attempt at humour had fallen well short of its target. As usual, I continued to dig myself a deeper hole.

I raised my eyebrows, my voice climbing an octave. 'Womb envy?'

She slowly rocked her head from side to side, straightening the newspaper. 'I wonder if you really are my brother sometimes.'

I sighed. 'Can I ask you a question?'

'Depends what it is.'

I took a breath. 'Does Charles keep a diary?'

'Why do you ask?'

I nervously wrung my hands together; this could be awkward. I could hardly tell her the truth. Not at this stage. 'I read somewhere that men who keep diaries find it hard to express their emotions,' I said, and quite possibly the lie of the month.

She shifted in her seat, put down the paper and grinned for the first time. 'Now you have my attention, Wills.' She picked an invisible thread from her dress, smoothing down the fabric. 'I must say, you seem to learn an awful lot from those Motor Cycle Weekly magazines you read.'

I smiled. 'You'd be surprised. Well?'

'Well what? I was waiting for you to tell me more. I'm intrigued.'

Bugger. 'Er...they...er...tend to put all their thoughts and feelings in writing rather than sharing them with those they care for.' I sat back feeling pleased with myself.

'You've just made that up.'

I tried not to laugh. 'Perhaps you should read it, Pattie.' I raised an eyebrow. 'Then you'll know what his true feelings really are.'

'Chance would be a fine thing.' She tutted. 'He wouldn't let me near it anyway.'

I was on a roll. 'Do you know where he keeps it?'

Patricia pulled a face and gave a slight jerk of her shoulders. 'I have no idea. Everything he does is shrouded in secrecy.'

'You knew he had a diary,' I countered.

'Only because I've seen him writing in it.' She sniggered. 'He once left it on the dining room table and went upstairs,' she pinched a thumb and forefinger together, 'and I was this close to having a peek.'

'Why didn't…'

'I thought I'd find you skulking in here. What lame excuse do you have this time, boy?' Charles was standing by the door, arms crossed; a small tic below his right eye began to twitch.

'I asked him to join me, Charles. I needed to...'

He rounded on her, eyes bolting. 'Shut your mouth, woman,' he snarled, 'I didn't ask you to speak. The boy can answer for himself.'

'Steady on, Charles, it was me who chose to be here.' I eyed the chair. 'You wouldn't expect Patricia to move that by herself, would you? Not in her condition.'

The muscles in each side of his jaw flexed as he ground down on his teeth. 'Don't try to be clever with me, boy, you know very well you were idling.'

I saw red. 'And what if I was, Charles? Exactly what difference would it make?'

'A lot, considering the Nazis are almost upon us.' He jabbed a finger in my direction. 'And you should be taking every opportunity to put an end to their murderous ambitions, instead of acting like you've been gifted some sort of sabbatical.'

I was speechless. I had nowhere to go, no comeback, no historical memory to make a valid defence, and consequently, no excuse worth its salt. I glared at Charles. He was now wearing a ghost of a smirk, a man replete in conquest.

'You're operational next week, so you'd better get your act together, good men get themselves killed because of chancers like you. Do you understand me, boy?'

I nodded but said nothing. It was difficult not be emotionally disturbed by the way he tore into me, the words he used. Charles was good at that, an abuser honed to perfection. I looked at Patricia; she was staring out the window. It was easy to see how he bullied her into compliance. I did the only thing I could do. Leave. I looked over to Patricia. 'I'll be in my room if you need me.' A whisper of a nod was all she could give me; words could be dangerous, especially when used in front of a man like Charles.

I opened the door to my room and stared at the space inside. Impossible was a word I rarely used, but it was becoming one that accurately described this untenable situation I found myself. It was abundantly clear I was in an unending loop, fraught with twists, turns, forked roads, and blind alleys. I paused and shook my head; self-pity was getting me nowhere. I had to get back to level-headed thinking; William's operational status meant I had possibly dropped back to a week before William's "planned" abduction, and possible death. The necessity to find Charles' diary and hand it to the relevant authority, if it contained damning evidence, had become the imperative.

I wandered over to the window, resting my forehead on the cool glass, watching, but not seeing, the world in all its summer glory; if only there was another way. Charles was not acting alone, I knew that, but was he guilty, together with his father, Edmund, of singularly dispatching my great grandfather's brother and his wife, or were others involved in that too?

'Are you all right, Wills?' Her voice was comfortably familiar, but its suddenness still made me jump.

'It's me who should be asking that. Where's Charles?'

'He left about five minutes ago.'

'Do you know where he was going?'

Patricia shrugged. 'No, but he took the car.'

'You'd better come in and sit down, you're looking pale. Do you feel okay?'

'I'm not entirely sure. I feel like I'm about to explode,' she said, blowing out her cheeks. She carefully sat on the edge of the bed. 'I was all right until Charles, well, you know.'

I nodded sombrely. 'Did he say anything before he left?'

'He wanted me to iron his shirts before he got back.'

'Really? I thought Mrs Hughes did that sort of thing.'

'Not when Charles believes it's my wifely duty, she doesn't'

'I don't know how you put up with it.'

'I have no choice, especially now.'

I looked at her. 'You could leave him, file for divorce, claim maintenance for you and Sylvia. Find a place of your own.' I glanced round the room. 'This estate must be worth a small fortune; you must be at least entitled to half of it.'

I caught her eye; she was staring at me. 'What are you talking about, Wills? That's not how it works. I'd be on the streets with a flea in my ear, and you know it. We both would.'

I closed my eyes. She was right. The mid-twentieth century view of divorce and an equitable arrangement was dire if you were a woman. I allowed my emotions to run away with themselves. Patricia was not finished with me yet.

'And where did you get the name Sylvia from?' she snapped, 'I've never discussed anything like that with you.'

I shrugged. 'No idea, it was just a guess,' I lied. A change of subject was needed. 'If Charles is going to be out for a while, perhaps we should look for the diary.' I raised my eyebrows.

'I'm sorry, Wills, but looking for a blasted diary is the last thing on my mind at the moment. Anyway, why are you so interested in it? It's hardly going to change anything.'

'It might.'

She frowned. 'What do you mean?'

I took a deep breath; it was time to reveal a little of what I knew. This could be tricky. 'I think Charles had something to do with...er...our parent's disappearance, maybe worse. He could well have documented it. Charles is basically a bad man, Pattie, and would do absolutely anything to get what he wants. So if he has been up to no good, and it can be proved, there's a possibility he could go to prison for a very long time. You could then divorce him easily and assume control of the estate. Let's face it, Pattie, it should have been yours...I mean...ours anyway.'

Patricia didn't look as shocked as I thought she would. 'Is that what you really think, Wills, that Charles did away with our parents so he could get his hands on the estate.'

'Yes. Yes, I do. And I don't believe Charles acted alone.'

'But Father owed Edmund money and couldn't pay it back, so why would he need to?'

'I have no proof, but I have a feeling Alex...er...Father found the money he owed Edmund and was either about to, or in the process of paying it back. I think Edmund saw the prize of Althurian about to vanish before his eyes and decided to take matters into his own hands. He got the loan paid back *and* took the prize. It was win-win.'

Patricia was silent for a moment. 'Charles doesn't keep a diary, Wills. He calls it a journal and is as obsessed about writing in it as you are about finding it. I have no doubt it's full of things he'd rather not be made public. Where he keeps the current one, I have no idea.' She smirked. 'But I have an inkling to where he's hidden the old ones.'

'You do? How?'

'When we cleared out Mothers old room on the west wing, Charles became overprotective of an old iron chest she used to keep in there. He emptied it almost immediately and put it upstairs in the attic room. It has a key which he never lets it out of his sight.'

My eyes widened. 'We have an attic room?'

Patricia laughed for once. 'You are funny, Wills, it's where you used to hide from Mrs Hughes. Surely you haven't forgotten.'

'Ah, yes, I remember,' I lied, not too convincingly. 'That attic.'

Patricia arched her back a little, yawned, cupping a hand to her mouth. 'I'm sorry, Wills, I know this is important, but I think I need a little nap. We'll have to leave this for another time.' She slowly, and awkwardly, got to her feet, closing her eyes briefly while she took a breath; it looked a real effort. I suddenly had this impulse to rush across to her, possibly help in some way. I would have too, if my feet were able to unglue themselves from the floor. A tingling sensation began to slowly make its way up my spine. I too closed my eyes; I knew very well what was coming next.

Chapter 15
Discovery

Sparkles of light flickered in and out of my dark universe, seen not with my eyes, but with my mind; if that makes sense. I felt sublimely calm, almost devoid of fear, anxiety or even thought, itself. Only for a few seconds did this luxurious Zen like state last. My awakening was to be a most memorable experience.

'It won't take you more than a few minutes, John; I don't know why you're putting it off.'

I think I was looking in the direction of the vaguely familiar voice, it was difficult to tell. A messy, soup like image began to form as I blinked continually in an attempt to expedite whatever process was taking place. I wanted to answer, but had no idea what the questioner wanted, or was talking about; not that it mattered; speech was only one of a host of senses unavailable to me.

'John. Did you hear me?'

I slowly began to feel the aura of my body, its presence, its very being, and its place in the now. I took a sudden intake of breath and my vision returned in an instant; as did everything else. Skye was staring at me. I couldn't make up my mind if I wanted to laugh or cry. I looked down, in my hand a mobile phone, my mobile phone. I looked up and frowned. 'Larry,' I said. 'I...was about to phone Larry, wasn't I?'

'Well, I thought that was the idea,' she said.

'You were going to buy chocolate cake...and a barbecue.'

'Are you feeling all right, John? You're acting a bit weird.'

I pulled a face. 'I feel weird. Perhaps I need to sit down for a minute.' I shuffled to one of the wicker chairs and unceremoniously parked myself on it. I felt as if I'd been away from my own time for weeks, it was really odd ("my own time" is the only way I can describe my anchor with reality). She was staring at me, concerned, arms folded, and I didn't really know what to say to her.

'Has something happened to you, John?'

'There's almost too much to tell, and I don't know where to start.'

'From the beginning?' She raised her eyebrows. 'Shall I make us a coffee?'

'Love one. Sorry about this.'

She touched a finger to her lips. 'You don't need to say sorry; it'll only take a minute.'

I smiled as she disappeared into the kitchen; it was good to be back. I looked down at my phone and thought I really should call Larry. I could do with some help, even if some of it proved to be less than useful. But first, I needed to share my latest disjointed adventure while it was still fresh in my memory.

♦

She listened attentively, as I tried to relate this almost epic series of events I'd become part of; I'm sure there were gaps, there always was. When I'd finished, she looked totally shell-shocked, and it was hardly surprising.

'I can't believe this all happened to you in just a few seconds, John.'

'Neither can I.'

She stood up. 'I need another drink.' She paused. 'You'd better ring Larry.'

I sighed, picked up my phone, turning it over in my hand. 'I'm not sure if I can be bothered. I'd rather us talk some more.' I was beginning to miss her presence in my life. A lot.

'We can do that later, sweetie. You'll feel better once you've called him.'

'I know,' I said, gloomily tapping in his number. It rang twice before he answered.

'Morning, John,' he said cheerfully. 'Thanks for returning my call. You okay to chat for a few minutes?'

'Sure thing, Larry,' I lied. 'What have you got?'

'You remember I said the signal appeared to be carrying intelligent information, well, it was. Without getting too technical, I ran the results through a piece of software that kind of separates the wheat from the chaff.' He paused; I could hear his heavy, excited breath easily. 'Well I was right, it was modulated. At first I thought the equipment had somehow picked up a stray carrier wave from a local mast because of its sinusoidal nature, but after carefully evaluating the strength of the signal, and the sensors proximity to the two central monoliths it's pretty conclusive where the source was located. Isn't it fantastic?'

'Right.' He'd lost me. 'So, what does that actually mean? Can we...er...tune into it in some way?'

'Not sure yet. Have you heard of an Enigma machine? The Germans used them in the Second World War to send encrypted signals between their various military units.'

'Yes, Larry,' I said, trying not to roll my eyes, even though he couldn't see me. Skye came from the kitchen and placed our freshly refilled cups on the table; she sat on the chair opposite.

'Well, this signal is like that. It has information buried in there, but not in a form we can easily get at; if at all.'

I took a sip of coffee. 'Which leaves us where, Larry?'

'It means the source of the signal was created by an intelligence, John. Quite what form that takes we may never know, but we might, just might, discover its language. I'm picking up a piece of equipment from a friend of mine tomorrow. It's a kind of signal processor cum analytical computer that uses a sort of fractal algorithm to process data. I have a feeling we might get lucky.'

If I'm honest, I was a little disappointed, I had hoped for something more conclusive, proof that it wasn't all in my head; tangible evidence of an external force outside of my control. I needed something to blame. Still, there was always hope. 'Interesting,' I said. 'When will you know?'

'Day after tomorrow; it'll need at least twenty-four hours, maybe a little longer.' He paused. 'There's something else, John. About six years ago I was asked to check out a site near the Welsh border, can't remember the name, but it had a very similar electromagnetic characteristic to yours; nothing quite as dramatic mind, but close enough. While I was there, I met a guy from Edinburgh University, he was a researcher from an in-house parapsychology unit. He was investigating claims by locals who lived near the monument that it was causing them to have vivid dreams of past lives.'

I almost choked on my coffee. 'What did you just say?' I barked.

'Which bit?'

'Past lives?' I could feel my pulse suddenly quicken; it was doing that a lot lately.

'Right. Well, like Althurian, their houses, which were a mixed bag of properties from different ages, had been built fairly close to the site. According to the residents I spoke to, many, but not all, had suffered recurring lucid dreams of past lives. They were not on their own either, according to some, the area had a history of it. It was uncanny.'

I had to get a grip; this was too weird for words. 'This researcher, does he have a name?'

'Edward Fairchild.'

'Do you have a number for him?'

Larry chuckled. 'I thought you might ask that.'

'Why?'

'When I saw the similarity in the data, I had an idea you might want to talk to him.' He took another excited breath. 'Am I right in thinking something similar has happened to you?'

He was an astute observer, more than I gave him credit for. 'I'd like to say it wasn't true, Larry, but it is. Almost from the first day we set foot here.'

'Is it just you?'

'Mostly, it is. Skye, my partner, has had a couple of weird moments, though.'

'So, what kind of things have you and, er...Skye, experienced?'

The directness of the question threw me, and I felt exposed. I almost didn't want to tell him, although another part of me was desperate to share it, find common ground. Quite frankly, before Althurian, if I was listening to someone relating the same story, I'd probably conclude they were barking mad, or had some sort of pathological delusion disorder. I may have been pondering his question a little longer than I realised.

'Are you still there, John?'

'S-sorry,' I stammered.

'Well?'

'It's complicated, Larry.' I think he may have sensed my reluctance.

'I see.' Larry was silent for a moment. 'Listen, I'm speaking to Edward later, would you like me to set up a meeting with him. He might even want to visit the site.'

'Do you think he would?'

'Absolutely, Althurian is right up his street. You'll like him, John. Although he's a science grounded academic, he's one that thinks outside the box, willing to stick his neck out for the truth. Edward is also a local man, so it's not out of his way.'

'Okay, Larry, do it, and let me know what he says.'

♦

I stared at the phone before laying it down. Skye was right, I felt relieved, as if I'd been putting off making an appointment for the dentist. The Edward Fairchild connection was a result; I didn't realise parapsychology was a recognised academic subject. Skye was first to speak.

'Are we expecting another visitor?'

'How did you know?'

She tapped the side of her nose. 'Intuition, and a smidgen of deductive reasoning, Watson,' she said, coughing a laugh. 'When is he coming over?'

'You're too clever for your own good.' I laughed too. 'Soon, and he's bringing a friend.' I paused. 'Did you know we have an attic room?'

She narrowed her eyes. 'That was random, even for you?'

I sighed. 'Bear with me. Those Victorian travel chests, did either of them contain journals or dairies?'

She slowly shook her head. 'Not so far as I know, although there's still a pile of stuff in one of them; mostly paperwork and photos. Why?'

'Charles Forsyth kept a journal and he probably used a travel chest or trunk as an archive. I think those journals hold a significant number of secrets between their pages and finding them might explain a lot about what happened here.' I stretched my legs out, clasping my hands behind my head. 'I doubt if Charles had thought to dispose of them before his untimely disappearance, and if Patricia had overlooked their importance, then they could still be around somewhere.'

'I think it's highly unlikely Patricia overlooked anything.'

'I agree, but I doubt if she would have destroyed them.'

'Why not?' She raised an eyebrow. 'Family secrets can be dangerous.'

I shook my head. 'I still can't see it.'

She looked at me curiously. 'I suppose it could explain why Sylvia left everything to you?'

'Possibly.' I had a sudden thought: If I had really foiled Charles' attempt to have William removed, then why had I returned to Althurian and not back to my flat supping a glass of Shiraz? Life had become so full of imponderables. My train of thought was rudely interrupted by a loud knock at the front door. I scowled and glanced at my watch as if the intrusion was untimely. Skye spotted my irritation.

'Shall I get that?'

I got to my feet. 'No, it's okay.'

I ambled through the kitchen and into the hall. I was feeling back to my normal self, the return of memories from this space in time was almost complete. I opened the door. Outside, a smartly dressed, overly thin woman, possibly in her late sixties, stood with her arms folded, a small leather bag hanging from her shoulder; she was wearing the sort of expression one expects from someone who has been kept waiting. She spoke first.

'John Warrener I assume?'

Helpful as always, but never one to give too much away when asked something personal by a complete stranger, I asked, 'And you are?'

'Bridget Green,' she answered haughtily, 'Sylvia wrote to you about me.' She took a breath, straightened her shoulders, and lifted her chin. 'I was to be expected.'

I remembered the letter I'd found in the desk drawer. 'You were her friend,' I said, trying not to sound too incredulous; she wasn't exactly the sort of "friend" I was expecting.

Her face softened a little. 'Fifty-two years this November.'

'Really?' I stepped back from the doorway. 'Would you like to come in, Bridget?'

'Thank you,' she said, brushing past me with short, sharp steps, her heeled shoes clip clopping across the wooden floor. She stopped short at the interconnecting door and turned. 'Garden room, we always sat in the garden room, it was her favourite,' she said, matter of fact.

I puffed out my cheeks. This was going to be fun. 'Yes. Yes, of course. Be my guest.' I really couldn't be bothered to argue either way.

Without saying another word, Bridget sauntered through the doorway and disappeared into the kitchen. Skye was in for a surprise. By the time I got to the garden room, Bridget had already found a chair and was sat bolt upright, hands clasped neatly in her lap. Skye gave me an old-fashioned look and shrugged. I gathered Ms Green had decided not to introduce herself. I couldn't help thinking Sylvia was having a laugh at our expense. I took a deep breath.

'By the way, this is my partner, Skye Tolhurst.' I've no idea why I found it necessary to give her surname. Bridget was obviously carrying something infectious.

Bridget nodded in her direction. 'Pleased to make your acquaintance. Not wed, then?'

Skye looked at me wide eyed. 'Er...no...Not yet.'

'Would you like something to drink, Bridget,' I asked, hoping she had a penchant for alcohol, or some other drug of choice. Crystal Meth perhaps?

'Tea please, milk no sugar, and Earl Grey if you have any. Sylvia always kept Earl Grey.'

'I'll have a look for you, Bridget,' said Skye, giving me one of those "I need to talk to you NOW" expressions.

I chimed in. 'I'll give her a hand.' Yes, it was lame, I know that. In the kitchen, Skye pulled me to one side, her voice just above a whisper.

'Who on earth is that woman?'

'I think she was the friend Sylvia mentioned in her letter.'

'NO WAY,' she hissed.

I pulled a face. 'I may have let in the wrong one. Perhaps she'll go soon. Make the tea and I'll try to entertain her.'

Bridget hadn't moved, and still rigidly upright. She looked the sort of woman who should've owned a small, snappy dog and talked endlessly about bunions. I took the chair opposite and sat down.

'So, how did you and Sylvia meet?'

'I used to deliver groceries to Althurian on my bicycle. Father ran the local store in the village, you see.' She smiled for the first time. 'Sylvia liked cooking and was always in the kitchen helping the cook. She'd take the groceries from me and we used to talk, we had lots in common, being about the same age.'

I frowned. 'You were same age?'

Bridget nodded. 'Well, almost. Sylvia was twenty-five, I was twenty-two.'

'Well I never.' I was surprised; Bridget was certainly older than she looked. I decided to check if she really was the "friend" we were expecting. 'It must have come as quite a shock when Sylvia passed away.'

Bridget dropped her eyes, gazing at the floor. 'It was a terrible, terrible loss, but not totally unexpected.' She looked up, her eyes meeting mine; I saw real pain in them. 'Sylvia had been ill for some time, you know, kept it to her-self, told no one except for a few people. She wanted it that way, said she had important business to deal with before it became public. Sylvia was like that, secretive. Had to be, I suppose.'

'Had to be? Why do you say that?'

'She said dark forces were working behind the scenes, although she never revealed what they were. I used to think maybe she was imagining it.' She raised her neatly trimmed eyebrows. 'Suffering abuse from the very people you'd least suspect of doing such things didn't help.'

'Her father and stepfather?'

She nodded. 'You're very well informed.' She unbuckled her shoulder bag and began to rummage inside.

I watched with some amusement, her dyed auburn hair, tied in a bun, was almost as stiff as she was. I shook the image from my head. It was becoming clear Bridget *was* close to Sylvia, her earlier haughtiness possibly due to nerves. Even so, I was not prepared to share anything more than I had to. 'I need to see how Skye is getting on with the tea, I think she might have lost her way to the kettle.' I chuckled, getting to my feet. 'Excuse me for a minute.'

The kitchen was deserted, the kettle cold, and no attempt had been made to prepare tea, or anything else for that matter. I wandered into the hall and stood for a moment, it was silent, eerily so. 'Skye,' I called, where are you, love. Nothing. I went to the stairwell, looked up and called out again. 'Skye, where are you?' A light, warm breeze tickled the side of my face as if a door had been opened somewhere behind me; although I heard no sound. It was odd; she wouldn't have just wandered off without telling me, she just wouldn't. I made my way back to the kitchen, checked the kettle for water and switched it on. I found the Earl Grey teabags and popped two in the pot. I craned my neck back. 'Sorry about the wait, Bridget, it won't be long, I promise.' A featureless silhouette suddenly appeared within the doorway.

'Did you call me?'

The voice was unmistakable. 'Where have you been?'

Skye stepped into the kitchen wearing a frown. 'Where do you think?'

I lowered my voice. 'You were supposed to be making tea for Bridget.' I glanced over her shoulder, nodding in the direction of the garden room.

She inclined her head inquisitively, smiled and folded her arms. 'Would this be Bridget the Midget by any chance, because I haven't seen her for days?'

'What?' I glanced over her shoulder again. 'What are you talking about,' I hissed, terrified (yes, terrified!) Bridget had heard her.

'I went upstairs, found the travel chest and brought it down with me.' She raised an eyebrow. 'The journals? Charles Forsyth?'

'Yes. Yes. I hadn't forgotten,' I said, slightly miffed. At this point I hadn't quite grasped that a change had occurred; there were no signs, and for a brief moment I thought she was playing with me. Finally, reality caught up. I stared at her.

'I thought you were in the bathroom,' she said. 'Why did you call me Bridget?'

I smiled limply. 'It was meant as a joke,' I lied.

Her eyes narrowed. 'I wonder about you sometimes.'

'I wonder about myself.' A quick change of subject was needed; it was becoming another necessary habit. 'So, did you find the journals?'

'I was waiting for you.' Her expression changed to one of concern. 'Are you feeling okay?'

'I'm not sure.' I'd suddenly become nauseous but didn't want to worry her. It wasn't a good sign. 'I think I need some fresh air. Would you mind making a start without me?'

'Of course not. Are you sure you'll be all right on your own?'

'I'll try not to get lost; I promise. I won't be long.'

♦

It was still warm outside, the sun a little higher than I remembered; my last visit to the garden seemed a lifetime ago. This need to be outside was unusually strong; not the suffocating need for space, but an urge to be somewhere else, and not knowing where. I took a deep lungful of fragrant air and started in the direction of the treeline. I reached the gate, which again, was open, and followed the path through to the stones. I was surprised the route, unlike everything else lately, had not changed. I experienced an unexpected lift in my mood as I wandered slowly across the centre of the circle. I closed my eyes, clasped my hands together, and stood motionless; waiting. It didn't take long. The temperature changed, dropping suddenly, not enough to feel cold, but enough to notice. I continued to keep my eyes closed, feeling the world round me with a kind of sixth sense. Suddenly, I knew deep within my core why I was there, why I had come, and where I was destined to go. I took a deep breath and opened my eyes.

I looked round, the landscape had changed radically; gone were the trees, manicured lawns, and flower beds, and finally, the place called Althurian. Everything had simply vanished. Instead, a smooth panorama of undulating wild grassland punctuated with clumps of gorse was all that was left. Strangely, I felt at home, at peace in this barren world, a world without pain, greed, and torment.

'You have returned.' Becket was standing next to one of the taller monoliths; he had an aura of serenity about him.

I smiled; I was relieved to see him. 'I believe I'm here for a reason, Julius.'

'Yes. The Celopea is finally within you, and is now permanent, with you always.'

'Yes. I can feel it.' And I could; not that I could point to anything specific.

He nodded sagely, like he knew. 'At times it will be a burden, a burden of great suffering, at others, a prize beyond imagination.'

'Why has this gift been given to me?'

'You were chosen, John. To question why is immaterial, a valueless concept. A child has the gift of speech but has to learn to talk. We do not have to ask why this is so, it just is. Your destiny was written long ago and cannot be changed. In time, you will understand this.'

It was another cringe worthy platitude, but I kind of understood where he was coming from. 'Where has Althurian gone?'

'Only time has changed, John. Your place in the universe hasn't. Althurian is still here, just not of this century. Time is rigid, you are fluid, remember this. As I have said before, you may not always have a choice to where your presence is required, but you do have a choice as to what you do. There will be challenges ahead, challenges that will test your ability to endure hardship. Know this.'

I was beginning to think Becket had spent too much time on his own, dreaming up riddles for gullible time travellers like me. Yes, I was a time traveller, albeit a reluctant one. I knew sooner or later Becket was going to tell me my time was running out, and I had one question that was bugging me: one that had to be voiced. 'May I ask you something, Julius?'

He smiled. 'It is your privilege.'

'Why do I end up in William's body, or his head, or his mind, or whatever you want to call it?'

I saw him pause and take a long, slow breath; no doubt deliberating his answer. 'Each soul requires a vessel, an anchor in which to live a functioning, practical existence on this earth. Without it, we can only exist in the ethereal. At times it is possible to replace one soul with the spirit of another.' He paused again. 'Each soul has a unique signature, and some are almost identical, identical enough to allow a degree of joint stewardship. I saw his expression change, that almost imperceptible glance to a place I could not see; our time was nearly up. He raised a hand.

'Until we meet again, John, take care.'

I nodded. Something inside me knew this was how it was meant to be. I closed my eyes and heard the sound of machinery somewhere distant, the chirrup of birdsong, and the familiar creak and rustle of the trees. I was back.

♦

The walk to the house, climbing the incline, was easier than I remembered it; my feet light, and my leg muscles remarkably tireless. I could see Skye sitting in the garden room busily sifting through some papers on her lap. It appeared I had returned to my own time. She looked up and smiled.

'You were quick,' she said. 'How are you feeling now?'

'Much better. Any luck?'

She shook her head. 'No, but I did find these,' she said, holding up several cards with small photographs attached to each of them. 'I think you'll find these properties are part of the Althurian estate.'

I took them from her. They looked as if they belonged to a manual filing system. Each one had a photograph of a property, an address, a brief description, when it was bought, a value, and a unique reference number. I looked up. 'What makes you say that?'

'I found invoices for maintenance work carried out on each of them. They were signed off as paid by Sylvia Forsyth. Looks like you have your hands full, John.'

There were five of these cards, one had a black and white photograph, the other four were colour, and almost all were bought in the late eighties. Each looked a sizeable lump of real estate, and one in particular caught my eye. I held it up for her to see. 'One with a sea view. Nice.'

'I saw that. Not far from here either. Fifty miles or so.'

Something inside of me wanted to jump in the car and go. The thought of unfinished business kept me from doing so. I flipped through the rest, checking off the details; nothing seemed to suggest the properties were occupied. I was about to hand them back when I noticed a small hand drawn symbol in the bottom-left corner of the one I'd just held up: it looked like three scrolls with their ends tied at the centre, sort of club shaped. 'What do make of that?'

'It's called a Triskele, John, a Celtic symbol.' She pulled a face. 'Odd thing to doodle on an index card.' She chuckled. 'They must have been bored.'

I was always impressed by her knowledge of such things; travelling the length and breadth of the country helped, I guess. 'It seems familiar somehow. Any idea what it means?'

'Not a clue, but you can find carvings of them all over the place. There's even one at Newgrange.'

'I thought Newgrange was Neolithic.'

'It is. I think the Celts borrowed the pattern and made it their own. Most people recognise it as Celtic though.' She inclined her head. 'Now you come to mention it, it does look familiar.' She tapped the card with a finger. 'I'm sure I've seen this recently.' She jumped up and padded towards the kitchen. 'Won't be a sec.'

I half expected the world to change when she disappeared and was relieved when I heard the hall door slam. When she returned, she was grinning and had her hands behind her back. 'Guess what I've found?'

I touched a finger to my lips. 'Now let me see.'

'Close your eyes and hold out your hand.'

I complied with a chuckle. 'You are such a child sometimes.'

'I know.'

I felt whatever it was tickle the palm of my hand. I opened my eyes. What I saw was unexpected, and a sharp intake of breath caught the back of my throat. I was holding a small disc shaped pendant on a gold chain. William had been the true recipient, but the emotion brought on by this gift from Patricia suddenly overwhelmed me.

'A Triskele amulet,' she said. 'Spooky eh?'

'Patricia gave this to William. It was to help keep him safe.'

'You didn't tell me.'

I smiled limply. 'It slipped my mind. There was a lot going on at the time. Strange it found its way back here; I thought it might have passed down to his children.' I saw a frown appear across her smooth, unlined face; the reason hadn't occurred to me.

'Children? William had children?'

I nodded. A boy and a girl. And a granddaughter.'

'Hang on a minute; this is not something you've shared with me.' I spotted a ghost of indignation. 'Are you sure about this?'

I gave her an old-fashioned look. 'Yes,' I said. 'Of course, I am.' Her challenge was immediate; she should have been a lawyer.

'Then why did Sylvia leave the entire estate to you?'

She had a point. Possibly I'd slipped into a world with an entirely different outcome. I responded the only way I could. I shrugged. 'Can't answer that.' And it was the truth, I couldn't. 'Anyway, we've found a connection. Perhaps they adopted the Triskele as a family symbol.'

'You said Patricia gave it to him.'

I nodded and frowned. 'Yes.'

'Then perhaps William and the property have something in common. Maybe he used to live there. Maybe he still does.'

I laughed. 'He'd be nearly a hundred years old.'

'It's possible.'

'Yes, but unlikely. His kids might though.'

'We could always drive over there.' She grinned and held up a string of keys, each with a separate label. 'We can even check it out if it's empty.'

At first this seemed like a crazy idea, a spontaneous waste of time considering how little we knew of Althurian. A little voice inside my head was telling me different, and Skye's enthusiasm for adventure wasn't helping. 'How far did you say this place was?'

Chapter 16
Persons Unknown

For once, nothing out of the ordinary had happened since my last visit to the stones, an event in itself. We forego the barbecue and bought some easy food we could throw in the oven. However, Skye insisted on the bottle of Australian Shiraz, and it would have been rude not to share it with her. We turned in early and slept like babies. We left the next morning after a lazy wake up, and an even lazier breakfast. This overly relaxed state probably explained why I forgot my watch.

A decision was made to take the Aston. Hang on; allow me to correct that statement. Skye unilaterally decided we should take it; I was still smarting from the two hundred pounds plus I'd already spent filling it up and was more than happy to take the Toyota. I have to say though, it was good to get back behind the wheel; although I wasn't so sure how long that joy would last, I could already feel those envious eyes boring into the side of my head the moment I slumped into the driver's seat.

The journey took a little over two and a half hours; rubbish map reading on my part, lack of road signage (for a moment I thought I was back in wartime Britain), and that all-pervasive enemy, heavy traffic, slowed us down considerably. A narrow, and thankfully deserted, coastal road wound its way through the rocky, partially grass covered terrain to the sleepy hamlet of Tynsly Farn; the turning to the cottage almost hidden by a dense thicket on either side of it. We pulled up well before the front gate and just stared for a while, not saying a word. It was difficult to tell if it was occupied or not. Sharply rendered in smooth, white painted concrete, this singular detached property in the middle of nowhere looked out of place. Perched not more than a hundred yards from a cliff edge, it had an unobstructed view of the sea and surrounding countryside. It was the product of a whim, and eccentricity was written all over it. At first glance it appeared to have been well maintained, showing none of the tell-tale signs of neglect.

We decided to leave the car where it was and walk. Aware that the cottage could be occupied, although we hadn't found anything to suggest it was, we tried not to make ourselves look too obvious as we casually sauntered past the gate. Actually, it probably didn't look casual at all, as we were both craning our necks in an attempt to peer through the windows at the same time. Skye leaned her head close to mine. 'It looks empty to me,' she whispered from the corner of her mouth.

'Shall we walk a little farther before we turn back?' Always one to err on the side of caution. Skye, as usual, had a different plan.

'Sod it. Why don't we just knock on the bloody door?'

I smiled limply and tutted. Of course, that was the most sensible approach; I just wished I had thought of it. I bowed slightly, sweeping my hand in an arc. 'After you, M'lady.'

Everything appeared to be in a fairly decent condition. Even so, I had to lift the gate a little before it would open. The lawn, the two square patches of grass either side of the entrance path, looked as though it needed a cut; not enough to be viewed as a sign of disuse though. As we approached the door, Skye had already removed the key from her waist bag. There was no bell push, only a large ornamental door knocker in the shape of a lion's head. I gave it two sharp raps and listened. For some peculiar reason I expected to hear a dog bark. Silence. I rapped again. Skye had wandered over to the window and had her nose pressed against the glass.

'It's still furnished,' she said, 'but looks empty, if that makes sense. Why don't we let ourselves in anyway?'

I winced. 'I'm not keen on doing that. I'd be really pissed if someone let themselves into the flat without my knowledge.'

'But you own it, John. You can do what you like with it.'

'Not if it's rented out. In the eyes of the law it's trespassing, and we'd need a court order.'

'But we don't know if it is.'

'True.' I sighed. 'We still have to be careful, though.'

'We could plead ignorance.'

'Ignorance of the law isn't a defence; you should know that.'

She gave me a sideways glance and giggled. 'I wanted to be sure you did. Are we going in or not?'

I took a deep breath, arguing was pointless when up against overwhelming odds. 'I suppose so. But I'll blame you if the boys in blue turn up.'

♦

Our earlier debate had proved a fruitless exercise once inside. Despite its well-maintained exterior, it was evident the property had not been occupied for some considerable time; a sizeable collection of post lay strewn across the floor, some jamming under the door as it opened. In the hall, next to the stairs, an equally large pile of dusty, unread post sat on an equally dust covered chair; in fact, the whole place looked as though it had been the victim of a dust storm. Abandoned grey cobwebs hung drearily from every corner, shelf, and door head, and the whole place had a damp, musty, empty of life smell about it.

We tiptoed, both experiencing the need to respect this undiscovered space, from the hall to the first of two reception rooms; a large, box square room with a relatively high ceiling, and clearly once a dining area. It was stacked high with cardboard boxes of various sizes, and had a rectangular, smoked glass table, and four tubular chrome chairs set to one side; a piece of furniture reflecting the decade of its purchase.

Skye peeked in one of the boxes, pushing up a cover flap with her finger. 'Looks like someone was moving out.'

I joined her. 'Or moving in?'

She shook her head. 'I doubt it somehow. Nothing written on them, not even a name and address.'

Most of the boxes contained books, some held old newspapers, others, knick-knacks and ornaments. Nothing, as far as I could see, alluded to an owner. Yet. The next room was undoubtedly used as a study, complete with a seventies must have: the ubiquitous roll-top writing bureau.

Skye let out a hoot. Quite frankly, the suddenness of it made me jump. 'If we'd bothered to look at the post, we wouldn't be having this conversation.'

I sighed. It was obvious, wasn't it? No, really it was. We wandered back to the hall and picked up a handful each. Finding a clean place to sit was a challenge, so we chose to stand instead. Most of the letters were addressed to the occupier, or lacked any sort of title, or chancer post as my dad used to call them. The rest, as you have probably guessed, were circulars and bin trash. Only two of the envelopes were addressed fully. I scooped another handful from the floor and continued.

Skye held up her batch and pulled a face. 'One here for a Mr G Garennier, the rest are rubbish.'

'Yep, two here have the same name.'

'Maybe we should open them up, see who this guy is.'

I winced again. 'I'm not entirely comfortable with that.'

'You are a wuss, John.' She laughed. 'Look, if it makes you feel any better, why not think of it as a kindness. All this stuff belongs to someone, and we have a duty to find them and return it. We can only do that if we know who this fella is. And we can only do that by.' She raised her eyebrows and smirked.

I stared at her, nodding glumly. 'Yeah, okay.' I knew she had a point. I couldn't help feeling a little disappointed. I was sure William had been here.

'Cheer up; this had to be done at some stage. It might as well be now rather than later. Anyway, you never know what we might find.'

♦

It would've helped if we had electricity to boil a kettle, not that we had tea bags or milk without finding a shop first. I thought it had been turned off at the fuse box until I noticed the cables from the meter had been disconnected and the main fuse removed. An act of vandalism I thought, especially when one needs a brew; it was just as well we still had daylight. Before starting this letter opening endeavour, we decided to first explore the rest of the house.

Apart from the front room, which looked the most habitable, everywhere else was in various stages of disassembly; it was evident Mr Garennier had been interrupted before he had finished packing. Very little, if any, personal information was present; even the boxes we found in the study only contained empty lever arch files, and some unused stationary. We returned to the hall and gathered up the rest of the mail and headed back to the front room. I noticed earlier the sofa had a cover draped over it, and once removed, even though the upholstery felt a little damp, was a comfortable perch to begin our investigations.

Skye said, 'I could murder a glass of wine.'

I looked up. 'Well, you've certainly murdered enough of those in your time.'

She stuck her tongue out. 'I didn't realise you were keeping a tally.' Her expression changed suddenly. 'You'll never guess this guy's Christian name.'

I half smiled. 'Graham?'

'Very funny. It's Gulielmus.'

'What?' I chuckled. 'What sort of name is that?'

'Sounds Roman to me.'

'Emperor Gulielmus, eh?'

'Well, it definitely has a Latin ring to it. Have you found anything yet?'

'I might have,' I said, resting a small clutch of papers on my lap; I had removed them from an official looking brown envelope. It had been sent by the firm of solicitors, Ashton & Tobias of Harwick. It was an odd read.

Farthing Cottage
Seaview Croft
Tynsly Farn
Northumberland

Dear Mr G Garennier

I hope this letter finds you well.
In response to our recent telephone conversation, and further to your instructions, I have today, May 2nd, 2014, written to Parminter and Simpson concerning the disputed ownership of Althurian Manor. I have issued a twenty-eight-day limitation to the order and indicated that we will be applying for a First-tier Tribunal hearing if this notice is ignored by their client. Hopefully, it won't come to this and an out of court settlement can be agreed.

Yours Sincerely

Steve Ashton

I handed it to her before casting an eye over the other papers. A line drawn diagram showing Althurian and the estate, which was huge, far larger than I had realised, and a section from an Ordinance Survey map indicating its geographical position within the surrounding countryside. No mention of Sylvia or any other name I recognised. Clearly, this Garennier character believed he had a claim, and Ashton & Tobias were going along with it.

She looked up. 'Whoever this fella is, he's pretty chummy with his solicitor. Never known one to ask about my health before, and he signed off as Steve.' She frowned. 'Did Parminter mention a dispute to you?'

'I'm sure I would've remembered if he had. I'm clutching at straws, but maybe his family owned Althurian before the Warrener's and there were historical irregularities with the legal title.'

'Can't see how he'd get away with a claim like that. Not after so long.'

'It was just a thought.'

'Could it have been used as security? It was once.'

'I doubt it, but who knows? This was written two years before Sylvia's death so it must have been resolved by now, surely.'

She snorted a laugh. 'Perhaps Sylvia had him abducted by aliens. Job done.'

I laughed but had a feeling the facts may turn out to be even stranger than the fiction; the man had disappeared leaving most of his possessions behind. 'He could have been sent to prison. Perhaps he was trying to scam Sylvia and got found out.'

'It's interesting he was one of her tenants.' She stared at me. 'What are you going to do, John?'

'I don't know. Unless he was a squatter, which I doubt, Sylvia must have known about him. There's probably a record of his tenancy somewhere and possibly in one of those boxes back at Althurian.' I paused. 'I suppose I could always ring Steve Ashton and ask him for a forwarding address, perhaps even a phone number.'

'Good luck with that.' She raised her eyebrows. 'Client confidentiality?'

'He could pass a message to him.' I grinned. 'Or we could find a pub. It worked the last time.'

She snorted. 'What are you talking about?'

'The Jolly Archer? Gerry Phillips and the news article?'

The penny dropped. 'Yes! James Dixon.'

'It's worth a try.'

'You just want a drink.'

'I know, but so did you earlier.'

'Damn, you're good.'

♦

We gathered up the remaining unopened post and left two neat piles on the sofa, one for each of us; we had every intention of finishing the task the moment we got back. A chilly south easterly breeze met us as we emerged from the cottage. Tynsly Farn was less than a mile away, and larger than the name "Hamlet" suggested. To be honest, I was doubtful it had a pub, and surprised when one came into view. The Viking was not the largest drinking house I'd ever visited; in fact, it was probably the smallest, perhaps reflecting the surrounding population. A building no bigger than a detached, three-bedroom family home, and probably why it wasn't heaving with patrons. Its white, rendered exterior, vaguely similar to Farthing Cottage, and every other building we passed, was clean and bright, as if it had only just received a lick of paint. There was no car park and we had to pull up in the road opposite.

Skye peered through the passenger side window. 'Cosy little place, eh?'

I chuckled. 'And a hive of gossip, I'd lay money on it.'

We entered through the front door and walked directly into the saloon; a lobby would clearly have used up too much drinking space! We counted only five wooden tables, each with two chairs. An attempt had been made to make the experience a little more comfortable by the casual placement of several padded seat covers (upholstered would have been overdoing the description a bit), to which we laid claim as soon as they were spotted; as an added bonus the table we chose was next to a glowing coal fire. The place was empty apart from two haggard looking individuals propping up the bar, glass in hand; they appeared to care not of our entrance and continued to silently stare at a space above the beer pumps. We smiled at each other and sat down. Skye was the first to speak, leaning forward as if to share a secret.

'Friendly here, innit,' she said mockingly.

I glanced over her head; I'd bagged the chair closest the fire. 'Hopefully, neither of them is the owner, or my cunning plan is in ruins.'

She scoffed. 'You had a plan?'

'I might have,' I said, feigning indignation. I was just about to extol the virtues of gossip and its place in an

English village pub when we heard a shuffling, heavy footed sound coming from somewhere behind the bar; the source, and its location, unclear. Suddenly, a disembodied voice called out.

'Wull, Ah canny find it, Jimmy. Ye musta taken it back with ye.'

'Impossible, you can't be lookin' in the right place, Cameron,' answered one of the men from our side of the bar. 'I knows where I left it.' He finally glanced in our direction and rolled his eyes. We both smiled and nodded automatically and had no idea why.

'Wull, come an' have a look fer ye-self then.'

The man glanced at us again and winked. 'I will, but you'd better come up an' do some serving, Cameron. You have customers up 'ere, an' they look mighty thirsty to me.'

Within seconds, a head bobbed up from behind the bar, and a man of about sixty, round faced with an untidy mop of thinning, salt and pepper hair, fixed us with a look of some amazement, and the mystery behind his disembodiment was soon to be revealed. After several more heavy footsteps, the man, who we assumed to be Cameron, and the landlord, appeared in full stature. A hidden trapdoor to the cellar was responsible. He gave us a wave.

'Ah'll be with ye as soon as Ah wash ma hands, Ah wull.'

I gave a little wave back. 'Seems friendly enough.'
'And a Scott no less.'
'Well, we are only ten miles from the border.'
'What are you going to ask him, John?'

I shrugged. 'I hadn't thought that far ahead. He might get a little suspicious if I ask him outright about Garennier. He doesn't know us from Adam.'

'You could just tell him the truth. Tell him that you've taken over Farthing Cottage and you're trying to locate the previous tenant because he left some of his gear behind. There you go, sorted.'

'Now, what canny Ah be gettin' ye?'

I jumped slightly; Cameron had been a lot quieter walking across the floor than he was clumping up the cellar stairs. 'Yes. Sorry.' I glanced at Skye and raised my eyebrows. 'Shall we have a coffee?'

'I thought you wanted a real drink.'

'Okay, if I must.' I grinned. 'You'll have to drive back though.'

'Ha! That'll teach me to open my mouth.'

I turned back to the landlord, who was by now looking slightly bemused. 'May I have a pint of Guinness and an Americano for the lady, please.'

'Would ye be eatin?'

'Not yet, thank you, not at the moment.'

'Right ye are.' He hesitated. 'Not from round 'ere, are ye?'

I smiled limply, I felt like a fraud. 'I've...er...we've taken over Farthing Cottage.' I pointed in the general direction. 'Up on the hill.'

Cameron frowned. 'Tha knoll ye mean?'

'I suppose so.' I had no idea what he meant. 'Seaview Croft.'

'Goatee's auld place?'

I shrugged, pulling a face. 'I only know of a Mr Garennier.'

'Aye, Goatee.'

'Right, Goatee.' I paused. 'You know him, then?'

'Aye. Once.'

It was my turn to frown. 'Once?'

'Aye, Ah did before he took a tumble.' His head rocked sombrely from side to side. 'Och, terrible business, it were.'

'What do you mean?'

'They found him on tha shoreline, below Chilworth Crag.'

I was shocked, and it showed. 'He's dead?'

'Aye. Deed as a doore nail.'

As I gathered my thoughts, Skye, who seemed to take these sort of things in her stride, chipped in. 'Do you know if he had any relatives?'

Cameron stroked his chin. 'Och, not that Ah can remember, lassie. Mostly kept hisself to hisself, he did.'

'What *do you* know about him?' I asked, a hint of frustration bubbling up behind the words. Skye gave me a sidelong glance, attuned to my impatience.

'Been 'ere as long as Ah have. Longer maybe, Aye. Knew he'd been fightin' some legal battle over some property or other.'

The two men had now leant their backs against the bar and had begun to take notice of our conversation; one in particular had not touched his pint since we started and was the first to speak. 'There are some of us round here who think he was bumped off.'

I looked across at him. 'Why do you say that?'

'We had some strangers turn up, looking for him. Next day he was found dead.'

Skye asked, 'When was this?'

'Couple of years back.'

I said, 'I assume there was an investigation.'

'The police said his death was accidental, slipped and fell, so they say. Can't see it myself, nor others that knew him. Goatee knew this coastline better than those born here.'

'He lived here a while, then?'

'Forty years, some say.'

'How old was...er...Goatee?'

The man shrugged. 'No idea, but he was getting on a bit.'

Then the other man at the bar spoke. 'Must have been in his eighties, I reckon. Sprightly fella too, kept himself fit. We were all shocked when we heard the verdict.'

I tried a long shot. 'Was he much of a talker?'

'Not about himself. Mostly about the world: politics, that sort of thing. Though, he did have a thing about old ruins, and weird mystical stuff.' He gave a derisory laugh. 'Woo-woo nonsense, mainly.'

My ears pricked up. 'What sort of nonsense...um...I mean...mystical stuff?'

'Magical powers, the ability to cure the sick, curses, and old wives tales. You name it, Goatee believed it. Don't get me wrong, I liked the fella, but he did have some strange ideas. He even thought there were these ancient stones somewhere in England, I can't remember where now. He reckoned they could send you back in time.'

I stared at him wide eyed. My mouth could have been open, and I think Skye's might have been too.

He lifted his pint to his lips. 'Yeah, exactly, weird stuff.'

'A pint of Guinness an' a coffee for tha wee lassie.' I had been so engrossed in the conversation I had missed Cameron's absence. He placed our order on the table, stepping back with his hands on his hips. 'Come ta think of it, Ah think Goatee had a niece, but Ah canny be sure.'

♦

Cameron returned to the bar, disappearing through a door to the side and the two men had gone back to wordlessly staring at the optics. It was almost as if the conversation had never happened. We finished our drinks and left soon after. This time, both men bid us farewell before continuing their vigil. We crossed the road in silence, not speaking until we were both inside the Aston. Skye, of course, was driving.

I puffed out my cheeks. 'Althurian, standing stones, and time travel. I rolled my head from side to side to release the tension in my neck. 'We need to go through the rest of that post, there's more to the mysterious Mr Garennier than we thought.'

'And he has a niece.'

I nodded. 'Strange she didn't pick up any of his stuff.'

'Maybe she's not with us anymore. It depends how long ago Garennier told Cameron about her.'

'True.'

'You up for a thought experiment?'

'Go on.' After a pint of Guinness had hit my empty stomach, I was willing to listen to anything.

'If Garennier had anything to do with Althurian, William might have known about him. Yes?'

I nodded. 'I guess so.'

'Well, if he was in his eighties, that makes him a little older than Sylvia. Could they have been married, or perhaps a couple at some point? Perhaps he lent her some money and she reneged on the debt.'

I laughed. 'And she hired contract killers to take him out.'

'Stranger things have happened. Althurian is a lot to lose; the threat of penury makes people desperate.'

I screwed up my face. 'I've just inherited an absolute fortune, and Althurian is just a small part of it; most of it old money. Sylvia, by my reckoning, has never had to borrow money in her life.' I paused thoughtfully. 'I suppose they could have had a relationship though. Anyway, what has that got to do with William?'

'If he did know Garennier, possibly you have a latent memory of him.'

'It doesn't work that way, love. I'd actually have to meet him for myself. Listen, we could sit here all day discussing what we don't know. Time better spent going through the rest of that post.'

'I know, but you can't beat a bit of wild speculation, can you?'

'Ha, we're getting good at that!'

♦

As we approached the turning for the cottage, we noticed a heavy band of dark storm clouds gathering over the North Sea. I guessed we had less than a couple of hours before the lack of useful light would make it impossible to see much of anything. We pulled up outside, and yes, I did check the glove box and boot for a torch!

Skye looked across to me as we emerged from the car. 'We could take the post back to Althurian. That just leaves the boxes.'

'I should have thought of that.'

She laughed. 'It's because you're an academic and I'm a practical thinker.'

I had a feeling she was right, not that I'd admit to it. 'Is that so. Then you can choose where we start. Upstairs or downstairs?'

'Upstairs. The windows are higher, and we can make the most of the light.'

My eyes narrowed and I tried not to laugh. 'Did you just make that up?'

'Of course, I did.' She giggled this time. 'And before I do that, and to prove my practical thinking prowess, I'll see if I can find us some candles for later on.'

'Good luck.'

♦

The cottage was colder than either of us expected; sitting by an open fire and driving back in a warm car didn't help. Skye yawned, extending her arms in a cat like stretch. 'Sod the candles, I could easily curl up and go to sleep. It's a pity the beds are so minging.' She hung the car keys on a hook by the front door, stood back and inclined her head. 'You could do with one of those in your flat. I've lost count how many times we've been late because you've lost your keys.'

I rolled my eyes. 'I'll bear it in mind.'

Chapter 17
The Bluff

There were five rooms upstairs, including a separate toilet and bathroom. All were furnished; even the beds were made up. Each room had a compliment of boxes, some full, some empty, and some just started; one of the rooms even had a large suitcase lying on the bed. The boxes were little different to the one's downstairs; almost all the items contained in them were carefully wrapped in newspaper or old towels. It was obvious this had been done by someone who intended to stay in the land of the living. As we stood on the landing debating who was going to do what, I found myself staring at the suitcase. It looked vaguely familiar, and I'd already decided where I was about to start.

It had seen a bit of life. A shabby, dark brown colour, scuffed in places, with one of its corner protectors missing; it was not of this century, for that I was certain. The catches opened easily, flipping up with a reassuring click. I hesitated before lifting the lid, I was hoping to find a photograph, or even better, one with a name on it; something tangible to identify the enigmatic Mr Garennier. What I found was a suitcase full of neatly folded clothes. I caught the faint, woody smell of camphor as the lid flopped back onto the bed, and a surprisingly familiar smell. I stared at the smooth woollen and cotton fabrics, the colours, their distinct antiquity; these were not modern clothes.

Rather than empty the contents out, I dug my hands down the inside of the case, feeling for anything other than garments. I found nothing. I stood back and looked round with the hope that maybe where there was one suitcase, there might be another. I checked under the bed and looked inside the walnut veneered Art Deco wardrobe standing in the corner, even on top of it, and still found nothing. It was only when my eyes settled back to the one on the bed, something caught my eye, the ribbed hem of a burgundy woollen jumper. I was about to pull the rest of it out when Skye popped her head round the door.

'Found anything?'

'Old clothes mostly. You?'

She held out a grubby polythene bag full of candles, and an equally tatty box of matches. 'Let there be light.' She laughed. 'They were under the kitchen sink.'

'Not a moment too soon by the look of it,' I said, glancing out the window.

'And guess what I found in the toilet?'

I screwed up my face. 'I'm not sure I want to know.'

She snorted. 'No, nothing like that, you fool. An old newspaper, it was on the window sill. I thought for a minute it might have something newsworthy like the one Gerry gave you. But it was just full of war stuff.'

I stared at her. 'What sort of war stuff?'

'Honestly, it has nothing in it worth looking at. You can see for yourself if you like.'

'I will, if you don't mind.'

She grinned. 'You are funny sometimes.'

As she left the room to fetch it, the hairs on the back of my neck began to prickle. I thought for a second, I was about to travel. I was feeling odd. I glanced at the suitcase, the clothes, and especially the jumper. Yes, it all felt very odd.

'Here it is,' she said, handing it over.

I gasped. The headline on the yellowing front page was enough.

GRAF SPEE BEGINS TO WEIGH ANCHOR.

My eyes turned directly to the date: Monday 18th December 1939. The eerie feeling had been replaced by a cold, clammy sweat.

'You okay?'

I looked up, pressing a finger to the paper. 'I've seen this before. I've touched this, picked it up, read these headlines.' I knew I was rambling but couldn't help myself. I took a long, deep breath to calm myself down. 'The confrontation with Charles, the one I had before I rang Janice Bergan.' I was now babbling. 'When Patricia announced she was pregnant. This was the paper I...'

Skye made a soothing gesture with her hands. 'Slowly, John, slowly.'

'Sorry.' I took another breath. It was strange relating a life she had no knowledge of. 'Patricia gave me this before going to see Janice's mother.'

She smiled placatingly. 'It could just be another copy, John. I'm pretty sure they printed more than one; thousands, in fact.'

I couldn't argue with the logic. Then I remembered something and handed it back to her; I couldn't bring myself to look. 'The back page, j-just look at the back page,' I jabbered impatiently. I knew very well what she was about to find.

She cursorily examined the paper and pulled a face. 'War news, an ad for biscuits, and one to say Marsh ham is off the menu for Christmas. It was obviously important at the time, but what has this got to do with you.'

'The quick crossword,' I hissed. 'The answer to one across is "Mail". I wrote that. I saw her eyes drop to the bottom of the page, pause, then look up, her expression was one of incredulity.

'You did this?'

'William…or me.'

'It wasn't a dream?'

'No,' I said, 'it wasn't.'

'So why is it here? How did Garennier get hold of it?'

I gave a sideways glance towards the suitcase. 'I haven't even the beginnings of a clue.' I paused. 'He certainly had a connection to Althurian, and it was more than just a passing interest because he saw a profit in it. No. This is something else.' At that very second, a peculiar tingling sensation swept from the soles of my feet, up through my legs, streaming into my body as if a switch had been thrown, I thought I was about to pass out until my grip on reality came back in a rush. Skye seemed not to have noticed.

'I loved storms when I was a kid; the louder and heavier the better. Dad used to hate them. He was worried about the roof, the gutters, whether we'd be flooded, that sort of thing.' She shook her head, solemn suddenly. 'It's a strange world, isn't it?'

My brow furrowed, my head still a little woolly. I thought I caught the sour smell of spent alcohol. 'I-I'm not sure I'm with you.' I chuckled for no apparent reason. 'What changed his mind?'

She glared at me. 'It isn't funny, John,' she said, her voice breaking. I saw a small tear travel down her cheek, dropping silently onto the carpet. 'I miss them terribly, and all you can do is laugh.'

'What?' I raised my hands defensively; this reaction was completely out of the blue. 'I had no idea you were missing them so much. Sorry, love.' I paused to gather my thoughts. 'Listen, why don't you drive back in the morning? Check they're okay and come back in a couple of days. You can take the Aston if you like; let your dad have that blast around the block.'

She put a hand to her mouth, her eyes weirdly accusing. 'What are you talking about, John?'

I sighed. 'Take the Aston, drive back to Faversham, spend a couple of days with your parents, more if you like, and come back when you're ready.' I grinned. 'I'm sure I can fend for myself for a few nights.'

She looked away. 'I need some air,' she mumbled.

I was a little taken aback. 'Okay. Perhaps we ought to finish up here and go back to Althurian.'

'You can do what you like, I'm going for a walk,' she growled.

'What...now?'

She turned without saying a word and stomped off; a few seconds later I heard the front door slam. It was bizarre, out of character, and downright puzzling. Unlike me, Skye was not one for temperamental outbursts, a sarcastic response would have been more her style. Quite frankly, it was so odd; I didn't know what to do. My first instinct was to run after her but knew this would only make matters worse. The room had darkened appreciably, and looking from the window I could see the storm clouds were now directly overhead. I consoled myself with the belief that once the first few drops of rain started to fall, she would make her way back.

Unsettled and feeling quite helpless, I decided to carry on with the search, it was a pointless exercise doing nothing but look at my phone every few minutes to check the time. However, my concerns started after the first half hour had passed, panic set in after an hour, turning to blind panic thirty minutes later; especially as it had been raining for at least half of that time. I checked for calls or texts, and even tried her number a couple of times; nothing, apart from an automated voicemail greeting. I was now kicking myself; I should have followed her right from the start. What was I thinking?

I tried to calm my rising anxiety by taking a few deep breaths and tried convincing myself that a simple explanation for her prolonged absence existed somewhere: neither worked. I slipped on my jacket, checked the phone again and headed for the door. Fortunately, the rain had stopped. There were only three ways she could have chosen: the lane leading back to the main road, or either of the two clifftop routes. I couldn't see why she'd take the former, so I took a chance and headed north, as it looked the most straightforward.

After about two miles or so of barren emptiness, and the fact I could see a fair distance ahead of me, even in the poor light, I decided to turn back. I was now confident she had returned to the cottage and was likely to be sporting one of her silly grins as soon as I walked in. The thought cheered me up no end and I picked up the pace accordingly; how could it possibly turn out differently? This happy little fantasy continued when I caught the glint of something shiny in the mud, and far enough from the cottage to suggest this was the route she'd taken. It was the Triskele, and a sobering discovery considering the circumstances. I stuffed the amulet into my pocket and, uncharacteristically, broke into a steady trot. My faith in hope was not to be rewarded.

♦

My call to the police was handled very sensitively, although I initially made the mistake of calling 999. After explaining the details, I was told politely by the call taker that it was technically a non-emergency and was swiftly passed to another handler. Nevertheless, my report was taken seriously, and the officer decided the circumstances warranted a visit; I later discovered, a patrol was on route before the call had finished. I remember thinking how prophetic my earlier reference to the "boys in blue" was. It was now out of my hands, and all I could do was wait and pray she returned before the police arrived. I'm not sure what I was expecting. Surprisingly, this was the first time in forty-four years I needed to call the police, and apart from being stopped once for a minor traffic offence, not had face to face contact with a uniformed police officer since. I can't say I was looking forward to it. I spent the time mindlessly poking around the contents of the remaining boxes, not really noticing anything, and not really caring. I found myself upstairs again; the suitcase was bugging me. Whether it was in fear, anger, or frustration, or a little slice of each, I turned it upside down and emptied the lot onto the bed. I stared at the pile for a few seconds wondering why I bothered; a psychologist would probably say I was responding to the situation by trying to control a small part of it. Possibly this was true, or maybe I was just treading water. I began to sift through the garments one by one, neatly refolding each, and returning them to the case. I continued until I came to the burgundy jumper; it was identical to the one I wore when first united with William, and probably why I was drawn to it. There was no way to confirm it was the same one, although it was quite a coincidence turning up in the same house as the newspaper; the one thing tying the two together came later. Three loud knocks on the door finally ended the painful wait.

♦

I kind of expected to see two of them; I'd obviously seen too many TV crime dramas. I was also a little surprised to see a female officer standing before me. Why this was so, I cannot, and could not fathom; age and a male dominated society has a lot to answer for. Nevertheless, her authority and presence was undeniable; a little shorter than me, with dark, tied back hair and a fresh round face, Constable Stewart was impeccably turned out.

'Mr Warrener?' She smiled. 'Mr John Warrener?'

I could feel my heart quicken. 'Yes,' I answered, somewhat nervously. 'Would you like to come in?' On reflection, it was a daft question in the circumstances. I turned and led the way to the front room, and the only place in the house where we could sit dust free. 'Sorry about the mess, we were in the middle of sorting it out.' I gathered up the post from the sofa, putting it on the floor by the window. 'Please, take a seat. I'd offer you a cup of tea, but the electricity has been disconnected.'

Stewart sat down, removing a notebook and pen from the waist pocket of her tactical vest. She looked up and frowned. 'How do you manage without electricity?'

I smiled limply. 'We don't actually live here; I inherited it from a relative. This was our first visit.'

She jotted a few lines before looking up. 'Okay, John, I just need to take down some personal details before we start; which she did, with almost clinical efficiency. Names, addresses, dates of birth, Skye's description, distinguishing marks, you name it, I answered it. It took a while, longer than you'd think.

'Was everything okay between you two?'

I hesitated. 'Yes. Yes, of course it was.'

'Has she ever done anything like this before?'

'Not in the eight years I've known her. This is well out of character.'

'Had you had an argument?'

I shook my head. 'No.' I considered her grumpy departure somewhat odd, but I'd hardly call it an argument. Also, I wanted to keep the anomaly regarding her parents to myself.

'Is she poorly, or has a condition that might affect her judgement?'

'No.'

'Were you the last person to see her, and the last person to talk to her at any length?'

'That would be me,' I said. 'Although we'd only just come back from the pub. The Viking; It's in the village.'

'Right.' She nodded as if she knew it. 'What time was this?'

'Two thirty. Three o'clock.'

'Had she been drinking?'

I shook my head. 'Only coffee.'

♦

I was exhausted by the time she left. I even had to complete some of the interview in her patrol car – a scary experience at the best of times – as the light indoors had diminished to almost nothing. I'd completely forgotten about the candles, and only remembered them after watching the tail lights of the patrol car disappear along the lane.

I closed the door and used the glow from my phone's screen to pick my way up the stairs and into the room where Skye had left the candles; there was no way I could leave, or go anywhere until I knew she was safe. The matches were old, and I must have broken the heads off nearly half of them before I got one to strike.

As the candle flame lengthened, it glowed eerily round the walls, adding a kind of Gothic menace to the whole situation. Wandering round in search of a bowl or plate to put the candle, I felt as if I'd fallen from the pages of *Stories for the Fireside, Wee Willie Winkie* had nothing on me! It was during a visit to the bathroom, a place where such things can sometimes be found, I noticed a faint glimmer coming from the floor, at first, I thought my eyes were playing tricks. Unsure of what it was, I pushed this unknown item with my toe before bending down to pick it up.

I could feel my pulse quicken as I turned the Omega Weems over in my hand. Its weight, the smooth metal case, its dark leather strap; all these things I was familiar with, including the minor scuffs and dents. It had, of course, stopped. I knew this to be William's timepiece, and a fine mechanical chronograph issued to pilots in 1940, and the one *we* both wore during *our* escape. He was here once, I'd known it all along, but unravelling the clues to prove it, was the issue. I carefully leaned the burning candle against one of the basin taps; I had no doubt the watch was there for me to find. I strapped the Weems to my wrist, wound it up, checked my phone, and set the time.

It was now a little after 8pm, and I was tired of being exhausted, if that makes sense. I wandered onto the landing, and the bed on which I'd dumped the clothes looked weirdly inviting. In times of difficulty my mother used to take to her bed, as if sleep made her problems easier to deal with, or perhaps she hoped they would simply disappear altogether. After all these years, I was beginning to see the logic behind her thinking. I couldn't even be bothered to move the clothes. I snuffed out the candle, lifted the musty smelling over-blanket, slid underneath, and went out like a light.

♦

I was breathlessly running down corridors banging on doors with a hammer so large I could hardly lift it. Even when I stopped to look back, I could still hear the banging. It was a ceaseless cacophony of sound, and it was getting louder, and louder, until. I sat bolt upright, had no idea where I was, and tried to work out where the infernal noise was coming from.

'Mr Warrener,' the voice bellowed. 'It's the police.'

This had the desired effect. I shot out of the bed, almost without thinking. Within seconds I had become fully awake, even my eyes had adjusted to the dim light. I thundered down the stairs and opened the door. This time I was facing two officers, and PC Stewart was one of them. Both had grim faces, especially the male.

Stewart cleared her throat. 'May we come in?' she asked. Missing was the smile; it had not gone unnoticed, and my worst fears were about to be confirmed without either saying a word. As they both turned on their tactical vest lights, all I could say was, 'Sorry about the electricity.'

They followed me to the front room, light beams bobbing round the walls as if a search was taking place; the whole thing was surreal. I sat on the edge of a spindly legged chair, they on the sofa. I knew what was coming. PC Stewart was the first to speak.

'We have some bad news for you, John.'

'She's dead, isn't she?'

Stewart nodded. 'Yes, I'm afraid so.'

I took a deep breath, feeling strangely calm. 'How?'

'It appears she fell from Anton's Bluff.'

This was a place that meant nothing to me. 'I don't know where that is.' I massaged my eyes with a finger and thumb without looking up. 'When was this?'

'A dog walker spotted her body on the beach, somewhere between 6 and 6.45pm.'

'How do you know it's her?' I'm not sure why I asked, desperate I suppose.

'Your description, personal belongings, her phone, purse, credit cards...'

I held up my hand, it was becoming all too much. 'Yes. Yes. Sorry. I get the picture.'

Her face softened. 'Is there anyone you can talk to tonight, somewhere you can go, be amongst family or friends?'

I shook my head; I was now truly alone. 'No,' I whispered. 'It's just me.'

'Do you feel up to a couple of questions, John?'

'I-I think so.'

'Does Skye have any family?'

I closed my eyes. This could be difficult. 'She has a brother.'

'Do you have a name and address for him?'

'Not a name, but I think he lives with her.' Not the best answer I could have given. I thought I'd ask a question before she queried my answer. 'What happens now, Officer?'

'You may be asked to identify the body at some stage. There will be an investigation to determine the cause of death, and it's possible the coroner may hold an inquest.' She paused and took a breath. 'Did Skye have any religious needs that you know of?'

Again, I shook my head. 'No. She was more spiritual than religious.' I stared at a space just above the officer's heads for absolutely no apparent reason. I felt wretched, more wretched than I'd ever felt in my entire life. I wanted to shout, cry, punch the wall, run, and keep running.

'Are you okay, John?'

To my grief addled brain, the voice appeared to come from nowhere. 'Uh!' My eyes refocussed. 'Sorry. I...er...sorry, what did you say?'

'I asked if you were feeling okay.'

'I don't know.' I puffed out my cheeks, preparing to put on a brave face. To lie. 'No, I'm all right. Just need a bit of time, that's all.'

Stewart glanced at her colleague, then back to me; I caught a genuine sorrow in her eyes. 'We'll have to leave you now, John. Will you be staying here for the rest of the night?'

I nodded limply. 'Probably.'

She stared at me. 'Look, if it helps, I know someone in the village with a B&B. I know it's late, but I can have a word with them if you like.'

I had a feeling she was acting outside her remit, an edge to her authority had softened. I did my best to smile. 'Thank you. You are very kind, but as gloomy as this place looks, I'd like to stay here.'

'Okay, it was just a thought.' She flipped the cover of her notebook, plucked a small card from inside, jotted something on the back, and handed it to me. 'If you need to contact me for any reason, John, my number is on the front. I've written the incident number on the back if you need to reference it anytime.'

♦

I closed the door behind them, resting my forehead on the cool wooden frame. I checked my watch, its luminous dial the only unnatural light in the room. I groaned. It was 1.47am. This time, sleep was far from my mind, and I was thirsty. I ambled through to the kitchen and turned on the single, wall mounted tap overhanging the white butler sink. It coughed and spluttered several times before issuing a steady stream of what I hoped to be water; all I had to do now was find something to drink from (I had tried to scoop it up with my hand). I used the dim light from my phone to check the cupboards. I wasn't holding my breath on finding anything, so I was surprised...no...Astonished, to discover an upturned glass tumbler sitting over the neck of a bottle of whisky; it was a fine twelve year old single malt, and almost full. I was equally surprised Skye had missed it during her search for the candles.

Now, I knew there were many, many reasons why this discovery was in the wrong place at the wrong time, but could not think of one, as I un-stoppered the bottle and poured myself a rather large, and possibly unwise, measure. As with the earlier Guinness, and a stomach containing even less, the alcohol made an immediate dash towards my brain's vulnerable nerve centre; as usual, it wasn't long before I was pouring another. Alcohol never helps though, does it? No, we just think it does. The runaway train had started its descent, and there was nothing I wanted to do to stop it.

The truth was, I was more than just alone, if that's a credible statement to make. A voice in my head was saying this was all a dream, another anomalous strand of time, a game to be replayed over and over until the desired outcome is achieved. Did I really believe this? Mentally, I was at a crossroads. If I was to describe what I was feeling right that second, I'd have to say it was like living with a chronic mind-altering disease, and that I was existing in a paracosm: a sophisticated projection of reality not of my making. Was I losing my mind? I had no idea; I had no one to ask, no help to seek, and certainly no one I could trust. I poured myself another.

I must have stood, ruminating, for some time. I shivered, not from cold, but the helplessness of my place in the universe. I wandered back to the front room, bottle in hand, and slumped heavily onto the sofa. The walls were bathed in a ghostly bluish light; clear skies and a full moon were now the celestial heroes, the storm clouds and thunderous rain long gone. I sat in relative darkness; a brain numb with over thinking. I was trapped, caught in a never-ending loop of time, permanently living almost parallel realities laced with alternate outcomes. Was it even possible to break the cycle? I really didn't know.

I got to my feet, then sat down again. Crossed my legs, then did the opposite. I was frustrated, and needed to see a way forward, when there didn't seem to be one. Then I remembered a friend of mind, a devout Buddhist, saying the best ideas come from an empty mind. To me, this always appeared an impossible task as my mind had always danced about, randomly jumping from one thought to another with neither rhyme nor reason. Maybe this was the way. I lifted the bottle; one more won't hurt. No, of course it won't.

I stared at the window, listening to the increasing breeze whistling through the gaps, the gentle click of the front door as it moved in its frame. I noticed the not so fragrant upholstery, the ethereal dance of shadows on the walls, even the steady rhythm of my heart. I took a deep breath. From somewhere unknown, a thought occurred to me. I was the common denominator, the axis to which this continued existence turned, and not just as a visitor; lives had changed because of me. I thought of Skye's parents, the brother I never knew, and William's narrow escape from death. It was me who was changing the shape of reality. Not Sylvia, not Patricia, Charles, or Julius Becket. Me.

A rumble of what I thought was thunder temporarily shook these ideas from my head. The room darkened once more, the breeze turning to gusts; the front door's earlier calm ambivalence had turned vocal and was now rattling noisily in its captivity. I got to my feet, wobbled slightly, and looked out; the earlier moonlit vista had been replaced by deepening cloud. I suddenly had the need to be amongst this elemental force of nature, to face it head on.

I pulled up my coat collar and locked the door behind me. The wind was now biting. A divided sky lay overhead, light and dark separated by a glistening ribbon of deep indigo and vermilion; sunrise was some way off but still announcing its presence way up in the outer troposphere. Without giving it a second thought, I took the same route as before, marching on as if I had a mission to fulfil. Maybe I had. Refreshingly light flecks of rain began to tickle the bare skin of my face as I plodded along the muddied footpath, my prized bottle slapping hard against my thigh. Who needs a glass anyway?

For now, I was insulated from the grief, or at least thinking about it in any meaningful way, in fact, I wasn't thinking about anything of any consequence, the whisky had seen to that. I wasn't even sure where I was trying to go, and must have travelled farther than I had before, as nothing appeared remotely familiar. The wind, which had been driving inland with an increasing velocity, suddenly abated. I continued until I stumbled across a grassed area enclosed by a number of short white posts. In the dim light I could just make out several randomly placed, grey boulders, a bench, and a concrete path running towards the cliff edge. I wandered slowly across to the middle and stared towards the dark horizon.

It was now eerily quiet, and the moon was, again, edging out from behind a band of cloud, casting everything a bluish hue. I stood for several minutes before pulling the bottle from my coat pocket. I rolled it over in the palm of my hand; even in my intoxicated numbness I knew I shouldn't. And I was right. The bottle hit the grass with a dull thud, and I cupped my face in my hands, squeezing my eyes tightly shut. Enough was enough.

Way, way in the distance, a crackle of lightning broke the chains of my silent stupor. I'd like to say I came to my senses, but I hadn't. Trance-like, I shuffled thoughtlessly towards the cliff edge and the waist height timber barrier placed across it; a strange and somewhat useless safety feature considering how easy it was to walk round or climb over. Which is exactly what I did; of course, the actual edge was somewhat farther away, and a steady downward gradient had first to be negotiated. As I neared the precipice, I started to feel lifted somewhat, as if an end was in sight. I came to a stop, the tips of my shoes overhanging slightly.

All I needed was to take just one more step, and that would be the end of it; the end of pain, the torment, the need for explanation, the end of the struggle. I closed my eyes. I could hear the might of the sea below, feel its power thundering inside my chest, and taste its saltiness on my lips. Mariners knew it demanded respect and were right to be afraid. For me it was different, for this brief moment I had the courage to step towards the unknown, become one with the elemental forces all about me. What was there to fear anymore? I smiled inexplicably; my recent fatalistic view of life didn't help as I teetered on the edge of oblivion. I opened my eyes and leant forward; the sheer sides of the black Cambrian façade plunged deep into the white, frothing turmoil of the sea, churning menacingly below. I lifted my arm and squinted at my watch; its face was now covered with a fine mist; spray carried by the wind. I carefully brushed a fingertip delicately across the glass, its vintage luminous dial still glowing eerily after all these years. It was 3am. I shivered. Several of my coat buttons had come unfastened and the chilly easterly breeze cut through the thin fabric of my exposed shirt; it occurred to me I should have put something warm underneath, like a jumper. I smiled again; a ridiculous thought considering my intention. What was I waiting for? Why did it matter? Alcohol does that, doesn't it? Confuses things, right? I took my last conscious breath, closed my eyes and prepared to take the final step.

Chapter 18
Revelation

Suddenly, the sounds of the sea were all round me; the rush and churn of sand on rocks, the heave of the tide, the thrust of the incoming wave, even the nasal chattering of nearby kittiwakes. I could hear everything, everything in the minutest detail. But sound was all I had. I felt no pain; in fact, I had no feeling at all. My sense of smell was no more, I had no taste, and sight was but a dim kaleidoscope of coloured mush; I was even unsure if my eyes were open. I had the oddest belief that I was surrounded by light, cosseted from the world in a bubble, held in a state of suspended animation. Did I remember? Yes, I did. Was death like this or had I finally fallen through the fabric of reality and entered another world? I was conscious, and knew I was conscious; this was no dream, or slip of time, and sure I was not about to wake up in a damp cellar; if "wake" was the right word to use. I was tired beyond words, but unable to close my eyes. I smiled inwardly at the absurdity. Sleep, if that's what it was, came in an instant.

♦

'Yer can't stay 'ere, lad.'

'Eh?'

'I said, yer can't stay 'ere. It's private property. Belongs ta the Trust, it do.'

I could feel my eyelids pulling against each other, trying to open. 'W-where am I?' I stumbled.

'Oh Lord, don't yer know?'

My eyes flickered open in an instant. The grey bearded man leaning over me had a kindly but concerned look on his face; he was down on one knee, and I assumed I must have been on the ground. I attempted to move, hoist myself up using my elbows, but it was impossible to physically do so. 'I-I think I may n-need a hand,' I mumbled.

'Been drinking, 'ave we?'

I felt a strong, surprisingly large hand hook itself under my armpit. 'Er...a...little,' I rambled.

The man let out a guttural laugh. 'We can all say that, me lad. Right, one..two...three...hup yer get.' I was on my feet in seconds, and weirdly able to stand, although unsteadily at first. The man recognised my instability and encircled my waist with his other arm. 'By 'eck, lad, yer musta knocked back tha whole bottle.' He chuckled quietly to himself. 'Sit yerself down over thar for a minute.' He steered me towards a wooden bench and carefully settled me onto it. I had up until then taken little notice of my surroundings, anything outside my immediate vicinity had been blurred and indistinct. I thought the old man must have found me on the beach, or amongst the rocks, so it came as a shock to discover the truth. I was still within the circle of posts; the empty bottle of whisky, now only an arm's length away. I eyed it wearily and shook my head. Surely, I couldn't have been so drunk that I...

'So, where yer from, lad?'

The question was simple and shouldn't have confused me, but it did. 'Whitstable,' I said.

The old man massaged his whiskered chin thoughtfully. 'Whitstable, yer say. Yer a longs way from 'ome, ain't yer?'

I winced. 'I was...I mean...I'm just visiting really.' Without warning, memories from the night before came flooding back. Reality hit me like a hammer blow, and I muttered a single word, a name. 'Skye.'

The old man frowned. 'What yer say?'

'Where's Anton's Bluff?' I asked, somewhat randomly.

He scratched the back of his head and looked at me awkwardly. 'Why, it's 'ere, lad. This is Anton's Bluff. Yer on it.'

I could feel the bile begin to rise from my stomach, I felt like I was about to throw up. I took a deep breath and swallowed, fighting this sudden nauseous impulse. 'The woman,' I hissed. 'Last night…she was...' I needed to tell him, somehow share my grief, the pain tearing me apart inside; I had to make him understand I wasn't some drunk after a night on the tiles.

'Yer na talkin' sense. What woman? Are yer tryin' ta tell me yer weren't up 'ere on yer own?'

'Y-yes, I mean, no. It wasn't like that.' I shook my head again. 'They found a woman, here on the beach last night.' Those words caught horribly in my throat.

He shrugged, eyeing me suspiciously 'Na, lad, 'eard owt about a woman bein' found anywheres round 'ere. Yer sure yer got that reet?'

I was irritated by the question and wanted to shout at him. I took a breath to calm myself. 'She was found on the beach after falling from the cliff, from here. Surely you must know something.'

He scratched the back of his head again. 'If she 'ad, I would have 'eard about it. Yer sees, I'm warden of tha estate, an' if sommat like that 'ad 'appened 'ere, I'd be tha first ta know.'

I closed my eyes; my head was swimming. Either he was mad, or it was me, and there was no way on God's earth I had imagined it. When I opened my eyes again, the old man was watching me, and seemed to be reading my face, as if its features were lines and characters on a page. In my heart I still wanted to pursue it, but the whole matter between us was now becoming moot, and beyond argument. I returned his gaze. 'I must have been mistaken. Rumours, eh?'

'Aye.' He chuckled. 'Plenty of 'em round 'ere. How yer feelin' now?'

'Better, thanks to you.' I smiled and gingerly got to my feet. 'I suppose I'd better get back. I've things to do,' I said limply. 'Sorry if I've held you up in any way.'

The old man waved a dismissive hand. 'Never thee mind, lad.' He laughed and began to walk away. 'Jus' be sure yer stay indoors next time yer takes to tha bottle.'

'I will, I promise,' I said, thinking I should have asked his name, and wondering why I hadn't. I watched him amble away until he disappeared behind a dense thicket of tall, leafy shrubs. I bent down and picked up the discarded whisky bottle, taking it to the waste bin I'd failed to see the night before. I stopped when I got to the path, something inside of me wanted to go to the cliff edge and look down, not that I was likely to see anything anyway. Even if I could, I sensibly chose not to, a physical reminder of last night was unnecessarily stupid and emotionally fraught, and I had experienced plenty of that already. I took a moment to look out to sea; the air was fresh, the sun was out, and the skies were clear. I considered removing my coat it was so warm.

The day was quite pleasant, and surprisingly calm, and in complete contrast to how I felt. It's funny how the rest of the world continues undisturbed even in our darkest hour. When my parents passed away, I expected ear-splitting crashes of thunder, jagged lightening, and to feel the tremor of the earth below my feet; a sign their lives meant something more than just the love of a son. I know this is likely to come across as childlike, but I think you can probably see where I'm coming from.

The path back to the cottage was firm and dry, and very few signs of the rain were in evidence. I checked my pockets for my phone, house keys and wallet, and something I should have done before I left. All were there, as was my "borrowed" watch. It was 10:26am, later than I thought, and seven and a half hours since I took that leap into the unknown; if in fact it had happened, and something I was beginning to doubt. I'd had none of the usual physical signs of shifting time, and again, concluded that a perfectly rational explanation may account for why I ended up where I was. I was thrown by the old man's claim about the accident, but this too could be explained, however much I needed to believe him.

So far, my return to the cottage was the only plan I had; thoughts to whether I should remain at Farthing Cottage, go back to Althurian, or my flat in Whitstable, were in flux; emotionally, I wanted to stay close to Skye, as strange as that may sound. But, a house without electricity was a trial in itself, ignoring what an absolute mess it was. Whitstable was just too far, so Althurian seemed the only sensible choice, a halfway house.

♦

I was reassured when the cottage, with the Aston parked outside, came into view; I expected it not to be the case. I unlocked the door, hesitating before opening it fully. Once inside, it was obvious nothing had changed and was exactly how I had left it; even the hastily gathered post by the front room window confirmed the visit by the police. This silent and empty world was not where I wanted to be, the loss of Skye was palpable, and my life had become soulless because of it.

I slipped the phone from my pocket and cursed; the screen was blank and flashed a critical battery warning icon when I tried to switch it on; not a problem if I'd remembered to bring a charger, or the Toyota. Losing this connection with the outside world made the return to Althurian even more important, and one I needed to make sooner rather than later. I eyed the keys to the Aston where Skye had left them, a sobering memory never to be forgotten. With my decision clear in my mind, I made a quick check to see if we'd left anything in any of the rooms, and left.

♦

The journey, as you can imagine, was a lonely affair, broken only by a brief visit to a service station. It took less than two hours this time; with fewer traffic hold ups and a slightly heavier right foot the likely protagonists, I was pulling up outside Althurian a little after one o'clock. As with the cottage, nothing seemed out of place. It was certainly a lot warmer. I made a beeline for the kitchen to find the coffee pot; a pint of Guinness, a whole bottle of whisky, and a few handfuls of insipid water didn't quite cut it! As I waited for the percolator to do the business, and debated what I should do next, there came a sudden, and urgent, knock at the front door.

On the steps stood a fresh-faced man of around thirty, beaming as if he'd just cashed a scratch card. He had three neatly stacked crates next to him and was holding a device similar to a labelling machine. 'Good afternoon, governor,' he said. 'Nice one, innit?'

I inclined my head, looking at him with suspicion; he was a little too friendly for my liking. 'And you are?' I asked, possibly a tad rudely, I thought.

His smile fell away. 'Er...your Tesco delivery, Mr Warrener. I'm sorry if I'm a bit early, the drop before yours cancelled at the last minute.' He rolled his eyes. 'Tried to ring but I couldn't get through. I'm really sorry.'

I nodded. Possibly I'd missed something. Although it was not something we discussed, Skye may have put in an order before we left for the cottage. Supermarkets were not on my list of places to visit, so food deliveries were a common event at the Warrener household. I smiled, so not to appear foolish, and shook my head. 'Ah, Yes,' I said, 'the delivery. How could I have forgotten?' I knew I was probably overdoing it, and I stepped to one side. 'If you bring the crates into the hall for me, I'll unload them.'

The man duly complied with my request and appeared to cheer up immeasurably during our brief interaction, giving me a cheery wave as he left. I stared at the bags of fresh vegetables: jars, tins and packets of various sizes, a nine pack of toilet rolls, and the obligatory bottle of Sauvignon Blanc. Almost all of it familiar, and brands I'd buy myself. I checked the receipt. I had indeed ordered it and paid with my credit card. It was not unusual for Skye to use my account from time to time, so it came as no surprise; although a little odd under the circumstances, I thought little of it.

With everything packed away, even the random box of Cheerios, I decided a shower was definitely on the cards; twenty-four hours in the same clothes, and a night spent out of doors in a drunken stupor wasn't entirely conducive to personal hygiene. The bedroom was unusually tidy, more so than when we left, and it caught me off guard when I opened the door and walked in. Brushing these anomalies aside with a simple explanation was becoming my forte, and this one was no different. Rachael, the waitress we met at the Royal Oak, was continuing her duties. Yes, that was it, because I had told her so. Simple.

After I'd washed and scraped the last twenty-four hours from my body, and put away two mugs of delicious coffee, I felt marginally revitalised; although the massive shot of caffeine gave me one hell of a headache. I finally got around to putting my phone on charge once I'd found the charger, an item I seem to lose with increasing efficiency. It took a few minutes to respond before I could turn it on and check for any pending texts or voicemail messages. Nothing. Althurian appeared to be a victim of random "no fly zones" where mobile coverage was concerned, the signal dipping in and out, and sometimes vanishing altogether when it felt like it. I sighed. Staring at its screen was unlikely to achieve anything but acute neck ache. Anyway, I had other things to do, or so I'd convinced myself. Basically, I was treading water, or "all at sea", a term my mother often used when she was out of sorts. I knew what she meant. It's said that shock doesn't register immediately, and I think this was part of the problem. I couldn't think straight and needed something to focus on, a direction to move in. Some say the universe moves in mysterious ways, this was to prove remarkably accurate when this latest ruminative state was suddenly broken by the sound of a vehicle pulling up outside.

I quickly skipped downstairs, through to the dining room, and surreptitiously peeped from behind the curtain. I was surprised to see two vehicles parked opposite the steps. I became quite protective when I saw that one of them, a white, slightly scruffy Ford Transit van, had parked so close to the front of the Aston, I was sure it must have nudged it, and almost broke cover. The other, was a smart looking, green SUV with tinted windows; hardly the sort of vehicles usually seen together unless stationary at traffic lights. A sharply dressed woman of about forty climbed out of the SUV, while a man of the same age, wearing jeans and a light blue rugby shirt, stepped down from the van. They appeared to know each other, perhaps not very well; only a nod and smile exchanged between them. I had the feeling the man looked a little defensive, edgy maybe. I waited until I heard a knock at the door.

The woman introduced herself first, while the man stood behind her; I think this was an indication of her authority rather than an act of chivalry on his part. She smiled and held out her hand. 'Mr Warrener, I presume?' She raised an eyebrow. 'Glenis Brooks, Selkirk Herald. Sorry to turn up unannounced.' Her light green eyes bored into mine as she waited for an answer; it was quite unnerving.

I ignored the presumption, but returned her polite gesture, her grip was surprisingly firm. 'You're from a newspaper,' I said.

She looked surprised. 'My editor contacted you. Right?'

I shook my head. 'Phone has been out for a while. What's this about?' I had a horrible apprehension this was about Skye, and I could feel my hackles begin to rise. Not that I had a clue as to why a newspaper would be interested in such a story.

'The Althurian Circle, of course.' She glanced somewhat nervously at the man behind her. I got the feeling this meeting wasn't as prearranged as she was trying to make out.

I relaxed a little. 'What about it?'

'Well, your decision to have the stones removed is in direct violation of a county protection order. That's pretty newsworthy stuff, don't you think?'

'It is, but I've made no such decision.' From over the woman's shoulder I could see the man was looking a little peeved. 'Where did this information come from?'

She unfastened the small clutch bag she carried and removed a notebook and pen. She looked up. 'So, you are now withdrawing the statement you made outside County Hall. Yes?'

This last sentence pushed me well and truly into a corner. This wasn't the set up I thought it was. 'I'm neither withdrawing nor denying anything at this present time,' I said, feeling quite clever with myself; I should have been a politician.

She grinned triumphantly. 'But Mr Hughes here,' she jabbed a thumb in his direction, 'has confirmed you and he had already entered into an agreement over how and when it was to be done.'

'Well, if that's the case, you clearly know more than me.' Before she had time to answer, I added, 'Now, if you don't mind, I have some business I need to attend to.' I smiled and went to close the door.

Hughes stepped forward, touching the door with his fingertips. 'Sorry, John, is it okay if have a quick word with you,' he gave Brooks a sideways glance, 'in private.'

'Sure.' I opened the door a little wider. 'Come through.' I looked at Brooks and raised my eyebrows. 'I'm sorry if my answers weren't what you were expecting.'

Brooks tucked the notebook back into her bag and grinned again. 'Not at all, Mr Warrener, to the contrary, I shall look forward to taking my seat in the press gallery at the County Court.'

Damn it, I thought, she knew exactly how to needle me. I gave my best "I don't give a toss" smile. 'We'll have to wait and see, won't we?' I closed the door and puffed out my cheeks; for a second, I'd forgotten about Hughes.

'John?'

'Yes. Sorry. I was miles away. What can I do for you?' There was a look on his face, the kind of look that said we were more acquainted than my response suggested.

'She tricked me, John,' he said. 'It wasn't like that, like what she made it out to be.'

I stared at him. There were so many questions I needed answers to, and none I could ask him. It was now obvious, reality had taken another fork in the road, and not one far removed from the one I had left; unfortunately, the gaping void once filled by another human being was still there. 'I can well believe it.' I laid a comforting hand on his shoulder. 'Try not to worry about it, the press can be a devious lot.'

'Are you still going through with it?'

'We'll have to wait and see.'

'But you were so into this, John. What changed your mind?'

'I haven't actually changed my mind.' This was true. 'It's complicated.' Yes, it certainly was that!

Hughes looked troubled. 'So it might be, but I gave up a lot of work, good work, to do this for you, John. Work I can ill afford to lose if this goes pear shaped.'

I eyed him squarely. I was struggling for answers, and it would help if I knew his name. I could hardly call him Mr Hughes. 'Listen, you'll get paid whatever the outcome. I promise you.'

'Really?'

'Yes, really.'

♦

I watched Hughes clamber into his van; I'm surprised he chose not to ask more than he did, possibly my overly generous offer was enough. I wandered through to the kitchen and into the garden room. It was odd how everything looked the same, but different in the sense of day to day existence. Something had happened to make me consider taking such radical action, and that this decision had come to the attention of the authorities. I also had the impression "my other me" was quite happy to break the rules and suffer the consequences, and expensive ones at that.

I wandered back to the kitchen, my stomach grumbling for food; a liquid diet had left it empty and wanting. I gave silent thanks to the Tesco delivery driver as I grabbed the cheese and a wholemeal loaf from the fridge. With my plate loaded with sustenance, I climbed back up the stairs, hoping to at least have a few moments to myself, but half expecting another interruption. As I sat on the edge of the bed in quiet contemplation, wondering what other surprises were in store, I noticed a handwritten note on the bedside table; in my haste to get showered I must have missed it. I leaned across and picked it up. It was from Skye.

> *John*
> *Don't forget to make that call to Dewars and order the "you know what". The last thing we need on Tuesday is another tantrum! And make sure it's a red one.*
> *Sorry 'bout this but knowing how rubbish your memory is I thought I'd leave you this little reminder. And don't tut, you know I'm right!*
> *Hugs*

I scratched that place behind my ear, the place my hand goes when I'm clueless; I think I may have pulled a face and shook my head at the same time. Only one thing in the note to make sense, was my not so hot ability to remember stuff. Dewars, orders, tantrums, and items that need to be coloured red, made none at all. Clearly, she expected me to know what the note was about, that was obvious, and whoever we were trying to appease had control issues, but that was about it. As to when she wrote it, and if it mattered, well, it was a question I was unable to answer. She was gone now, and I had to stop torturing myself. My phone bleeped; a blessing in itself. Those bothersome electronic winds must have changed direction! It was a text from Larry Talbot.

Are you okay for a visit today? Edward Fairchild is with me

At least Larry was someone I knew, and a distraction; I was in danger of sinking even further into my maudlin-ness, if there is such a word. I decided to call him back, I never have been much of a text person, a medium so easily misinterpreted, but that's probably down to me. Anyway, it had occurred to me he may have got wind of my plan to flatten the circle, we may have even discussed it for all I knew. I'd have to play it by ear.

As before, his phone rang twice. 'Hello, John, thanks for calling back. I wasn't sure you'd be there today.'

'Me too,' I mumbled. 'Larry. How goes it?'
'Good, John. So, are you up for a visit?'
'Sure thing. When?'

'Two o'clock?'

I checked my watch; it was a few minutes after one. 'Two's good for me, Larry. Is Edward bringing any equipment with him?'

Larry chuckled. 'If a voice recorder and notebook count, then yes. No, Edward travels light. You'll find him full of questions, but he will be ready with some pretty cool answers to go with them. I think you'll enjoy the visit.'

'Sounds good to me, I'll get the tea and biscuits ready.'

♦

Just before the call finished, I heard what I thought was the sound of footsteps, and they appeared to be coming from somewhere downstairs. I left the phone on the bedside table and wandered to the landing, cocking an ear in the general direction. After a brief pause the footsteps started again; I was fairly certain that whoever it was, was moving from room to room, noisily crossing the wooden floor of the hall as they did so. I was tempted to call out but thought better of it. I was sure I had locked the door after Brooks and Hughes had left. I took a deep breath and stealthily made my way downstairs, heart in mouth, and looking for anything I could use as a weapon.

The door leading to the hall was open as usual, held in place by an old cast iron scale weight. Keeping close to the wall, I tiptoed towards the opening and peered out for several seconds. Nothing. Complete silence, and not a hint of movement. I was about to give up, putting it down to a rare form of tinnitus, when the door opposite, the one to the bathroom, slowly creaked open. I stood like a rabbit caught in headlights, unable to move, eyes rigid, heart thumping as it usually did at times like this. I could just make out a figure in the gloom, a woman. We stared at each other, neither saying a word; she looked as shocked as I did.

'Mr Warrener, sir, you give me the frit of me life, you did. Didn't expect you home quite so sudden.' She stepped into the light of the hall, closing the door behind her; she was carrying a bright yellow bucket full of bottles, sponges, and dusters. 'Are you on your own, sir?'

I should have recognised her sooner. And odd my presence at Althurian was a surprise to her. 'Rachael?'

She smiled. 'Yes, sir.'

'What are you doing here?'

'Cleaning, sir, it's Thursday.' She looked confused. 'Was there something else I should be doing, sir?'

It might have helped if I'd remembered my earlier deductive reasoning. 'No, sorry, Rachael, I forgot it was your day today,' I lied. 'When did you get in?'

'About ten minutes ago, sir. I had to take me mum to the hairdressers, then take Pickles to have her nails done.'

'Pickles?'

'Me mum's cat. Twenty-five quid it cost.'

'Right.'

'I did tell you I was going.'

I smiled limply. 'It's been a difficult week.' I winced.

'It has, sir,' she replied, nodding solemnly. 'I'll do upstairs now if you don't mind.'

'Yes. Yes, of course.' I stepped to one side to let her pass. I'd said too much, but was surprised by her response, it was like she knew about the accident, or had heard something. Not that it mattered, it was going to come out sooner or later; I just didn't need it to be now, the wound was far too deep, and far too raw. I checked my watch. 1:50pm. Larry and Edward were due at any moment.

♦

I chose to wait for them in the garden room. The sky was clear and the sun full and warming, although I was puzzled by how low it appeared to the horizon. I quickly dismissed the thought with a shake of my head. I had started to question everything; my place in the universe was uncertain, turbulent, and transient, so no surprises there. I closed my eyes.

'Hello.'

I snapped upright and turned around; I may have dozed off briefly. Larry, with another man I assumed to be Fairchild, were standing in the doorway to the kitchen. I was shocked and irritated by this sudden intrusion, and it showed.

'Sorry, John,' Larry gave a weak smile and thumbed over his shoulder, 'Skye let us in, told us where to find you.'

I got to my feet and stared at him. 'Skye? What on earth are you talking about?' My outburst wobbled him. Even I was unsure where it came.

He physically took a backward step. 'Y-your wife, s-she answered the door,' he stammered.

I took a deep breath and allowed my anger to subside. I lowered my voice. 'Rachael, it was Rachael. She cleans the house for us.' I paused. 'My...er...wife is not here at the moment.' Not the most credible explanation for my explosive reaction, and now it was me who was rocking on the back foot. 'Please, come in and take a seat. I'll make us something to drink. Tea or coffee?'

♦

I had a feeling Fairchild was wary of me. A tall, slim, bespectacled man, with a smooth featured face and thinning brushed over hair; he looked every bit the academic he was; even the slightly oversized, charcoal two-piece suit, had the stamp of scholarly appearance. Larry and he sat together saying little until I returned from the kitchen. Edward was the first to speak, his voice surprisingly deep and gravelly. He got straight to the point.

'Larry tells me you want to bulldoze the site.'

I took a sip from my cup and eyed him carefully. 'I haven't made up my mind. It depends.' I was fishing.

He raised his eyebrows. 'On what?'

I half smiled. 'If I can get away with it.'

Edward leaned back; I saw a ghost of a smile pass his lips. He clasped his hands together, making a church like steeple with his fingers, touching them lightly against his lips; he looked like a disciple of Sigmund Freud. 'What do you blame them for?' It was another unexpectedly direct question.

My answer was equally unexpected; it was as if it came from outside of me, not of my making. 'Everything.' I briefly thought of Patricia.

He took a breath. 'Have you ever considered it may be the location and not what's built on it?' He unclasped his hands, fingers outstretched. 'This whole area has been the subject of folklore and legend for aeons, so it's hardly surprising that people, who had little understanding of the laws governing nature, considered the supernatural responsible for any misfortune that beset them. The people who placed those stones here were reacting to forces they had little knowledge of.'

I felt my eyes narrow. 'Old wives' tales and superstition, eh?'

'Some of it, but that's not where I was going with this, John.' He paused. 'Try to think of the circle as a talisman, a physical construction, be it a large one, built by people to harness magical powers and bring luck to those who visit it. Removing the stones won't change anything.'

'So, you believe in magic, then?'

'No. I believe in science. What you are experiencing here has an explanation based on undiscovered natural laws. To believe otherwise makes us no better than those who allowed women to be executed for witchcraft. And it wasn't that long ago either, scarily so, in fact.'

'I get that, but how does this knowledge help me?' I had that "other worldly" feeling again. 'I'm experiencing things that are beyond normal and I need to find a practical solution for them.' I paused for breath. 'Answer me this: If science is designed to challenge ideas through research and experimentation, then tell me, has anyone removed a stone circle to prove the point either way.'

Edward stared at me. 'Anecdotally they have.' He nodded sagely. 'Admittedly, these tales were not from recent times.'

'But there is no scientific proof behind anecdotes, is there, Edward?'

'True. But without a scientific approach, finding a solution could only ever be by trial and error. Flattening the stones may solve your problem. But what if it doesn't? Turn the bulldozers towards Althurian, flatten this too?'

Larry chipped in for the first time. 'They'd never allow you to do it anyway. Ancient standing stones are protected under the Archaeological Areas Act 1979.' Judging by his response, and the stony grey expression, this was tantamount to an act of vandalism. 'Wouldn't it be easier if you just moved out, John?'

Larry had a point, it would. I'm not sure why I was arguing the point. It really wasn't me who had decided this course of action; although this manifestation of who I'd become clearly had, and a detail I was unlikely to share with anyone. I sighed; I was also becoming bored with the conversation. Personally, for me, it was too late. Skye had become a victim of Althurian, a result of an inheritance, and nothing was going to change that.

'John.'

I blinked. 'Sorry, Larry. Yes, you're right.'

Larry frowned. 'I am?'

I nodded. I had no cause to be there, no ties, no history, apart from my brief exploits to a past life that was nothing more than a shared experience with an identity I hardly knew. There was far more to Althurian than I was capable of understanding. It was time to make a decision, it was time to leave.

Chapter 19
Homeward

Larry and Edward took it well, better than I expected. They had come with high expectations and left, I should think, more than a little disappointed. Larry was the more buoyant of the two, smiling cheerfully to himself as he climbed in the passenger seat of Edward's car; no doubt pleased he was able to change my mind. I felt sorry for Edward though, he was obviously a very clever man who took his studies deadly seriously. Althurian and its legendry stones, if he had known, was possibly the greatest missed opportunity he was likely to have in his lifetime. I watched their car until it disappeared from sight before closing the door.

I stood facing the full length of the hall, the gilt framed paintings, the panelled doors, its gloriously high ceilings, taking in the wonderful feel of its antiquity. This truly was a magnificent building. I opened the door to the room we first explored together. I remembered Skye's infectious enthusiasm, her childish excitement for anything and everything. I think she had embraced Althurian way before me, if I ever really did. As I was about to leave, I spotted an item I hadn't noticed before, on the mantel, above the fireplace, stood a small wooden photo frame. I wandered over and gazed at the image behind the glass; bare legged and wearing a tiny red duffle coat and matching wellingtons, a pretty blonde-haired little girl of about five looked out. There was something endearing about her, and a likeness that was more than just familiar, eerily so. I took down the frame and moved to the window to get a better look. The more I stared at it, the more familiar the face became; I wondered if I was trying to identify a likeness when there wasn't one, a kind of face pareidolia. She looked like Skye, there was no mistake. I returned to the fireplace, unable to shift my eyes from her image. I lingered for a minute or two before carefully returning it.

I quietly left the room, closing the door behind me. Something inside of me wanted to scream, shout at the top of my voice; I was trying to suppress an anger that needed to come out and was losing the battle. At least I had made a decision, albeit an emotional one. I would leave Althurian, possibly sell it and move to somewhere familiar, somewhere near people; isolation wasn't for me, especially now. Deep inside I knew my time at Althurian had come to an end, the experience was over, the game was up, and my journeys to the past were to become just a cluster of faded memories.

I took myself back to the garden room, procrastinating as is usual when I have a hundred and one things to do, and stood looking out. The season seemed to had shifted a little, and probably accounted for the sun being lower than I remembered it; I had not checked, or noticed, the date since my return, even when using my phone, and may have become oblivious to the path of time in my wanderings. Several cardboard boxes and a steel trunk lay on the floor by the back wall; I'd spotted them during my meeting with Larry and Edward, and were similar to the ones Skye had been looking through before we left, and a task I knew I would have to continue whether it was here or somewhere else. Truthfully, the emotional side of me wanted to dump the lot and forget they ever existed, the other, pragmatic side of me, was still curious, and maybe a little concerned I could throw away something of real value. For now, though, they would have to wait. I needed a walk.

The air was quite frigid, far colder than I expected. Bracing was a word my father used often and described the atmosphere outside perfectly; I had decided to make one more trip to the circle regardless of how long I was to remain at Althurian. Now feeling quite calm, I took my time, a leisurely stroll, driven by nothing. It was remarkably quiet, broken only by the odd caw of a rook cruising over the treetops or the flutelike whistle of a song thrush hiding amongst the conifers. I was soon facing the line of trees, the gate was pegged open, and the earlier rut running the length of the path had disappeared, replaced by a smooth carpet of thinning grass; someone had been busy, and looked as if it had recently experienced a fair amount of foot traffic. My heart quickened as I caught sight of the larger of the two monoliths; beating a little less so after emerging from the wood as the circle seemed strangely benign.

I clasped my hands behind my back and stood motionless, unsure as to why I'd bothered to come here in the first place. As I allowed my eyes to wander untethered to anything in particular, I caught sight of something partially hidden behind the large recumbent stone. At first, I thought it may have been a tool or device left out by the gardeners. A closer look proved otherwise. It was a small blue and red tricycle, and fairly new by the look of it; its shiny, unblemished paintwork covered only by droplets from an earlier shower.

'Tha nipper 'as left her bike out again, ain't she, Mr Warrener.' I turned sharply. Standing on the opposite side of the circle, a short, rounded man of about fifty, wearing shabby blue overalls and a baseball cap, raised his hand and smiled. He began to shake his head as he started walking towards me. 'If I 'ad a quid fer every time I put it away, I'd be a rich man, I would.'

I tried to laugh convincingly, having absolutely no idea who he was talking about, or who was addressing me; it was a fair assumption he was one of the gardeners, and the tricycle likely belonging to a grandchild. I clicked my tongue. 'Kids, eh?'

'Aye, you can say that again,' he said. 'I'll put it in tha garage, shall I?'

I nodded. 'Probably best,' I answered feebly.

'Aye, probably best,' he repeated. Picking it up by one end of its handlebars, he looked at me and inclined his head. 'I knows this is none of ma business, Mr Warrener, but does thee know when we should expect tha first visitors ta arrive. I knows it's next month, but a date would be handy.'

I stared at him. 'Not off hand, I'll have to check. It's all in the air at the moment. Sorry.' I was pleased with the answer, but not entirely sure he believed me.

He gave me a sideways look. 'Right you are. I'll wait 'till I'm told.'

I watched him amble away, the tricycle scraping the ground occasionally, his slightly awkward gait possibly due to an old injury. I closed my eyes and slowly dragged my palms down my face; my need to run away was becoming an acute psychological disorder. I had returned to a world not of my making, and needed to undo the changes somehow, and had no idea where to start, or what those changes were likely to be.

I had an idea. Unlike me, Skye was quite well organised; where I would keep everything in my head, she would write down anything important, be it a plumbing issue, taxing the car, or the one hundred and one jobs we all have to find time to do. She did so in a small day book, and if my search was to start anywhere, it needed to start there. Bar interruptions, I would begin upstairs and make my way through each room until I found it, or anything else I believed relevant. I now had a plan and felt better for it. I made my way back to the house thinking of little else.

I chose to search our bedroom first, and an obvious place to look before moving on to the other rooms in the likelihood they were now being utilised. Rachael had been busy; the fresh smell of bleach and wood polish was like a signature. A neat pile of recently pressed clothes lay on the bed; I recognised most of them as belonging to Skye and found it difficult to even look at them without tearing up. Rachael was very thorough, and little was left out of place. Skye was a bedtime list maker, so I checked the bedside cabinets first, and it was somewhat reassuring to find we were still keeping to "our own side" of the bed. Apart from a rather scruffy, well-thumbed copy of *Ned the Lonely Donkey* and a small bag of coloured plastic beads, I found nothing unusual. Okay, the book and beads were odd, but she made weird attachments to things, it's who she was. No lists though, or daybook. I checked the wardrobe only to find it empty apart from a couple of garments on hangers; I was a little surprised by this because Skye had brought a suitcase with her as well as an overnight bag, which I had not retrieved from the car yet. There should have been more, much more; another anomaly with a simple solution?

The bedroom opposite looked much the same as it did when we first arrived at Althurian, although I had the feeling it had been slept in recently. I gave it the once over nonetheless, and again, found nothing. The rest of upstairs was no different, I even searched for an entrance to the attic room Patricia had mentioned, and still found nothing, so I won't bore you with the details. So, apart from the boxes and travel chests we found originally, and the many paintings, there was very little left to discover. I plodded heavy footed down the stairs; I had believed I was about to stumble across an Aladdin's cave of answers, a compendium of Althurian secrets, written in a simple language, even I could understand. But it was not to be.

I took my dispirited self, back to the garden room and sat down again; it was becoming an important "go to" rendezvous for my thoughts. Unfortunately, those thoughts didn't quite receive the time they deserved.

'Just finished, Mr Warrener, sir. I cleaned up that mess the decorators left behind, untidy beggars. Made up for the time I lost droppin' me mum at the hairdressers.'

I almost cricked my neck. 'Rachael,' I said, with a start. 'I thought you'd already gone home.'

'Sorry, my fault, Mr Warrener, sir, I shoulda told you I was stayin' on a bit later. You here tomorrow?'

I nodded. 'Yes, as far as I know.'

Her face lit up. 'I'll be pickin' up the cake for Little Dove in the morning. Can't wait to see it.'

I slowly rocked my head as if I knew what she was talking about. 'Oh right...Little Dove...Well, that's good then.'

'Shall I put it in the fridge or leave it on the side. S'pose they'll put it in a box for me.'

'I...should think so, Rachael, why wouldn't they.' I began to feel like an imposter.

'That's what I thought. Don't want the flies gettin' on it before the big day.'

I shook my head. 'Heaven forbid.'

'Well?'

I stared at her. 'Well what?'

'The fridge or the worktop?'

'Oh yes.' I raised my eyebrows. 'The fridge?' What did I know?

'Thought so. Okay then, must dash. Got to pick up Ms Bergan's prescription before I gets home.'

'Janice Bergan?' At last, a name I recognised.

'Yes.' She chuckled. 'It's a bit of a trek, but I don't mind. Be seeing ya.'

She was gone before I had time to answer. I blew out my cheeks. Rachael was like a whirlwind, appearing to be one of those selfless people driven always to help others. Little Dove was another unknown, although it wouldn't have surprised me if it was the name given to Pickles' companion (Her mum's cat to save you looking). I remembered the cryptic note from Skye. Perhaps it was the cake and I had asked Rachael to collect it for me. Cats see things differently; maybe a red cake looks delicious to them and gross to us. I shrugged. Who cares? I glanced at the boxes, daylight was fading, I was getting hungry, and not just a little tired, and probably why I was feeling grumpy.

    I got to my feet, shuffled my way over to one of the boxes, pushed a flap to the side with a fingertip, and peered in; to be honest, it was a half-hearted attempt because a part of me really couldn't be bothered. It must have been a lucky hit, for at the top was the very thing I was looking for: The daybook. I slipped back to my seat feeling more than pleased with myself, forgot my grumbling stomach, even my tiredness. I put my feet on the chair opposite, leaned back and sunk into the cushion; it would be a difficult read, but was sure it might help explain the disparity between my life as it was and what it had now become.

    I held the fabric covered notebook for a few seconds before opening it. I had a weird, uncomfortable feeling in the pit of my stomach; I considered her notebook like a journal, diary, or shoulder bag, it was a personal space with an inviolable law of privacy, and one I had no right to break. I took a deep breath and opened the cover. The first few pages of jottings contained nothing out of the ordinary, no unfamiliar names, destinations, or projects we hadn't discussed a million times together. But as I turned the pages certain side notes, usually in a pencil drawn margin, appeared odd and quite random, and related to a subject we'd hardly ever discussed. As was becoming the norm, and just lately, somewhat predictable, the inevitable interruption. It came as two sharp raps on the half-glazed garden room door. Outside, nose almost pressed to the glass, was a face I recognised relatively easily; but still a surprise. I lifted a hand and beckoned him in.

Edward Fairchild looked more than a little awkward as he opened the door. 'I hope this is not an imposition,' he said. 'I didn't know how else to contact you.'

I felt my eyes narrow. 'Larry has my number; you could have asked him for it.'

'Ah, yes.' He paused to take a breath. 'I'll get around to that in a moment.'

'Please, take a seat,' I said, gesturing towards the chair opposite. Yes, I had removed my size nines from it. I watched as he took off his jacket, hanging it over the back of the chair in one, smooth sweeping action. I folded my arms as he took his seat; this was going to be interesting; I could feel it. I looked at him curiously.

'I expect you're wondering what this is all about?' he said. 'His vocal manner was clipped; he had an officer class lilt Charles Forsyth would have recognised.

I assume Larry doesn't know you're here.'

He shifted in his seat, pinching his nose. 'Larry is a good man; we've been friends for a few years now.' He paused. 'He takes the world of archaeology very seriously, and so he should. It's a serious subject. But,' he paused again, appearing to struggle to find the right words, 'when confronted with complex, and baffling paranormal activities in and around some ancient sites he can let his emotions get the better of him. He raised his eyebrows. 'You saw it for yourself.'

'Did I?'

'Basically, Larry considers these sites more important than the people who live near them and has a rather simplistic solution to their issues.'

'Move away?'

'Precisely.'

'And you see it differently?'

'Oh, yes, I do indeed.' He nodded. 'Paranormal activity can destroy lives, and does so with alarming regularity, far more than you can imagine. It is conveniently disregarded as a cause, brushed away and conveniently attributed to a host of other factors rather than its true source. So, people who suffer egregiously from this abuse, and it is abuse, fear ridicule and social isolation if they come forward and tell it how it is. If you can up sticks and walk away. Good. If you can't, where do you go? Who do you talk to? Who will listen after you've told them you regularly interact with,' he gestured with his fingers, "visitors from the other side"? He pursed his lips. 'Sadly, psychological counselling and prescription drugs are the predictable outcomes.'

'So, why did you come back, Edward?'

'You were willing to stick your neck out, fight the system because you believed it was right to do so. That not only said a lot about you but told me there's more going on here than just the electromagnetic disturbances picked up by Larry's equipment.' He stared over me, lost in thought for more than a few seconds.

'Edward?'

He shook his head and looked me directly in the eyes. 'Have you visited the past yet, John?'

Another direct question I was unprepared for. 'Yet?' I said, raising an eyebrow. There was more to Edward than I thought; Althurian interested him, it was written all over his face.

He leaned forward as if to share a confidence. 'What you're experiencing here at Althurian is not unusual,

John. It's everywhere. I've conducted hundreds of interviews with people who all tell identical stories. I'll ask you again. Have you visited the past yet?'

I had nowhere to go. 'Yes,' I said.

'As someone other than yourself?'

I nodded but stayed silent.

'Were most of these scenarios set in the early nineteen forties?'

I frowned. 'Yes. But how did you know that?'

'I'll come to that later. Do you only assume this character?'

'Yes. But I have travelled in time as myself.'

He stroked his chin thoughtfully. 'Interesting, how often has this happened?'

'Once' I said, then remembered my brief visit to the distant past with Becket. 'Maybe twice.'

'Okay.' He took a breath, touching a finger to his lips. 'Were the situations you found yourself surrounded by conflict? Clashes of personality, sibling rivalry, family disputes et cetera, and were these sometimes violent, even life threatening?'

I was astonished and perplexed at the same time. 'Yes. Yes, they were; almost every one of them. This is incredible, I-I thought...'

He smiled. 'It was unique?'

'But why, Edward, how can this be? Are you saying what happened to me was some kind of shared experience?'

'In a way,' he said. 'A preconfigured storyline played by different actors, all faced with the same obstacles and challenges.'

'A game?'

'Pretty much,' he said. 'A sophisticated one, but a game nonetheless.'

'But my life is different now.' I jabbed my finger at the table. 'If this was a weird kind of game, then why have I returned to a world where everything I once knew has changed?'

He gave a knowing smile. 'Maybe it hasn't. Maybe the world is exactly how you left it.'

I felt giddy at the implication. 'But I don't remember it being like this.'

'You weren't meant to, John.' His eyes softened. 'Sometimes it's necessary to forget before we can relive the beauty of the life we once took for granted. Look at it as a gift, and one to cherish for the rest of your life.' He glanced over his shoulder, turned back and smiled again. 'I believe it's time to leave.'

I stared at him. 'But you've only just got here.'

'Not me, John. You.'

♦

I couldn't open my eyes, and I had no memory of closing them. My skin tingled as if I was immersed in a warm, soft liquid; buoyant, but not knowing which way was up. I was aware of my breath, the gentle pulse of my heart, my place in the universe, even the relentless tick of time. My earlier anxiety had vanished, and I could only feel gratitude for the life I had within me. I felt serene for the first time in my relatively short existence.

Birdsong was the only sound I remembered just before my eyes flickered open; my view filled with a blurred medley of disjointed colours. I had no clue to where I was, my back hurt, my legs and arms were numb with cold, and I was far from comfortable. But, little by little, I could feel a real sensory energy begin to flow throughout my body. I watched, fascinated, as the mishmash of colour before my eyes sharpened into recognisable shapes. As the seconds, then minutes ticked by, one by one each of the nine stones of the Althurian Circle came into crisp focus, and there was only one place where I could view them in perfect symmetry: on or very near the large recumbent. My ability to move was painfully slow to return, and started with my toes, gradually creeping up through my legs and into my body, feeling like I was being inflated with electrically charged particles. Strangely the experience was quite pleasant. Once I was able to move my eyes again, it was evident I was sitting on the recumbent, and accounts for how cold I felt. At first, I struggled a little, to get my limbs to do what I wanted them to do; I probably looked like an uncoordinated toddler attempting a new physical skill, and swinging my legs from this huge lump of rock, and putting my feet to the ground, felt just like that.

Apart from seeing the stones, this was the first time I was awake to the world round me. My return to conscious awareness must have been a gradual process because there was a marked change in the surrounding environment; the sun was high, the air warm, and very little breeze to speak of. I also picked up the scent of newly mown grass; it was summer again, and the seasons had shifted once more. Once my legs and feet were up to it, I wandered across the centre of the circle, making my way towards the grass covered path. I had the eerie feeling someone was behind me and nervously glanced over my shoulder.

I emerged from the treeline and into a garden full of glorious bloom, its heady aroma almost taking my breath away. I was particularly surprised I hadn't picked up the intense scent of lilac and jasmine, two of Skye's absolute favourites. It was difficult not to smile as I ambled towards the house; a sense of well-being had replaced my earlier deep melancholia. It shouldn't have been so, but it was. I stopped a little way from the house and took a moment just to look; all my negative feelings seemed to have ebbed away, as if they belonged to a dream I once had. In a funny sort of way, I kind of knew they were part of me, but couldn't quite work out why. I caught sight of movement within the garden room, it looked like someone picking up a tray and taking it through to the kitchen; the reflection of the garden in the window panes obscured any real detail.

For some unknown reason I removed my shoes before stepping through the open door, not something I'd previously considered. I thought the scent of the garden had followed me until I noticed several green earthenware vases full of freshly cut flowers of abundant colour, lined up where the boxes had once stood. Someone had been busy, and Rachael came to mind, more so when I heard the clinking sound of washing up coming from the kitchen.

Suddenly, a head popped out from the doorway. 'Spooky,' she said. 'I was just about to come and get you. Tea or coffee?'

I stared at the face looking at me; the pale blue eyes, the small lines of her smile, the fall of her hair. It was too much to take in. I immediately felt the rush of blood to my temples, and could feel my conscious self, slipping away. I took a step backwards.

'Whoa, no you don't, my lad,' she said, hooking an arm undermine; it was surprisingly strong. 'You need to sit down, I told you not to go far.' She carefully guided me to a chair, gently controlled me until it was safe to let go, then laid a comforting hand on my shoulder. I turned to look up at her and tried to speak, but she shook her head and touched a finger to her lips. 'I'll make the coffee.'

A wave of anxiety washed over me; it came from nowhere. What if she didn't come back? I tried to blot it out, but it kept returning like an angry wasp. I took a deep breath and closed my eyes, had my life really become the game Edward Fairchild spoke of, some kind of sick joke created by a cruel universe?

'How do you feel now?' She placed two cups of steaming coffee on the table.

'It is you, isn't it?'

I could see her eyes moisten as she looked at me, her lips quivering imperceptibly as she prepared her answer. She smiled benignly. 'Yes, it is, my love.' I was surprised she wasn't fazed by the question; in hindsight, it was an odd thing to ask. She checked her watch. 'I really don't know where the time goes these days.' She looked up. 'It's just as well the clinic cancelled your appointment.'

I frowned. 'W-what appointment?'

Her face softened. 'To see Dr Arcturus. Don't you remember?'

'Ah yes, Dr Arcturus. Sorry, it had slipped my mind,' I lied. I lifted my cup and smiled. 'More time to drink coffee.'

'For you maybe.' She laughed. 'I still have Jemma to pick up. Would you like to come?'

The name was vaguely familiar, but I was unsure how long I could keep this bluff going. 'I'd like that. When do we leave?'

Her expression changed. 'You don't remember, do you?'

I sighed. 'No.'

'How much *do* you remember?'

What was the point? I'd soon be in a corner again. 'Not much.' I paused. 'Why do I need to see a doctor?'

'Because of your accident.' Her expression implied this had been said a thousand times. 'You sustained a head injury, John. We thought you'd never recover. We're lucky you're here at all.'

Those were chilling words, but I had missed one small and important detail. 'How long have I been like this?'

'A year this September.'

I wiped a hand across my face. 'I don't know what to say.'

'Then say nothing.'

'It'll be different this time, I can feel it.' It was true, I did; something had changed in me.

She smiled. 'I hope so, I really do. We have this conversation every day, and every night I pray you'll remember everything I've told you.'

'I remember us.'

'I know you do.'

'I love you, Skye.'

A small tear fell from an eyelash to her cheek; she wiped it away with the back of her hand. 'I have always loved you, John, and always will.' She laughed nasally. 'Just look at us, an old married couple before our time. I thought it would be years before we had conversations like this.'

'We're married?'

She held up her left hand, a surprisingly wide band of gold glinted in the sunlight. I recognised the intricate design instantly but struggled to remember where from. 'Five years this autumn.'

I stared at her. She looked a little older, not by much though. I needed to know more. 'What year is this?' I shuddered as an acute sense of déjà vu rippled through me.

'Twenty-twenty-two.'

Was it possible I had lost six years and not remembered any of it? Was this really Skye, or another actor? My joy at seeing her again was beyond imaginable, but if this was just another stage in some bizarre experiment where I was the objective, a prisoner condemned to wander in time, living and reliving the pain of loss, I'd rather decide my future on that cliff edge.

'John? Are you okay?'

'Do you remember our visit to Farthing Cottage?'

Her face hardened. 'It was hardly a place I could easily forget. I was more than happy to see the back of it.'

'We sold it?'

She nodded. 'Yes.'

I frowned. 'Why?'

'You thought there was something sinister lurking there after we discovered what had happened to your cousin.'

'My cousin?'

'William. You had this wild idea the house was built on some ancient ley line and was the cause of his insanity. You had a real bee in your bonnet about it. A lot of it due to that pile of notes we found.'

'But William didn't live there, it was a guy called Garennier.'

'Garennier is an old French name for Warrener. William changed it for some obscure reason.'

'Really.' I stared at her. 'And Gulielmus?'

'Another name for William. German, I think.'

'Jesus. And these notes?'

'A collection of his thoughts, he even had a name for it: The Celopea. Sadly, it was the last thing he ever wrote.' She rocked her head gravely. 'He was a troubled man; thought he could travel through time; must have tipped him over the edge.'

My heart quickened, my face flushed, and was sure I was about to be sick. I closed my eyes and took a deep breath in an effort to quell the nauseous feeling deep in the pit of my stomach. This knowledge of William hit me unexpectedly hard. I had no idea we had been fellow travellers, separated only by time. Destiny had brought us together, choices had finally, and fatally, torn us apart. I eyed her steadily, was this about to happen again? I sincerely hoped not. I'd had enough.

'Are you okay, sweetie?'

'Sorry, I was thinking about William.' I was tired and could sleep for England, and it probably showed. I was also confused by her response to William's claim. I suddenly needed to change the subject. 'Rachael said she's picking up a cake tomorrow.'

She stared at me. 'Cake?'

I nodded. 'She said it was for Little Dove.'

Her eyes moistened. 'That was over a year ago, John, a month before we decided to move here permanently.' She sighed. 'Rachael doesn't even work for us anymore.'

I combed my fingers through my hair, then smiled limply. 'Sorry.' I now felt hopelessly lost. 'How did it happen? My accident?'

Her bottom lip trembled. 'Y-you've never asked me that before.'

'Sorry.' Apologies were becoming a habit.

'No,' she said, shaking her head. 'It's good you want to know. It...surprised me, that's all.' She took a deep breath. 'You'd had too much to drink, we both had. You left…'

'This was at the cottage, wasn't it?'

She gasped. 'Y-you...remembered. I went to look for you. I lost my way. I didn't know what to do.'

'I fell?'

'Y-yes.'

'Anton's Bluff?'

Her eyes widened. 'My God, John, they said the memory of it would never return. Can you recall anything else?'

'Only what I've already told you,' I lied.

She continued to stare at me. 'You can see why it had to be sold.'

'Yes. I understand.'

She glanced at her watch, then back to me. 'It's time we made a move, John.'

'Why? Where are we going?'

She smiled. 'To pick up Jemma.'

'Really? What now!' I couldn't work out why there was such a rush. Surely the woman could wait a few minutes longer.

She tapped her watch. 'It's quarter past three already. Your smart shoes are in the hall, you're not wearing the ones you've had on in the garden. Oh, and your jacket's still in the car from yesterday.'

'We picked Jemma up yesterday?'

'We do every day, John; it's called the school run.' She laughed. 'It's time for our Little Dove to come home.'

My heart lifted. 'We have a daughter?'

'Oh yes.' She grinned. 'And the prettiest thing you'll ever see.'

The End
Possibly

If you have enjoyed this novel I would be thrilled if you consider leaving a favourable review on Amazon or Good Reads. As an independent, self-published author, reviews are very important in order to promote my work in an extremely competitive market. Also, please check out my other titles listed at the front of this book.

Kind Regards

Antony

Printed in Great Britain
by Amazon